AFTER DARK

THE AFTER DARK SERIES
BOOK ONE

DEAN ALAN CONRAD

AFTER DARK

The homeless disappear. It happens every day in a large city. Have they moved away? Gone into rehab? Died of overdoses and carted away, nameless, to the city morgue?

No one seems to care except a small band of people who live in tents and boxes on the sidewalks. They know the Whistlers have taken their friends, animals that hunt in the park to feed their vampire masters. The homeless in the know have escaped from the Whistlers and the vampires who *live* in the basement of After Dark, a historic restaurant near the city's new baseball stadium, a hub of city life.

With limited resources, junkies with names like Overboard George, Mad Maggie, and Old Harriet, using an old horror movie fan magazine as a guide, join forces to fight the undead.

ACKNOWLEDGMENTS

After Dark is the first of a trilogy of vampire novels I hope will be published sooner than later. Characters who survive *After Dark* will continue to fight the undead in subsequent books. It's been quite a trip for them and me, a journey that crosses the United States and comes halfway back, although I didn't stray too far away from my computer to write these novels. I want to thank my family for their continued support and interest, including my wife Maureen, daughter Meredith, and son Spencer, who also designed the cover artwork.

Special thanks to Gail Delaney, my editor, who correctly challenged some of my writing decisions. Also, novelist J.A. Stein, who showed me a path to publication.

CHAPTER ONE

Bo Bentwood roared into the city in his new Dodge Charger, the Hemi howling under the hood as he passed car after car. The sleek auto was a twenty-first birthday present from his parents. As usual, Bo's friends TJ and Ridge were along for the ride. They fist-bumped while they planned the night's escapade, hollering above the engine's roar.

Bo was thirsty and looked forward to an ice-cold IPA. He was also anxious. Bo hoped the female bartender at After Dark would be there. Tonight he would ask her out. There was a tingle in his groin every time he thought about her. After the date was scheduled, the trio would cause mayhem on the street and in the park among the city's homeless drug users.

Hot, reeking city air blew in their faces through open car windows. Bo hit the exit ramp and navigated the mostly quiet city streets, hitting the gas every time a traffic light ahead turned yellow. They cheered when the bright yellow Charger bolted through intersections just before the red. From the back seat, TJ recorded street life with his cell phone camera. Eventually, Bo slowed the car, slid the shifter into neutral, gunned the engine a few times, and engaged the transmission back into drive to creep into a parking place near the baseball stadium. The stadium was empty. The home team was on the road.

The stadium, now five years old, was supposed to be a boon for the city and the rundown section where it was built; and it was, in a way. Blocks of mostly empty, burned-out tenements had been razed. The homeless were pushed out. New construction popped up. Bars and restaurants opened. Bus and subway lines were extended and stopped at shiny new terminals near the stadium. A park with fountains and exotic shrubs and grasses added color to a once drab landscape. Office buildings and two hotels with conference centers dominated as much space as the stadium and its environs.

Bo and his buddies spilled from the car and walked the block to After Dark, a bar and restaurant that had become their favorite hangout. It attracted pretty women 'on the make' for ball players and the occasional alky who managed to scrounge enough money for a drink or two. Fast talkers hoped to con a draft from fans eager to hear about their supposed run-ins with such stars as Barry Bonds, Hank Aaron, and Roger Clemens. The young men walked quickly along the dirty street and passed tents, shanties, and sleepers. TJ hung back to record the images on his phone. A few panhandlers were out. The sidewalk smelled of urine, feces, and dirty clothes. A trail of trash lined the sidewalk near the gutter like a giant snake. A constant hot wind scattered rubbish as if it were fall leaves.

The trio stepped over a junkie passed out on the sidewalk. "I thought the city was supposed to keep the homeless away from the stadium," TJ said, pausing to get a close-up of the sleeping man's face and then a dirty sock on a shoeless foot.

"That plan didn't last long," Bo said, twisting his head toward his friends. He sneered, "The city spent all that money to build the park, and plant exotic trees and grasses," he pointed across the street to the park entrance and a group of camped homeless. "They extended the train and bus service to the stadium, but they didn't give a shit about the homeless."

"You got that right. The dopers got pushed out and then they pushed back," Ridge said. "Had nowhere to go while more homeless hit the area. They invaded the park and got their old streets back."

They passed a series of tents covered with tarps and flimsy structures made of cardboard and thin plywood. Shopping carts overflowed with brightly colored bags filled with who knew what. The homeless hoarded and littered. Chairs and sofas lined the walls of nearby buildings and deserted shops. Graffiti-covered park walls, new trains, and bus station tile, just about anywhere graffiti finds a home.

The men were dressed in dark, tight-fitting jeans and T-shirts. Bo wore a black hoodie, despite the heat. It made him feel like a hoodlum about to break the law. When they reached After Dark, the bouncer, a big black man with a shaved head, was stationed near the door inside and nodded in their direction. He knew they were all at least twenty-one. Had seen them many times.

"Man, when you gonna shave that melon?" the bouncer called to TJ. "That red hair is too much." The bouncer laughed.

TJ smiled and raised his arms, palms up as if to say *who knows,* and continued to the bar with his friends. Nobody screwed with Big Benjamin, and everyone laughed at his jokes and accepted his insults. Rumor had it that Big Benjamin – never Ben – had been a defensive end at either Alabama or Clemson. Knee injuries and a penchant for drugs ended his chance for a job on Sundays. It also was rumored he wore a knee brace under his pants and walked with a limp, but the trio had never seen him walk. They were happy to stay on his good side.

Big Benjamin was always perched on a high-back chair near the door. Neither had they seen him in action, ejecting a trouble-making patron. Big Benjamin's reputation preceded him, and the rumors persisted. *Big Benjamin sacked a couple of guys the other night. Both were carted away in ambulances. Blood everywhere. Compound fractures. Broken bones right out in the open. Pushed through their clothes. After Big Benjamin whispered something in their ears while they were hauled out on gurneys, the guys never filed charges. Admitted they were in the wrong.* And so it went.

After Dark had been a hotel, *The Gracie*, and was one of the few old buildings in the area that escaped the wrecking ball during the city's redevelopment, mostly because it was historic and had an ornate façade that was still in good condition. It sat cattycorner across the street from the stadium's home plate end. The first floor included two dining rooms separated by a long bar, which was dark and scarred, supposedly original to the building. If you looked hard enough there were bullet holes in the wood from Prohibition times. Exposed brick walls added ambiance. Tourists inspected the old brick, inserted fingers in spaces they believed were bullet holes, and stood for photos where hoodlums supposedly died.

An irregular gash in one wall led to the kitchen. The lighting was dim. In addition, there were potted trees and marble statues here and there. The statues, angels, and shrouded grieving mourners, either kneeling or prostrate, were pulled from a cemetery under what was now the outfield and parking lot beyond the stadium.

Rumor had it the statuary stressed the first-floor structure. Although graves were moved outside the city, some dead preferred to remain with their ornate monuments rather than with their respectfully reinterred remains, so the stories went. Some of those spirits were said to be mean and scratched or shoved workers and patrons.

Rumor also had it that the dead didn't appreciate hanging around now in the bar's noisy atmosphere. Dining among the dead had a certain allure, even among rabid baseball fans. If After Dark guests weren't touched, a salad fork or butterknife didn't disappear, or a shadow figure wasn't seen crossing a dark wall near them, friendly waitresses and busboys were happy to share *their* hauntings. Patrons who exited the restaurant with full bellies, leftover food for another meal, and the willies usually left nice tips. Anything to make a buck.

Occupied offices filled After Dark's upper two floors. Among the barristers, psychologists, an elderly dentist with ancient equipment, and various counseling services, it was rumored all manner of things, from important files to paperweights, disappeared temporarily, only to reappear the next day on another desk, sometimes in a different office. It was said, that because there was much rumor surrounding After Dark, employees from the upper floors accepted these abnormalities cheerfully or blamed pranksters. Still, truth be told these businesses were always looking for new employees.

Bo Brentwood noticed the help-wanted signs inside the bar entrance. Bo had the hots for Lisa, a new After Dark bartender, and scanned the bar's length for her. "I don't see her," he said to his friends.

"Maybe she's off tonight," Ridge said, "or on break. They have to give the girl time off, even a break."

"She takes her breaks over there," Bo said, pointing to a small corner table now empty. "A salad and soda. Sometimes she splurges on a pasta dish. Probably from the kids' menu." Tonight would be the night Bo would approach Lisa, strike up a conversation, and ask her out. He had come close before, but he waited too long and she scurried away to another patron in need of a drink. Then he lost his resolve.

"This man's in love," TJ crooned. "He can already order for her."

"He's a stalker, if you ask me," Ridge said.

"Fuck off, you guys," Bo said. "What will you do for rides when I take her out?"

"There'll be plenty of room for us in the back seat as long as you don't have her horizontal in it," TJ said. He smiled with his wide mouth of bright white teeth.

"Get a room!" Ridge shouted. "We have dibs on the back seat."

Ridge was a little chunky and gained weight after three years of college life and eating better food than he had found at home.

"Let's get on with the plan," Bo said, still looking up and down the bar. His shoulders dropped and he looked disappointed. Another lost opportunity with Lisa.

They ordered IPAs and tequila shots. After three rounds there was still no sign of Lisa. Before they left After Dark forty-five minutes later, Bo learned after laying down a nice tip for the male bartender on duty that Lisa would be working days from now on. It was midnight when they returned to Bo's Charger. Bo removed two bamboo canes, a short kayak paddle, and box cutters from the car's trunk. He kept the paddle and handed out the canes and box cutters. Bo closed his trunk silently, even though no one was nearby. It added to the mystery, the drama, of their mission. They walked up the street slowly, whispering, weapons ticked at their sides, slipping on black latex gloves. Drunks and users staggered along the filthy sidewalk, oblivious to the trio. People napped in lawn chairs or wheelchairs. Others with hollow stares perched on blankets or sleeping bags. A few lay passed out on the middle of the sidewalk. Passersby stepped over or around them. A sliver of a moon emerged from the clouds on a hot humid night in the city.

"We should have some dippers up the block," TJ said, grinning. "I recorded them on the drive. I know we'll find some. If not, we can try the park. It's darker there."

"I don't understand why they dip," Ridge said. "It seems physically impossible, bent at the waist like that. You'd think they'd fall over."

"That's all the shit they mix with the heroin," Bo said. "Fentanyl and tranq, animal tranquilizers, especially Xylazine."

"Whatever it is, the dopers defy gravity," Ridge said. "They get into some weird positions."

TJ added, "The dope gives them the urge to take a dump. That's why they pull down their pants."

Across the street, a white woman in shorts dipped, bent over at the waist. It was difficult to determine an age. She was thin. Her hair was unkempt. Sores covered her bare legs and dangling arms. Her face was not visible, folded against her thighs. As the men approached it was evident she had shit herself. Bo moved closer. The woman dipped silently, oblivious to them. Bo raised the paddle and struck her across the ass. She howled and straightened, arched her back in pain. TJ caned her behind the knees and she crumbled to the sidewalk. Her face hit the concrete with a thud. She rolled on her side and moaned. The boys howled and Bo added two sharp blows between her shoulders. Someone stirred inside a tent nearby, stuck out their head, then retreated quickly, and the trio trotted down the block where a spindly, shirtless white dude dipped, his pants pulled down around his thighs.

"This doper thinks he has to go," Bo laughed. "When you gotta go, you gotta go!" Bo got a running start and whacked the man's bare ass with his paddle. The junkie stumbled forward a few steps, tripping on the pants, and was ready to dip again when Ridge hit him across the shoulders and TJ swung for his knees. The man fell immediately and rolled into the gutter, his long, disheveled hair picked up dirt and debris like a magnet. He winced after a discarded needle stuck him in the stomach.

"Oh, God, help me!" he cried. "The devil's back!" He blew little clouds of dust into the air from the dirty street.

Meanwhile, the tent dweller emerged where the woman still floundered on the sidewalk and shook his fist, cursing. "Get off our street! You bastards. Get out of here."

He charged up the block as fast as he could on two bad legs, but the boys had already trotted away in search of new victims. The tent dweller, a rotund old man, stopped to help the spindly guy, who screamed incoherently and rolled in pain from side to side. The old man picked the needle from the man's concave stomach and threw it aside. The noise brought others to the sidewalk from their concrete mattresses with blankets or tarp coverings.

The next dipper the trio encountered was a black man. The

Beaters stopped a moment to size him up before attacking. They set upon him, bringing blow after blow until he dropped to his knees, crying. The black man was big and had long arms. He swung at them from his knees, but the attackers laughed and skipped away. When he managed to stand, they returned and beat him more until he went down and curled into a fetal position.

When the boys ran out of helpless dippers, they flattened tents, using box cutters to slash the nylon fabrics, and beat the homeless where they lay inside. They avoided those who had dogs or were crowded together, crossing the street to attack loners. The men laughed all the way. The homeless who weren't attacked huddled in fear, whether in tents or in the open, because this was not the first time the Beaters appeared on *their* street, and no one was fast enough to either catch or evade them. The Beaters moved like phantoms in their dark clothing, attacking and fleeing without leaving a trace.

After working both sides of the avenue, the men returned to Bo's Charger, sweating and breathless, stowed their bloodied weapons in the trunk on plastic sheeting, stripped off their latex gloves, and dropped them in the gutter. Bo handed out ice-cold pounders from a cooler. They stood in the shadows like tailgaters reliving their exploits, laughing, shouting. They swung invisible weapons, pretending to strike imaginary prostrate homeless.

"That skinny cunt dropped like a bag of bricks," TJ said, between gulps of beer. He tomahawked his free hand as if inflicting more injury on the woman.

"What about the black dude swinging like a boxer from his knees," Bo shouted. "He almost caught me with a right." Bo imitated his recent move. "But I jumped out of the way and clipped him with my paddle until he fell on his face. He was no Ali. No rope-a-dope. Just a dope."

Ridge kicked a syringe with his toe. "Look at this. The city gives out free needles and the homeless use them and drop them like cigarette butts. I'd hate to work in the street department."

"You hate to work. Period," TJ roared.

The men laughed but stopped suddenly. "You hear that?" Bo said.

Was it a whistle?" TJ asked.

"I don't know. Something like that," Ridge said. "It sounded like a whistle, but not a whistle."

"Yeah," Bo said. "There it goes again. It's a whistle."

"That's another one," Ridge said. "The first one came from behind us." He pointed over his shoulder. "That one is on the left." He pointed again.

"Now it's on the right," Bo said. "There are definitely more than one, and they're moving, circling. It's like they're trying to surround us. What the fuck?"

The long, low whistles modulated up and down, as if communicating. The whistles grew louder and closer every time they sounded. The trio stood motionless and stared at one another.

"Maybe the homeless are ganging up on us. Maybe it's a code they have."

"No junkie sounds like that. They're animals. Maybe coyotes. The city has coyotes. I saw it on the news. They live off garbage and stray dogs and cats."

"Coyotes don't whistle, man."

"They can make a lot of noises when they hunt. Communicate."

"We ought to see what it is. For future reference."

"Grab the cooler. Let's get out of here before we attract attention," Bo said. "I don't like this noise."

They piled into the Charger and roared back to the safety of their fraternity house a few miles up the interstate. The cooler was moved to the back seat between TJ and Ridge and provided more ice-cold beer.

CHAPTER TWO

OVERBOARD GEORGE CRAWLED FROM HIS BOX ON FIFTH Street, a block from the stadium. The street had been Fifth Street for as long as anyone remembered, and its name hadn't been changed when the stadium was built. For that George was happy. It gave some normalcy to his life. His box was stiff and strong and once contained a side-by-side refrigerator that had an ice maker and water dispenser, according to the sides; amenities he wished he had now in the summer heat. Still, he thought it was a sweet deal because the box still contained Styrofoam, which made a nice pillow, and it sat on two wooden pallets he had hauled in his shopping cart a quarter mile from the bridge overpass. The pallets kept the box's bottom dry, even in the winter. In addition, he had a bright blue tarp to preserve the top and sides. The tarp flapped noisily in the wind, but it kept the box's interior dry.

To complete this sweet deal George had pulled a torn yoga mat from someone's trash and received a sleeping bag from a church volunteer. All Overboard George feared was the city chasing him, sending his home to the landfill, but now there were the Beaters who attacked at night. He was coming out of his last heroin injection, but today his knees were bloodied, he had a welt above his left eye, and his back throbbed from the beating he took last night. He couldn't remember how many there were: one, two, three, or maybe more, who had dropped him on the sidewalk. He swung like the old Navy boxing champion he had been but didn't know if he hit any of them. His knuckles were bloodied, but the damage probably came from hitting the sidewalk, not a haymaker that connected.

Overboard George knew he was late. The sun climbed in the sky. It was never easy, but the walk to Burger King would be more painful today. His spot near the drive-thru window pick-up, where he begged for money and scooped up change that fell to the ground, coins people in a hurry didn't bother to leave their cars to retrieve. His spot would be taken by another, probably Mad Maggie, who wasn't a user but just mentally ill. If he fought with her for the spot, the manager would chase them both, maybe ban them forever from the restaurant drive-thru.

As long as George didn't harass the customers, the manager left him alone unless someone complained. After all, the manager had been a Navy man.

When customers complained it was usually about George's body odor, which could be stronger than the smell of french fries and burgers frying and at times wafted into their vehicles while they waited for their orders to be assembled. Then he would struggle off to the bus stop bathroom to bathe in the cleanest toilet bowl he could find. He kept track of the bathroom's cleaning schedule, with dates and times posted on a paper next to the entrance door, which recorded when toilets were last cleaned. It wasn't difficult to find a toilet that hadn't been used since it was disinfected. The locking toilet stall door provided him a little privacy.

Then he'd dry himself with the bathroom's paper hand towels, change clothes, and wash his filthy ones in a sink. It was not a difficult operation if completed between bus arrivals and during nice weather. It was not uncommon for him to wash alongside other homeless. He had most of the bus schedule memorized. Washing in the winter was a last resort.

George would have to settle for a less busy spot and hold his sign that read *Navy Veteran Homeless & Hungry Please Help.* Above *Navy Veteran* he had scribbled *Disabled.* The letters were scrawled with crayon on old cardboard. The sign was irregularly shaped and dirty at the edges where his fingers held it. The Burger King dumpster would be picked clean by now. The best breakfast sandwiches would be gone, the ones bought for children who took one bite and refused to eat more. Generally, he ate around the little teeth marks in the buns and hoped the people who bought the food had kids with clean hands. But when you're hungry you tend not to worry about the clean hands of others. He couldn't remember when he had washed his. Didn't think about it much.

The day was already hot and George knew his body would feel worse by night. He didn't have the money for a fix and needed one. As he approached Burger King, he thought he saw his wife sitting on the ground near the pick-up window. His glasses were long gone, and he remembered through the bright sunlight that hurt his eyes his wife had kicked him out before the Navy kicked him out. Even his kids were only a memory. His family hadn't bothered with him in years, even though they knew where to find him. After all, all the homeless knew Overboard George.

Upon closer inspection, the panhandler proved to be Mad Maggie, sitting on the concrete in her soiled dress, a blanket spread before her to collect thrown money before the coins rolled away.

"I'm not moving," she chirped as George approached, wagging a finger. "Start your nonsense and we'll both go hungry."

George bowed. "You were here first, Maggie. I don't want no trouble. Couldn't cause any if I wanted."

Maggie looked up at him. Her face was scraped and bruised. She cried softly.

"They get you, too?" Overboard George said.

She nodded. Tears filled her eyes. "Caved in my tent. Tore it to pieces. Beat me almost senseless. Then killed my cat. Broke its back with sticks. Then stepped on its poor head."

"It was a mean cat," George said, showing a grimace. "Bit me once."

"It was a mean cat. Bit me, too. But it was a comfort."

"Something has to be done," George said, shaking his head, sitting slowly, painfully next to Maggie, letting his back partially support him as he slid down the wall.

"Don't get too comfortable. Any money thrown this way is mine." She collected the coins on her blanket and pushed them into a small purse that hung around her neck.

"Just a minute's rest," George said. "We gotta do something about these Beaters. They don't even rob us—not that we have much to steal."

"I got—*had*—plenty of valuables," Maggie said with a wink.

George looked at her thin, drawn face.

"Your face looks sore," George said.

"It is. Hunter John gave me a tube of ointment this morning to stop infections. It's out of date two years, but..." Maggie smoothed her hands over the wrinkles in her lap. "Hunter John says the Beaters are college kids on a fling. Nothing better to do for the summer, so he says. Maybe it will stop when they go back to school in the fall. That's what he thinks."

"Nothing to do? I thought they were making something of theyselves. We ought to go to the city."

"That'll get us nowhere. I'm not going back to the psych ward, and they'll take your box. Wait and see. Your sweet box, those pallets it took you a day to push from the overpass, and that nice tarp will all go to the landfill. That nice tarp will be flapping in the wind at the landfill. They'll put you in a shelter. Maybe jail."

George rose stiffly. "You're right, Mad Maggie, and pretty smart at that. The city won't do nothing. For all we know they be paying the Beaters to clobber us. I'm going over to that After Dark restaurant. They say the grub's good. I'm getting tired of fast food anyway." George walked away.

"How you feeling?" Maggie said.

"Rough."

"Here," she said. "I can't spare anymore. So don't ask." Maggie pulled a five-dollar bill from her purse and handed it to George. "Found it on the street this morning. The wind blew it right at me. When does that ever happen? Something for nothing. I hope it helps."

George took the money. "If you ever need a dry place to sleep, there's plenty of room for you in my box."

"Only if you keep your hands to yourself," Maggie cackled. "I'm not that kind of girl. I'm not easy." George threw back his head and laughed.

"Okay, Maggie." He kissed the five-dollar bill and stuffed it in his T-shirt pocket.

———

THE WALK to the After Dark was agonizing. George's muscles hurt from the beating. Withdrawal symptoms were setting in. He found a gated dumpster at the back of the restaurant in the nearly empty parking lot. The gate was difficult to open. The chain link fence around the dumpster was woven with vinyl strips that hid him once he was inside and pulled the gate shut. Inside the dumpster were bags of food that lay on newspaper. One contained a hamburger and french fries. Another had a chicken sandwich. A third just fries. Bottles of water lay beside the dumpster. George ate the chicken sandwich and drank some water. Then he found a spot on the asphalt in the shade behind the dumpster, out of sight, hidden by the fence's fabric cover. In a moment he was asleep.

It was dark when George woke. It had to be after midnight, he thought. He had pawned his good watch years ago after time no longer mattered, and he needed money for drugs. His cell phone needed a charge. Only the fixes mattered. Noise from the bar filtered outside when a door opened. That meant it wasn't closing time yet—two a.m. George took the hamburger and fries from the dumpster. Food for tomorrow. More garbage had been tossed inside, but George hadn't heard the deposits or the lid slam shut. He was really out of it. He opened the gate slowly and slid through the opening. Then he closed the gate, fastened it, and stole to the front of the restaurant and along the street. He was sure no one had seen him. Although the walk was long, the food was good. Worth it. He already had a meal for tomorrow. It would be worth revisiting this dumpster, he thought, and would remain his secret. He wondered who had put fresh food inside it. Not a single tooth mark.

Overboard George proceeded along Fifth Street in front of the silent stadium. The street was nearly deserted. Pangs of withdrawal continued. His head hurt and his stomach cramped. He thought something rushed across the street behind him. He turned, but nothing was there. He heard something across the street. Overboard George froze. Were the Beaters back? No. They couldn't move that fast. Nothing could. A dark blur crossed the street in front of him a half block away. There was no way he could see clearly that far without glasses. He blinked several times. Rubbed his eyes. Salt from the french fries stuck on his fingers stung his eyes. He was afraid to continue but knew he would be safe in his box with other people around, if he could reach it. The remnants of his last fix, hidden in a secret Styrofoam cavity, might get him through the night. Just don't get caught on the sidewalk again. He couldn't stand another beating. He took more painful steps. There was a flurry of activity around him, heard but unseen, possibly footsteps, scraping noises, and shrill whistling, clicking, the gnashing of teeth.

Someone new was fucking with him. He clenched his fists, ready for a fight. Tonight, his punches would land, despite the sore knuckles and his throbbing muscles. His hands would run red with the beating he'd unleash on his pursuers. Then all the separate noises converged on him. He didn't know where to turn. He saw blurs all around. He was overwhelmed in an instant, held immobile, suffocated. The air stank. Everything went dark. Overboard George never returned to his sweet box. The hamburger and french fries lay flattened in a greasy smear on the sidewalk where they dropped.

CHAPTER THREE

Lisa Van der Meer stood behind the After Dark bar cutting lime wedges that would slip into Corona beer bottles or garnish any number of cocktails she could make. Occasionally, she caught a spritz of lime juice in the eye.

"Have to get some sharp knives," she muttered. "They want me to order stuff. The first thing on my first list is some new sharp knives. Really sharp."

She stopped slicing and retrieved her order list. *Some sharp knives,* she added to the list at the top and smiled. Then she resumed slicing. Lisa wasn't happy when the manager asked her to take over the bar's daytime duties after working a month at night, getting to know the regulars by name, having their drinks poured and set on the bar where they always sat by the time they walked from the entrance to their stools. That little act drew smiles from the clientele. Lisa catered to the regulars and even one-time patrons, whether they drank draft beer or Manhattans, were college kids or businessmen. She knew how to earn her tips. A smile, a wink, a knowing nod, a chuckle at lame jokes that didn't make sense, and feigned interest in a recently concluded, boring presentation at one of the convention centers, all opened the purse strings. She considered herself an actor of sorts. Regardless of how she felt, she always had a smile. Working days meant fewer tips and more responsibility. She hoped the increase in salary and bar manager's title would be worth it in the end. If her job had one imperative, it was that she couldn't forget to order anything the restaurant or bar needed.

Bart, the restaurant boss—He liked being called *boss*—had said, "Lisa, I need you to take over the bar, work days, do all the ordering, make the schedules for me. The other girl...didn't...had to be let go. She didn't fit in."

"You mean Geisel?"

"Yeah." He twisted his face as if her name recalled an unpleasant memory.

"She's training me, right, before she leaves?"

"She's already gone. You'll have to pick it up on your own." His words had a sound of finality. Lisa knew the case was closed. If she wanted a job, she would be the new daytime bar manager.

"I like working at night," Lisa said. "It keeps my days free."

"Please, Lisa. Give it a try. If you don't like it, I'll *try* to find someone else. To be honest, you're too good not to be a boss." He stepped back and looked her over. "After all, someday you might have my job."

After a month at After Dark, Lisa knew Bart's smile was a command that better be followed. She needed this job in a down-town location.

The other girls at the bar had concluded Bart was gay and made fun of him when he wasn't around. He was pudgy and balding with a rather bulbous nose, over which his thick eyebrows almost met. His pallor was accentuated by his dark clothing. He wore no wedding band, no jewelry at all, had no photographs on his desk or the walls of his office, and never talked about himself or his family, including a wife and children. Lisa thought otherwise of Bart. He wasn't gay. If he were, Bart would be a better actor than she was. He rarely looked her in the eye, instead focused on her breasts or crotch, and had a habit of wetting his bloodless lips before he talked. Bart reminded her of a fat constricting snake. When Lisa heard him approach from behind, in his quick small-stepped gait, she felt his eyes all over her.

Lisa accepted the new job and picked it up on her own in a few days, although she had help from the head chef Jose, the building manager Jake, and various waitresses. They all had suggestions. It seemed everyone wanted sharper knives. Lisa needed a job, one that allowed her time to follow her true purpose.

The restaurant would open its doors in fifteen minutes. Lisa covered her sliced limes with a towel and placed them in the cooler. Then she went to the kitchen. It was like an oven already. Jose saw her coming, wiped his forehead with a towel stuffed in his belt, and pulled three small bags, neatly folded, from the freezer.

"You hungry already?" Jose said. "I never saw a girl eat so much."

"Is that it?" she said, taking the bags.

"So far. The ends of some beef I can't serve on day-old bread. It's going to the dumpster one way or another." Jose smiled, which made it appear his pencil-line-thin mustache turned up on the ends.

Lisa smiled and touched the chef's moist forearm. "Thank you, Jose."

"Lisa, why you feed these people too lazy to work?"

"I appreciate your help, but that's my problem," Lisa said.

"If Bart finds out it will be my problem. Bart would say let the homeless save their money, or beg for it, and buy a take-out meal. I don't want to disappear like Geisel."

"Disappear?"

"She doesn't come to work. She never come back. Not even to pick up her pay. Nobody does that. Leave a check? I see the check and her purse at the table over there where nobody sits. Where all the junk collects. Now the check and the purse are gone."

"That doesn't mean she disappeared. Bart said he fired her. She could have collected her stuff when you weren't here."

"Nobody see her come back. Nobody. I asked around. Geisel not fired. She snoop around downstairs where nobody goes. She find the key to the door that is always locked. The big key to the old door." Jose pointed at the old door outside the kitchen. "She disappear. Then the key disappear. It was always over there with the other keys that don't open anything. Old doors from before the remodeling. The police were here. They talk to me. I don't tell them about how she snoops. I don't tell them about the key and how it disappear. Bart tell the police Geisel runs away. Have man problems. Bart says Geisel's man slap her around and she returns home to her mother. Where's that, police ask? Where is her home? Nobody knows. Where is boyfriend, police ask? Nobody knows. What is his name? Nobody knows."

"I really didn't know Geisel," Lisa said, frowning. "When I came on duty she was leaving. Sometimes, we didn't work the same days and I didn't see her at all. When we talked it was only about work. She filled me in on what was going on and what the specials were for the night. That kind of thing. She was all business. She never mentioned a boyfriend or her mother. Not even a hometown. I would have thought she did a good job. Was efficient."

"She was a snoop. Better for you. The less you know, the better you are. Well, Geisel disappear. Now, you do Geisel's job, which I like better. You don't forget to add things I need to your list. I get low on something, Bart tells *me* to go to the store after work. *Me!* You don't snoop around, but you feed the poor. That is not good either. It could land us both in trouble. But...you are prettier than Geisel. Have nice smile, not teeth fucked up by drugs."

"Thank you, Jose. I'll take that as a compliment."

Jose smiled again. "You better make your trip to the dumpster before we open. Or you get caught. I leave a garbage bag by the door for you to take out in case Bart see you. The bag is light. It's full of paper. Bart like to snoop around, too. Problem is he don't disappear. Poof." Jose threw open his hands.

They laughed at the thought of Bart disappearing in front of them in a puff of smoke. Lisa took the frozen sandwiches and picked up the trash bag. She left the kitchen by the back door and headed to the dumpster. Mad Maggie was there, trying to unfasten the gate latch. Maggie jumped when Lisa introduced herself.

"I'm here to find Overboard George," Maggie said, backing away from Lisa until she bumped against the gate. "This is his private driveway gate."

"That gate hides the restaurant garbage dumpster." Lisa put her hands on her hips and cocked her head. She couldn't help smiling.

"Do tell?" Maggie said, placing a dirty index finger in her mouth. "Last time I was here George lived in a palace behind a gate like this. There was a call box to contact his servants. Now the call box is gone. Probably Overboard George ran the call box over with his Mercedes Benz. Thought I'd open the gate, let myself in, and surprise Overboard George."

Lisa smiled. "Let me show you how the gate works. Then you can visit any time."

A bemused Mad Maggie smiled like a child.

Lisa opened the gate for Maggie and handed her one of the sandwich bags. "You like roast beef?"

"Who doesn't? I could take one for a friend."

Lisa pressed the two remaining sandwiches into Maggie's hands. Maggie rummaged through the bags. Looked up at Lisa. "No *au jus*?"

"Sorry," Lisa said with a smile. "Not today."

"Bless you anyway, child."

"I don't think I'm much younger than you," Lisa said.

"I'm twenty-three," Maggie said.

"And I'm twenty-five."

"Grandma!"

The women laughed.

"To be honest, I'm looking for Overboard George. Yesterday, he said he was coming to this dumpster for a meal. He was hanging out at Burger King and was tired of fast food, so he told me. Last night he never came back to his box. I gave him five bucks I found so he could get his fix. But now I want the money back. This money came right up the sidewalk to me, blowing on the wind. Usually, I got to chase paper money a mile before I catch it. came Do you know George?"

Lisa shook her head.

"He's a big black man, was wearing bright red shorts and a bright red T-shirt. Not all that clean. A little faded, too. Chlorine in the toilets will do that to your clothes."

"I don't remember seeing anyone like that around," Lisa said.

"First, Overboard George says I can stay in his box because the Beaters destroyed my tent. Killed my cat, too. It was a mean cat, Overboard George said because the cat bit him. But he bit me, too. Bit almost everybody that fooled with it."

"Overboard George?" Lisa asked, screwing up her face, "bit you?"

"No. The cat bit me. Now I have some cat food to eat for a day or two, maybe longer with this spread in my arms. So, Overboard George takes off with my five bucks."

"Why do you call him Overboard George?" Lisa said.

"I suppose that's his name," Maggie said.

"I mean *Overboard.*"

"He was in the Navy. Jumped ship. Went what they call AWOL. He's been AWOL ever since. For years."

Mad Maggie opened one of the bags Lisa gave her and pulled out a sandwich, examined it. "How's business inside?" She replaced the sandwich.

"We're busy," Lisa said, "especially with conventions and home games at the stadium."

"I guess so," Mad Maggie answered. "Everybody's busy. I read in the newspaper—it was a week old before I picked it off the sidewalk—that attendance at games is up, especially after the team got those *marquis players*. That means concessions are up. Souvenir sales are up. Go anywhere in the city and you see team T-shirts and hats. That means tax revenues are up. The city leaders are happy. They go, *wink, wink*. Now there's talk of building a new football stadium in the same neighborhood. You know, one hand washes the other. The city will make a fortune, but that doesn't help the homeless. They'll get pushed out again—maybe for good this time. Nothing'll get fixed. I think the bodies will just pile up. Instead of people stepping over the prostrate, they'll step on them, like they're walking down a cobblestone path."

"I don't think the city would allow that," Lisa said. "After all..."

"Who cares about overdoses? There won't be enough police, firemen, paramedics, or church volunteers to find the overdoses." Mad Maggie pointed a finger at Lisa. "it's just another John or Jane Doe carted away to the morgue."

"I see," Lisa said. "Listen, I have to get inside. The restaurant is opening."

Bart was at the kitchen door. "Lisa, you there? You have customers!"

Lisa slipped around the dumpster enclosure and raised the garbage bag to show Bart. Then she disappeared behind it again, flipped the garbage bag into the dumpster, and let the lid slam shut. Mad Maggie jumped. Lisa was sure Bart would hear the bang. She secured the gate. "I try to keep food in here and water on the ground," she told Maggie. "It's best if you come after the restaurant is closed. Come back. I want to talk to you again. Tonight."

Bart waited in the kitchen when Lisa returned. Sweat stood in beads on his forehead. He wagged a finger under her nose. "I don't want you carrying out garbage. We have staff for that. Remember? You're management now."

"Just helping," Lisa said, trying to sound cheerful, squeezing by Bart, who blocked the doorway. He licked his lips when she couldn't avoid brushing against his lavender-colored shirt already wet with sweat under the arms.

"Who was that old bitch out there? Never seen anybody so filthy."

"She's twenty-three and homeless."

"Makes the place look bad."

"I chased her, Bart. You won't have to worry about her.."

"Good work, Lisa. Get back to the bar. You have a Bloody Mary to make. There's a convention in town. Casket makers, I believe. They drink like fish. You can expect to be busy. Don't forget to play up the ghost angle. Creeps like that will love it."

Lisa walked toward the bar. She said to herself, "I don't think she's a druggy, but someone sure beat the hell out of her."

CHAPTER FOUR

MAD MAGGIE RETURNED TO FIFTH STREET TO CLAIM Overboard George's sweet box. She pushed the shopping cart filled with all her possessions to the box, now that her tent had been slashed and her mean cat killed by the Beaters. She had left the cart hidden among some abandoned tents on the sidewalk while she went to After Dark.

She thought about taking one of the tents, one larger than her own had been, but decided the sweet box would offer more protection, especially in the winter. She thought, too, about getting a new cart because this one had a wheel that wobbled and sometimes froze, making it difficult to push.

She'd really like to have a garden wagon, the kind with large, fat tires that wouldn't get stuck in intersection potholes when traffic barreled down on her. She had seen such a wagon in a discarded garden catalog. Her old shopping cart had been hit once, a cart that had four good wheels, spewing its contents over the road. She barely avoided being hit herself, but her cart was destroyed and most of her stuff was ruined. While she ran in circles, trying to pick up scattered bags, cars blared their horns and some drivers shouted obscenities. A passing cop stopped to chase her, making her abandon everything. He tossed the flattened cart between two tents, raising the ire of the homeless. The cart she had now wobbled so much it made her head shake, which caused her to appear madder than perhaps she was.

When Mad Maggie reached Overboard George's sweet box, Old Harriet was examining it, lifting a corner of the tarp to inspect the cardboard for stains, which meant leaks, kicking at the pallet foundation for sturdiness. Old Harriet seemed pleased and smiled. Maggie rammed her cart into the box with a thump. The noise startled Old Harriet.

"Don't think about claiming this box for yourself. It's mine," Mad Maggie shouted.

"Says who?" Harriet responded, equally loud, puffing out her chest.

The commotion attracted several homeless who crawled from sleeping bags or tents and stopped in their tracks to see something amusing, to have something to talk about later. An argument witnessed was often just the thing to help fill the long empty days on the street.

"He said if anything happened to him the box was mine," Mad Maggie saidm raising her fist.

"He told me the same thing," Old Harriet called back. "First come, first served!"

"I have a sharp knife that could carve you to pieces in an instant," Mad Maggie hissed.

"Show me!"

"It's up my sleeve. I'll show you when I slit your throat and fill the sidewalk with blood, carve out your eyeballs and give 'em to Hunter John's dog to eat. Remove your hairy snatch and wear it as a hat this winter."

The bystanders withdrew. The argument was no longer amusing. Everyone knew Mad Maggie was mad and had castrated Fred, her childhood abuser. A sharp knife in her hands could take out the whole block. Even Old Harriet took a step back as if waiting for the knife to appear.

"Okay! Okay! I already have a nice tent," Old Harriet screamed. "Take your old box. I hope it's full of fleas."

"That's no way to talk about Overboard George," Mad Maggie said, calming herself somewhat by breathing deeply. "He was a good man. My cat liked him well enough, and my cat was a good judge of character."

"Your cat bit him," Old Harriet said. "It was as crazy as you."

"What if it did bite him? A sign of love. I'll bite you if you don't shut up. That mean old cat and me had a lot in common. We didn't like being fucked with."

"You keep that knife wherever it is," Old Harriet said. "I don't want any trouble. Any trouble and we'll both end up in the psych ward." Old Harriet gave Mad Maggie a knowing nod and wink. Old Harriet pushed at the beehive hairdo piled askew on her head.

"Don't worry. You're safe with me, Old Harriet. I only take out that knife when the Whistlers or the Beaters are about. Or, when somebody might decide to take my sweet new box."

Old Harriet changed the subject suddenly. "You want to come in my tent and share a can of stew? It's too much for me," Old Harriet said, sweetly. She pushed at her wild hair. "I'm afraid it will go bad in this heat."

"I have some tuna," Mad Maggie said. "Cat food, but it's not all that bad. I prefer Spam, but that's expensive anymore. But Alpo will do in a pinch."

"The stew's enough for me. Plus, I have some bread. We'll have to eat around the mold. Hunter John found it in a dumpster. A whole loaf. Never touched, only slightly moldy. What a waste."

Mad Maggie smiled. The women backed into Old Harriet's tent and squatted on overturned five-gallon buckets. Old Harriet called attention to her *new furniture.* The air inside was hot and smelly. Old Harriet opened the stew, spilled half into a Styrofoam cup, and handed the cup and a large spoon to Mad Maggie. Maggie wiped off crusted food on the spoon with her dirty dress hem. The women ate silently until the stew was consumed. Then they ate the bread, avoiding the mold, and threw the crusts outside on the sidewalk.

"We can do some bird watching from in here if you like," Old Harriet said.

"My mean old cat liked birds. Caught one now and then," Mad Maggie said. "Say, I'll take that stew can if you don't want it."

Old Harriet paused and thought for a moment. "Well, I kind of collect them. You never know when you're going to need a good stew can."

"Humph, It's a shame about Overboard George. I say the Whistlers got him," Mad Maggie said. "It's not like him to not return at night."

"When you disappear like he did, leaving all your stuff behind, I'm certain it was the Whistlers," Old Harriet said. "But I hope aliens took him instead, not the Whistlers, and he's on a spaceship, having the time of his life, on his way to another galaxy. Those female aliens are insatiable." She winked at Mad Maggie. Then she added matter-of-factly, "Overboard George would have a good time with them. They say some of them have two vaginas."

"I hope so," Mad Maggie said, smoothing the wrinkles in her lap, brushing a few crumbs on the tent's floor, "but I wouldn't want aliens or the Whistlers to take me."

"Me neither. I'm happy enough here," Old Harriet said.

"I should go," Mad Maggie said. "I have to straighten out my box. Get rid of Overboard George's stuff I can't use. Then I have to go out tonight. Have an appointment."

"Appointment? Well, aren't you all hoity-toity? Is it with a man?" Old Harriet said with a grin, leaning forward.

"I ain't saying who it's with."

"You better be careful, going out by yourself, Mad Maggie, or the Whistlers will take you, too. If not them, the Beaters will get you again. They don't keep score. They don't care how many times they beat you or how often."

"The Beaters got me once already this week. I'll carry my knife where I can use it fast. The Whistlers won't touch me, once they find out how mad I really am. I'll castrate them, too, if they have any junk to snip."

The two women laughed, and Old Harriet touched Mad Maggie affectionately on the back.

"You just take care of yourself," Old Harriet said.

CHAPTER FIVE

After her shift, Lisa returned to the restaurant at night and stood in the shadows in a corner of the parking lot. The asphalt was tacky after baking in the sun all day, and heat still rose from it. She sweated profusely.

The parking lot had been packed with cars, but the number had thinned. Lisa knew there would be open tables and barstools inside. If she saw someone approach, she could back into the bushes, vault over a small fence, and melt into the surrounding neighborhood, a warren of buildings, alleys, and sheds in diminutive backyards. Such a strategy wasn't safe but it was better than explaining her presence to Bart, who was never there when you needed him but always there when you wanted to avoid him.

It seemed she waited an eternity for Mad Maggie. Kitchen exhaust fans hummed noisily, spewing the odor of frying food into the humid night air. Occasionally, a busboy or dishwasher brought garbage bags to the dumpster. Lisa knew them all. One worker managed to linger on each trip long enough to light and take a couple of hits on a joint he kept squirreled in a shirt pocket. He was Jose's brother Miguel, a nice enough kid, Lisa thought, a little lazy, someone who hadn't reached a point where he took life seriously or planned a future.

After Miguel returned to the kitchen, a sudden commotion caught Lisa's attention. Three young men staggered around the side of the restaurant and angled unsteadily toward Lisa and a bright yellow Dodge Charger. They were boisterous, talking over one another. Their conversation was incomprehensible.

Frat brothers, Lisa thought.

One was cute but creepy. He was the one who had stared at her on different occasions when he was in the bar with his two friends. The one with the blond hair. A good-looking guy. Lisa edged deeper into the shadows, hoping the car lights wouldn't expose her when they drove away. Something moved behind her through the bushes, something fast, possibly a cat, but it seemed larger and emitted a low, strange whistle, which was answered by a similar whistle farther away. Lisa froze in fear.

The men approached weaving, still talking. Lisa could understand them now.

"She stood you up, Bo," a red-haired youth said. "Let's face it. She dumped you."

"Fuck you," Bo said. "She didn't work tonight."

"Maybe she got canned," the third man said. "Wouldn't put out. She probably won't put out for you, either."

"Miguel said her name is Lisa and she got a promotion, opens the restaurant for lunch now. Makes the schedules. Orders supplies." Bo tapped the side of his head with a finger.

"Miguel?"

"Miguel the dishwasher," Bo said. "He supplies our weed. Why do you think we come to this dump?"

"I say Bo's in love," the redhead said. "Again."

"It's not love, but I will take her out and fuck her. I always do."

"I never saw you fuck anyone since I've known you," the redhead said.

"And how much ass did you get since you joined the frat?" Bo said. "I don't remember any females in your room. Yours either, Ridge."

Lisa fumed in her hiding place. What assholes, she thought.

Bo reached the driver's side of his Charger. He fumbled for the key fob, dropped it, and picked it off the ground. The whistle sounded again, long, low, and closer. Bo turned from the car and stared into the bushes. Stared directly at Lisa hidden in the shadows.

Lisa raised a hand to her mouth. She was afraid to move. Bo took a step toward her, squinted, and leaned forward as he scanned the darkness. Lisa's heart pounded. Sweat stood on her face and trickled down her back. Another whistle answered the first from her left. Bo straightened and shifted his gaze in the second whistle's direction. Lisa followed the noise, too. She feared what made the sound more than being discovered by the drunk frat boys. She started to take a step and froze.

The redhead puked. A fountain of beer and bar food arced through the air and hit the asphalt with a splat. Bo groaned. The third man gaged. The redhead hurled again and a third time. The smell of vomit filled the air. In the bushes, the whistling turned to chatter, a clicking noise. Whatever it was seemed excited, possibly by the odor of vomit. Two became three. Three became four. The things were close. They had a horrible odor. It smelled like wet hair and entrails. It was worse than the dumpster on a hot day. Worse than vomit.

Lisa gagged. She wanted to bolt—jump the fence and take off. The men would hear her, though. She doubted whether they would pursue her. The things in the bushes would hear her. She had been a sprinter in high school. She knew she could outrun three drunks because she was still in pretty good shape. She wasn't sure about the other things. Were they fast? How many were there? How were they spread out? What were they? In a split second, she decided to remain still.

Bo shouted, "You puke in my car, faggot, and you'll walk back to campus."

The third man giggled.

The redhead moaned and spit several times. "I'm done. You hear that whistling? Same as the other night. Those things are all over. Let's go."

Bo opened the car doors with his key fob. "Don't track that puke in my car. I just cleaned the fucking mats."

The third man piled into the back seat. The redhead fell into the passenger side's front seat, closed the door, and slumped down. Bo walked around the front of the car to examine the vomit on the ground. He made a face and returned to the driver's side. Before climbing behind the wheel, he looked back into the bushes. "It looks like the homeless get a break tonight," he said, smiling. "Sleep soundly, motherfuckers. You cock suckers. We'll make it up to you next time." He delivered the last words with a sneer. Then he climbed inside the car. After a moment of gunning the engine, the trio roared off. Bo chirped the tires on the curb when he pulled onto Fifth Street and flew away.

Lisa breathed a sigh of relief. Just as the Charger's engine faded from earshot, Mad Maggie stepped into the parking lot. She approached the dumpster cautiously, looking around, talking to herself, and occasionally raising a finger in the air as if to make a point.

Lisa stepped from the shadows, waved to Maggie, and motioned for her to join her. Lisa had studied restaurant surveillance cameras in Bart's office and learned the dead spots inside and outside, where camera lenses didn't reach.

Maggie was sweaty from her long walk and smelled. Lisa handed her a lunch bag and a five dollar bill.

"I can't," Maggie said, returning the money but keeping the lunch.

"I found it by the dumpster," Lisa lied. "I figured George dropped it when he was here. Technically, it's your money."

Maggie looked at the folded money in Lisa's hand, thought a moment, and snatched it, stuffed it into a small purse that hung on her shoulder. "Technically, it is mine. I shouldn't have given it to Overboard George so he could buy a fix. You know. Contributing to his addiction and maybe even his demise. Even though we argued, I always had a soft spot for OG."

Lisa smiled at Maggie, who was thin and frail-looking, the bruises from her beating still visible.

"I hope this food is good," Maggie said. "Did you throw up over there?"

"No," Lisa laughed. "A college kid who got drunk inside. This food is good. If you find lunch bags in the dumpster, they might still be frozen. Just let them thaw. It's all good food. All fresh. We freeze them so they last longer, especially in this heat."

"College kids. Throw up good paid-for food. What a waste." Maggie shook her head. "Word on the street is that college kids are doing the beatings. Three boys. Come at night in a noisy car. Now, we run like hell when we hear a noisy engine, even if it's a big truck. It's the sound. Try to get into groups, if we're awake. They seem to go after the dippers or people alone. Sometimes the users pass out in the open, on the sidewalk, or in the park. That tranq hits them hard.

"Tranq?" Lisa asked.

"That's right. Tranquilizers they use on big animals like horses. It's mixed in with the dope."

"It's no wonder the users drop."

Mad Maggie continued. "Then they're at the mercy of anyone who wants to hurt them. At their complete mercy. The Beaters wouldn't be man enough to take on someone like Overboard George when he's not all tuned up."

"Is the car yellow?"

Maggie looked into the sticky night sky for a moment. "Could be. But I never heard anyone mention a color. The Beaters are always on foot. I wouldn't want to be run over by a noisy car. You know, the homeless have time on their hands to discuss things—everything that concerns them—like where to get needles or food or help with problems."

"Would you like to get help, Maggie? Maybe I can help you." Lisa touched Maggie's sweat-stained thin forearm.

Maggie recoiled. "I don't need help. The help I got once landed me in the psych ward."

"That's none of my business," Lisa said. "But I will help if I can, if you want help."

Mad Maggie said, "After my dad died and my mom got a new boyfriend, I was persona non grata to Mom if you know what I mean. I was a *Lolita* for the boyfriend—Fred—I saw the movie, both versions. Peter Sellers was a hoot. Anyway, when it came down to me or the boyfriend, Mom chose Fred. I acted out and went to the psych ward."

Maggie raised a finger in front of Lisa. "I was going to go to college, you know. Dad was saving money, but after I acted out Fred spent my college money, with my mom's permission, on a car for himself. Then he totaled it. I acted out even more because I really wanted to go to college. When he wanted me to blow him, I stabbed Fred five times. College was over before it started, and I went to the psych ward."

"That's terrible," Lisa said. "I'm sorry." This time Mad Maggie let Lisa touch her hand.

"But believe it or not," Mad Maggie said, wagging her finger back and forth, "I had a plan and escaped the psych ward. It took a while. They thought they had me converted to their way of thinking. I was a minor and couldn't get out until I was eighteen at the earliest. Maybe never. Probably would have gone to another psych ward after I turned eighteen. But I became their model patient. Yes sir. No ma'am. So polite. They even brought other doctors —and students, too—to talk to me. When I got them in the palm of my hand, just where I wanted them, I slipped away one night and been on the lam since I was sixteen, that's seven years ago."

"Maggie, how did you survive?" Lisa said. "I don't think I could have made it on the streets."

Maggie smiled. "Anything's better than the psych ward. Maggie's not my real name. They call me mad because I was in the psych ward after I killed Fred." She paused a moment. "I don't think anybody looks for me anymore. You never know. They probably think I'm dead, murdered by some creep, or overdosed. I think sometimes they get tired of looking for certain people. I had a dog once, but it was hit by a bus. So, like I was saying, Mad Maggie isn't my real name, but I like the alliteration." She smiled. "See I could have gone to college. I know what alliteration is.

"I can tell you're intelligent, Maggie."

"I was thinking of getting a bigger dog, one that a bus driver could see, but the Beaters slashed my tent and killed my cat. I've moved into Overboard George's box. I could still get a dog. I'd prefer a dog over another cat, even though I have some cat food— but I could eat the cat food myself. It's overrated but not too bad. Cats seem to like it well enough. I was telling Old Harriet I like Spam but will make do with Alpo. Overboard George had a sweet box. Now I have it. He's not coming back. I might have to fight to keep that box, but the users aren't that strong. They're mostly wasted away. Even though I'm small, most of the users are afraid of me because I'm mad. I tell them about stabbing Fred five times."

"No wonder you're crazy," Lisa blurted and immediately regretted saying it.

Mad Maggie didn't seem to notice. "I got him in the chest and neck and once in the eye. The one in the eye was last and did him in immediately. Not that the other stabs wouldn't have, but the one in the eye pretty much killed him immediately. I even pulled down his pants and sawed off the privates he used to make me taste. And he wasn't a clean man, either, when it came to privates. Mine are cleaner and I live on the street. I don't know how my mom could stand to be in bed with him. Fred's either rotting in the ground or a pile of ashes. I went off to the psych ward and nobody told me what happened to Fred. I suppose there was a funeral, even though he didn't deserve one. It didn't matter that he molested me, starting when I was twelve, only that I killed him so horrifically. Fred's not coming back either."

Lisa put up her hands to interrupt Mad Maggie. "Where's your mother now?" Lisa said, trying to be kind.

"Mom was a user. I don't know where she is. Maybe she got a dose of fentanyl and died. Mom always wanted to be a pile of ashes. Fred wasn't a user. I wish he was a user, then maybe he would have cared more about dope instead of molesting me. I might be in college now, but if Fred was a user he probably would have spent my college money on dope. Either way, I was fucked, unless Mom and Fred both OD'd on fentanyl." Mad Maggie thought a moment and smiled. "Then there might be college money. I'd be living off a trust, or something. At my age now, I'd already be graduated."

Mad Maggie let out a great sigh. "The way it is now, most people are afraid of me because I'm mad and cut off Fred's privates and flushed them. I don't think they could have sewn them back because he was already dead when I cut them. I flushed them to make sure. I tell everybody about all the blood there was. Now I have Overboard George's sweet box."

"What about George?"

Mad Maggie grimaced. She looked at Lisa as if she were all-knowing. "Word on the street is that if you disappear the Whistlers take you. Not the Beaters, or the police, or even the men in white coats. *Word on the street* is wise. It sounds like this: Maggie imitated the whistle Lisa heard earlier.

Even though the whistle was not loud, a similar whistle responded from a distance.

Maggie jumped up and down and clapped her hands. "Just as I was saying! I've heard them. They're here."

Lisa was scared. Whatever *they* were they had been close to her when the drunk college kids were in the parking lot. She smelled their stench. "Do you know what they look like?"

Maggie raised a dirty index finger to her lips. Her nails were long, dirty, and ragged. She whispered, "Nobody does. They move too fast. Always in the dark. Not in the light. Never, never be alone. That's when they take you.

"We try to stay together—the homeless. After dark we camp in bunches. Walk in bunches or don't go out. The users—they get separated sometimes. They get their fixes and can't wait to get in a crowd to shoot up. The addiction is that strong. To be honest, I'd rather be mad than addicted. They say years ago you could get brown dope and it was good. You could function. Now there is no brown dope. It's white. It's mixed with fentanyl or animal tranquilizers, or crazy shit. The new dope drops you like a rock. That's why the junkies dip. They're dipping or passed out on the sidewalks. All alone. Easy prey for the Whistlers. That's how they disappear. Nobody ever sees them again."

"Who would take junkies?" Lisa asked.

"Who wouldn't? Old Harriet says it might be aliens, but I know better. Old Harriet has a sister who's well off and gives her money here and there. Then Old Harriet gets a motel room and cleans herself up until the money runs out. She spends all day watching TV, especially those alien shows. She is quite the expert on UFOs, you know, at least that's what she claims. She's going to South America someday to look at ruins, so she says, because the aliens left carvings down there. She thinks she can translate the symbols. But I know she ain't going nowhere. I say all she has to do is look around here if she wants to see ruins. Ruined buildings, ruined streets, ruined people. I'd let the aliens take me on a trip to another world, but I'd want a sharp knife, the kind I used on old Fred, in case they got smart with me, start pushing their sex organs at me. You probably have plenty of sharp knives in that restaurant. I wouldn't mind seeing a couple of sharp knives. Just to look at."

Mad Maggie ended the conversation abruptly. "I got to get

going. Have to be up early and get my spot at Burger King, even though I don't have to compete anymore with Overboard George. I miss OG. We had our arguments, especially when we got to Burger King at the same time. Then we raced as best we could. A tie. One would have to leave. Yes, I miss OG."

Maggie hurried away. Lisa sidled along the restaurant wall to avoid the security cameras, returned to the street, climbed in her car, and drove to her apartment. She had to work the next morning.

MAD MAGGIE KNEW she was out late and alone. She had to walk about ten blocks and along the edge of the park, to people and her sweet box. The sidewalk was deserted. The park was dark. In the distance, she heard a whistle. She chortled to herself and whistled back. She thought, *no Whistlers can get me. I have a sweet box and a good spot to beg. Life is good on the street.* She pulled a small paring knife from her bag and carried it concealed in her palm. New whistling joined the original sound from several points in the park.

Mad Maggie gripped her knife handle and hurried her step. She had arrived at the corner of the park. The ornamental grass parted, and Mad Maggie was swallowed into the foliage. The only sound was the swooshing noise the grass made when it returned to its original upright state.

CHAPTER SIX

The next morning before work, Lisa explored Fifth Street, walking among the homeless, their makeshift shelters, and their shopping carts filled with junk. She avoided dippers, the unconscious, trash piles, and feces on the sidewalk. Drunks already staggered about. Others peered at her with hollow eyes from seats on the concrete or from sleeping bags and blankets, where they had rolled themselves the night before. The street smelled like a sewer, and occasionally the pungent odors made Lisa cough.

Lisa looked inside the tents and shook sleepers to see their faces. Eventually, she spotted what she imagined was Overboard George's sweet box, complete with a bright blue tarp cover. Lying inside as proud as a peacock was a woman who proved to be Old Harriet, a user with long, limp hair piled on her head. Lisa imagined she was called Old Harriet more for her old-fashioned hairdo than her age. Harriet was thin. Dirt smeared her bare arms and forehead.

Lisa smiled at the woman. "I'm looking for Overboard George and Mad Maggie. Have you seen them?

"You from the city?" Harriet said. She looked at Lisa suspiciously.

"Of course not."

Old Harriet raised a skeptical bushy eyebrow. A large mole on her forehead sprouted a single, black hair. "Never heard of such people."

"I'm trying to help. I talked to Mad Maggie last night and she mentioned you. Is it Harriet?"

"Oh?" The old woman twisted her mouth and retreated into the box. "Nobody mentions me. It's the code of the streets. You don't talk about people you know."

Lisa squatted to better see Harriet. The smell inside the box was intense, along with the odors of the plastic tarp and dirty clothing. "This is one sweet box." Lisa coughed.

"It's mine," Harriet countered, shaking her fist at Lisa. She squirmed to the back of the box.

"What do they say? Possession is nine-tenths of the law." Lisa smiled at Harriet.

"Damn right!"

"I was hoping to talk to Maggie again. Can you help me?"

Harriet paused a moment, studying Lisa's face. "What was Maggie looking for?" Harriet said finally. "Tell me that."

Lisa blew out a deep breath and then paused. "Maggie wanted a sharp knife to take on the spaceship to other worlds."

Harriet pursed her lips. "That fool. Everybody knows you can't take a sharp knife on a spaceship. It's absolutely *verboten*. The aliens got metal detectors. You might puncture the side. Let all the air out. Those spaceships are paper thin." Old Harriet wagged her head. "*That* allows them to travel so fast, go so far on next to no fuel."

"So, you know Mad Maggie?"

"Course I do. And Overboard George. They are both fools or should I say *were* fools, going out alone with the Whistlers around.

One night George doesn't come back. Maggie claims his box. Then she goes out to an *appointment*, all hoity-toity as she was, and doesn't come back. Now the box is mine. I ain't going out at night. I can tell you that much."

"Do you know this?" Lisa pursed her lips and tried to imitate Mad Maggie's whistle.

"Stop! Stop it!" Harriet screamed, covering her ears with her hands. "Are you crazy?" She looked frightened and spun around in the box.

"I heard the whistling last night," Lisa said. "Then I talked to Maggie. She whistled it and got an answer from far away in the night. In the dark."

Harriet nodded. "You're damn lucky if you heard the Whistlers. It's foolish to call them. They'll be on you in a second. Take you away, where you end up on the Whistler's menu."

"Eaten?"

"Sure," old Harriet said. "Not right away, though." She inspected her long, dirty nails, pursed her lipstick-smeared red mouth, and cleared her throat, adding to the dramatic effect. "They put you in a cage. Clean you up. Let the dope or booze or whatever addiction you have clear out of your veins. Withdrawal is painful. Extremely. Everybody taken goes through it. Only then are you consumed, once the flesh, especially the blood, is clean. Not everybody survives the withdrawal. *They* never get consumed. They die in captivity first."

"Does all this take place on the spaceship?" Lisa said, suppressing a laugh.

"Of course not! I'm beginning to think you're as foolish as Overboard George and Mad Maggie. There are aliens, all right. *They exist.* The Whistlers aren't aliens. They take you underground, deep underground, where your screams won't be heard. Once your blood is clean you become dinner."

"Really?" Lisa tapped her temple with her index finger.

"Really! Bad Nelson told me. He told everybody. He told the police and he told the city man. Even told the church volunteers. He told all of us addicts. The city man and the police wrote his information down and smiled. Then they walked away and laughed, laughed up their sleeves as they used to say because they thought he was a crazy addict. Then they dropped those carefully written pages in the closest garbage can. We found them." Old Harriet spread out her arms. "The people on the street are the only ones who believed Bad Nelson. I believe him."

"Well," Lisa said, not knowing where her questions should go next. "How'd Bad Nelson know all this?"

Old Harriet groaned, shook her head, rolled her eyes, and hit her palm on her forehead. Her beehive hairdo shimmied. "How do you think he knew? He was taken himself. He was gone a long time. Nobody saw him. He lost his tent, his cart, and everything that was in them. He was gone for weeks. Then he came back one day. He was clean and sober. He escaped from the Whistlers. Pretended he was dead, he told me. They kicked and prodded him. He made no moves, no sounds, and absorbed the blows. After all, the Beaters worked him over a few times. He knew how to take a hit or two. How to play dead. The Whistlers were pissed he died because they wanted to drain his blood.

"His blood?"

"They howled and howled. They didn't want *dead* blood. They're particular, have a discerning palate, is what Bad Nelson called it." Old Harriet raised her arms over her head and shook them as if dancing. "Quite hoity-toity they must be. They threw his body out in the street, early in the morning, like it was garbage, when it was still dark. He was naked. Not a stitch on. Dumped him in the gutter. He saw all these kinds of things transpire while he was in the cage. He seen the homeless come and go. He seen them stripped and hosed down. Watched them go through withdrawal, while he went through his own withdrawal. It was mostly dark in the cage. He heard the homeless being sniffed by the Whistlers, just as they sniffed him. Sniffed in the pitch dark sometimes. He couldn't see a thing, but he could hear things. Hear their claws scraping the concrete floor. Smell their horrid breath. He thought they sniffed to see how clean his blood was. He thought they could sniff clean blood. Then when the homeless were ripe, when their blood was clean, they were dragged away, kicking and screaming, and consumed. He heard their screams. The Whistlers whistled. The others laughed."

"Others?" Lisa screwed up her mouth.

"By *others*, I mean beings that sounded like people," Old Harriet continued. "Had their own language. Not English, according to Bad Nelson. Then the homeless person was quiet. And he heard everybody feeding, sucking, gulping, gnashing their teeth. Ever been to a banquet where everybody gets quiet while they eat? That's how it was, Bad Nelson said."

Lisa got tired of squatting and sat cross-legged on the sidewalk outside Overboard George's sweet box. The air temperature seemed to rise by the minute. Old Harriet offered Lisa a filthy blanket to sit on, but Lisa thought she'd take her chances on the hot concrete baked in the sun. It would be another hot and humid day. Perspiration stood in beads on Lisa's forehead, arms, and even her hands.

"Bad Nelson watched homeless person after homeless person dry out and go to their demise. Some of them he knew. Pure Penny —who claimed she was still a virgin at thirty-five—was one. I can tell you she weren't no virgin. Hunter John slept with her in his tent. Her stuff is long gone. She had a nice tent down the block and two beach chairs." Old Harriet smiled, "One chair was for company, don't you know. They were so eager to get at her, they didn't bother to close the door between the big room with the cages and what Bad Nelson called the feeding or *dining* room. It had been a while since they fed. The *others* get famished after a few days without feeding. They strung Pure Penny upside down, bare as a newborn. She twisted and thrashed like a fish out of water, Bad Nelson said, screamed for her life, while the Whistlers and the others watched and licked their lips, shivering with anticipation. After Pure Penny was exhausted, too tired to move around much, the others, who looked like you or me, so Bad Nelson claimed, only they *looked dead* and had a strange dialect that sounded hollow, as if they spoke with an echo inside them, they took the first bites and drank their fill of blood."

Lisa shook her head. "This is hard to believe Old Harriet."

Old Harriet raised a finger. "There's more. Eventually, the Whistlers were invited in. The Whistlers lunged at her like vicious animals, hung on every part of her, dug their claws in, and bit her all over until you couldn't see her body, only her toes above the rope that held her. Eventually, even those toes stopped wiggling. They drank their fill, opened her up, pulled out the inners, sucked and ate everything. After they could hold no more, they dropped on the floor, one by one, like leeches, until all that was left was a shrunken corpse, small as a child, *desiccated*, Bad Nelson called it, full of bite marks. Bad Nelson is a scholar. Those creatures even licked up the blood from the wounds, and anything that splattered on the floor was consumed. It was hideous, Bad Nelson said. It was hard for him to get the story out."

Old Harriet paused and raised her finger again. "Now occasionally the Whistlers will take a regular person off the street, not many, but not a junkie, someone who wasn't careful where they walked. Got off the beaten path. They were consumed immediately, ahead of even a junkie who was ready to be eaten, who now had clean blood themselves."

"Do the Whistlers beat the ones they take?" Lisa wanted to know.

"Not at all. Bad Nelson said they even got good food in the cages, better than shelter food. Once, he got a steak, although it was a little overcooked for his liking. Bad Nelson has a discerning palate, too." Old Harriet shrugged her shoulders. "Mashed potatoes, vegetables—freshly steamed, not canned—and occasionally a piece of pie or sliver of cake. It was like the stuff came from a restaurant. Bad Nelson thought the food was discarded but taken before it reached the dumpster because sometimes there might be a bite out of a piece of bread or meat. Like it was off somebody's plate. Food someone didn't finish."

Old Harriet thought for a moment. "I don't know. Where would they get food like that? Restaurant food?"

"I wonder," Lisa said.

Old Harriet grunted. "The funny thing was a man brought them their food. Gave them bottled water to drink, as if to plump them up like Hansel and Gretel. The man exchanged their bathroom buckets. Gave them pans of fresh water to wash in or hosed them down with cold water. Bad Nelson pleaded with the man to let him go, but the man," Old Harriet waved her hands back and forth in front of her face, "didn't, couldn't, wouldn't talk. Just did his job, and coughed occasionally, though, that was his only reaction. Probably the smell. Bad Nelson said the place had a terrible stink. Worse than the street."

"And the Whistlers?"

"What about them?"

"What did they do? How many were there?"

"Bad Nelson didn't know. The Whistlers brought the junkies in from the street. They brought him in, but he didn't remember much. He believed they were the hunters. He saw them when they consumed Pure Penny. There were enough to crawl up her body and cover it, so you couldn't see Pure Penny like she was wearing a big fur coat, he said, just her toes wiggling upside down below the ceiling. After the Whistlers ate, they fell in a pile, couldn't tell one from the other, like they were full of Thanksgiving Day dinners, paralyzed, like a junkie with a fresh fix."

"What did they..."

"I know what you want to ask. What did they look like? Bad

Nelson said they were *ugly*." Old Harriet hissed the word ugly. "Everybody wanted to know what they looked like. Every time he tried to tell us he cried, cried uncontrollably. He couldn't explain it."

"Where's Bad Nelson now?

Old Harriet smiled and rolled her eyes. "Nobody knows. They say he moved away. He was sober, so he got some clothes at the shelter and hitched a ride to another city. Some believe he went to Hollywood to sell his story to the movies. But I know he had a big secret stash of cans and bottles. Turned them in for the recycling money and got a bottle. Bad Nelson liked the booze, you see. Went off alone somewhere to forget his problems inside the bottle. Forget the horrors he saw. I say the Whistlers took him a second time while he was unconscious. Dead drunk. Senseless. By now he's been consumed."

Lisa wiped the sweat from her forehead. "Just because you haven't seen Bad Nelson doesn't mean..."

Old Harriet said matter-of-factly, "Consuming him would have been their number one priority. They didn't have to wait weeks for his blood to clear the second time they got him. Maybe only a couple of days the second time. Alcohol leaves the body faster than dope. Bad Nelson talked too much, even though nobody in power believed him. But, what if just one person believed him? Just one. That could mean the end for the Whistlers. I think *the others*, who might have been like us at one time and changed into monsters, have spies on the streets to pick up gossip. *They* want to know if people on the street know they exist. See what I mean?"

Lisa wiped the sweat from her forehead again. This was all incredible. How could she believe such a story from the likes of Old Harriet? In the previous weeks, she had talked to police officers and church volunteers. Although the homeless moved around and could be difficult to trace, some seemed to disappear. They often hid their identities because they had criminal backgrounds. That's why they went by street names like Overboard George and Pure Penny.

Jimmy Young, a Lutheran church volunteer, had met Lisa outside After Dark a week ago while she began her walk among the homeless. She was armed with sandwiches and bottled water. Jimmy admitted some homeless dropped off the map. "Part of the attraction of being homeless is having no ties, being independent, not being accountable to anyone. If people disappear, we never know whether they move away, are reunited with their families, die from an overdose, or go into rehab," he said. "Often, they make decisions on the spur of the moment and don't let anybody know where they're going. Keeping track of the homeless is impossible because they don't keep track of one another, although lately, with claims about Whistlers kidnapping the homeless and Beaters assaulting them, more of the addicts are banding together. At least that's what I've seen."

"What do you think about Whistlers and Beaters?" Lisa said.

"I haven't seen any evidence of it, although the homeless seem genuinely upset. Some appear to be bruised and scraped up as if they've been beaten. But..." Jimmy blew a stream of air through his pursed lips. "They fall a lot, have accidents. They might imagine they were beat up."

Lisa frowned.

"Are you affiliated with some group or on a personal crusade?" Jimmy said.

Lisa exhaled deeply. "I'm looking for my father. He's Charles Van der Meer. Have you run across him?

"The name doesn't ring a bell. Is he an addict?"

"Alcoholic."

"I'm sorry."

Lisa shrugged her shoulders. "I'm trying to reach him before he kills himself. A friend said she thought she saw him downtown. Then I started to watch these videos on YouTube about the city's homeless and I thought I saw him passing on the sidewalk while a junkie was interviewed. I've been looking ever since. Even got a job at After Dark, hoping he'd turn up there someday. The video I saw was recent, so I believe he's still alive."

"I'll pass his name among all the volunteers I know. From the church and city. But what if he doesn't want your help?" Jimmy asked.

"I've got to try. He's my dad."

CHAPTER SEVEN

The bright yellow Dodge Charger traveled down Fifth Street under the speed limit. Occasionally, Bo gunned the engine, always keeping the car in motion. Every time he revved the engine the homeless scattered and the Beaters howled inside the car. From the passenger seat, TJ aimed his cell phone camera at dippers and fleeing homeless.

"Look at them go," TJ called. "Every time Bo revs the Hemi they scatter. This is great."

"You better be careful about filming those fuckers," Ridge called from the back seat. "You lose that phone *we* could be in a world of hurt. What if some asshole finds it and turns it over to the police? They'll see us and the car."

"Don't worry," TJ said, turning the phone toward Ridge.

"Get that out of my face, you prick. We'll all be identified," Ridge said. "I don't want to get thrown out of school for fucking with drug addicts."

Bo chuckled while he drove.

"The last thing the homeless would do is turn over your phone to the police," TJ said. "They avoid the police like the plague. A lot of them have warrants on them. They'd be hauled off to jail or an insane asylum."

"Somebody could try to sell a nice phone like TJ's. I'd hock it if I found it in the gutter," Ridge said.

"If I stopped the car right now and we laid the phone at the curb, in plain sight, do you think anybody could find it with all this trash?" Bo shook his head and laughed. "Do you think *we* could find it if we drove around the block once and stopped where we dropped it?"

Ridge pointed a finger at TJ. "I don't care. But you better be careful with that phone."

Bo pulled into After Dark's parking lot a little too fast and chirped the tires on the low curb. The parking lot was mostly deserted. The baseball team was out of town for a brief road series. Bo navigated the car around the lot, revving the engine occasionally, and coasted into a parking space near the bushes away from other vehicles. He turned off the engine and looked at his friends.

"Let's make it quick in here," Bo said. "We want to have time to lay some beatings on the idiots. Watch where you walk. Don't step in any shit and drag it into my car. Otherwise, the perp will be detailing the interior tomorrow."

"Hey man, your puke's gone," Ridge said. "Wasn't it right here? Maybe a junkie ate it."

"The last time anybody stepped in something it was you," Ridge said, fist-bumping TJ. "Then we had to smell it on the way home."

"Call an Uber if you don't want to ride with me," Bo said. "I don't even charge you gas money."

The men walked toward After Dark. A whistling noise was audible in the distance. "There's that noise again," Bo said. "What the fuck?"

"There's another one," TJ said, stopping suddenly. "It's an answer."

"Probably a cicada, or even a cricket," Ridge said. "Some kind of insect."

"Insects don't whistle," Bo said. "You need lungs to whistle. After it whistles it gets a reply. Then others seem to join in. It seems they converge from different areas. Whatever that is it's communicating, moving. Insects don't talk like that, or that loud. And they're too dumb to talk."

"That's pretty definite," TJ said, resuming his steps to the bar. "Almost like wolves or coyotes. Maybe they run in packs, chasing rats and stray cats."

"The last cat I saw was the one I stepped on up on Fifth Street."

"That was sweet," TJ said. "A fucking eye popped out." The men chuckled as they approached After Dark's entrance.

The bar was mostly deserted. Some old-timers clung to barstools over their drinks, which they held tight-fisted as if they were afraid someone might steal their glasses. A few giddy couples were scattered along the bar's long length. One young man rubbed his girlfriend's bare shoulders. Bo imagined Lisa in such a dress, caressing her shoulders and arms.

Bo climbed on a stool near the tapping station, where he hoped to get better service. The men ordered beer and tequila shots. They drained them quickly and ordered another round. Then Bo asked for their bill. He wanted to get going.

The men returned to the Charger to secure their weapons. Tonight they would cover the park, which they hadn't visited in two weeks. The homeless should be caught unaware. They walked out of the parking lot, crossed Fifth Street, and hugged the sidewalk away from the street, shielding their weapons from view.

The night was still. Few people were on the street. Even the traffic seemed to be at a crawl and intermittent. It was too hot to be outside. They jumped over a small wall into the park with high grass littered with empty bottles and cans. A dozen homeless stood or sat around a small fire off the asphalt path ahead. Occasionally, a deep voice reached them followed by muffled laughter. A few seemed to be unconscious on the ground. Two dipped, leaning toward and against each other as if offering support. The others talked quietly and poked the fire with sticks. Their sweaty faces shined in the firelight.

"This is the first time in a while," Bo said. "I hope we're not out of shape."

"You'll never get out of shape for this," TJ said. "This is your passion, man."

"I can't wait to lay into one of these fuckers. Put one on the ground."

The Beaters veered away from the group and their fire. They raised their hoodies while they walked slowly. Dark silhouettes with hidden faces fit in the park. Their presence sparked no alarm. Members of the group around the fire gave the Beaters a casual glance and returned to their conversations. The fire had an acrid smell of burning rags, plastic, paper, and wood scraps.

The Beaters moved over a rise and saw a thin white man dipping off the path near a large oak. They stopped, checked the surroundings for witnesses, and after a nod from Bo, fell on the man with fury.

The switches fell like hammer blows. The dipper was young enough to be a college student, perhaps a fraternity brother. He crumbled to the ground with a cry and rolled into a fetal position, cradling his head in his arms. The blows fell fast and furiously, raising large red welts on his shirtless body. The man moaned. Occasionally, a strike found an unprotected spot on his face, lacerating his cheek or forehead. When the man cried for mercy, Bo renewed his attack.

Finally, Ridge interrupted the flailing. "Enough. Enough. You're going to kill him, Bo." Ridge stepped between Bo and the prostrate man, who oozed blood from his head and torso. "You know the rules—a couple of swats and move on. Find another target."

Bo was breathless and sweating. He wiped his arm across his forehead and sneered at the beaten man. "He asked for mercy. My club's name is *Mercy*." Bo leaned on the kayak paddle. "Yeah. This one had enough."

The Beaters walked backward away from the junkie, who lay sobbing now, taking one last look at their handiwork before spinning and jogging away up the path.

"I don't see him breathing now," TJ said.

"Who the fuck cares," Bo said. "That's one less maggot."

"I just saw him move," Ridge said. "Thank God. He moved a leg. I swear."

Next, they encountered a seated woman leaning against a large oak. She seemed to be fifty but was probably younger. Probably someone propped her up to prevent her from choking on her own vomit. They fell on her, lashing her legs and torso with the switches. She made no sound, no movement. The Beaters stopped after a few lashes. Her head dropped to her shoulder. Her mouth hung open. The men looked at one another. Finally, Ridge felt her neck for a pulse.

"Dude, this one's dead," Ridge said. "No pulse. No breathing." He wiped his fingers on the grass and then inspected them as if the body had imparted something nasty on his skin.

"Maybe we should call for help," Bo said. "TJ–start CPR."

"Fuck you," TJ said. "Look at that mouth. She puked." TJ pulled out his phone, switched on the flashlight, and shined it on her face. "Dude, she's blue. Nothing's gonna help her."

"Fuck her," Bo said. He laughed, stepped forward, and lashed her across the face with his paddle, broke her nose with an audible snap.

"Woah! Woah!" Ridge said. "Why the fuck did you do that?"

"Because I wanted to," Bo said. "Fucking stupid junkie."

"It's one thing to beat the living, but the dead? That's abuse of a corpse," Ridge said. "You're crazy."

"Some cop you're going to make," Bo said, pointing his bloodied paddle at Ridge. "Criminal justice major, my ass."

"The medical examiner will know she was beaten after she died," Ridge said.

"We didn't kill her. She killed herself. I didn't put a needle in that infected arm. She did. Stupid bitch."

"It's still a crime!"

"Like beating these junkies isn't?" Bo said. "You were always up for it. What did you call it? 'Blowing off steam.' Now you have a conscience."

"With the living, the wounds get better," Ridge snapped. "Maybe a beating will make them decide on rehab. This was wrong." Ridge stepped toward the body and pointed at her. "Dude, this was somebody's daughter, sister, maybe a mother herself."

"She was a junkie," Bo said. "It was the end of the line. She couldn't get any lower. If an overdose didn't take her, the effects of drugs would kill her eventually. Any way you look at it, she was going to have a short life."

"Let's get out of here," TJ said, "before somebody comes along and sees her."

"We'll dump her over in those bushes," Bo said. "That should keep her for a day or so. The cops will think she fell and died. Do you think they're going to launch a full-scale investigation after they see the needle marks in her arms? She's going directly to Potter's field."

"I'm not moving a body," Ridge said. "That's a crime, too."

"Bo, let's go back to the car," TJ said.

"I'm with TJ," Ridge said. "I've had enough of these beatings. I'm done with them. Forever."

Bo put his hands on his hips. "Well, I'm not done. I'm having a fucking hell of a time, and I'm going to beat some more junkies, alive or dead. Nobody gives a shit."

Bo walked away on the path. After about ten yards he stopped and turned. "You coming?"

"No," said TJ.

"Suit yourself." Bo turned and walked away.

"We'll get an Uber," Ridge told TJ. "You can pay me later. Let's go back to After Dark. Maybe Bo will show up. Maybe he won't stay out long."

Bo continued up the path. A male dipper was bent over ahead of him. He was short, thin, and young, with short blond hair. Occasionally, the man opened a plastic bag on the ground and searched through it, slowly, cautiously, as if taking inventory of his possessions. Then he closed the bag and dipped some more. The man's jeans had slid down his thighs and hung about halfway to his knees.

Bo smiled. This would be an easy mark. Bo stepped off the path and watched the man dip for several minutes. Bo made sure there were no witnesses nearby. The park was quiet. Moonlight shined on the path, illuminating the man as if he were meant to be a target. Bo approached the dipper from the side.

The first blow caught the dipper on the back of the neck. The dipper straightened and grimaced. He made a choking noise. Several holes showed in the grin where teeth had once been. The second strike caught the man in the kidneys. He howled and staggered forward, his loose pants impeding his attempt to get away. Bo next struck him behind the knees, and the junkie fell to the ground. His forehead made a thump on the asphalt path.

The man rolled over on his side, facing Bo. "Why are you doing this?" he cried. "I didn't hurt you. Please stop. Let me alone."

"Maybe you're the fucker who sold my little brother dope. Maybe you got him hooked on heroin. Maybe you're the one responsible for *his* OD, you puke."

"I never sold H," the man mumbled between heaving breaths. Tears ran down his face. "I sold speed a long time ago. That's what I got hooked on, man. Now I just use."

Bo rapped him again across the head and smashed his ear, which spouted blood. The man covered up, crying, moaning. "Man, I never knew your brother. Please stop."

Bo beat the man across the back. Blood showed through his dirty T-shirt. Bo beat the man across his legs until he was breathless, and his arms were tired. Bo stood over the man, who was still breathing, crying silently.

Exhausted, Bo moved on. He sweated profusely. Leaning on his paddle, he was ready to return to his car when he saw a female dipper in the distance. *One more, for good measure*, he thought.

He approached her cautiously, fearing the male dipper's cries for help might have alerted others. Bo moved off the path and stood behind a large tree, one that predated the park, waiting to ensure no one was nearby. He was more cautious than he would have been when his friends had been along.

Bo leaned against the giant tree. He imagined he had melted into the park and was invisible. A moth flew into his hair and startled him. He spat and brushed the bug away.

He stood by the tree for several minutes. He breathed normally now and was ready to attack the young woman who had long dark hair and wore a light-colored blouse, dark shorts, and flip-flops. A backpack rested on the ground near her. She dipped silently.

Just as he was ready to step from behind the tree the first whistle sounded. It was close, in front of the dipper. It was followed by two more whistles from farther away. Each was long and low and modulated up and down. The distant whistles grew closer. It seemed they traveled fast.

They were joined by a fourth and then a fifth.

Bo froze in place. When he had heard the whistles before he had always had Ridge and TJ with him. Now he was alone with a dipper who would be no help in a fight.

The Whistlers seemed to gather. Bo heard scratches and movement in the bushes nearby. They no longer whistled but chattered and made clicking noises among themselves. He peaked around the oak enough to train one eye on the dipper. In the distance, Bo thought he heard a human cough. He raised his paddle over his head, holding it in both hands, wishing he had brought a baseball bat, a nice light aluminum one he could use to crush a skull or two.

The clicking stopped. The park was quiet. A wan glow filtered through the trees from a distant light on Fifth Street, dimly illuminating the dipper and the path in front of Bo. Her diffused shadow spread in front of her, much taller than her actual height. The dipper dipped, her forehead pressed against her knees. Her curled fingers brushed the ground. Bo squinted the eye that peaked around the tree trunk. He breathed in short shallow gasps.

Suddenly, several dark forms burst from the bushes on the right side, crossed the path, moved like a giant tumbleweed, and swept the girl away into the shrubs on the other side. Neither she nor the creatures made a noise. The only sound was the scraping of long claws on the asphalt the instant they crossed the path.

The Whistlers were gone.

Silence was restored.

Bo's heart pounded. He slid down the tree and sat in the grass, leaning against the trunk. A mosquito buzzed near his ear. He batted it away. After several minutes, Bo stood and moved to the path. The dipper was gone. Her backpack was gone. Only a single, small flip-flop remained on the path. Bo walked to the spot where she had stood. He picked up the flip-flop and examined the toe impressions worn on the sole. He dropped the shoe.

Bo collected his thoughts.

The creatures moved so fast that it was difficult to see them. However, he knew they were dark and small, and ran on two legs, sometimes on four.

Had one seen him peaking around the tree? Did it stare at him for a split second? Did it have long, pointed ears and a short snout? Were there sharp teeth in the mouth and long claws on the finger-like appendages? Or was it his imagination? It was dark. Did his mind create a creature? Something took the woman because she was swept away. Why not the hideous creatures?

Could the animals have been wolves or coyotes? He wanted to

believe the creatures were short-legged, bat-like creatures, nimble and able to communicate among themselves, but he told himself the city around the ballpark had a wolf problem, even though he knew wolves don't whistle or run on two legs, or even live in this part of the country.

RIDGE AND TJ threw away their canes, launching them into a patch of high ornamental grass. They kept to the path and saw the fire they passed when they entered the park, a glowing speck in the distance. They looked at each other and smiled. They'd be out of the park before long.

"I'm done with these beatings," Ridge said. "It was fun when we took a few swats at the junkies, surprised them, heard them scream, roll on the ground, but Bo went too far tonight, beating a guy half to death and hitting a corpse in the face. Somebody might want to see her features. Give her a funeral."

"I'm with you, man. I'm done, too. I don't need this shit and Bo making all the decisions just because he has money and a nice car."

After a few more steps they heard the first Whistlers. They froze.

"Hear that?" Ridge said.

"Yeah."

"Probably the homeless fucking with us. It didn't seem real. They're imitating that whistle. They think this is *their* park."

"It's a city park," TJ said. "We have as much right here as anybody."

"Damn right."

The whistling continued. It grew louder and closer.

TJ and Ridge were out of sight of the homeless and their fire, where the path plunged. This part of the park was dark. The asphalt path was almost impossible to see. An overhead light on the path was out. Still, they pressed on.

"I don't like this whistling," Ridge said.

"Sounds like we're surrounded. Like the Alamo, amigo."

Bo walked slowly, cautiously back the way he came. There was no whistling. The junkies still had a fire going, although more of them had collapsed on the ground or dipped. He thought of joining them for a few minutes but decided to get back to campus and the safety of the frat house.

Bo hoped Ridge and TJ stopped at After Dark. Maybe they'd still be inside. However, After Dark was closed when Bo reached it. Fifth Street was empty, although a few cars were visible in the distance.

The restaurant parking lot was empty, too, except for his car, parked in a corner near thick bushes. Bo thought it was strange for the lot to be empty. Usually, a car or two remained after closing, sometimes overnight after an impromptu hook-up occurred inside or someone got too drunk to drive. He climbed in the Charger and gunned the engine. He pulled out slowly, hoping Ridge and TJ would hear the engine and appear around the corner, but he returned to campus alone.

Bo was surprised to learn his friends hadn't returned to the frat house before him. Although unlikely, perhaps the men hooked up with girls they met at After Dark—everybody horny and desperate at the end of the night. None of the trio had scored over the summer. Bo was obsessed with Lisa. Ridge and TJ were drunk most of the time. If TJ and Ridge had found girls, it was a story Bo didn't want to miss in the morning.

CHAPTER EIGHT

LISA WAS BEHIND THE BAR AT AFTER DARK, SLICING LIMES with one of her new sharp knives. She hadn't received one squirt to the eye so far and smiled.

It was an hour before opening. The bar was cool and empty except for Pete, who had no title but was the restaurant's jack-of-all-trades. If anything broke, he could fix it, but he mostly swept and mopped floors, and cleaned bathrooms. In a pinch, Pete could tap a new keg, shelve supplies in the right places, and even make a mean house salad for Jose. Everything Pete did was behind the scenes, out of sight of customers.

Pete was tall and lanky, prone to wearing sweatpants that were too short, exposing his bird-like legs, ragged T-shirts with stretched necks, sweat-stained baseball caps turned backward, and clownish, secondhand shoes too large with turned-up toes. He was somewhere between age forty and sixty and had a face that appeared to have collided with sidewalks or fists too many times. Pete was a drunk and looked like he was hurting now, but he always knew what to do when he came on duty and completed his daily chores without incident or complaints.

Pete had moved the stools away from the bar to sweep up peanut shells on the floor. His hands shook pushing the broom. Lisa noticed immediately. After all, her father was a drunk and she knew what it would take to get him functioning and out of pain. Lisa poured a double shot of rye and slid it up the bar toward Pete. He looked at Lisa, leaned the broom against the bar, grabbed the glass with two hands, wobbled it to his mouth, and drank the whiskey in one gulp. He stood a moment, head back, eyes closed, relishing the burn.

"Bless you, girl," Pete said.

After he slid it back, Lisa took the glass, poured a single shot, and walked the glass back to Pete, who drank it down. He nodded to her again. A tear formed in his eye.

"That's all," Lisa said. "I have a shipment coming in and need you to help me put it away. It will give you some more time. Then you can get Jose to make you something to eat."

Pete smiled. "What would I do without you?"

Lisa stowed the glass under the bar to be washed and sliced her last two limes. Pete returned to sweeping.

Pete would be homeless, except for the fact that he was indispensable to After Dark, and especially to Bart, who didn't like getting his hands dirty. For his handyman acumen and his willingness to do anything, including changing deep fryer oil, unblocking toilets, and cleaning up vomit, Bart let Pete sleep in an unused closet behind the kitchen. The spot was quiet and warm, a place to sleep off his daily jags and still be accessible when a job needed doing.

Pete was quiet and made no trouble. He drank his paycheck and stumbled off to bed before he got too sloppy and had to be carried away. When he got hungry, which wasn't often, Jose made Pete a meal. Pete liked soup and leftover specials.

Lisa had been out early that morning. At the Goodwill thrift shop, she bought Pete two pairs of sweatpants, four T-shirts, a pair of sneakers, a pack of new boxers, socks, and a clean baseball cap with the local team logo. She folded these neatly and placed them on his cot in an empty tomato paste carton, along with soap, deodorant, and a pack of disposable razors.

Just before the restaurant opened, Pete appeared at the kitchen door wearing his new clothes and freshly shaved. Tears rolled down his face. He pressed a palm over his heart and mouthed a silent thank you to Lisa. He stood a moment silently as if trying to decide what to do next, his scabby arms dangling at his side. He blew her a kiss and returned to his spot behind the kitchen.

Lisa followed Pete into the kitchen and went to Jose.

"No time for homeless meals now, Miss Lisa. We have a big takeout lunch for the convention center. Maybe later. Maybe not at all."

"Jose, what happens to the food that customers don't eat."

"Miguel and the busboys scrape the plates into the garbage. Then it goes to the dumpster. You should know that."

"Are you sure?"

"Where else would it go? Back on a plate? They say tomato sauce covers a multitude of sins, but that isn't one of them," Jose said with a smile. "It sounds like you want to set up a buffet in the parking lot for the homeless. Wait till Bart sees that!"

"No, Jose. I heard a story that someone might have got a piece of steak with a piece bit out of it. I wondered..."

"If someone sent back a steak with one bite out of it, I might eat it, but probably not. If I want a steak, I will make one for myself the way I like it. If Bart doesn't like me making a steak for myself, he can go fuck himself. Find himself someone else to be chef, work in this oven of a kitchen."

"What about desserts? You know, cake and pie?"

"I don't eat desserts. Lisa, I have to get this order out."

"Okay. I have to get to the bar."

"One more thing," Jose said. "Thanks for the new knives." He laughed. "They good and sharp. You take care of me. I like that very much."

After work, Lisa returned to her apartment and opened her laptop. There was a new posting among the city's homeless videos.

It included a drive-through of the streets around the stadium taken from a slow-moving car. The video picked up street noises, horns blaring, shouting voices, buses pulling out, and occasional sirens in the distance. There was even a *bang, bang, bang,* like gunfire in the distance. The only thing missing was the stink, Lisa thought. The car retraced a specific route, around several blocks. Usually, it stopped only for backed-up traffic, a red traffic light, or the occasional interview with a junkie.

The same buildings and intersections appeared again and again. The same tents, mounds of trash, squatters parked on discarded recliners, wheelchairs, or beach chairs. Some slept. Some watched the traffic go by. Dippers dipped, junkies walked ungainly, a man pushed a woman in a shopping cart. Some stood motionless, others passed out, lying across the sidewalks, in the sun, on the concrete. One man limped along wearing only one shoe. Another scratched his wooly hair furiously.

Scores of tents surrounded by litter lined the sidewalks as if they were a village. Tent neighbors argued, consoled one another, or chatted. Some tents had open flaps, revealing sitting or unconscious occupants. Occasionally, sober people walked quickly through the neighborhoods carrying backpacks, looking momentarily at junkies cooking their fixes, injecting themselves, or helping others find a vein to shoot up.

Lisa stopped the video sometimes to get a better look at the people. Her father had been a handsome man before her mother died of cancer and he turned to booze, unable to raise a rebellious teenage girl alone. Lisa was raised by her grandmother until she died. Then she was on her own. Charles Van der Meer lost their home and his job. He went to counseling and rehab but failed at both—several times. He lived out of his car for a while, but the vehicle inspection expired and the city towed it away eventually, while he sat down the block in a dive, and passed out at the bar.

As she scanned the video, Lisa wondered whether her father resembled Pete, whether she would recognize him if he passed on the street. Charles Van der Meer had always been resourceful. Lisa hoped he was still in the city and had found shelter somewhere. The car stopped in traffic. Horns blared. The camera zeroed in on Overboard George's sweet box. Old Harriet stood outside, her arms flailing, talking incoherently in a loud voice. No one was nearby. *To think, I half believed that crazy old hag, with her hair-sprouting mole and her frizzy gray hair.*

Just then, a tall man walked by with his head down. Lisa knew it was her father. Her heart skipped and she drew in a deep breath. Tears filled her eyes. Charles Van der Meer was grayer than she remembered and walked through the scene in a second. Although he walked slowly, he didn't stagger. Lisa couldn't see his entire face but he appeared to be clean-shaven. Even his hair seemed trimmed. The toiletries she gave Pete that morning she had collected for her father. It appeared now he had his own. The camera did not follow Charles Van der Meer but remained on Old Harriet as she ranted at the world. Her beehive stood at an odd angle.

Traffic moved and the car pulled out. The video continued. Old Harriet appeared to place a curse on someone as she disappeared from the frame. At the end of the block, the car pulled to the curb. The video stopped for a moment and restarted with the photographer interviewing a thin man with long straggly hair and beard. His hair was matted when he pulled off a dirty knit cap to dig at his scalp.

"This is Darren," the interviewer said. "We talked to him a few weeks ago."

Darren smiled and flashed a peace sign. His teeth were yellow and broken. He looked dirty. His eyes were dark and sunken.

"When we last spoke with you, Darren, you had an open sore on your leg. How's that doing?"

"It's still there," Darren said slowly, sleepily. "In fact, it seems to be bigger."

"May we see it?" the interviewer asked.

Darren rolled up his sweatpants leg, revealing a bandage above the ankle. He unwrapped the gauze, which was soaked with blood and a yellowish fluid. The bandage stuck to the open skinless wound. Darren winced when he pulled at it, thought better, and rewrapped it."

"That looks nasty, D."

"Yeah, it does," Darren agreed. "I wash it every day if I remember, but it doesn't get any better."

"How do you get around, D?"

"On this chair on wheels. It's easier if I push myself backward. The only thing is I gotta be careful on the street. It can get stuck in a pothole, even a big crack. The wheels are too small, more ornamental than useful, but I like the chair itself. It's fancy with leather and nice woodwork. It might be an antique. A pothole almost flipped me out a couple of times. And being so low, a truck or bus driver might not see me." Darren chuckled. "This here chair used to belong to a guy named Overboard George who lived in a box around the corner. But he's gone now, and I have it. It's very ornate, don't you think?"

"D, what happened to Overboard George?"

Darren cocked his head. "Who knows? People disappear, man. There's a woman named Old Harriet. She claims the Whistlers took Overboard George."

After an uneasy pause, the interviewer said, "Yeah. I heard about the Whistlers from a few people here on the street." He added, nonplused. "We'll save that subject for another video. Maybe next week after I do a little more research. Maybe we'll try to find Old Harriet and talk to her on this topic."

"Well, Old Harriet took Overboard George's sweet box. She wanted this chair on wheels, but she don't need it. She can get around on her own two legs. I need a chair like this, something on wheels, so I have it. When I get tired, which is often, I can sit for a while. You know. Take a break. Hey, I'm in the market for some bigger wheels for this chair. Bigger wheels will make it easier to push. These ornamental wheels look nice, but they ain't very useful in the real world."

"It's a sweet chair, D. Leather cushions on the seat and back with fancy woodwork on the arms and legs. What do you call that, D?"

"That's scrolling. Those pieces were made on a lathe. Very fancy, indeed. I have a plan to attach bigger wheels. It might take away from the value but I need bigger wheels."

"How old are you, D?"

"Twenty-three." Darren lit a cigarette and inhaled. He coughed immediately. "I'll be twenty-four this winter. Hope I make it."

"You'll be fine, D. I can see you digging into that birthday cake. I thought you were going to seek help for that wound, man."

"I looked into it like I said I would, but they wanted to admit me to the hospital. That was it. I was out of there. I can't take dope sickness. I can't go through withdrawal. It's like too painful." He chuckled. "I'd rather deal with the hole in my leg, as painful as that is, than withdrawal."

"How's your other leg, D?"

Darren rolled up his other pant leg. "It's about the same. Not as sore, though."

"All those holes, D. They look infected. Is that where you shot up."

"Most of the time. I don't know how they got so big and deep. Looks like bugs crawled inside. But all my veins are bad. It's hard to find a good vein."

Just then a black man pushed a shopping cart through the scene. A small woman sat inside.

"There goes Little Mary," Darren said, beaming. He called after them, but they continued up the street. "Mar! You need a cigarette? I got a new pack." Darren returned to the camera and shook his head. "She lost a leg, between diabetes and infections. I'm afraid I'm going to lose a leg or both legs. Maybe I got diabetes. At least she got somebody to push her around, but I don't. If I lose a leg it's going to be very bad on me. A chair on wheels won't do me no good if I have no legs to push it around. You know how it is? You need some kind of traction."

"Well, D, there is help out there."

Darren twitched and scratched his face with long, dirty fingernails. His head lolled from side to side while he spoke. "I know. And I'm going for help, but I want to try to heal these sores myself. I think they'll come along. Just needs some time. Some of these treatments are supposed to be good. I'll give it a try. Try to get clean again. To tell you the truth, shooting up ain't fun like it used to be. The brown dope was good. I'd be high for six, seven, eight hours. You'd get that rush and then that warm feeling." Darren smiled and looked skyward for a moment. "This shit now is bad. Even the fentanyl is bad now. They got all kinds of stuff mixed in it—meat tenderizer, research chemicals, animal tranquilizers. This stuff knocks you out and in an hour you're up and craving more. It just ain't fun no more, but it's an addiction. I want to get clean, but then I don't. Know what I mean?"

"Sure, D, I know. It sounds like you're using some nasty stuff. When was the last time you OD'd?"

"To be honest, yesterday. I got narced twice. They thought I was dead and started to walk away. Then I got that breath of life, a great big deep gasp, and came to. My chest is still sore from them rubbing it. That's what they do." Darren laughed and touched his chest gingerly. "I had some Narcan myself at one time. In case somebody found me OD'd. But that all got used up or stolen. I don't remember. Now I'm kind of on my own."

Lisa's father walked through the frame. Darren grabbed his hand, trying to pull him closer. "Chaz!"

Charles pulled free from the grip, looked at the camera for a second, and hurried down the street.

"That's my man Chaz," Darren said. He raised his arms over his head. "I love you, Chaz. Need a smoke? I got a new pack," he called after the man, before looking back at the camera. "He saved me yesterday. I went down like a ton of bricks. Most people are used to seeing that, but he called for help. One of the Lutherans showed up and hit me in the neck with a Narcan shot. It wasn't enough so when the cops arrived a minute later, they gave me another shot in the neck. They rubbed my chest so hard that they almost set it on fire because it's sore as hell today. Red, too." Darren lifted the dirty T-shirt to expose his inflamed skin. "Rubbed so hard they almost broke my ribs. The Narcan ruined my high, too. I was pissed. But at least I'm still breathing." Darren chuckled. "At least I'm still breathing." Darren lowered his voice to a whisper. "Way to go Chaz. I owe you one. I think I got some scratches from that nice ring of yours. But, hey, that's okay. You saved my life."

"With your permission, D, we'll revisit you in a week or so to see what progress you make," the anonymous interviewer said. "I'm concerned. I want to see what progress you make with those legs. I know my viewers commented *a lot* after my first visit with you. Can you walk at all?"

"Not much. Not more than a few steps at a time. Just enough to get inside and outside my tent. If I'm not on my chair on wheels, I'll be crawling around. That crawling is painful, too. I do appreciate the concern your viewers show. Thanks, guys. It means a lot to me. If you're in the mood to donate, I can always use cigarettes and clean bandages. Wouldn't mind having a cane, either."

"That's right. You can send donations directly to my link," the photographer said. "I'll see D gets them. I'll see you next week, D."

"I'll be here," Darren said, smiling broadly. Then he pointed. The camera followed his dirty fingers. "That's my tent. I don't stray too far. Everybody's welcome to stop and chat. Thank God for a chair on wheels. If anybody got some bigger wheels let me know. I made a drawing, an artist's concept, so they say, of how I'd put those bigger wheels on the chair. Someday, I might even get a motor for it."

The camera panned back to Darren's face and focused on his smile for a few seconds. The video ended.

Lisa was stunned. She rewound the video to the point where the video passed Overboard George's sweet box. Her eyes filled with tears again. She fast-forwarded to where the car pulled to the curb. She stopped the video and studied the street scene. *I know this place*, she thought. She had been through it numerous times. She moved the video forward again to the point where Darren grabbed her father's hand. Visible on the screen, although slightly out of focus, was her father's surprised face, as he looked at the camera for a moment, like an animal caught on a trail camera, and his right hand and signet ring, easily identifiable. Lisa bolted for the kitchen, grabbed a water bottle from the refrigerator, stuffed her keys into a pocket, left her apartment, and sprinted down the exterior stairs to the ground.

Lisa raced to After Dark and parked her car in the lot behind the restaurant. The video was made two days ago. Posted this morning. She jogged to Fifth Street and walked quickly passed the stadium and through the human quagmire, skirting tents and trash piles, dodging dippers and panhandlers, the mentally ill who wanted her to stop and talk. The street smell burned in her nostrils. In the distance, Lisa saw Overboard George's sweet box, the bright blue tarp flapping in the breeze. Beside the box and its bright blue tarp was Old Harriet perched on a chair. Lisa crossed the street to avoid Old Harriet and continued to the end of the block, where she turned the corner just as the car in the video had done and continued down the sidewalk. Eventually, she slowed her pace, caught her breath, and lined up her sight with the scene she recalled from the video. Then she arrived at the spot. The rusted chain-link fence Darren leaned against, with its plastic shopping bags caught in the mesh. The empty, overgrown lot behind the fence. The overturned green sofa that spewed stuffing into the lot like a disemboweled animal. The edge of a graffiti-covered brick wall on the right. However, Darren, his chair on wheels, and his tent were gone.

Lisa wondered if she had the wrong location. This must be the right place. Everything lined up–the lot, the fence, the brick wall, the old sofa. She doubted whether Darren could walk very far on his damaged legs. Perhaps Darren wasn't his name. She didn't even have a last name for him. She walked up and down the street stopping often to recalculate Darren's position in the video. Twice she stepped into the street for a better view and was accosted by blaring car horns. Despite how many times she recalculated the video angle, she always came back to the same spot.

Eventually, Lisa retraced her way back to Overboard George's sweet box. She was wet with perspiration. Old Harriet dipped in front of the box now. Lisa shook the woman. Old Harriet straightened and slumped forward to dip some more. Lisa straightened the woman and pushed her across the sidewalk and sat her on the chair with wheels. It was the same chair Darren used in the video, padded seat and back, and scrolled woodwork on the arms and legs, with small, decorative wheels.

Old Harriet's neighbor emerged from a green tent next to the sweet box. He was a thin black man and approached cautiously. "You from the city?" he wanted to know.

"I'm Lisa and I came to talk to Old Harriet."

"She not around."

"Well, there she is," Lisa said, pointing to the unconscious Old Harriet, her head resting sideways on her shoulder, her beehive pointing into the breeze like a weathervane. "I just put her there. She was dipping in the middle of the sidewalk."

"Old Harriet tends to do that," the man said, reflectively. He raised an eyebrow.

"I need to talk to her. Where did she get that chair?"

The man walked over to the chair. "Never seen it before. Nice chair, though. The wheels are kind of too small to be much good outside. Probably came from an old mansion. If you want to talk to Old Harriet, you can come back in an hour or two. She'll be cognizant then. Or you can wait. If you want a seat, we can stand her up and let her dip while you rest. Old Harriet's pretty clean. She got no bugs, at least none I know of. She cleaned herself up since she got that sweet box belonged to Overboard George."

"We'll let Old Harriet have the chair. I'll wait beside her.

"Suit yourself." Before the man returned to his tent, he asked Lisa for money. She declined.

Lisa poked Old Harriet a few times, but she was still out. Lisa settled on the sidewalk near the chair on wheels. Then Lisa remembered Jimmy Young, the volunteer from the Lutheran church. She still had his card in her phone case. Lisa called Jimmy. He picked up immediately. Lisa asked whether he remembered a guy named Darren who had bad legs.

"I know–*knew*–him," Jimmy corrected himself. "He OD'd. Was found in his chair with a needle in his leg. He's at the morgue now. I don't know if there's anyone to claim him. He might be at the morgue for a while. That happens sometimes. I came so close to getting him in rehab, getting those legs looked at, but in the end, he wouldn't give up the dope. Couldn't live without the high."

Lisa told Jimmy about seeing her father again in the city homeless video. Darren had known her father. He called her father Chaz. Her father had saved Darren's life last week.

"Did you narc Darren last week? Lisa said.

"I did. Then the cops gave him another shot."

"Was there a man there?"

"He was the one who called for help. I just happened to hear him. He had a fancy ring with initials. I remember the ring because he helped rub Darren's chest. It had a big black stone."

"That was my father. I saw him two times in that video. He was wearing his signet ring. I saw the ring in the video."

Lisa told Jimmy her location. Jimmy was two blocks away and

would join her in a few minutes. Jimmy was late. By the time he arrived, Old Harriet was coming to.

"It's you again," Old Harriet said when she saw Lisa. "What do you want?"

"What happened to Darren," Lisa demanded.

Old Harriet shrugged her shoulders. "He OD'd. Somebody told me he had Overboard George's chair on wheels. I went there to confront him. To find out how he got it. Darren was gone. Went to the morgue, they said, to wait to be claimed. Some guys were loading his tent into a truck. Probably government men after some technology Darren had in his tent. Darren was like that, you know. Always talking technology and computers and music systems, but never had any himself. No electricity. He was a smart cookie, though. While they were having trouble with the tent, I wheeled the chair away. Now it's mine. I'm sitting in it."

CHAPTER NINE

Overboard George woke with a moan. He felt chilled, rolled over, and struck his head on something hard. He rubbed his scalp and groaned. Suddenly he realized he was naked. His eyes focused slowly. He was not under the sky, as he was when he usually woke. He was in a large, high-ceilinged room. Huge wooden beams loomed overhead. The concrete floor he lay on was damp and cold. He was in a cage large enough to stand in but not big enough to stretch out. He lay curled. Eventually, he sat up, pressing his back against the cage, and extending his feet through the bars in front of him.

Overboard George tried to figure out where he was. The place was too clean and antiseptic smelling for a sewer. Too dark to be a hospital unless he had been taken mistakenly to the morgue. He hadn't shot up, so he didn't overdose. If it were the morgue, it wouldn't be necessary to put him in a cage. Dead people don't walk away. Dead people no longer need to be protected, unless they were serial killers in real life and their victims' families wanted to hack them apart. Maybe the real morgue was filled with dead righteous people and junkies were thrown in cages. Overboard George stood, using the cage bars for support. A stone wall was behind him, with just enough room to walk by. It leeched moisture and a green slime.

A row of similar cages was on both sides. In front of him, some distance away, was another stone wall and a large metal door. To his right a third rock wall was visible. To his left, the row of cages ended in darkness. A burned-out light, George thought. He was in a neglected part of some building, probably the basement. Maybe he was in an old police station. He didn't remember doing anything that would warrant him being hauled off to jail, even though shooting up dope was probably illegal by most accounts. Maybe the Navy caught up with him at last, but this was no way to treat someone, even a person AWOL for years. The police mostly ignored the homeless unless they caused problems. He raised his arms and pushed against the bars on the cage's ceiling. They didn't budge.

George relieved himself in a metal bucket in the corner. The piss stream sounded deafening as it hit the back of the bucket and fell inside. Up until now, Overboard George had been silent. He cleared his throat and in a low voice called. "Hello. Anybody there? It's Overboard George and I'm locked in this here cage. Will somebody help me?"

He waited for an answer but there was none.

"I'm just telling you I'm going to need a fix soon. Somebody has to leave me go." Overboard George shook the cage bars, but they didn't rattle. The cage was solid. The metal appeared newer. The welds still shined and were thick. Even the door refused to rattle. He soon tired and sank to the floor. "What the hell is going on?"

He heard a groan several cages away, near the point where the room went dark.

"Who's there?" George called. "I know somebody's there. I can hear you."

"Oh, help me," a woman's voice called. "I can't stand being locked up. I need to get out."

"Is that you, Mad Maggie?" George called. He stood and

turned toward the voice. "Mad Maggie. How'd you get down here? It's OG."

"George? What the hell. Where are we? Somebody took my clothes. I'm naked."

"Me, too!"

"The Whistlers got us, Overboard George. They took you one night, and they took me the next, after I moved into your sweet box. I was at After Dark, meeting with that Lisa girl. We went our own ways, and I heard the whistling. I hurried along Fifth Street, trying to find a crowd. They took me when I walked near the park entrance. I had my knife out but it didn't matter. They were on me so fast I dropped the knife. Then I was squeezed. There was a terrible stench. Like the dead. I could hardly breathe because I was squeezed so hard. I was surrounded by fur and off the ground. They squeezed me so hard I must have fainted. That's all I remember."

"That's more than I remember," George said. "I don't know what their game is, but they better supply me with dope. I'm not going through withdrawal sickness. If they want to see a mess I'll shake this fucking cage apart, pull those whistles right out of they throats."

"You ain't getting no dope, Overboard George. They're drying you out. You'll go through withdrawal. We'll wait and see what they do when you're sober."

"How you know that?"

"It's just a feeling. The thing is," Mad Maggie said, lowering her voice, "They don't know I'm sober, just crazy. If being crazy don't matter to them, I'll go first. It'll be a while before you sober up."

"Did you see the Whistlers?" George said. "They must be powerful because they carried me away and I'm a load. They didn't drag me 'cause I have no scrapes."

"Only for a second. They hit me fast. Knocked me over. Pushed the breath out of me with a strike to the stomach. They knew what they were doing. I couldn't scream. I couldn't get air in my lungs to scream. But one had his face in my face. Little beady eyes. Sharp teeth. Hairy bodies. Bristly, like an old, stiff brush. Not smooth hair like a cat has. Not as tall as me. Ugly as sin and breath that would shrivel a corpse. Dead breath. Breath that would make you think of old blood. Breath the way a corpse smells when you find one in a tent OD'd in the heat. Know what I mean?"

"I know," Overboard George said. "I smelled it enough."

"I know you have. Anyone homeless on the street a time knows what the dead smell like. In the summer. In the heat."

"I wonder if they did the same thing to me," Overboard George said. "Squeezed me until I passed out."

"You were probably dipping and senseless, Overboard George. Who knows what they did to you? Could have pulled your pants off and had their way with you. Probably did."

"Nobody has their way with me, Mad Maggie, unless I want it that way."

"I can tell you I wasn't the first they took. It was all very coordinated. Then it was lights out," Mad Maggie said.

"We gotta get out of here, Mad Maggie. Come up with a plan to distract them. Escape when they bring us food—there's a food tray in the cell on the other side of me—or empty these sloop buckets. So start thinking. I'm already thinking."

A lock rattled at the dark end of the room. A door opened, letting in a slice of dim moonlight on the damp floor. After a while, a man wheeled in a gurney with a young man, a redhead, strapped to it. He was gagged and struggled under the belts. The man left the gurney by the metal door opposite Overboard George and retreated until he disappeared into the darkness where he had come.

"See that?" Mad Maggie whispered.

"I got eyes."

"They got another one."

Overboard George and Mad Maggie pressed themselves

against their cell doors to watch. The man soon wheeled back a second gurney with another gagged young man. The tight straps that bound him pressed into his heavyset body. The man let the second gurney go and watched its progress until it bumped into the first. Both men renewed their efforts to get free, but the bonds held. The man retreated and carried back a young woman over his shoulder, dumped her in one of the empty cells, and locked it. He paused to cough and spit, and proceeded to a door in the corner which he unlocked by tugging on a lever. In a second, a tumbling black mass exited the door, crossed the floor, and covered the gurneys. It was difficult to see in the low light, but it soon was evident the black mass that rolled like tumbleweed was made of individual animals. They covered the gurneys, gnashing their teeth, pulling off shoes, tearing clothes off the men with their claws.

"Get back! Get back now, or I'll turn the lights on. I'll burn you to a crisp," the man hollered. The animals recoiled from the gurneys and massed themselves into a single lump a few feet away. They growled and clicked. Their blood-coated mouths and individual sharp teeth showed through the darkness as one by one they took turns poking out their snouts.

The mass rolled forward slowly. The creatures bared their fangs, seemingly challenging the man.

"I'll tell the master if you don't get out of here," the man screamed. "You did your job. Get back! You'll all get a share. Two with clean blood. Not junkies. You eat tonight."

The Whistlers moved in unison away from the gurneys. They crawled and leap-frogged one another. Their claws scrapped the concrete floor and must have dug into the other Whistlers, because they clicked, craned their necks to the animals on top, and barred their teeth. The bound men were scratched and bitten. They moaned. Both were mostly naked, with only a few scraps of material left dangling, a T-shirt neck, a sock, or an underwear waistband. Most of the clothes lay on the floor in shreds. The man opened the large metal door and wheeled the two gurneys into the room across from Overboard George. As soon as the man disappeared into the room with the second gurney the Whistlers charged Overboard George. He threw himself against the back of the cell. They attacked, clung to the bars, pressed their snouts through the openings, and salivated a foul-smelling drool.

While the beasts surrounded the cell, George moved to the center of the small enclosure. Occasionally, a sharp tongue licked across his stomach or back. Behind the tongues, their teeth snapped with fury. George recoiled. They inserted their long-fingered claws and pawed at George, coming within inches of his body. George threw a quick one-two punch, striking the snouts of two Whistlers. They howled in pain and withdrew from the cell. Down the row, Mad Maggie screamed. Several Whistlers dropped to the floor and attacked her cell, attaching themselves to the bars. George turned his head in her direction and saw her pressed against the back of her cell. She stood crying with her eyes closed. Her chest heaved. The Whistlers clawed at her body, barely missing her flesh.

Suddenly, a bright, bluish light illuminated the room. The Whistlers howled and withdrew to a mass on the floor. Their smoking hides stank. The man switched off the bright lights by throwing a knife-blade switch on the wall.

The man who controlled the knife-blade switch screamed incoherently at the Whistlers. They assembled into one unit, rolled to the corner, and disappeared through a small door. The man hurried to the door, pulled it closed, and locked it. He stood a moment coughing, leaning against the wall.

The Whistlers howled and clicked on the door's other side.

"You misfits will listen to me when I'm a master," the man yelled. "I'll teach you. I don't understand why Gerrard and Eva have a soft spot for you."

The man turned and looked at George for a moment. He walked toward the exit slowly, coughing again. George pressed himself against the back of his cage. He caught his breath and looked at Mad Maggie. She stood like a statue with her eyes closed.

"They're gone, Maggie," George called.

Maggie opened her eyes.

"You see that box on the wall by the door?

Maggie shook her head.

"That controls the blue light the Whistlers can't stand. Remember where it is, crazy girl. That might be our ticket out of here."

Sometime later, at least hours later, George was hurting. His bones ached. He had a fever. He sweated and shivered. He wanted to vomit but couldn't. Dry heaves racked his body. The pain was excruciating. He squatted over the bucket with diarrhea. Sometimes he missed. His cell smelled. As soon as he moved off the bucket, he had a violent urge to shit again. He couldn't remember eating to make him shit so much. He was in withdrawal.

Down the line, Mad Maggie sat on the floor talking to herself incoherently. Her fingers walked across the floor as if they were searching for something. Finally, she said, "I know there's a knife around here somewhere. The same knife I carved Fred with. Sharp as a razor. Maybe sharper."

The man arrived through the far door. First, he looked at Mad Maggie, who feigned withdrawal symptoms. She moaned and made herself shiver. Next, he stopped in front of George. George begged for a fix. He told the man he would die without one. The man showed no emotion, said nothing, and turned away. He entered the room across from Overboard George and closed the door.

Through his pain, George heard water run, possibly a hose. The men on the gurneys screamed, pleaded for help, and choked. George thought they were being hosed off. They howled in pain when it was apparent the man scrubbed them with a stiff brush. Chains rattled as if being pulled through blocks and tackles. At first, the chains moved easily, quickly, then more slowly, as if they encountered weight. Inside the room, the man coughed between tugs. The men screamed and thrashed. The noise was hideous.

Mad Maggie whimpered. Overboard George concentrated on what happened behind the closed door, as if some information could be gleaned to help him escape. He stood and clenched the cell door bars. Eventually, the men quieted. They sobbed, apparently exhausted. The door opened on creaking hinges. The man brought out one gurney at a time and parked them near the exit. While the door was open, Overhead George saw the naked men suspended upside down. Their wrists were bound behind their backs. They were gagged. Their movements were reduced to quivers. Their flesh was raw from the scrubbings, scratched from the Whistlers' attack. The keeper watched silently. Occasionally, he looked at his watch.

The far door opened near the Whistler den and two adults, a man and a woman, entered the basement. They were dressed formally. The clothing seemed odd, as if from an old movie. The man wore a tuxedo, the woman a gown with a frayed hem that nearly touched the floor. Long threads dragged across the floor behind her. Going to or just came from the opera, George thought. They walked slowly and stiffly. The keeper stood straight and bowed to the couple. They smiled in return, revealing sharp fangs among their teeth.

The woman walked to George. Although she appeared young, her flesh was wrinkled, and seemed ancient, as if it needed hydration and blood. The man was equally wrinkled. Their flesh sagged. They both appeared pale, dry husks. The female approached George's cage and looked him over.

"I ain't seeing this," George said. "This isn't real. It's the dope sickness having its way with me. This is a full-blown hallucination."

The woman licked her lips and examined his naked body, head to toe. She focused on his crotch, raised a small hand to her mouth, and tittered. She talked to the man in an unfamiliar language, and they laughed together.

The keeper rushed toward her as if Overboard George were dangerous.

"This one isn't ready, Madam," the keeper said. "He's still going through detox. But the two I hung have clean blood. They're university students, young. I think you will be..."

The woman raised a hand with an imperious flip of her wrist. The keeper fell silent. He nodded, bowed, and receded to the room where the young men were suspended. She and the male vampire followed, walking slowly, nodding, and talking in whispers George couldn't hear. The woman who found Overboard interesting, fondled Ridge's penis. Ridge screamed through his gag. She scratched his buttock. Drew blood. She collected several drops in her palm and licked it clean. Relished the taste. She turned to the male and nodded approvingly. The dangling men cried. By now they were exhausted and limp, positioned face-to-face. Their eyes showed disbelief and terror. The keeper returned outside the room and closed the door. He leaned against it, as if he were exhausted, too. He had a dry cough—no phlegm.

Through the heavy door, Overboard George heard muffled shrieks of pain, laughter, and sucking noises. After a while the door opened and the vampires strolled from the feeding room and exited, licking their lips, dabbing red stained handkerchiefs at the corners of their mouths. The woman who took an interest in Overboard George was now flushed. Her skin was taut and youthful looking. Overboard George saw the dangling men had numerous deep bite and claw marks. Blood trickled from the wounds in thin rivulets down their arms and legs and dripped on the floor. Their bodies were pale, drained of blood, but still alive enough to take shallow breaths and twitch. One man had been scalped. His red hair lay on the floor like a discarded mop. The other's penis was missing.

The vampires walked away slowly, just as they had come. The female burped and vomited a mouth full of blood on the floor. The two vampires chuckled and receded into the darkness, back from where they came.

With the vampires gone, the keeper released the Whistlers,

who rolled in one mass from their door in the corner to the feeding room. They clicked and clattered, whimpered with anticipation. Their talons scrapped the floor. The mass separated at the door and individual beasts leaped on the men, clinging to their bodies, sucking the remaining life from them. The tangle of bodies trembled as the boys' bodies twitched through the last moments of life. The entire collection of bodies swung back and forth. Overboard George saw more than he wanted before the keeper closed the feeding room door again.

Surprisingly, George slept. After he woke, he saw there was little left of the two bodies. The dehydrated cadavers were folded like laundry and wrapped together in one plastic parcel of clear plastic, smaller than one human, and pushed away on the gurney. The red, bloodied scalp pressed against the plastic shroud in one place. The other's face showed through at another spot, shrunken and dry-looking with a gaping mouth, still reflecting horror. After the bodies were whisked away, the keeper hosed down the feeding room. The chains were cleaned and made ready for the next meal. The keeper wore long rubber gloves, high boots, and a black rubber apron that extended below the boot tops. He worked methodically, pausing occasionally to cough.

As what seemed like days passed, the keeper paid more attention to Overboard George and Mad Maggie. He stood outside their cells, watching for signs of withdrawal symptoms. As usual, he was silent and refused to answer their pleas for help and freedom. George was still in withdrawal. Maggie was a good actor. She mimicked everything George did. The small female was exsanguinated soon after the young men were killed. George and Maggie knew they would be next. No other victims were in the basement.

One day, when they were alone, Mad Maggie, said, "You know that gurney man who pushed the boys inside, hoses us off, brings us food, carries away our shit?"

"Should I know him?"

"You should know him, O.G. It's Chazzy. Charles Van der Meer. It took me a while to put a name with his face."

"I thought he drank himself to death," Overboard George said slowly. "Seemed that's where he was going but he cleaned up. Looks good, too. No wonder I ain't seen him around. He been busy feeding monsters."

CHAPTER TEN

Bo Bentwood woke early. The frat house was quiet. Most of his fraternity brothers had left campus for the summer and returned to their hometowns. Bo was living at the fraternity, along with TJ, Ridge, and a few others. Bo didn't have a job, but Ridge and TJ did. Bo didn't need extra money. The other men did.

Bo had an uneasy feeling in the pit of his stomach. Dressed only in his boxers, Bo walked down the hall to the room Ridge and TJ shared. He approached the room hoping to find one or both had hooked up with women, possibly at After Dark. He might even get a look at the girls in some state of undress. He had an idea the girls might be twins, cousins, perhaps sorority sisters. He entered the room without knocking, pushing the door forward slowly, and found it empty, and dark, which was strange because the boys rarely turned off lights.

TJ's bed was made, as it always was. He was a neat freak. Ridge's was a tangle of sheets. It appeared like a whirling dervish had danced on the mattress. Empty beer cans lined Ridge's desk. TJ's desk had neatly stacked books in the corner, and a pile of folded clothes in the center. The room hadn't been slept in. The books and laundry were in those same positions when the trio left for downtown last night to beat the junkies.

Bo sat on TJ's bed and stared at a black television screen. He hoped the door would open any second and his friends would pile in, eager to tell stories of their overnight adventures. Maybe they stayed out, found a party, and eventually went for breakfast. Ridge was a breakfast guy. That was conceivable, Bo kept telling himself. The possibility he didn't want to admit was his friends were taken by the Whistlers.

Their penchant for beating the homeless had been Bo's idea. It started one night earlier in the summer when After Dark had closed for the night. Bo was in a sour mood because Lisa wasn't there. As they weaved out of the bar a junkie bumped into Bo. While the junkie bounced off Bo, Bo pushed him to the ground. The trio laughed and started to walk away, when Bo turned suddenly, ran back to the man, who was trying to stand, and kicked him repeatedly until he collapsed. Bo walked away. Ridge and TJ howled. The beaten man rolled back and forth from his back to his side.

"Come on," Bo said. "Let's have some fun with this fucker."

"Better be careful," Ridge said. "You might run into one who's your match."

"They're as weak as kittens," Bo said, laughing. "I hardly touched that asshole and he went down. Could hardly stand."

Bo pointed to a dipper up the street. Bo jogged up to the man and tipped him over. His head bounced off the sidewalk. Ridge and TJ followed and surrounded the prostrate man, watching him try to roll over. The man moved in slow motion, sloth-like.

"See what I mean," Bo said. He hauled back his leg and kicked him in the stomach. The junkie moaned and tightened into a fetal position. Bo threw back his head and laughed. The other men sniggered.

"Come on, old timer," Bo said gently. "Let me give you a hand." The man reached up and took Bo's outstretched hand. Bo started to lift the skinny man. He was halfway up when Bo let go, and the man hit the sidewalk again. The man groaned and tried to get to his hands and knees to crawl away.

"My bad," Bo said. He leaned over, suppressing a laugh. "My grip slipped. Let's try this again. We'll get you upright this time."

The man reached for Bo's hand, nodded his head, and talked in an unrecognizable flurry. Bo pulled the man to his feet. The man nodded again and acknowledged the help. Bo latched on his wrist, planted his feet, swung the junkie in a circle and let go. The man stumbled forward and fell on his face. His glasses flew across the concrete sidewalk.

The frat brothers howled. The junkie patted the sidewalk near him for his glasses. He found pieces. An arm and a lens were missing. He patted the concrete until he gathered all the pieces and drew them into his stomach, holding them in a fist.

"Here comes another," Ridge said. "Let's give him the works."

A short, shirtless man staggered down the sidewalk.

"Looks drunk," Bo said.

"Hey, buddy, can you spare a buck," the man mumbled.

"Sure," Bo said. "Anything for a friend."

"That's right. Do I know you?" the man said, twisting his face as if trying to remember. He smiled with teeth destroyed by meth.

Bo reached in his pocket. Came up empty. Dug his hand into another pocket. The drunk rubbed his hands in anticipation.

"I appreciate this, man. You're a real prince."

"Oh, too bad," Bo said showing the man his empty hands. He shoved the man to Ridge, who spun him around and pushed him at TJ. The chunky frat boy put his fist into the man's stomach, knocking the wind out of him. The drunk staggered toward Bo, who delivered a roundhouse kick to his face. The man collapsed to the sidewalk and was silent. He breathed in short gasps, scattering dust, then choking on it.

"Across the street," Bo said. "Another dipper. A cunt. Let's get her." The trio jogged across the street and shoved the woman into a pile of trash. She moaned while they covered her with leaking plastic garbage bags, letting the oily water run over her head before dropping the bags. The stench from the bags smelled like a landfill. Eventually, she was buried by trash, invisible from the sidewalk, without the strength to crawl out.

The next morning, Bo bought a highly varnished kayak paddle from a sporting goods center off campus. He secured the bamboo switches for TJ and Ridge from a dumpster where he saw their ends stick out. He also bought a box of neoprene disposable gloves, a container of antiseptic wipes, and box cutters. After all, none of the boys liked touching the homeless, even if it was only long enough to give them a good shove. Heaven forbid contacting the filthy humans once they were bloodied.

A smile cracked Bo's lips. He wondered whether the junkie ever escaped her tomb of garbage bags, or did the city scoop her up with a front-end loader and carry her to the dump.

After his friends did not return, Bo walked back to his room and sat on his bed. He had carried the kayak paddle with him. Held it like a guitar and strummed imaginary strings. What should he do? Go to university officials? The police? His friends' parents? He'd look foolish if the guys suddenly returned. He couldn't explain they were out beating junkies. They could all get kicked out of school.

Bo phoned TJ and then Ridge. Both calls went to cell phone voicemails. Bo wondered about TJ's videos. He knew TJ captured images of some of the beatings. All three had to be pictured. Even Bo's Charger appeared in some scenes. Bo went back to bed for an hour but couldn't sleep. Eventually, he got up, took a shower, and dressed—shorts, T-shirt, and Nike sneakers. His friends should be at work by now. Both had jobs at the convention center near the baseball stadium. They did janitorial work and helped set up and break down tables and chairs for events, move room partitions, and anything that might require a couple of young, strong backs.

When he arrived at the convention center, Bo found neither

Ridge nor TJ clocked in for work, and neither called in. They were dependable, another worker told Bo, even when it appeared they were hungover.

Bo decided to go to After Dark. He was hungry and hadn't eaten. He could ask if anyone remembered seeing his friends, and he might get the chance to see Lisa.

Inside After Dark, Bo sat at the bar and ordered a dozen wings and a draft IPA. After all, it was time for brunch. The bar had just opened and was mostly deserted. A few barflies sat at a distance. People scurried in and out of the kitchen. Waitresses set out silverware, napkins, and water glasses on tables.

An older man carried a bucket of ice behind the bar and dumped it in a cooler.

"Hey, Dude, what's your name?" Bo said.

"It's Pete." The man eyed Bo warily.

"Pete, is Lisa working today?"

"Day off," Pete said. He wiped his hands on a towel he carried over his shoulder. The man looked hungover himself.

"I'm a friend," Bo said. "Thought I might talk to her. Buy her lunch. You look like a man in the know. Why don't you get me Lisa's schedule?"

Pete cocked an eyebrow toward Bo. "I would think a real friend would know Lisa's schedule. After all, she makes the schedules."

Bo sucked the sauce off a chicken bone and drained his beer. "Hey, chief, suppose you get me a refill. Pour yourself one, too."

"I'm not the bartender," Pete said. He turned to walk away.

"How about Miguel? Is he working today?" Bo called after the quickly retreating Pete.

"He's in the kitchen," Pete said.

"Tell him a friend wants to see him."

"I'm not a messenger, either," Pete said. "Find him yourself." Pete moved his towel from one shoulder to the other and continued on his way.

Bo muttered, "Fucking old drunk. I can't wait to get you on the sidewalk some night."

Bo finished off the plate of wings and crunched the celery stalks dipped in bleu cheese dressing that came with the chicken. Meanwhile, the bartender returned, and Bo ordered another draft.

He, too, feigned no knowledge about Lisa. "Dude, I only work here. Take orders and do my job."

More customers filed in. Some were seated at tables. Others bellied up to the bar. There was an afternoon game with a 1:30 start. Some fans wanted a buzz before the game started without paying the high prices for beer inside the stadium. Bo paid his bill with plastic and stiffed the bartender.

Bo returned to his Charger in the After Dark parking lot. Instead of climbing in, he checked the interior and walked into the bushes where they had heard the night whistling, scaled a concrete block wall, and dropped over its side. *There might be some evidence of what made that noise.* The wall Bo climbed was about five feet high and constructed of concrete blocks. It and a parallel wall made a narrow alley that continued for blocks in both directions, interrupted only by cross streets. The trash-strewn alley defined the ends of small concrete-paved yards each home had, barely larger than interior rooms. Although some homes were vacant, with no curtains or blinds on the windows, the neighborhood teamed with life. The little yards had grills, patio furniture with colorful cushions, tiki torches, and strings of colored electric lights. There was also the sound of traffic moving on Sixth Street one block over. Bo weaved his way through the alley, and avoided a mattress folded in half and stacks of garbage bags. Here and there, rats scurried away in the distance. Weeds and trees grew from the path. The area smelled of dampness and rot. Bo slapped at mosquitos that attacked his exposed flesh. There were sirens in the east. What sounded like gunfire in the south. A few quick pops followed by more. Bo peered over the walls into the little yards, moved slowly, and looked for signs of the strange whistling creatures. However, he saw none and didn't know what to look for. He was no outdoorsman. Couldn't tell a bear's track from a cougar's, although neither would be inside the city and neither would make the kind of noises he had heard. The concrete walkway revealed no tracks, even in flattened piles of wet leaves. Scores of used needles surrounded an abandoned sofa. When Bo could take the bugs no more, he returned the way he came.

Just as Bo entered the brush near After Dark's parking lot, he saw a trap door open on the grassy lot about fifteen yards from the side of the restaurant. A tall man emerged, looked around cautiously, and let the door fall shut before hurrying off across the lot. Bo watched him recede through the high grass. The man was no junkie. However, he looked familiar. His face reminded Bo of someone, but he couldn't place it. Even more unusual was the fact that the man came out of the ground, as if from a grave, through a door near no buildings. He had to have gone through a tunnel to reach the door. The closest building, which wasn't that close, was After Dark. If it hadn't been for his missing friends, the tunnel wouldn't have concerned Bo. He went to the spot, felt through the long grass, found the door and its metal handle, and lifted it a few inches. His nose was accosted with a stench worse than the smell in the alley. Bo dropped the door and tried to find some landmarks to use if he ever had to open it again. This was suspicious. A familiar-looking man emerged from a secret door before sneaking away.

Bo returned to his car, started the engine, and sat in the air conditioning for several minutes before pulling out. He scratched at mosquito bites—some real, some imagined—that covered his arms and legs. He pondered what he could do to find his friends. Everything he imagined implicated him in multiple crimes, his friends' disappearances, and beating the homeless. In the end, he decided to wait and see what happened. After all, Bo was sure Ridge and TJ would show up eventually and all would be explained.

CHAPTER ELEVEN

Lisa had the day off. She ate a quick breakfast, packed a lunch, and drove to After Dark. She parked at the edge of the lot, where her car should go unnoticed, even by the security cameras. A day game meant the restaurant would be busy. She grabbed her folding beach chair, umbrella, and backpack and headed to Darren's spot on the sidewalk where she planned to wait for her father. She had seen him walk through the location twice on videos. There was a good chance he would pass through the area again; that it might be part of his routine. She had no idea where he was going or where he came from, but he had had enough time to call for help when Darren overdosed and stay long enough to see him recover after the Narcan shots. Although Lisa hadn't seen her father in years, she imagined he still had some humanity left inside him. She knew no other way to find her father than to wait and confront him.

The stadium was already open. Foot traffic increased. Herds of people crossed and recrossed Fifth Street. Scalpers milled around, bought and sold tickets. Men and boys hawked ice-cold bottles of water from coolers on wagons. Peddlers pushed carts loaded with hats, T-shirts, cheap sunglasses, and team pennants. Panhandlers had their choice spots picked and their buckets placed to catch donations. In a small plaza across the street from the stadium, a black man sat on an overturned five-gallon bucket and drummed wildly on other buckets. The crowd applauded when he paused, stood to bow, and a few dropped change or singles on a towel at his feet. Larger tips elicited furious drum rolls. The passersby loved it.

Lisa hurried, weaving through the crowds, passed the stadium, up the street, and eventually around the corner. Occasionally, a man or woman stepped in front of her begging for money. She side-stepped them with the alacrity of a seasoned city dweller. Darren's spot was still vacant. Lisa set up her chair, positioned her umbrella in the fence to provide shade, and sat down with her backpack within reach. It was a perfect day for reconnaissance. The humidity had dropped and there was a steady breeze that tumbled Styrofoam cups, paper plates, plastic bags, newspapers, and food wrappers in a constant parade. Occasionally, the city's sour smell of human refuse reached Lisa's nose. A procession of homeless limped by, some with bandaged arms and legs. People dipped on both sides of Lisa. One woman hung clothes on hangers attached to the chain-link fence. Lisa wondered if the clothing was displayed for sale, left to dry after being washed, or hung there because there was no better place to put it. Within fifteen minutes after sitting, three men offered to sell Lisa drugs. Two more wanted sex. Other home-less just wanted money. Lisa felt depressed. She pulled her large-brimmed hat over her face, feigned sleep, and kept her eyes on both sides of the street.

No one familiar moved through the neighborhood. Eventually, despite shouting voices, an occasional horn, and frequent sirens in the distance, she dozed off. Lisa woke suddenly when something bumped her leg. It was Old Harriet rummaging through her backpack.

"May I help you, Old Harriet?" Lisa said from under her hat brim.

"I thought this pack was for anybody. Thought the Lutherans left it for me," Old Harriet said. She straightened stiffly. Primped her wiry hair.

Lisa raised her hat. "It's my backpack."

"Lisa, isn't it?"

Lisa nodded.

Harriet continued to rummage. "She put in her thumb and pulled out a plum!" Harriet held up Lisa's sandwich. "Will you look at that? Finders' keepers."

"You can have it, Old Harriet. But leave me one bottle of water." Lisa fanned herself with her hat.

"I'll take the small water. Just so you know, I prefer Diet Coke. A girl has to watch her figure. I told the Lutheran boy that, but all he ever has is water. At least he hands out tampons occasionally." Old Harriet laughed. "There was a time it embarrassed him to ask if we needed tampons. He'd have boxes of them in his car. He'd turn red as a beet. 'Of course, we need tampons,' I'd say. 'Rather have a tampon at *that* time of the month than a good meal.' You know, I used to make my own—pads, that is—out of toilet paper and plastic shopping bags. A real mess. Now, the Lutheran boy takes care of me. I promised him I'd come to church sometime."

Old Harriet opened the sandwich and took a bite. She chewed slowly, methodically, and swallowed. "Damn good sandwich," Old Harriet said.

"It came from After Dark."

"Oh yes. I've heard of it. This is very good. I'm accustomed to dumpster food when I can get it."

"I'll see that you get more food. I work at After Dark. I'm a manager."

"After Dark," Old Harriet said. "*That was* the place Bad Nelson thought he was taken, where the Whistlers live, where the homeless are consumed to the point they're like old King Tut, every drop of moisture drained from them. Dry as dust."

"That's impossible," Lisa laughed. "I've been through the entire building, even most of the offices on the upper floors. They're all rented. Have respectable businesses." Lisa thought a moment. "If there's one place I haven't been it's the..."

"The basement," Old Harriet interrupted, after swallowing another bite. She nodded her head conspiratorially.

Lisa remembered Jose's story about Geisel snooping around, the big key, the door that's never opened, the basement where nobody goes. She stared at Old Harriet.

"The basement," Harriet said. "That's where all the hanky-panky goes on if you know what I mean."

"Are you sure?" Lisa said.

"Bad Nelson never got a chance to finish his story. He went through the dope sickness and all, and then he gets recycle money for his can and bottle stash. He might be alive somewhere, but I say he was consumed by the Whistlers. They caught up to him."

"None of this makes sense. For example, what would they do with the bodies?"

"Bad Nelson said they grind them up. The flesh is dry as punk. Almost turns to dust by itself. The bones are ground up. Bad Nelson said he could hear the grinder going. The grinder would wail, especially when it got ahold of something big like a leg bone or a skull. Maybe even a denture. He thought they scattered the dust on the street or in the vacant lots. Who would know? With this wind today, we could be sniffing Overboard George and Mad Maggie. They could be in the dust as the wind picks up.

Lisa gagged.

"There, there," Old Harriet said, leaning over to pat Lisa's leg. "It's nasty stuff. I know. I couldn't tell you how many people have come and gone, died, in the time I've been on the street in this city. I thought I was doing myself a favor by moving here." Old Harriet scratched her beehive hairdo with dirty fingers, then examined her ragged nails. "They come; they go. Some of them are nice friends, while they last. Some ain't nice. Have ulterior motives, if you know what I mean."

"I don't know what you mean," Lisa said.

Old Harriet looked at her with amazed eyes. "Well, there are people—men and women—

who'll sell you drugs, find you sex, get you anything you want. Someone old, someone young. I always said it takes all kinds, but some of the worst kinds are on the streets in this city. Some, like Bad Nelson, said the worst of all live underground."

CHAPTER TWELVE

Lisa sat in Darren's spot for the rest of the day. Old Harriet shot up nearby, dipped for more than an hour, then wandered off. Charles Van der Meer never showed. The next morning, Lisa went to work early. It was order day and she had to get her requests in early to get supplies delivered the next day. She used Bart's office to call her vendors. His massive desk let her spread out lists in separate piles, which avoided confusion and saved time. Calling in orders, deciphering the array of handwriting she got from Jose, Julie, the head waitress, even Pete, and her own scribbled penmanship could be difficult. Items were often added to the list on the fly and the papers could be stained by anything from ketchup to soup. Any list could have a multitude of different handwriting, as various workers added items when they noticed supplies ran low. At times, the same staples were ordered by different people. Still, Lisa had to take her own inventory because something was always left off the list.

Today, someone wanted fluorescent light bulbs, thirty-six inches long, but Lisa did not recognize the writing. It wasn't Pete's. Pete always signed his name when he asked for something. Actually, he signed his name twice—*Pete and re-Pete*, a private joke he had with Lisa. The lightbulb request was written in an elegant hand, very old-fashioned looking, Lisa thought, a kind of penmanship that had not been taught for years.

Lisa called Pete as he walked up the hall and by Bart's open office door to show him the list. "I didn't order long lightbulbs," Pete said. "I don't know if we have lights that size in the building."

"It's okay. They're on your list," Lisa said. "But it doesn't look like your handwriting. You didn't give me a *Pete and re-Pete*." Lisa smiled.

Pete walked behind Lisa, bent over the desk, and scanned the list. "You're right. That isn't my handwriting," Pete said, shaking his head. He was clean-shaven and had recently had his hair cut. He even smelled good in his new clothes. "I don't need lightbulbs. If you want to cancel..."

"They could have been added to the wrong list," Lisa said, raising a pencil to her lips.

"Maybe somebody needs light bulbs at home and thought After Dark should pay for them." Pete looked at Lisa and raised his eyebrows. "My home's right here. You could barely fit a light that size in my little space."

"Still, I've never seen this script before," Lisa said.

"Nor me," Pete added. "Not that I'd recognize anybody's handwriting. I don't pay attention to things like that." Then he added hurriedly, "Unless it's a disguise. You know. If I'm right-handed, I might use my left hand to write on the list. Throw everybody off." He tapped an index finger on the graceful penmanship with its comely looped letters. "It looks like a hand that someone long ago would have written. Don't order the bulbs and somebody's sure to complain. That way you'll know who the culprit is."

They stared at each other for a moment. Lisa smiled again. Then they laughed.

Pete said, "The only other thing I can think of is the ghosts want them. If you believe in ghosts. It's a possibility. Or, somebody needs bulbs downstairs."

"I didn't think anyone went downstairs to the basement." Lisa looked intently at Pete.

"That's what I was told, but there *is* activity down there. I hear it at night. Sometimes it wakes me."

"What kind of activity?"

Pete raised his hands near his ears, moving them in circles at the sides of his head. "There are noises. I can't tell what it is. Sometimes I think it sounds like screams, or someone laughing, or somebody shouting orders, or somebody banging. My cot is low, almost on the floor. I think I hear it, but it's all muffled. The floors must be thick, almost soundproof. But, if I can just about detect it up here, it must be quite loud in the basement."

"I don't like to involve him, but I'll ask Bart what he wants to do about the bulbs," Lisa said. She threw up her hands. "Did you ever mention the noise downstairs to Bart?"

Pete smiled and winked. "I don't talk to Bart unless I have to. Getting him involved won't get you anywhere." He left the office but turned suddenly at the doorway and faced Lisa again. "This is an awful place," he said motioning to the office interior. "So dark. Cold even in the summer, even with it being so close to the kitchen. It gives me the creeps. If there's a haunted room in this old building, it must be Bart's office."

After she called in the orders, except for the lightbulbs, Lisa took her list and searched for Bart.

Lisa found Bart in the kitchen talking to Jose. Lisa waited for Bart to finish before she approached him. Bart tried to avoid her and started to walk away, but Lisa insisted. Bart stopped, spun around, and blew through his pursed lips. She explained the order as fast as she could. Lisa knew she wouldn't hold Bart's attention long.

"I've never seen this handwriting," Lisa said in summation. "I wanted to run it by you before I order something we don't need. Possibly something that can't be returned."

Bart grabbed the list from Lisa's hand and sighed. He flushed when he saw the writing. "I don't recognize it either," he said quickly.

"Pete said the bulbs might have been ordered for the basement," Lisa said.

Bart dismissed the idea with a humph and a wave of his hand. "What would that old drunk know?"

"Pete told me he hears noises in the basement. That there's *activity* down there. That sometimes the noise wakes him."

"Impossible!" Bart threw up his hands, dismissing the possibility. He looked at Lisa sharply. "Nobody, I mean nobody, goes in that basement."

"Isn't that the door?" Lisa asked, pointing to the large, dark, paneled wooden door behind Bart.

"That's the door, Lisa." Bart sounded exasperated. "It's locked. It's the only way in and out of the basement. There is no *activity* down there, despite what Pete thinks he hears. His brain is addled from years of alcohol abuse. The door is locked for safety reasons. The steps to the basement are rickety to the point of being hazardous. I wouldn't walk down them if you paid me. They could collapse on their own. At some point, we might have them replaced, but the basement is cold and damp. We couldn't even use it for storage. Anything you put down there would be ruined, either rust or waterlogged. It's easier to keep the place locked and forgotten."

"Well, what about the light bulbs?" Lisa said.

Bart stared at Lisa for a moment. Then he said sharply, "Order them. We'll see who claims them, and the mystery will be solved." He flashed a quick smile and walked away in his funny short-stepped gait.

Jose hurried to Lisa's side. "Trouble with the patron?"

"He's an asshole," Lisa said.

"He's a big asshole," Jose added.

She motioned Jose to follow her into a corner, pointing to a ceiling-mounted camera that covered most of the kitchen. Jose nodded and followed Lisa.

"Have you ever been in the basement?" Lisa said.

"Nobody goes in the basement. Except Geisel, and she disappeared. You don't want to go into the basement. Don't even try to go there."

"The steps?"

"Worse than that," Jose said, shaking his head. "Evil. There is evil in that basement. I can feel it through the floor."

"It's just a dirty, damp basement, full of cobwebs. Maybe it's filled with junk. Broken equipment."

"No. It's evil down there. If you try to go down there you will disappear, Lisa. There is nothing wrong with the steps. Bart goes down to the basement. I have seen him. He takes the big key from his pocket and opens the old wooden door. The door is heavy because he pushes hard against it." Jose pushed his palms in front of him to simulate the effort Bart needed to open the door. He reminded Lisa of a mime.

"You saw him?"

"Of course. He thinks no one is near. He goes through the door and locks it again from the inside. Sometimes he is gone for only a minute. Other times it might be almost an hour. But always, when he comes back, he opens the big door an inch to make sure no one is around before he sneaks out. Then he locks the door again. He used to keep the big key in the kitchen until Geisel found it. Now, he carries it in his pocket."

"I have to get down there, Jose." Lisa put her hands on her hips.

"No! It is evil! As long as the door is locked the evil stays downstairs. You don't want the evil upstairs with us."

"Did you ever hear noises from the basement?"

Jose looked at her carefully, sadly, Lisa thought.

"No, I never hear nothing. The exhaust fans here in the kitchen are too loud. I can't even hear myself think. I'm telling you something. Stay away from the big door, or you will disappear. I will miss you, and especially, the homeless you feed will miss you. Think of them if not yourself."

Later in the day, after the lunch rush, Bart approached Lisa, as usual, from behind.

"I didn't mean to blow you off this morning, Lisa. In fact, I wanted to tell you what a good job you're doing," Bart said, nodding, smiling, and undressing her with his eyes.

"Thank you, Bart."

"There really is no activity down there. If Pete hears things in his room, he might be hallucinating. Had an old man who lived next to me when I was growing up. Said he saw pink elephants when he drank." Bart laughed at the memory. "Really! He told me they were in his basement. Believing him and being a child, I said, how did they get in? He said, they always were there because I guess, he always was loaded."

"Actually, Pete hasn't been drinking that much," Lisa said.

"Since you cleaned him up. I noticed. It's a big improvement. He doesn't look like your run-of-the-mill bum anymore."

"It wasn't much. Just a few things from the thrift store."

"That was nice of you. It seems like it worked," Bart said. "Gave him back some pride in himself."

"I hope so. I think he's a nice man. An honest man."

"Well, that's why I try to keep him here," Bart said, smiling, staring at Lisa's breasts.

"That's why I tend to believe him when he said he heard noise downstairs," Lisa said.

"Just the old steam boiler rattling, the heat pipes banging. Air gets in them."

"I thought you turned off the heat in the summer and just used the gas water heaters for the kitchen and bathrooms upstairs. The pipes shouldn't bang now. Should they?"

Bart smiled again, as his eyes glazed over. "Then it has to be the ghosts."

CHAPTER THIRTEEN

Bo sat on his bed in the frat house. Five days had passed since Ridge and TJ disappeared. He was convinced they shared the same fate as the dipper in the park he saw carried away.

What was the thing, the things, that grabbed the woman and her bag, as she stood helpless, bent at the waist, blissfully sedated by a mixture of heroin, fentanyl, and God knows what else, fingers dragging on the ground, and sped off with her through the park, silently, with only the occasional clicking the thing or things made? Bo had talked to Ridge and TJ's parents yesterday afternoon. He told both sets of anxious adults he had no idea where the young men were. Which was true. They had gone their separate ways downtown while walking in the park near the stadium. Which was true. They had not been to a baseball game. Ridge and TJ had decided to return to campus. Bo wanted to remain downtown. Bo did not have a date or a ticket for the game. All was true. He had told no lies. However, he left out what he did know.

Working together, the two sets of parents had made flyers with their son's photos. They planned to make separate long drives to the city, meet, and canvass the stadium area. They would post the flyers anywhere they could, on every bulletin board and telephone pole they passed. Both families had new staple guns and boxes of staples. They would hand out flyers to those they encountered, stopping to ask if they had seen the young men. No one believed the duo had become junkies. They were not exceptional students, but they were not stupid enough to get mixed up with drugs, either as users or sellers. Bo, their closest college friend, attested to that.

Bo said he would accompany the distraught parents. That was the least he could do. He would reconstruct his and the boys'–that's what all four parents called them–nocturnal wanderings that fateful night. They would treat Bo to a meal as recompense and hoped they were not taking him away from important studying. Bo reminded them he wasn't taking classes over the summer. If they thought it was strange Bo neither worked nor had classes, they didn't say anything. While Bo waited for the parents to arrive at the frat house, campus, and city police interviewed him. He told the cops the same things he told the parents. Even though the police questioning was more detailed than the phone conversations he had with the parents, Bo didn't tell a single lie, because he really did not know what happened to his friends.

Bo knew the parents' quest for another witness would be fruitless. The posters would go unnoticed. The homeless they encountered wouldn't recognize the boys' faces unless they hoped to secure a few dollars for some cockamamie story they whipped up on the spot.

It would go something like this, Bo Imagined, with numerous pauses, eye rolls, and hand gestures.

"I seen both of them. They were standing on the corner over there. One pointed down the street. The other pointed up the street. Thought maybe they were lost. I was going to interject myself into the mix, was on my way to help them, you understand? I was close, just ready to say something, when they crossed the street straight over. Almost got hit by a city bus if I hadn't shouted a warning. I might have saved they lives, because they both had to run a few steps

to avoid being struck. I don't think the bus seen them. They were thankful and gave me a wave from the other side, called me over, and gave me a few dollars. Real nice boys. After that, I lost sight of them in the crowd near the bus terminal. There was a ball game and the crowd was heavy. I couldn't say whether they got on a bus. No. They just melted into the crowd. That's the last I saw them. I sure was thankful for the money they gave me."

Bo thought Ridge and TJ's folks would end up more confused by the end of the day. He was sure his friends would never be seen alive, probably never seen at all.

Ridge and TJ both came from blue-collar families. As far as they knew, the boys were the first to attend college, although the Hudsons, TJ's parents, claimed they had legitimate claims to the Hudson automobile fortune. The Hudson family, scions of the defunct car, still had a fortune, they claimed, and a direct heir to the Hudson money was disinherited wrongly. The Hudsons were the first to arrive and promptly told Bo about the fortune their branch of the family had lost. They were tall and slender. Both worked at the same plant for an international company. Jenny—Mrs. Hudson—offered Bo a small bag of sample lipsticks, facial balms, and perfumes from the high-end department store, where she moonlighted. The cosmetics could be divided between Bo's mother and girlfriend, Jenny said with a wink. Jenny's husband Tom had a missing front tooth. Bo feigned interest in the lip gloss colors and fragrances before he stashed the bag on his cluttered desk, without explaining any girlfriend's existence.

The Phonics, Fred and Carol, arrived soon after, bearing no gifts, but they said they would spring for lunch. Both sets of parents had armloads of flyers with Ridge and TJ's earnest staring faces, high school graduation photos, it seemed. Neither photo was especially flattering. The Phonics were somewhat chunky, like Ridge. Fred seemed especially florid, the victim of hypertension, and Bo imagined his head would explode before the day's end.

Fred was an auto mechanic at a Chevy dealership and worked

as a late-night short-order cook in an all-night diner. Carol was a beautician and worked out of an addition attached to the Phonic home.

Both sets of parents filed missing person reports with the campus and then city police departments. Now, with the police interviews completed, the searchers headed to the stadium. Bo rode with the Phonics. Although their car was older, it was larger. They all ate lunch at After Dark. Unsweetened iced tea was the drink of choice, although Bo was dying for an IPA. Burgers and fries all around.

Bo noticed immediately Lisa was behind the bar. Fortunately, they sat nearby where he could watch her. She shook a cocktail and poured it over ice, garnished it with olives speared on a long stick, and served it to a man at the bar in a business suit.

"You know the bartender, Bo?" Jenny Hudson wanted to know.

"I've seen her here a few times." TJ's mother didn't miss a thing, Bo imagined.

"Do you think she might know one or both of our boys?" Jenny said.

"I doubt it. She doesn't interact with the customers much, from what I've seen," Bo said.

"That's strange. Being friendly is how you make tips," Carol said. "I did my stint as a waitress. I hate some of my hair customers, but I still know their kids' names, who they went to the prom with, their social skill problems, allergies, and all that nonsense. When they ask for a new style, I give it to them, no matter how funny it looks."

"It won't hurt to ask," Jenny said, "especially if this is your hangout." She stood and pulled a flyer from her purse, along with a bag of cosmetic samples. Carol handed her another with a nod and a smile. "I'm sure a couple of handsome young men wouldn't go unnoticed in a place like this."

Jenny turned to the bar and discovered Lisa had disappeared. "She's gone. What the heck."

"If there's time we can stop back," Tom said. "We better hit the street."

Fred paid the lunch bill and left a measly tip for the plump, harried waitress. He strolled out as if he were the last of the big-time spenders after grabbing a toothpick at the cash register.

Outside in the smelly heat, they divided the flyers so everyone would have photos of each missing man. The Hudsons worked on one side of the street, the Phonics on the other. Bo ran back and forth between them, refilling flyer supplies among the adults and helping staple or tape flyers to any flat surface that would hold a staple or tape. In addition, they passed out flyers to the homeless, even pressing pages to the faces of dippers, insisting they look, shaking their shoulders. To unload his allotment, Bo flung flyers inside tents or dropped them in the laps of unconscious junkies. Some flyers drifted away immediately in the stiff breeze and blended into the garbage or cartwheeled down the street along with paper cups and plates. Before long, most would melt to mush outside in the elements.

Old Harriet was unconscious in her chair on wheels. Bo dropped a flyer in her lap and threw another inside her foul-smelling box before moving on. Across the street, Carol handed flyers to Jimmy Young, who was distributing boxes of tampons among the homeless women. Jimmy stopped and scanned the faces carefully, thoughtfully, before shaking his head no. However, he kept the flyers, took several copies of each, and held Carol's hands for a moment. After a brief chat, Carol waved to the others to join her.

"Mr. Young is from the Lutheran church," Carol said. "He wants to pray for God's protection and the boys' safe return."

The group bowed their heads as Jimmy prayed. After he finished, he handed the five cards with his name and telephone number.

"Don't be afraid to call me...any time," Jimmy said. "After all, it's my job. I'm an alcoholic. Been sober for two years. Every day is a struggle. So I understand what your sons are going through."

"Our sons aren't alcoholics or addicts, Mr. Young. They are college students. They don't have the time for such stuff," Carol said. "Ridge and TJ have summer jobs at the convention center." The other parents nodded in agreement.

"I'm sorry," Jimmy said. "Of course."

An awkward moment followed. Jenny dug into her oversized purse and pulled out a bag like the one she gave Bo.

"Do you have a girlfriend, Jimmy?" Jenny wanted to know, pressing the bag into his hands.

"Not exactly, but I have a date tonight with a girl who works at After Dark," Jimmy said. He smiled and then laughed. "Of all things, she's a bartender. Imagine that. It's not the kind of place you would think an alcoholic should go. Her name is Lisa."

Bo narrowed his eyes and stared at Jimmy.

CHAPTER FOURTEEN

Exhausted from the heat, their flyer supplies diminished to a few pages, the five decided to return to campus in their stylish plaids and stripes. It was approaching dusk and both families had long drives ahead of them. The group exchanged hugs and handshakes. The women sobbed. The men sniffed and wiped tears from their eyes. They all vowed to keep one another up to date on any news about the boys. The parents now had police contacts and Bo. Then they were gone.

Bo stood in the frat house parking lot and watched their cars disappear in the distance. He felt lonely for the first time away at college. His yellow Charger was the only remaining car in the lot. It was time to set in motion a plan he hatched that morning. He returned to his room, changed into dark clothes, and grabbed a backpack with a camera, tripod, water, and snacks. He would wait out the things that carried away the junkie in the park and possibly got Ridge and TJ. He drove to Fifth Street and slid his car into a spot near the park entrance. The sun, a large red ball, had slipped below the horizon. Its rays still provided a wan illumination, the gray light tinted orange just before dark. The park entrance was clustered with homeless, sprawled along a low wall. Some sat, digging through their bags. Some lay on the ground on blankets or sleeping bags. Others dipped.

Bo hurried through the entrance, two large columns, and headed into the tree-and-shrub-laden interior. A half dozen men built a fire along the asphalt pathway at the same spot there was a fire the night Ridge and TJ disappeared. The fire seemed like a nightly ritual. They didn't notice Bo, so he imagined, too preoccupied with the correct placement of kindling. Here and there dippers dipped. Junkies with bad legs limped, bent over their shopping carts loaded with junk. The grass was high and strewn with cans, bottles, paper, and the remnants of old clothes.

Bo approached the spot where the woman was taken. He had stopped there today with his friends' parents for a breather. The men had smoked. Bo recognized the tree he had hidden behind when the girl was captured. Although the tree was large and must have been a part of the old neighborhood, it offered little protection, especially if someone—or something—approached from the rear. But a nearby obelisk with a surrounding hedge was the perfect spot to hide with his camera. He was prepared to wait all night if necessary.

It was just about dark in the park. When no one was within eyesight, Bo shouldered his way through the hedge into the clear place at the obelisk's base. He found a spot where the hedge was thin enough to set up his camera and record a large swath of the path, including the exact spot where the woman was taken. There was enough room for him to sit cross-legged in front of the monument and set up the tripod and camera. Then he took out his water bottle and protein bars and laid them in a row beside him. They might be difficult to find after nightfall, and he didn't want to make noise digging through his pack.

As darkness fell, a few final people hurried through the park. They were not junkies but people on a mission to get through the wooded area as fast as possible. Still, their eyes were glued to their cell phones more than they watched where they stepped. Bo watched one last homeless man push his cart along the path, painfully slow, shuffling on bandaged legs. Bo watched the man's progress, hoping he wouldn't be taken. In the distance, he stopped to rouse a dipping female. She straightened. With difficulty, the man guided the woman and his cart, pushing one, then the other, a few steps at a time. Eventually, Bo lost sight of them in the distance to the dark and the path's gentle downward slope.

The park was quiet, although occasionally the bleat from a distant motorcycle or loud car split the silence. Bo settled in for his surveillance. He had no idea how long it would take. If necessary, he would remain all night. Bo checked his camera again. It had a full battery and a fully charged backup. The flash was turned off. Whether he shot a photo or video, the camera would work virtually silently. He leaned against the cool stone of the obelisk. It was a nice alternative to the heat still left in the park.

Bo's mind wandered. He saw his friends' faces. Remembered Ridge's goofy laugh. He recalled how once TJ missed his mouth with a shot of tequila and spilled the drink on his shirt. How they laughed. That was the same night TJ puked in the parking lot at After Dark. What a hurl. What a couple of guys. Then he thought back to their rides in the Charger, their prowling the street and park near the stadium, weapons ready to beat the homeless. How the junkies shrieked when beaten, how they wailed when he hit them with his kayak paddle. How they shrank into fetal positions as Ridge and TJ worked them over with their bamboo canes. Bo couldn't help smiling.

They were brave when it was the three of them marching through the park with their weapons. They feared nothing. Now Bo's throat was dry. He had difficulty swallowing. Every noise alerted him. A dog barking in the distance. A bird settling to roost for the night in a tree near him. The wail of a siren heading deep into the city.

Suddenly, Bo saw his younger brother's face. Blond hair, blue eyes, toothy smile, much as his own was, only Boop, as he was called among family members, had freckles across his nose. No one had seen the change in Boop. After all, Bo had his own fish to fry, getting ready for college. Boop developed new friends. Friends who didn't come around the Bentwood home like the old ones did, needing a ride, staying for supper, laughing around the dinner table. The new friends seemed older. It was not clear whether they were still in school or even had jobs. So little was known and shared about them. What little time Boop spent at home was in his bedroom with the door closed and sometimes locked. They discovered later that all Boop's old friends knew he was using, but none said anything. None raised an alarm. They watched Boop dissolve before them at a distance. Bo was away at college, a freshman when Boop was discovered under the visiting team's bleachers after football's homecoming game, a needle in his arm that injected a lethal potion of heroin and fentanyl, among other substances, into a vein. Another boy with him was resuscitated with Narcan. Boop was too far gone. No one in Bo's family knew the other boy named Jackson. In fact, they didn't know whether Jackson was a first or last name.

Bo's mind drifted back to the present. Here he was sitting on hard ground when Jimmy the alky was out somewhere, possibly seated on a soft-cushioned chair, working his way into Lisa's pants. Imagine that. A drunk taking out a bartender. "Would you like an aperitif?" "Yes, please, a Coke." And for dessert?"

"A glass of buttermilk."

Bo checked his camera *again*. Turned it on, turned it off. His eyes had become accustomed to the dark. The rising moon offered occasional illumination as clouds slipped by overhead. The first mosquito arrived and buzzed at his left ear. Bo waved at it noiselessly, but it returned after a few seconds. He hadn't thought of insect repellant. A scented repellant might mask his human odor, he now realized, if the things relied on scent. Also, it occurred to him he had no means to safely leave the park before dawn. If the things returned and discovered him, he would have no escape route back to his car. His key fob would open the door. He could hit the locks and dive in. Gun the engine and take off. But it was a long run back to the park entrance. If he could make it to the fire, there would be safety in numbers. If he had to run, he would make for the fire and wait out the night among the homeless. He would sprint if he had to, even though he was never especially fast, never especially an athlete. He'd run in a straight line. Leave the path where it made the wide curve, cut through the trees, despite the potential danger, high grass, and its hidden can and bottle pitfalls, then eventually return to the path with its hard asphalt, and bolt to the fire. The straight line was still the shortest way between two points. If the high grass slowed him, it would impede anything chasing him. He'd leave his backpack and camera in the hedge and return for them in the safety of daylight. It sounded like a plan. He realized now he should have thought about this all before coming to the park at night.

Mosquitos continued to plague Bo. They buzzed around both ears. He swatted them away, but they returned almost immediately. He felt a sudden bite on his left forearm and slapped instinctively. The noise was surprisingly loud. It frightened Bo in the park's dead silence. He lifted his palm slowly and in the wan light saw a flattened black mosquito, its smashed wings and legs at crazy angles, and a dash of red. The mosquito had fed before Bo realized it was on his arm. The blood didn't even amount to a drop. He flicked away the mosquito and wiped the blood between his fingers. Then he dribbled a line of spit on the bitten area and rubbed it in. Slowly, carefully, he cracked open the water bottle for a drink. Should have done this before, in the car, he thought. Next, he opened a power bar excruciatingly slowly, tearing the foil wrapper a centimeter at a time. After all, he hadn't eaten since lunch. This, too, should have been done beforehand. He took a big bite. The power bar crunched. Another mistake. Should have bought a soft one. Now that it was in his mouth he had little recourse. Bo had to swallow, especially if it became necessary to run. He would need a clear airway. He chewed slowly, trying to mask the crunching by using his tongue to mix and soften the bar with saliva. Finally, he swallowed and washed the granola down his throat with a swig of water. He leaned his head against the obelisk for a moment. Its coolness held no comfort now. He dashed water on his arms where he thought mosquitos landed rather than slapping at them again. He'd incapacitate them long enough to squash them with a finger. He splashed more water on his head. The humid air was oppressive, but he would have to conserve the water, because this bottle had to last all night. What would he do if he needed to piss? Bo squashed another mosquito on his cheek. When he rubbed the area another small spot of blood was visible on the tip of his index finger. He rubbed the blood with his thumb.

That's when he heard the first whistle, low and modulating, from far away. After a moment, it was answered by another. Then a third and a fourth, all from different directions. Bo froze. *You gotta do this, Bo, for Ridge, TJ, and even Boop. Even Boop.* Bo got his camera ready. Had his finger on the record button. He waited. Several minutes passed. The park was silent. Bo heard a noise, as if claws scratched on the asphalt. In the distance he could see a large mass on the path, emerging from the darkness. At first, it appeared solid, but as it approached Bo could see it undulated, rolled, and shimmied. It moved like a giant caterpillar. The thing now made clicking noises. Bo swung the camera to his right and turned on the recorder. He watched the thing's progress in the camera's view screen. The focus adjusted automatically, zooming in or out as needed. As it grew closer Bo almost choked on an incredible stench. He wanted to cover his nose but had nothing to use.

Bo moved the camera, keeping the mass in the screen's center. Now it was directly across from him. The mass stopped and chattered with a long series of clicks. Slowly, the thing disassembled, separating into parts. Each segment moved independently. They were dog sized. As big as Bo's Labrador Nellie. Some were smaller. They walked on four legs but could rise on their hind feet and sniff the air. They had large, pointed ears, short snouts, gleaming teeth, and short stumpy tails. Their forearms were shorter than the back legs but had long yellowish claws. There appeared to be eight in number. They formed a circle about ten feet in diameter and rose on hind legs, pointed snouts upward to sniff the air. They clicked and chattered. Bo realized they were hunting.

They were hunting Bo. Had they smelled his blood? The minute flecks of blood left over from the mosquito bites? Heard the noises he made? Smelled his protein bar? Heard him chew? Or was it just his human scent? The two closest creatures turned in Bo's direction and scanned the hedge. He continued to record. They took a cautious step toward Bo. He pressed his back against the obelisk as if he could pass through the stone and exit through the back. The two creatures stopped and chattered. The rest dropped to four legs and turned toward Bo. They took a single step in unison toward him. They tested the air from four legs, their snouts thrust upwards, their long teeth gleaming in the low light. They clicked again back and forth. Creatures from the back of the group spread to the sides as if to thwart any escape. The two creatures in front licked their thin lips and swallowed. They lowered their hindquarters. Their muscles tensed under the dark fur, ready to pounce.

Then a siren wailed on Fifth Street. The creatures turned in unison toward the sound. The siren grew louder. The creatures became agitated. Clicked, chattered, squeaked. They sniffed the air. Returned their collective gaze toward Bo. Some appeared ready to spring. A few retreated. The smaller ones held their clawed hands over pointed ears. The siren changed its tempo. Not only was it getting louder, closer, but it was also wailing faster, adding an occasional WOOP, WOOP, WOOP to the sound.

The things arranged themselves into a single mass and rolled off into the woods, away from Bo, snarling, crying in apparent pain. Bo charged through the hedge, stumbled, took a header, and hit the ground. A bottle in the grass tripped him. His legs felt like lead after sitting cross-legged for so long. He jumped up immediately and tore as fast as possible down the path, his arms pumping, his heart racing. When he reached the path's curve, two things happened: the things detected his flight and the siren stopped suddenly. The creatures wheeled en masse to chase Bo. They chattered louder than ever. Bo cut through the grass. He kicked a bottle, almost causing him to fall again, made him stumble, which slowed him momentarily, consumed energy. After a few more steps he flattened an empty aluminum can with a crunch. He wished he had kept to the path, even though that route was longer.

Bo was not in good shape for someone so young. His lungs heaved. His thigh muscles burned. He felt like he was moving in slow motion through the high grass that seemed to clutch at his ankles. He heard the mass growing closer, clicking, chattering, whimpering with expectation. They rolled on an angle, trying to cut him off. He could see it now when he looked over his shoulder, closing the distance between them. Finally, Bo returned to the path and the long straightaway to the fire and safety. Bo crested a knoll. He dashed onward. He expected to see the fire. He shouted as loud as he could between heaving breaths to warn the homeless. He was coming in. The animals were closing. They were running individually now, still trying to cut him off. They stayed in the grass, where their claws dug into the soft earth, propelling them faster than ever. Their heads bobbed on short necks. Bo shouted again. No one was there. There was no fire, only a few gray wisps of smoke trailing upwards. Maybe the cops chased the homeless or perhaps the Whistlers themselves scattered them. Bo turned at the intersecting path, sliding on rain-washed gravel. He went down hard on a hip, scraped his palm, and bounced up. His knees wanted to buckle. He streaked toward the park entrance. The car was parked twenty-five yards ahead. The Charger was visible, parked at the curb. He dug for his key fob. That slowed him. The fastest creature nipped at Bo's heels, and almost tripped him when its teeth raked across a shoe. Another sailed over his head, rolled across the path, and slammed into a tree, screaming in pain. The distance to the car closed. Bo had the fob in his hand. He opened the car locks. The creatures were in a frenzy. Another one vaulted over Bo's head and was impaled on the ornate wrought iron gates. All the creatures wailed. He had ten yards to go. Through the gates and across the sidewalk. Five yards to go. Creatures were closing from both sides. They had outraced him.

Bo hit the car alarm. The bleating horn shattered the night air. Flashing lights blinded. The creatures shrieked and retreated. Bo tugged open the passenger-side door, fell into the car, and pulled the door closed. One final creature, overcoming the alarm and lights, slammed into the car door. It howled before limping back into the park. Bo lay stretched out the best he could. His heart raced. His chest heaved. Sweat poured off him. After several minutes he sat up and looked through the gates. The park was quiet again. Several pairs of eyes watched him, burning red, from the bushes. Eventually, he crawled into the driver's seat and started the engine. After another several minutes, with the AC blasting, Bo felt strong enough to drive back to the frat house.

CHAPTER FIFTEEN

Lisa and Jimmy sat at a secluded table in After Dark. The table was around a corner and near an ornamental tree growing in a pot. Also close was a grieving angel, praying on its knees, one of the several cemetery statuaries in the restaurant. Its weight caused a ripple in the floor. Their table was close to the kitchen and Pete's closet. By design, the bar was not visible from where they sat. Lisa had reserved the spot earlier that day. Jimmy was an alcoholic, and although the restaurant served booze, there was no need to tempt him, she thought, by sitting where trays of drinks passed them, where shelves laden with liquor were visible. The restaurant was crowded. There was a game tonight and the team's ace would take the mound.

Now that they were seated over sweating glasses of iced tea and as Lisa played with the straw's paper sleeve, she regretted selecting After Dark, even though the food was good. Her co-workers took every opportunity to glide around the corner to get a look at Lisa's *boyfriend*. They smiled and tittered. Jimmy noticed, and Lisa was annoyed at the sophomoric behavior. She hadn't warned anyone she would return after work to dine with a man. If she had, the entire staff would be there to gawk. She supposed it was a way to get back at their boss, although most employees said they liked Lisa as a manager better than Geisel, who—as Jose had claimed—

disappeared suddenly from After Dark with her strange accent and rumored man problems. Even Bart glided by on his short legs, never pausing his diminutive quick steps, but managing to get an eyeful—Lisa in shorts and a nice blouse that showed a little cleavage.

After all, this was a first date, not at all romantic. Not even a date: more of a business meeting, but Jimmy was handsome, Lisa thought. He had a nice smile, an unruly crop of light-colored hair, and an easy laugh. The fact that he was an alcoholic didn't matter. Alcoholism ran in her family, but she had yet to learn whether Jimmy was a mean drunk, which her father was, always looking for a fight, or a happy drunk, the life of the party, funny for a while, but obnoxious when the volume got louder and the one-liners repeated like the news cycle. Her last boyfriend was the happy drunk, which didn't sound too bad, but then it played out nightly, ramping up from binge drinker to alky. After he refused treatment, had two DUIs—one that totaled Lisa's car—and eventually lost his job, Lisa had had enough. She knew what her mother had gone through. Although the old boyfriend had never hit her, he did put her head through Lisa's windshield on the second DUI, after he picked her up from work, refused to let her drive, weaved his way home through the streets, and passed out behind the wheel.

Now she smiled at Jimmy. They split a dozen wings with diablo sauce and waited for their entrees to arrive. Lisa waved her hand in front of her mouth to cool her lips. Jose made a killer hot sauce.

"You need some more iced tea?" Jimmy said.

"A bucket full, please."

They laughed.

"It is hot," Jimmy said, "and so good."

"Just what we need," Lisa said, taking another wing to her mouth. "More heat. Today wasn't hot enough."

"Ninety-four in the shade," Jimmy said. "Dew point almost as high. I keep track, you know. Try to adjust what I give out to the homeless. More bottled water than tampons today. That doesn't make the females happy. Most would rather have the tampons."

"I think even I'd be embarrassed handing out tampons," Lisa said. She wrinkled her nose.

"I was at first, too. But that's what women need. They're expensive to buy. They want tampons and socks. They'd rather have a box of tampons in their tent than a case of water, risk dehydration and heat stroke." He rolled his eyes. "Everything embarrassed me when I first started work among the homeless." He smiled. "But I got used to it."

"The smell?"

"You never get used to that. Pastor Shenkel says street duty is like working in a morgue. He should know. He was a cop before the ministry called him."

Jimmy flagged the waitress and ordered more iced tea. Their waitress Lulu was heavy set and tattooed. She flirted with Jimmy, resting a beringed, long-nailed hand on his shoulder while they made small talk. Lisa shot daggers at her through her eyes, but Lulu didn't notice.

After Lulu arrived with their After Dark Burgers and more iced tea, Lisa gave the waitress the evil eye. Lulu smirked and walked away. *I'm going to kill that bitch tomorrow,* Lisa thought and then smiled. *He's not even my boyfriend. Maybe he never will be, but...*

"What's wrong?" Jimmy wanted to know. He leaned across the table toward her.

"So, the morgue didn't call Pastor Shenkel to the ministry?"

"Hardly."

"What called you?" Lisa picked up a fry with her fingers, swept it through a dab of ketchup on her plate, and popped it in her mouth. She knew it would be good. Pete had changed the oil in the fryers that morning. One fryer was dedicated to french fries. Then she took a bite of her burger, which included, in addition to the ground meat, bacon, lettuce, tomato, avocado, a fried egg, and Juan's special sweet sauce. It was impossible to grab all the ingredients in one bite.

Jimmy took a bite of his burger. A bacon strip slipped from the sandwich and dangled like a tongue from his mouth. Lisa lost it. They both did. Bart, who was making another pass, rolled his eyes as Jimmy restacked his burger.

"You should have left the skewer in it," Lisa offered. She pointed to her burger. "Helps keep it from falling apart."

"I'll know better next time. But, to answer your question," Jimmy started, after swallowing and taking a swig of iced tea.

"If you don't want to..." Lisa said.

"I don't mind," Jimmy interrupted. "I share my story at AA meetings...almost every day, to anyone who wants to listen. I was in a bad place. On the street. I was a drunk. Would drink anything. As much as I could get until I passed out. I lived out of my car until I cracked it up. I staggered away. The cops didn't find me but towed away my car. That's why I don't have a record. When they tracked me down a day later, I was sober and said the car was stolen. By that time, I had flunked out of college in my senior year. My parents disowned me. Without a car, I was sleeping on the street. I panhandled for booze money. Some days I could buy a gallon of cheap vino. The next, maybe an airplane-sized bottle of schnapps. It went on for almost a year. I lost track of my family and friends. One day, my dad found me and gave me fifty bucks to clean myself up. He invited me home. There was a condition. No booze. I told him I'd think about it."

Jimmy paused and wiped his mouth with the napkin that had rested on his lap. Then he continued. "I took that fifty and went straight to the liquor store. I told myself I needed a treat. That's what those fifty bucks represented. Not a meal. Not some better clothes. Not to save some. I got a good bottle of bourbon, at least what I thought was good stuff. Drank the whole damn thing.

Passed out in the gutter, so far gone I didn't know it had rained and the water ran around me. The dirty, muddy, filthy gutter water from the street, where people spit and shit, was in my mouth. I was choking it down. Vomiting it, the bourbon, everything, all up. It was cold and Pastor Shenkel grabbed my coat collar, dragged me out of the gutter, and held me in the rain while I puked up everything and went through the dry heaves. Then he bought me something to eat —I don't remember what—and I puked that up in his car. He took me to the parsonage, got me some clean clothes, let me sleep it off."

Lisa wiped tears from her eyes. "You can stop...Please. I don't want to hear it." They stared at each other a long moment.

"No. I want you to know. I slept almost twenty-four hours on the parsonage sofa. Blood red leather. Pastor Bob Shenkel and his wife Sadie looked after me. Gave me beer to ward off the DTs. Weaned me off the alcohol until I didn't have the shakes. But oh, how I wanted a drink. Despite the nice place to stay and the good cooking, I had no money. Decided to go back to the street. Panhandle to buy more booze. This time, like a hundred times before, I was going to do things in moderation. Not be dependent on booze. I felt I had licked the drinking problem. I wanted to thank Pastor Bob and let him know I was leaving. Sadie said he was in the church next door, in his office, writing Sunday's sermon. It was the first time I was in that church. I came in silently. Pastor Bob's office door was ajar. I saw him bent over his desk, hand on his forehead. He was writing out the sermon in longhand. He's old school. That's how he did it, even though he had a computer next to him.

"There's a lot to be said about *old school*," Lisa said, with a smile. "I'm kind of that way."

"I didn't want to bother him when he was concentrating, so I went back into the nave and sat down on a pew near the front. I was amazed at how quiet it was. The air didn't seem to move. I could smell candle wax and, I imagined, the aroma of flowers, sweet-smelling flowers from a past service. It would be so nice to hear this sermon the pastor was working on. The pastor had a rough look about him. A scar on his forehead. After all, he had been a cop. He could talk tough, too. Talked tough to me. But yet, he was a mild man. He could be soft-spoken, too. He talked softly to me when I needed it. I was thinking about this sermon he was working on when the church around me filled with light, the sun must have come through the clouds, and I was bathed in colors from the stained-glass windows."

Jimmy's eyes filled with tears.

"That must have been beautiful," Lisa said, taking his hand.

"The sudden light startled me. I must have made a noise of surprise, maybe a sob, because in a moment the pastor was at my side. I didn't hear or see him coming down the aisle. 'Isn't the light, the colors, wonderful?' I said to him. And he said to me, 'God has blessed you, Jimmy. Come into my office.' His voice was so soft, so quiet, I would have followed him anywhere.

"I sat next to the desk in his office. He wrote his sermon on a legal pad. He flipped the pages over when he got to the bottom. The page he was halfway through had wet spots. I knew he had been crying. I cried, too, and thanked him for his and Sadie's help. Instead of saying goodbye, I told him I looked forward to Sunday and hearing his sermon."

"I hope I can meet Pastor Bob someday," Lisa said. "I'm sure I'd like him."

"When Sunday came, I was surprised to see Pastor Bob in his vestments. He looked different. More ministerial, you could say. The sermon was about me. He didn't mention me by name, of course, but told the congregation my story and how I had been blessed by God in the church that week. At Sunday dinner, I told Bob and Sadie I needed to get a job and a place of my own. I offered to volunteer at the church. Bob set it up for me to work at a trucking company one of the parishioners owned. I started taking orders over the phone. Before long, I was a dispatcher. Now, I'm head dispatcher. I tell the drivers where to go and what to pick up or deliver. I try to get out for a part of every day on the street, as long as my work is done."

Lulu returned to the table. "Something wrong with the food?" she wanted to know, a petulant look on her face as if she had cooked their meals. She knew bad food would affect her tip.

"We were talking," Jimmy said. "Lost track of time. They're actually very good."

"You talking nice or dirty?" Lulu said. Her index finger pushed her lips into a smile. "If it's not, it should be dirty." She smiled. "Want boxes?"

"No. We're going to eat them," Jimmy said. "I got a little long-winded with a story I told Lisa."

"Okay. I like *long* stories." Lulu touched Jimmy's shoulder, pushed her pencil behind an ear, and sauntered away.

CHAPTER SIXTEEN

A light rain fell outside After Dark and the temperature had fallen. Just as thunder rumbled in the distance, a cheer erupted from the stadium. One of the hometown boys must have gone yard. Luckily, the rain was too light to delay the game. After Dark was already crowded. People scurried along the sidewalk. Lisa and Jimmy stood on Fifth Street under the canopy at After Dark. Their date had been in the works for a week but postponed twice. Once arrangements were finally made, they had planned for everything – except rain.

"We're going to get wet, no matter what we do," Jimmy said.

"I don't care," Lisa said, although she hated the idea of getting her new sandals wet, even though they were cheapies bought from the clearance rack. She had had a good time and didn't want the night to end so soon. "We could go for a drin-oh, sorry."

"A drink? You can have one. I'll have something else, say coffee. If it weren't raining, we could go for a walk."

"No bars. Not tonight," Lisa said. She was cold and pressed herself against Jimmy.

"Don't be sorry. It's not your fault I'm an addict. The world is full of alcohol. So much revolves around *having a drink*. Aperitifs. Happy hour. Nightcap. Tailgating. I can't ignore it. I can't avoid it. I'd cut off my left leg for a drink right now. This minute. But I don't have to imbibe. I've fallen off the wagon in the past. Might fall off again. But my path is clear. I have a good life. It's better without alcohol. It's been a lot better since I met you, Lisa. I don't want to screw it up."

Jimmy held Lisa closer. "We could go to my place. Watch the rest of the game. See who hit the donger."

"My place is closer," Lisa said. "And I'm parked closer. In the restaurant lot."

"Sounds like a plan."

Just as they prepared to run for Lisa's car, a man bumped into Jimmy.

"Sorry, chief," he said. "It won't happen again." The man put down his head and continued with a cough.

At that moment after the accidental bump, both the man and Lisa registered a flash of recognition. The man continued into the rain.

"Dad? Dad!"

The man stopped and turned around. He raised his head. There was a look of surprise on his face. "Lisa? Can it be?"

"Daddy! You're here," Lisa said. She ran and hugged him.

The tall man, rugged-looking, seemed embarrassed and pushed Lisa away. "It is you. I can't believe this."

"I've been looking for you, Dad." She wiped tears from her eyes. Jimmy stood in the background smiling. "Chelsea Gibbons, you remember her, from down the street? We talk on Facebook. She said she saw you on a newscast. You walked through the frame. Then, I saw you on videos about the downtown. So I moved here to find you."

"Baby, I have to go. I'm busy."

"You have a job?" Lisa couldn't remember her father working. This sounded like good news.

"You could call it that." He laughed nervously and edged away into the rain.

"Wait, Dad. Where do you live?"

"Here and there. In a...shelter now. But I'm looking for a permanent place." He coughed again and cleared his throat.

"I work at After Dark."

"No." He looked shocked.

"Yes. I'm the bar manager. We have to get together."

"Sure, but I have to go now."

"Are you drinking?"

"No. I quit."

"That's great. I'm so proud." Lisa wanted to continue the conversation. She looked her father over from head to foot. He looked respectable. Clean shaven. Nice clothes. Hair neatly cut. Immaculate nails. He hadn't appeared like that since before her mother died and he went on an extended binge. "So, where do you work?" She wanted to keep him here all night. Tears of joy streamed down her face. He clasped her hands.

Charles Van der Meer edged farther away. Held her at arm's length. Lisa caught his arm. "I'm getting soaked out here," he said, anger rising in his voice.

"Come under the canopy, Daddy. We can go inside."

"I can't. Have to go. I'm late already."

Lisa tugged him, pulling him off balance, and he stepped out of the rain. "For work?"

"An appointment. I must go. I'll be in touch."

"How do I reach you, Daddy?"

"I'll contact *you* at After Dark."

Charles Van der Meer shook his arm free. Stepped backward. "Look for a new job, baby. Be careful in this place. It's no good. I'll check in on you soon." He spun and walked away, coughing into his fist.

Lisa covered her mouth with a palm as if trying to stifle a scream—of joy or dread. She turned to Jimmy, who had remained frozen during the reunion. Her eyes were wide. She stood on her toes.

"Well? Jimmy smiled.

"What do we do?" Lisa said.

"Let's go for that walk. Even if it is raining. We'll follow him."

"Really?"

"Of course."

She hugged Jimmy and they left the canopy's protection. A cold rain soaked them immediately as they weaved through the crowded sidewalk and ducked around umbrellas.

"Do you see him?" Lisa said. "He already has a good start on us."

"I'm looking, but we don't want to get too close and have him spot us. That wouldn't be good. Like I told you when we first met, he might not want to be found."

"Why wouldn't he? I'm his daughter. He's sober. Has a job." She looked at Jimmy, expecting he wouldn't have an answer. "What could be wrong?"

"He might be mixed up in something he doesn't want you to know."

That was the answer Lisa thought to herself. The answer she hoped Jimmy wouldn't think. An answer blatantly wrong.

"Do you want to split up?" Lisa said.

"No. You keep an eye on the other side of the street. I'll watch this side. It's so crowded we don't want to bump into him again. That's too much of a coincidence."

"Really. After all these years."

Lisa couldn't take the smile off her face. She didn't want to. Mission accomplished. She had found her dad. He hadn't been the world's greatest father, but he was all she had left of her family. He was mean when he drank. But he never hit them. He got into barfights. Had a record. Assault, breaking property, etc. Not exactly public enemy number one, but his rap sheet would prevent him, even now, from getting a good job, Lisa realized. Perhaps Charles Van der Meer's job was a little seedy. Maybe he had dropped off the radar. Got paid under the table for...who knows? Lisa thought her father would never do anything criminal. Maybe marginally legal.

The last Lisa heard, her father worked for a funeral director. The owner of the funeral home was elderly, and Lisa's father assisted him when he picked up bodies, carted them around the embalming room, and even helped dress the stiffs. He worked, too, at funerals, moving cars, opening the front door for grievers as they filed in and out, and even filling in as a pallbearer. Soon, however, his drinking caused problems. He dented a client's fender and the hearse's bumper and insulted a client. He was let go.

But when he was sober, Charles Van der Meer had been a good father. Lisa remembered he was soft-spoken. He smiled a lot. He played checkers and Parcheesi with his daughter at the kitchen table on rainy days. Watched scary movies on Saturday nights. Was always the first customer when Lisa sold lemonade on the sidewalk in front of their home.

But her classmates didn't know that Charles Van der Meer. They only knew the man their parents chuckled about over supper, what they picked up in neighborhood gossip. Growing up in a small town, Lisa was teased at school. "Where's your father headlining this weekend?" boys would ask. "Van der Meer versus Ali, Madison Square Garden. Or, Van der Meer versus another drunk at Chick's Bar and Grille." The boys doubled over laughing, swearing more, calling Lisa a cunt and a whore, words they hardly understood, and white trash, which they and their parents certainly were.

Lisa stood her ground and cursed in reply, calling them faggots and eunuchs. That's how she got the moniker *Potty Mouth*, although being vulgar was part of the boys' rite of passage. She didn't miss her hometown of Mammoth, Pennsylvania. She had no intention of going back, ever. Her roots in that city in the heart of the anthracite coal region were cut when she left her boyfriend. Besides, Mammoth was the type of place where almost anything could happen.

The rain had stopped suddenly. It felt muggy already. They both heard Charles's cough before they saw him. They froze immediately and moved to a building entrance and scanned the sidewalk around them. They didn't want Charles to see them. There was more coughing, violently this time. *Cough it up*, Granny Van der Meer told Lisa's Pop-Pop during one of his coughing spells, *it might be a Ford.* It was a family joke until Pop-Pop was diagnosed with lung cancer. He went fast. Even the doctor had said at first it was bronchitis, that lingering, hacking cough that refused to let up, that seemed to turn him inside out the spasms were so fierce and prolonged. Eventually, more testing proved a different story. There was no automobile in his chest but a multitude of tumors.

Hidden in the doorway, they saw Charles at the end of the building, the start of a lot where the homeless had taken over, leaning on a wooden fence post, coughing up a lung. Lisa squeezed Jimmy's hand.

"I've seen enough," Lisa said. "I want to go back."

"We could go to him," Jimmy said. "Maybe help."

"No. He wouldn't take any help."

"He could have pneumonia, even in the summer."

"No. I think it's lung cancer," Lisa said, nonplused. In that instant, Lisa saw, heard in her mind, all the plans for a happy family reunion, dashed, and crashed into a million pieces. Holidays, birthdays, and barbecues together with her father, were gone before they could be planned. "He sounds like my Pop-Pop did when I was a girl. Exactly the same. That's what *he* had. First Pop-Pop with lung cancer and then my mom. Hers was breast cancer."

"I'm sorry, Lisa. That sucks."

"Yeah, it does."

Jimmy held Lisa in the building entrance. When she looked into his face, tears of sorrow streamed down her cheeks along with rain from her hair. After a while, they looked for Charles. He was gone. They walked back to After Dark. The rain had stopped and the setting sun peaked through the clouds. The couple was soaking wet. Lisa apologized, but she said the date was over. Too much had transpired in the last hour for her to be good company tonight.

CHAPTER SEVENTEEN

Bo woke with a groan. Bruised and sore from his encounter with the Whistlers, he had slept until noon. With difficulty, he stood and stretched, scratching at the red bumps on his arms and face. He had to return to the park to retrieve his camera. Otherwise, the video and the proof would be gone. Who would believe him without proof? Who would believe the junkies? Surely the homeless knew about the things that whistled.

He showered. Every joint and muscle ached. It hurt toweling off. His legs felt like rubber after the sprint through the park. His ribs were bruised, the result of slamming into the car's consul as he hurled himself inside the Charger. It even hurt to breathe. Bo wondered if he didn't have cracked ribs. Now he understood how the junkies felt after he and the boys worked them over.

Still, he could not help smiling. He made it. Beat the things that had hunted him. Outwitted the beasts, knowing enough to take the shortcut through the grass instead of the longer route on the asphalt path. Even though he gained only a few feet, that's all he needed to make it back to the car. Got the angle on the pack. In the end, he had outdistanced all of them, even the fastest. Those things had to be hurting, too. One slammed into a tree; another into his car. His parents wouldn't be happy about that damage. The one that got impaled on the park gate must be dead. Maybe it was still there. Hanging like a pelt on the ornate park entrance gate, surrounded by the homeless who poked it with sticks. Perhaps someone wore the foul-smelling pelt as a cape. Even better, Bo imagined the dead Whistler was surrounded by cops. That would be the ultimate proof.

Bo dressed slowly, painfully. If that camera was gone, he would be in trouble. The Nikon was new, expensive, bought for a film class he ended up dropping because it required what he considered too much work. The damage to his car he would blame on the homeless. His parents would understand. They always did. He could do little wrong since his brother died. Whatever deficit they had as parents—allowing a son to get involved with drugs—they tried to make up with Bo. He wanted for nothing. They weren't happy with his college grades, especially after he had done so well in high school, but seemed happy he was still alive with mediocre grades to show them.

Bo drove downtown and parked near the stadium. There was a good five hours before the baseball game started, and the visiting cellar team would not bring in a big crowd. Just as the heat increased, so did the city's smell, even in the park. Bo inspected the area around the gates for traces of blood, hair on the gate's wrought iron spires, prints in the dirt. There was nothing. Walking passed the remnants of the homeless campfire, he retraced his manic flight of the night before. Bo's legs ached. He imagined he had a slight limp. Looked like a well-dressed junkie himself, recently returned from a shelter or thrift store with new duds. If he had to run now, he wouldn't get far. Bo studied the asphalt as he proceeded. It was clean. At the very least, he expected to see scratches even on the hard surface. He remembered hearing the Whistlers' sharp talons, scraping, scuffing, on the asphalt as they dug for traction. Even in the dark, he saw the long, curved claws, longer than a bear's. The area where he cut through the grass in a last-ditch shortcut held little evidence, only a few small divots scattered about. They could have come from anything; perhaps a dog pawing the grass after it stopped to pee. It seemed his camera would be the only legitimate evidence he had, anybody had.

In the distance, a man poked in the hedge surrounding the obelisk. He retrieved Bo's camera and tripod, cradled them under his arm, gave a quick glance around the park, and walked off. A poop bag swung in his other hand. Rather than accost the man at a distance, Bo decided to follow him. The man was tall and thin and walked rather fast for an older guy. He coughed as he went. With his aching legs, Bo made up the ground slowly. Suddenly, the man stopped and had a coughing spell, long, dry heaves. He stepped to the side of the path and doubled over, transferred the poop bag to the side that cradled the camera, and leaned against the tree Bo hid behind the night the female dipper was carried off. Bo continued and closed the space between them. As Bo approached, the man got the coughing under control but continued to lean on the tree, catching his breath, his palm pressed on the bark. Bo noticed a large, ornate ring on the man's hand. After a moment, the man started to walk again. Bo passed him without a look. He had to continue. If he stopped suddenly and lagged behind, the man might get suspicious. If he confronted the man, a fight could ensue. Although there were few people in the park, the police might come. How could Bo prove the camera was his and not the man's? If Bo claimed he knew what was on the camera, the man could say Bo watched him filming. Bo decided to keep the man in sight. One thing was clear: the man he followed was the same one who emerged in the field through a trap door near After Dark. He was sure of that. It was odd that this stranger would seem familiar to Bo.

In addition, the scat on the asphalt path where one of the Whistlers defecated last night, was gone and probably swung in the poop bag. Only a smeared stain remained. No different from count-less other piles swept up by conscientious dog walkers. Perhaps the man, tall and slender, not a junkie, was the clean-up guy, Bo thought. Maybe the Whistlers weren't too smart, and he followed their trail after a hunt the next day to pick up the pieces and eliminate the evidence. It was also possible the man hunted with the beasts, hiding, noting where they passed, and waiting for the next day to fix things when he could see better. But his coughing would surely give him away at night, as well as the Whistlers, hinder their attempts. What if the beasts turned on him? The animals appeared to be savage, dominated by their lust for the kill. Even if the Whistlers were his, how would he control them?

Bo was confused. He heard a cough in the distance. He stopped, turned, and saw the man walking away at an angle. He no longer carried the camera and poop bag. There was a trash can nearby on the trail. Bo waited for the man to leave sight and limped to the trash can. Various rubbish lay on the top. Bo dug a little and found the poop bag. A little farther down his hand hit the tripod leg. He hauled it and the camera out. A junkie dipped nearby. Several couples sat in the grass up the path. Two argued over a pack of cigarettes. It appeared no one noticed the man.

Bo stowed his finds like the man had, cradling the camera and tripod under an arm, and returned the long, painful walk to his car. He thought of trailing the man, but he had disappeared among the trees. Once he got to Fifth Street, the man could go in any direction and blend in with the crowd. He'd never track him, especially among the baseball game's crowd. The important thing was Bo got his camera back. His backpack was gone. No telling who picked that up. It probably now held drugs that were dealt to the homeless.

Activity in the park increased as Bo walked. Addicts dipped here and there. Others walked painfully with backpacks or pushing shopping carts loaded with their belongings. Some people appeared clean. Others looked like they hadn't washed in weeks. Most had tattoos and smoked. Almost all conferred on cell phones, probably to line up the next drug deal, possibly a fatal one laced with fentanyl. Where were they going, Bo wondered. To early demises, the result of overdoses, malnutrition, and blood diseases from using dirty needles. To that seemingly endless list now, he knew, could be added the Whistlers. Bo was sure the Whistlers had taken Ridge and TJ, plucked them from the park as they had the female dipper, and whisked them away to some unknown destination, a secret lair. His friends were dead, Bo thought. In the case of Ridge and TJ, no evidence had been found. Perhaps they were chased through the park by the clicking fiends as Bo was. Perhaps his friends shrieked for help and found none. Perhaps the Whistlers toyed with the young men, letting them believe they were getting away before they pounced on them. At least Bo had a car to dive into and reach safety. The Whistlers had taken the dipper before she realized it, along with her backpack, leaving behind only a small, heavily worn flip-flop. It was obvious the Whistlers were predators. They didn't have sharp claws and teeth to look pretty. They were carnivores. They hunted in a pack. They communicated. From the little Bo had seen, it appeared they liked what they did and were especially dangerous.

Bo reached his car finally and slid in behind the wheel. He sweated heavily and turned on the engine and AC. He deposited the poop bag on the passenger side floor. Maybe the scat could be analyzed to determine what had been consumed. Bo didn't know. He knew no one who could do such an analysis other than brainy Martha Dong, a Chinese pre-med student who had been in one of his classes. She hadn't been interested in dating him and now had fled the city for the summer and was back home, wherever that was.

Bo examined his camera, which now had several scratches. He turned it on. It was dead. Impossible, he thought. Although he had recorded for quite a while, he had a fully charged battery when he started. There should be plenty of power left. He opened the camera and found the battery and memory card were gone. The old man must have swiped them before he ditched the camera. His compelling evidence was gone as if it never existed. And the poop bag? Who would suspect that was anything other than dog shit?

CHAPTER EIGHTEEN

Overboard George's sweats were gone. The pain had diminished. He knew his blood was clean. Still, he had an overpowering desire to get another fix. It would be the first thing he did when he got out if he survived this ordeal. Get some money and buy some dope. If he and Mad Maggie couldn't escape, they would be taken to the consuming room, hung upside down, and drained of every last drop of moisture. Then their remains would be ground and removed from the basement and who knew what. Were they destined for a landfill? Burial in a vacant lot? There were plenty of vacant lots in the city. Dumped over the side of a bridge?

Meanwhile, Mad Maggie continued to moan and shake as if in convulsions any time the man with the ring appeared. Since Mad Maggie had identified him, Charles Van der Meer rarely stopped long to see their conditions. He dropped off food and picked up the sloop buckets. Occasionally, he gave them soap and hosed them down with cold water. There were no towels or soft robes to wear. Charles ignored their pleas for help.

"Lather up. We don't want this place stinking to high heaven," he demanded. "It'll drive the creatures mad. Then you'll be sorry."

Most of the time, however, he ignored them as if they weren't even present.

While George napped, the burned-out lightbulbs in the distance were changed. The lights turned on and off as Charles came and went from the opposite direction. Now George saw the steps at the end of the basement against the wall that presumably led to a first floor. However, most of the time the basement was in darkness. It appeared no one used the steps, although a short, pudgy man occasionally ran down them, conferred with Charles Van der Meer, sometimes heatedly, and returned up them just as quickly. The man had a funny gait that made George smile. He was careful to turn away from the cages and not reveal his face. Still, Overboard George and Mad Maggie could have identified him by the way he walked. George's grandmother would have called the man a *sis*.

George and Maggie had no idea what time of day it was or how long they had been in captivity. George estimated they had been underground about two weeks because he had been through withdrawal before. He knew how long it lasted. They didn't know the dates they were taken. After all, there was no strict timetable—no timetable at all—on the street. Holidays, birthdays, and important events passed without notice. This didn't stop them from speculating endlessly about their plights when no one was around. Of one thing they were certain: no one looked for them or worried about what happened.

However, they decided it must be night when the creatures were released. That was when they were taken. That was what they believed. Sometimes the creatures came back without prey. That's when they howled especially loudly after they returned to their pen. The others—if they were present—gnashed their teeth and spoke in that foreign language. They would become agitated and gesticulate wildly. Sometimes they looked at the cages longingly. Occasionally, they walked over to the cages and peered in. When their flesh was slack, when it lay in folds, Overboard George knew they were famished. They needed to feed. In a way, they were not much different from a junkie. Overboard George believed either of them could tear the cages open and drain him or Maggie on the spot. With no sense of time, Overboard George couldn't tell how often they needed blood, but he knew before they fed sometimes they were shriveled. After they fed it appeared they had spent a long time in a hot bath and were pink with tight skin. The Whistlers got the leftovers. Overboard George concluded *the others* were vampires.

Another addict was taken from the street overnight, or so they imagined. She was awake when they grabbed her, not a dipper. Although the creatures could handle an adult easily, she was left in the basement alone with Charles. He chased her through the cavernous room, screaming all along. She ran up the steps and banged on the door repeatedly, calling for help. When Charles crawled up the steps, the woman threw herself at him. They tumbled to the floor. She was up and racing immediately toward the basement's other end. Charles was not as fast as the woman, but eventually, he managed to trip her and fall on her. Charles pulled her to her feet and hauled her to a metal gurney, which was really a mortuary table. He bent her backward over the table, leaned against her, as if they might have sex, and managed to tie her hands and arms to the table. All the while he heaved a dry hack, and she screamed louder than ever, thrashing from side to side. Mad Maggie held her hands over her ears.

Overboard George watched with interest. He would have to overcome Charles. He looked for a weakness in the man. Overboard George had been a boxer. It would take only one punch, what they called a one-punch massacre. George knew he had the strength. He had been doing push-ups and dips in his tiny cage since his withdrawal symptoms subsided, pressing his bulk against the bars to increase his endurance for the time he needed all his strength. Now it appeared Charles would wear out before the woman. Just as he managed to get her legs on the table she landed a kick to his midsection, crumpling him to the floor. She screamed and thrashed. Pulled over the mortuary table. She kicked so violently that her shoes sailed across the basement in high arcs. She called out to George for help. Charles got to his hands and knees and dropped to the floor again in a prolonged coughing spell. With her hands still tethered, she pulled the table across the floor. Charles coughed uncontrollably before gagging and almost passing out. His face was sanguine. Eventually, the coughing subsided and he was able to catch his breath.

George was surprised Charles didn't slug the woman and knock her out. It would have been easy to do, because she, too, was exhausted. With difficulty, Charles righted the table, hauled her to the top, and tied down the woman's legs. When she was finally secured, although she still thrashed, Charles leaned against the table and panted, coughed more. Apparently, the others don't like their victims injured much. Charles released the brake from the table wheels and pushed the woman into the consuming room. He used scissors to cut off her clothes. He put on his rubber apron and hosed her down. Then he scrubbed her body with soap and a stiff brush. The woman howled in pain.

After washing her thoroughly, Charles, coughing all the time, pushed her back to the cell next to Mad Maggie. Charles released the straps and rolled her off the table. She hit the floor with a thud. The woman was exhausted and had no fight left in her. Charles locked the cell and rolled away the table. He left the area but returned soon with a slop bucket, which he placed inside the cell. The woman was passed out. He watched her a while, leaning against the bars as if he were too tired to move.

Time passed. The woman went through withdrawal symptoms. She sat in a corner with her knees drawn up to her chest. She moaned in pain and sweated profusely. Although George could not see the woman clearly, Mad Maggie kept him apprised like a play-by-play sports announcer.

"Just retched again," Mad Maggie would chirp. "Missed the

bucket completely—again. Now she got the runs. It's a real geyser. Only got some of it in the bucket. What a mess. You must smell it, Overboard George. What that girl needs is a bigger bucket."

"I got a nose, don't I? Hope that Charles come around with his hose and cleans her up. It's not dignified the way she's kept."

"That's the way we were kept, Overboard George. Or can't you remember? You won't remember anything when those Whistlers suck your brain out your ear canals if they find any gray matter up there. Those long black tongues will penetrate your chest and wrap around your heart while it still beats. Squeeze all the goodness out."

"Never mind, Mad Maggie. Keep your mouth shut. Nobody's sucking anything from me. I'm getting out of here. If you behave, I'll think about taking you with me."

"That's nice of you, Overboard George. Thank you for being a true friend. I'll make it up to you when we get back on the street. I got some cat food you can have. It's tuna, and it's not too bad. Not as good as those sandwiches Lisa leaves at After Dark. But it's passable."

"Hey, Maggie, do you think our stuff is still out on the street?"

Maggie thought a moment. "No. It's gone. It's all gone. You know, when you disappeared I took over your sweet box right away, before somebody else could move in. I must admit some of your stuff I couldn't use, so I sold or traded for it. Hunter John took a little. Some I even gave away. I'm sorry now because I never thought I'd see you again."

"It's the way of the world, Mad Maggie," Overboard George said, thoughtfully. "Don't worry about it. We'll get new stuff when we're out of here. Maybe better stuff than we had. They're always people looking to help the homeless."

"When I disappeared, someone else took your box over, I'm sure," Mad Maggie continued, running a finger over her gums. "Maybe it was that shrew Old Harriet. Maybe she ate my tuna cat food in a can, so don't expect any until we get back on the street and find it. If I have it, it's yours. If it's gone, too bad. Know what I mean?"

"I understand, Mad Maggie. It's the way of the world."

"Not to mention my tampons. I had almost a full box. I'm sure they're all gone.

"It's the way of the world, Mad Maggie."

More time passed.

"Overboard George, if we don't make it out of here, do you think the psych folks will still look for me?"

"How do you know they're looking now?"

"I just have a feeling they'll never give up until they have a corpus delicti—that's a body."

"I know what it is," George said, shaking his head. "I wonder if the Navy's still looking for me. Not real active, but like if I got arrested they would get the word, somehow."

"Who knows," Mad Maggie said. "It is nice to think you're making the psych people and the Navy go to a lot of trouble to look for you even if you're no longer here. It's kind of like getting the last word in, even though you've said nothing and they ain't heard nothing."

There was a silence for a moment, and then they repeated together, "It's the way of the world."

Overboard George didn't mind being naked in the cell. After all, he had been in the Navy, showered with countless men, and slept with women of many nationalities. Being nude didn't seem to affect Mad Maggie either because, George thought, she was mad and Fred had molested her. Plus, most of their time they spent in the dark. During their seemingly endless conversations, the two decided they would make a run for it when Charles appeared. George would be ready and spring when Charles opened the cell to remove the slop bucket. They hoped he would go into one of his coughing spells. That would make him an easy target. The lights would be on when Charles was there. They would run in the direction Charles entered, even though they couldn't see a door or another passage. They'd avoid the steps to the first-floor interior because they always heard a key turn in the lock before the little man came skipping down from above. Running up the steps didn't do the new woman any good. She couldn't get out and had to come back down. If the beasts or the vampires were present, George would run to hit the bright lights they used to control the varmints. They'd take their chances in the direction Charles Van der Meer came from. There had to be an exit that way.

"You open this cell, Overboard George, and I'll be right behind you. At least we have a plan, and if Bad Nelson escaped, the way they say he did, we can do it ourselves."

CHAPTER NINETEEN

The vampires showed increased interest in Overboard George and Mad Maggie. They visited the basement alone or together, pressing their faces into the cells, sampling the air within the cages, and licking their bloodless, slack lips. When they pulled back to confer together in their foreign dialect, or with Charles Van der Meer in English, the bars left deep channels in their faces. They hadn't fed in a while. The beasts were out twice and returned without prey. The last woman they took was still in withdrawal, spending most of her time moaning, calling for help, screaming. Her noise agitated the vampires. They hollered back at her when she screamed, but the woman took little notice. George knew the horrors of withdrawal. It seemed the vampires had little sympathy for those with drug addictions.

The vampires returned to George and Maggie's cells, and stood to watch over them, motionless, like wax figures. Their faces were drawn. Flesh sagged. Their clothing hung limply on their bodies. The female's bare arms were flaccid. They looked hungry as if they were concentration camp inmates, but they were on the wrong side of confinement. Overboard George thought he might be able to take one of these vampires. He knew his exercising had increased his strength. He could do more reps now than when he first started. He imagined grabbing one of the living corpses and smashing a fist through the flabby body, hearing the bones shatter, watching the thing collapse and disintegrate on the floor before him. Perhaps it would expire in a sudden rush of flame like vampires did in films. Or maybe it would first glow and then disappear, leaving a faint residue on the ground in the shape of a body, as the aliens died in the old TV show *The Invaders*.

Overboard George might gain the upper hand over one vampire crippled by hunger but was he a match for two of the undead? He knew the strong lights would drive them away long enough for him to free Mad Maggie and make their escapes. George had his plan ready. He whispered it to Maggie several times in the basement darkness. Even though she acknowledged each detail with a quiet *uh, huh* after he paused, and a head nod, he imagined, George knew it was better to repeat the plan over and over, because, after all, Maggie was mad and might not remember it. All George needed was the chance.

When his cell opened, George would make his move, throw himself against the door with all his strength, and knock over Charles Van der Meer. While Charles lay dazed, George would pick up the slop bucket and crash it over his head. The bucket was heavy and surely it would knock Charles unconscious. If it didn't, he would hit him again and again until he was senseless. He'd take the key from Charles's belt—there was only one key on the ring, and it opened Overboard George's, Mad Maggie's, and the new girl's cells—and free Maggie. During their whispered discussions, Mad Maggie wanted to bring the new girl with them. In fact, they had begun to call her New Girl and she responded to it as if it might be her real name. That's the way it was on the street. A name attached itself to you, George thought, even if you didn't care for it.

George didn't like the name *Overboard*. It sounded like an accident had happened. That maybe he was clumsy. He also didn't like any connection to being AWOL. After all, the Navy still might be looking for him. Would be happy to catch him, throw him in another cell, and court martial his ass. That would mean more prison time. When this mess was over, George was determined to change his name to Admiral George, maybe General George, to avoid a connection to the Navy. It might take a while for the new name to stick, but it would work.

George wasn't sure about taking New Girl with them. She might not be able to keep up in the throes of withdrawal. She probably would be more trouble than help. The last thing Overboard George wanted to do was carry this woman to safety. But if he didn't take New Girl, Maggie might have a meltdown in the basement while the vampires regrouped. It might be better to free New Girl and let her on her own. By now New Girl should realize she'd have to follow George and Maggie and wouldn't have a chance on the steps again.

The three captives sat in the dark. All three were quiet, even New Girl, who snored softly. George knew the next time the lights came on the vampires would arrive to feed. He and Maggie would be the main course. They had one chance to escape. He had gone over the plan time after time. His exercise in the cell had made him stronger. Now he was ready. He hoped all three were ready. There was a noise from far away down the basement. George heard coughing. He recognized the dry hack. It was Charles Van der Meer. And he was followed by the noise of many paws and the scratching and scraping of claws on concrete. There also were multiple clicks and teeth gnashing. Charles cursed the beasts between coughs and seemed to strike them with a club because there were repeated thuds and immediate yelps.

Then the lights turned on. Overboard George was blinded temporarily. Mad Maggie cursed the sudden loss of vision. New Girl screamed. The beasts spilled into the basement from the far end and hauled a body to the table.

"Over there, over there," Charles gasped, "on the table. Hurry now! The masters are coming. Then you will feed." Charles leaned against George's cell, breathing heavily. He held a sawed-off baseball bat in his free hand.

George eyed the bat. It would work better than a bucket. He believed he could wrench the bat from Charles's hands and club him with it. George led his high school baseball team in home runs for three years. He still knew how to swing a bat. He'd have to be careful, or he'd bash in Charles's head, and spill his brains all over the floor. That could cause the beasts to go bat shit. He'd take the club from Charles's weak grip and hit him over the head hard enough to daze him. Maybe hit him twice, if necessary.

"What are you looking at?" Charles wanted to know. He gasped for breath after every few words. "You get a reprieve tonight. You and nutsy were set to go, but the Travelers got a fresh one, not an addict. *They'll* be happy. Young, pure blood."

"With that cough, you sound like you might not make the party, Charles," Overboard George said with a smile. "I wouldn't imagine they would want your blood. God knows what's in it."

"You idiot. You won't be here to see it, but before long this cough will be gone. I'll be cured, feeding on stupid people like you. For what I've done, helped set this thing up," Charles Van der Meer said, raising his hands toward the ceiling, "They'll make me one of them. My liver and lungs will be brand new. I will live through the ages. Young. Virile. You'll be dust. Not even a memory."

"Don't count on it, Chuck. You'll never be no Count Dracula," Overboard George hissed, pressing his face against the bars. "*They* ain't doin' shit for you. Wait and see. You'll be on the curb taking your last breath and they'll have some new monkey down here passing out room service and collecting shit. You can tell the cops everything you know, call it a death-bed confession, and they'll write every word down, eager as hell. Watch you with compassion. After they watch you expire, see you go whimpering to the afterlife, they'll tear those papers up and laugh their asses off."

Mad Maggie laughed. "You know it, Overboard George. The only future he's got is the one in his imagination. Silly old drunk."

"Shut up!" Charles barked and doubled over coughing. "I'd love to keep you two going, to let you see me young and strong again. Then I'd drain you from the jugular. I'd plant my lips over the wound and drain every drop of blood in your veins."

New girl howled. "I...need...a...fucking...fix! You bastards!"

"Everybody needs a fix, honey," Mad Maggie said, "of one kind or another."

New Girl screamed and beat her head against the bars.

Meanwhile, the beasts lifted and held down a woman on the table. They gnashed their teeth and nipped at the woman's fleshy arms, leaving tiny bite marks. Her clothes were torn to shreds by the Whistlers' sharp claws. A shoe was missing. Charles limped to the table and strapped her down.

He tried to chase away the beasts but they refused to leave. A few tried to climb on the woman and copulate, even though they had no apparent sex organs. She regained consciousness and screamed. New Girl howled. Mad Maggie held her head and shrieked.

"How am I going to do this alone?" George called, looking toward the ceiling.

Charles stumbled to the table and beat the animals with his bat to move them away. They were famished and returned to the table immediately. Charles coughed. He could no longer swing the bat. It seemed his lungs would explode, expel dust into the air, his hacking sounded so dry. He staggered to the wall and threw the knife blade switch on. The room filled instantaneously with dazzling ultraviolet light. The Whistlers shrieked and rolled this way and that over the floor. The odor of singed hair filled the air, and their short dark snouts burned pink. Unable to escape the light, they flapped their arms and legs and clawed at the concrete floor, as if trying to dig a hole to escape.

Charles coughed more and covered his nose with his arm. He

pulled the switch, sending the room back to its prior dimness. He pointed the bat toward the basement's darkened end. The beasts formed a mass and rolled toward the darkness, yelping and whimpering all the way. They dropped to the floor and one by one disappeared through the small door with an iron gate George had seen them emerge from on prior feedings. Charles limped to the door and locked the beasts inside. They continued to howl and throw themselves against the gate.

Charles returned to the table, unlocked the wheels, and pushed the woman into the feeding room. She was unconscious. As fast as his waning strength allowed, Charles stripped off the woman's remaining clothes. Then he secured her ankles with a strap connected to a chain. He released her other table bindings and hoisted her upside down. Charles rolled the table outside the feeding room, set its locks, and leaned against it. At last, the coughing stopped. He breathed deeply. It was obvious to George his keeper was worn out. Charles would have little strength for a fight. Still, he was able to hose her off and use a long-handled brush to clean the woman.

Suddenly, the basement became quiet. The beasts stopped, except for an occasional whimper. The woman hung like a pendulum in the feeding room, her massive breasts stretched to her shoulders. The sudden quiet caught New Girl by surprise. She listened intently.

"I don't think she's breathing," New Girl said, pointing to the human pendulum. She looked at Mad Maggie. "I can't see her chest move, and I have good eyesight."

A key turned in a lock at the top of the distant stairs. Then the massive wooden door creaked open. There were footsteps on the wooden steps. Slowly, the vampires came into view. Charles struggled to his feet as they descended the steps. He kicked the woman's shredded garments to the side toward a massive pie of clothing in a corner. He moved forward to welcome the ghouls. Despite their thirst, the pair walked slowly, elegantly, toward the feeding room.

They gnashed their teeth. Each bowed slightly as they passed Charles. He bowed deeply, suppressing a cough. They stopped a moment, turned toward Overboard George, and smiled in unison. Their teeth were stained, sharp, and crooked. Then they returned their attention to the hanging woman. The male approached the feeding room. The woman placed a hand on his arm. The movement made the female vampire's sagging flesh jiggle. She said something in their foreign language. The words sounded hollow as if her body were empty as a drum. The tall vampire stopped and she stepped in front of him. The duo sniffed the air as they proceeded.

"Must be the queen bee," Mad Maggie said, nodding toward George.

George shushed her.

Mad Maggie giggled.

New Girl sat transfixed, watching the parade of vampires in the ancient, threadbare, ill-fitting, stained, and dusty evening clothes.

The female vampire entered the feeding room. Sniffed the air more. And approached the dangling woman, who hung motionless. The female licked her lips, bent slightly at the knees, and inclined her head toward the woman's throat. She stood suddenly.

"Charles, this one is dead. It is useless," she said in her hollow voice, her words in English. "She's already turning blue. What have you done? We will not drink dead blood. We are nearly famished."

Charles looked dumbfounded. "She was alive when I hung her. I found a pulse on her neck. I swear it."

"You idiot. Bring the small woman. We will have the big man tomorrow." The hollow words seemed to ring off the basement walls.

The vampires were agitated. The beasts howled from their den.

"Hurry, Charles! We don't have all night," Gerrard said. "It will be morning soon. We can't wait any longer. Eva, this thirst is intolerable!"

"Please, Masters." Charles groveled before the vampires. "She was alive. I swear it. The Travelers were so hungry they wouldn't recede. I had to use the ultraviolet lights on them. She must have had a stroke. Maybe it was a bad heart. You can't always tell someone's health by looking at them. I'm sorry."

"Fool! You used the light in front of them!" Eva said, looking toward the three captives. The vampire's words echoed off the walls. She pointed to Overboard George.

"I had no choice. The Travelers were about to overpower me. They would have eaten her on the table. They might have scared her to death." Tears welled in Charles's eyes. He wrung his hands. "Please forgive me." A coughing spell started and Charles collapsed.

The male vampire pointed at Mad Maggie. "Get that woman and make it fast!" he shouted.

CHAPTER TWENTY

Bo placed the camera on the Charger's floor and positioned it with his foot where no one would see it. He left the car, locked it, and started back through the park to the garbage can where the man with the ring discarded the camera. He should have checked the camera at the can. The memory card might still be mixed with the trash. Now he had to return through the park in the heat, through the smell. His legs ached more than ever, and he was thirsty. The uphill climb through the park was excruciating.

What if someone saw him rummaging through the trash? Bo knew that was commonplace among the junkies. Every trash can, no matter what foul-smelling, greasy slop it contained, had at least one gem that could be added to a homeless person's shopping cart full of treasure. But what if an addict had already found the memory card, whether the man with the ring dropped it in the can or on the street? He would never be able to prove his claims. Who would believe him? Nobody. The cops who interviewed him about TJ and Ridge would think he was a college kid looking for attention. Perhaps a drug user himself.

Bo walked the long asphalt path to the can. The homeless, who sat or stood in clusters talking, looked away as he approached. Some lay unconscious on benches, or on the ground where they had passed out, the victims of an unknown cocktail of chemicals with an unknown potency. They had dirty faces and slack mouths that hung open for the world to see, for flies to explore. One man was in the process of stealing a woman's newish-looking Nikes off her feet. Another woman helped herself to a box of tampons from an unconscious addict's belongings stuffed in a plastic bag. Several people recorded the images with their cell phones, never stopping a thief or ensuring a junkie breathed. They recorded exactly what happened.

The obelisk he had hidden beside was visible now in the distance. That area of the park, which had no benches and walls, was devoid of people for the moment, although several homeless followed on the path behind him like zombies in a movie. Bo increased his pace. Each breath hurt his bruised ribs. Sweat rolled down his face and back. The Whistlers' scat smear was still visible on the asphalt near the obelisk, where it was dry and collected flies. Finally, Bo made it to the can. The can was empty and cleaned out except for a wet newspaper stuck to the barrel's sticky bottom.

Bo couldn't believe it. The city had emptied the can. He jogged to the next can along the path, its fluorescent green visible ahead. Bo was only halfway there when he slowed to a walk. His ribs and legs ached. He sweated more than ever. A man dipped by the can. Bo approached the man and trashcan cautiously. That can was empty, too. The hydraulics of a garbage truck sounded in the distance. Bo retraced his path to the point where the man with the ring walked through the park. Perhaps he dropped the memory card in the grass, not wanting it found with the camera. Bo walked slowly, eyes to the ground, sliding his lead foot back and forth through the long grass, hoping to turn over the small missing memory card and slightly larger camera battery. He knew the search was futile, because he had no idea whether he followed the exact path the man with the ring took. The memory card could have been dropped a few feet to his left or right or tossed a distance, and Bo would never know. Still, he had to continue the search for the memory card. He owed it to his missing friends, and he owed it to himself for the danger he put himself in.

Although he found no memory card, Bo did overturn aluminum cans, plastic bottles, snack wrappers, a dead bird, a cheap, silver-plated bracelet. As he approached Fifth Street, Bo decided he would ask some of the homeless if they knew of the Whistlers. As he stepped over a short wall onto the sidewalk, he immediately entered a tent city teaming with the homeless. The tents and tarps were every imaginable color, even camo. There were also flimsy shelters made of cardboard and plywood, none seeming able to withstand a strong wind. The homeless walked this way and that, some limping on bad legs wrapped with soiled bandages. Others sat in and around their shelters. They socialized and argued. Junkies tied off arms or legs to inject themselves or others.

A hot breeze flapped the tents and tarps like flags and rattled the ramshackle shanties. Trash pinwheeled along the sidewalk. Dust from the street rose in clouds. The homeless eyed Bo suspiciously. They knew he was an outsider. His clothing. His haircut. His cleanliness. Everyone he approached asked whether he was from the city. They begged for money, cigarettes, and food. None had ever heard of the Whistlers, but Bo saw the alarm in their eyes when he said, "Have you ever heard a whistling that comes from the park?"

It was as if acknowledging the Whistlers would doom them, Bo thought. The homeless were terrified of the night and the Whistlers. Some gasped before they denied knowing about the beasts or admitting to anyone who did. Bo decided to return to his car. At least he got his camera back. Regardless of what happened, he doubted he would go out again to capture more video.

Bo saw one more woman perched on an ornate chair on small wheels. The chair appeared like it came from an antique parlor.

She would be the last one he asked. As he approached, Bo couldn't determine whether the woman was awake or in a stupor. Still, she had a lit cigarette between her fingers.

"Hello," Bo said by way of introduction.

"You from the city?"

"No. I'm not even a city resident. My name is Bo. I go to the university."

"You can call me Old Harriet."

"Nice to meet you," Bo said. He smiled, but Old Harriet eyed him suspiciously.

"Are you one of the groups who goes around beating us homeless? You looking for some more easy targets? Aren't we helpless enough just after a fix?"

"Of course not," Bo said. "I never heard of *Beaters*."

"I can tell you all about them," Old Harriet said. "They got me good. Split my head open in the scalp. Beat me all over. It took a long time for the welts to go away."

"I'm sorry to hear that." Bo looked toward the ground.

"All the homeless know about the Beaters. They come dancing up the street, crash through the park, attack everybody they pass."

"Did you go to the police?" Bo found it difficult to swallow. He looked away from Old Harriet again.

"Police?" Old Harriet scoffed. "They don't care. The city don't care. What's a few less homeless to them? Nothing at all. They couldn't tell you who's out here at any one time or how many people are laying in a heap with an overdose."

"I'm sorry. That's too bad."

"Damn right, it is."

"Are you a user?" Bo asked, now looking at Old Harriet.

Old Harriet smiled. "A little, now and then." She twirled her fingers through her straggly beehive hair. Then she became fierce. "But I got none extra. You'll have to go elsewhere."

"I don't want drugs," Bo said, looking down. "My younger brother died from an overdose. He was just a high school kid."

"Shame. A lot of people do. The dope's no good. Nobody cares about the users. The sellers are happy to supply it, but they don't give a shit about us. When we croak, somebody else will take our place. Take my word. There'll always be somebody new lined up to buy dope."

"How long have you been on the street?" Bo asked.

"Long enough," Old Harriet fired back.

"Ever go to the park at night?"

"Hell, no," Old Harriet said. "Between the beaters and the Whistlers, I'm not going near the park, especially when I got a sweet box like that." Old Harriet pointed toward the bright blue flapping tarp.

"Then you know about the Whistlers," Bo said.

"Naturally," Old Harriet said with a smirk. "Being a college boy and living at the university, you wouldn't know about the Whistlers. But I know this..." She pointed a finger with its dirty, long nail, "If you hear the Whistlers, nine out of ten you disappear. You're never seen again. They're animals. They come at night. They talk to themselves in whistles we don't understand. They grab you and take you underground. They took Bad Nelson, but he got away. Escaped. He told me everything. They took Overboard George. That used to be his sweet box with the blue tarp over it. Then Mad Maggie took over the box. She had it one day. One day! But the Whistlers got her, too, so we believe because she also disappeared."

Old Harriet paused. She spread her arms as if to call attention to the tent city that surrounded them. "That's how it goes here on the street. It's, as they say, *the way of the world*. These stupid people go out at night and they don't come back. They got appointments, all hoity-toity like they were *somebody important*. Now I got this sweet box. And I got this chair on wheels that was Overboard George's. A kid named Darren took this chair on wheels after George went missing, because he had bad legs. After Darren overdosed and went to the morgue, I got the chair. I suspect he's still at the morgue. Maybe he'll stay there, if they allow such a thing."

"I believe you, Old Harriet. I think the Whistlers took my two friends. They've been gone a couple of weeks. The cops didn't think my friends were missing but met some girls and are shacked up somewhere."

Old Harriet winked at Bo. "That's the beauty. Nobody will believe animals take you underground to be consumed. The city thinks everyone down here screws like minks. Anyone goes missing, the city says they're shacked up somewhere. If that was true, the whole city'd be shacked up."

"I've seen them in the park. Twice. They took a girl. She was dipping. I recorded it with my camera, but I lost the memory card. Now there's no proof."

"I know a lot more about it, too. Bad Nelson said the animals belong to vampires. They take the addicts underground until their blood clears. Wait until the blood is pure, nice and tasty, just the way a vampire likes it. Then they drink them dry. I'm afraid your friends are dead."

"That's what I believe," Bo said. He lowered his head a moment and looked back at Old Harriet and her bizarre hair. "I wish I really knew what happened. Where they were taken."

"I can tell you. I know. They're all taken to After Dark."

CHAPTER TWENTY-ONE

"Take me, you son of a bitch," Overboard George shouted, shaking the cell door. "Leave Mad Maggie alone! My blood will fill your empty tanks! Hers won't move the needle to halfway. I dare you to take me!" George pressed against the cell door, ready to throw it open the second Charles's key turned in the lock. Even though he was outnumbered, the element of surprise was in his favor.

Charles Van der Meer paused and looked toward the female vampire. He seemed frightened. *Is he afraid of the vampires or me?* George thought. Charles tried to suppress a cough. Finally, he cleared his throat and swallowed. George knew he could push the hapless Charles over and run for the strong light switch. He had about forty feet to reach the wall and switch.

What he couldn't determine was how fast the vampires were. They were always fast in movies. Able to outrun their prey. Appear ahead of a fleeing person in a split second in foggy, trash-strewn alleys. These vampires were weak. They needed nourishment. He had never seen them move quickly on their forays to the basement. They walked slowly, dignified, George thought, on their way to and from the basement. Never in a hurry. Always at a slow pace, the way Bela Lugosi walked through London just before he seduced the young flower girl. However, these vampires didn't wear capes and top hats or carry sleek, polished canes. They moved slowly despite their crushing hunger. They were assured. Confident. Safe in their subterranean lair. They wouldn't expect prey, scared too senseless to fight, to attack *them*.

"Bring the woman," the female vampire demanded again, in her hollow-sounding voice that seemed to echo from an empty vessel. "We'll deal with the other one later."

It appeared to take all Charles's energy to move to Mad Maggie's cage.

"Charles!" the female vampire called. Her voice was harsh, impatient. It reverberated off the walls, seemingly louder than such a being could make.

Charles fumbled for the key ring on his belt.

The Whistlers howled, locked in their pen. They threw themselves at the door. Made a terrible racket.

Mad Maggie looked toward Overboard George. Tears ran down his cheeks. He mouthed a silent *Sorry* to Maggie. His large frame deflated in defeat. He watched, still gripping the cell door.

Mad Maggie winked at George. "Time for Plan B."

George looked at Maggie quizzically.

"Just made it up," Mad Maggie whispered. She nodded and smiled at George.

"Maybe you're not mad after all," Overboard George whispered.

The Whistlers howled. New Girl moaned and then screamed as if she suddenly realized what was about to happen.

The vampires licked their pale lips and watched with anticipation. Mad Maggie was not a person to them. She was only a meal no different from a platter served in a restaurant.

Mad Maggie pressed herself into the back of her cell.

Charles had the key in the lock. He paused, hacking more.

"Charles!" the female vampire called again. "We thirst." She was plaintive as if a child calling for her supper.

The moment the key turned in the lock and Charles put his free hand on the door to tug it open, Mad Maggie launched herself at the opening. She rammed the door with her shoulder, using all her might, pushing back the surprised Charles. A step outside the cell, Mad Maggie planted one bare foot on the damp concrete floor and delivered the other to Charles's groin. He shrieked in pain and crumpled, curling into a fetal position. His hands cupped his crotch. Mad Maggie howled and sprinted toward the knife switch. However, she found her legs, which were barely used in weeks of incarceration in the small cell, folded under her. She staggered toward the knife switch, waving her arms wildly to keep her balance. The vampires hissed, showed their fangs, and lunged toward Mad Maggie.

"Go girl, go!" Overboard George cried, hands on the cell door, shaking the bars furiously. Tears still ran down his face. Now he felt proud of the diminutive young woman who weaved her way to the wall like a running back, bent over to make a smaller target.

The Whistlers roared and banged on their den door, sensing prey was loose, throwing themselves headfirst at the iron gate. George shouted encouragement. New Girl screamed hysterically.

The female vampire grabbed Mad Maggie's arm. Her nails ripped the flesh. Maggie squealed in pain. The vampire pulled Maggie toward her as if she were a doll.

"Cunt!" Maggie shouted.

The vampire swept her other arm forward to grab Maggie in a titanic bearhug, but Maggie ducked below the claws and raked her own hand down the vampire's face, catching the sagging flesh under an eye. Maggie ripped away half the vampire's face, exposing the pallid, bloodless muscles underneath. The vampire screamed, let go of Maggie's arm to cover her face and the exposed eye socket.

"You little fucker!" Mad Maggie shouted in delight. She dropped the vampire's flesh and lurched toward the knife switch, but the male vampire lunged for Mad Maggie and caught her ankle. He pulled her across the floor away from the wall. He had immense strength even in his debilitated condition. Maggie rolled over and planted a heel in the vampire's face. Surprised, he let her go for an instant. When he grabbed at her again, Maggie was already scrambling backward toward the wall like a crab. She hit the wall hard and regained her feet, using the wall for support, as the female grabbed for her body. The vampires hissed, exposed their fangs, extended claws from their fingertips. They caught her legs and an arm, dug their claws into Mad Maggie's flesh, lifted her off the ground as if she were weightless. Maggie screamed in pain. The vampires stretched her limbs, pulling her in opposite directions, as if they were quartering her by horses in a medieval torture. Maggie thrashed, even though the movement caused her more pain. The vampires increased their grips, digging in their claws, and pulling harder on her extremities. Mad Maggie's knees, shoulders, and elbows were ready to pop from their sockets. Despite the pain, the flailing allowed Maggie to keep one arm free. The vampires were in a frenzy. They smelled blood. Sensed Maggie's terror. Except for one struggling arm, Mad Maggie was suspended in air, naked, spreadeagled over the floor. The vampires leaned in to feed on her body.

Maggie saw them lick their lips. She smelled their fetid breaths. George screamed. The Whistlers banged at their gate and fought among themselves to get their snouts through the bars to smell the blood, and sense the fear in the room. New Girl screamed in horror, her hands covering her head. Mad Maggie could fight no more. She couldn't even scream. She went limp. The vampires held her easily, perfectly still, suspended spreadeagled over the floor. Her head lolled backward, exposing her throat. The male vampire said a few words in his hollow voice, in their strange dialect. He held Mad Maggie by one bloodied ankle, where he had sunk in his claws. He used his index finger claw on the free hand to open a vein on the inside of Mad Maggie's leg just above the knee. A small flow of blood spurted out with Maggie's hammering heartbeat. The Whistlers renewed their attacks on the den door. Charles Van der Meer looked on in horror. The male vampire inclined his head toward the wound to drink, and caught a few spurts of blood in his open mouth. Smiled. The female vampire was transfixed by the sight. She licked her lips. Their faces were pale, waxen, expectant. The vampiress' face had begun to heal. Tissue grew slowly around the exposed eye socket.

Mad Maggie turned her head toward the wall, away from the male vampire and his lurid open mouth, the horrid black teeth. This would be her end. She would die as the other people she had seen drained in the basement. Her corpse, dry and shrunken to half its size, would disappear. There would be no funeral. No place of rest that people could visit to remember her. It would be as if she never existed. Was Fred, her monstrous stepfather, waiting for her? She felt herself receding into unconsciousness when out of the corner of her eye Mad Maggie saw the knife switch so close. Her mind jolted into action as if she had been shocked. The fiends held her shoulder height above the floor. She raised her head. None of the vampires noticed. Their eyes were glued on the bleeding wound on Maggie's leg, the spurting blood. Their mouths grew slack, opened in anticipation, as Gerrard planted his lips on Mad Maggie's thigh and sucked on the laceration. Neither did they see her grab the knife switch with her free hand and engage it.

The basement was filled with bright ultraviolet light. The vampires shrieked. They dropped Mad Maggie. Her head hit the concrete floor. Their faces bubbled with blisters in an instant. Their hands burned when they covered their faces. The woman's sagging, bare arms steamed in the light as flesh dripped off.

"Charles!" the female vampire shrieked. "Help us! Save us!" The vampires staggered to the feeding room, their smoking bodies half-crawling through the entrance. With the last of their remaining strength, they closed the door, sealing out the lethal light. Meanwhile, Charles struggled to stand. Mad Maggie had regained her own feet, squinted in the bright light, and delivered another kick to Charles's groin. He screamed and sank to the floor, curling into a ball again, moaning, coughing, his lungs seemingly ready to explode.

"What I wouldn't do for a knife right now," Mad Maggie howled, with her hands on her hips, looking over the prostrate Charles. "I'd snip those jewels and flush them down the nearest drain, let those vampires suck you dry, lap your blood off the floor."

"Please, Maggie," George called.

Mad Maggie limped toward her cell, holding the wound Gerrard gave her, removed the key from her cell lock, and freed Overboard George. He pushed open the door, took the key from Maggie, and opened New Girl's cell.

There's no way I'm going to leave anybody here to be pulled apart like a chicken at Sunday dinner, Overboard George thought. I'll get New Girl out if I have to carry her.

New Girl scrambled out of the cell and headed for the stairs, screaming all the way.

"No, fool," George said. "This way." He grabbed her arm and pulled her back. "You already tried that once and it didn't work."

As they passed Charles, who was still prone on the floor, Overboard George delivered his own kick to the man's ribs. He collected Mad Maggie and led New Girl to the basement's opposite end. There a crude hole was cut in the stone foundation. Beyond the hole a passage supported by wooden timbers continued for some thirty feet, ending at steps that led upwards. The place smelled of earth and the Whistlers. Overboard George went first up the steps. He put his shoulder against the horizontal door built into the ceiling and tested it. It didn't budge.

"Must be locked from the outside," George said, looking down the crude stairwell.

"Put some might behind it," Mad Maggie said. "I can't help. I'm all played out and New Girl is useless." New Girl stood last in line, her bare shoulders rounded and shaking. She sobbed. "You been in training for weeks to fight the undead, Overboard George. Now's your chance. Give that fucking door a shove!"

The bright lights in the basement turned off. Charles had regained some strength and was at the Whistlers' door, but he found it difficult to unlock while the beasts threw themselves against it.

The feeding room door must have opened because George could hear the strange hollow voices. *They must be cursing and in a lot of pain*, he thought. *They'll be here any time, no matter how bad the light hurt them. Now they control the light, not me.*

Finally, Charles threw open the Whistlers' lock and the creatures spilled into the basement, clicking and howling. The vampires' voices grew louder. They beat back the beasts. Cursed in English and their own tongue. Their voices reverberated off the walls and were high-pitched, painful for the living to hear. The Whistlers hurtled through the tunnel from the basement and appeared at the bottom of the steps. Mad Maggie and New Girl climbed the steps behind George and gathered around him until they were bent over under the door. A sharp command from the male vampire halted the Whistlers at the bottom of the stairs. Then the vampires appeared. Their eyes glowed. Their skin appeared melted. There were pustules on their faces and necks. More were on the vampiress' arms. They hissed at the sight of the humans and showed their teeth and claws. They mounted the steps with their usual deliberateness. Behind them, the pack of Travelers howled. The smell of their burned flesh gagged the humans.

"Hurry, George!" Mad Maggie called from a step below him. New Girl cried in terror.

Overboard George put his big, hairy shoulder against the door and shoved. The door flew open, admitting fresh air and early morning light. The vampires shrieked and retreated. A few Whistlers ventured into the light momentarily but withdrew in pain. From the top of the steps, bathed in cool air and morning light, George smelled burnt hair and flesh from below. He paused a moment to watch the rising sun. The trio stepped out and into the grass, wet with dew, in the lot next to After Dark. The long grass blades tickled his bare legs. They dropped and huddled together naked in the longish grass, invisible to anyone on the street. The city never smelled so wonderful. The door to the basement tunnel was open. All three sobbed, but they no longer were afraid. The vampires, the Whistlers, would never leave their lair during daylight. The only one who could come above ground was Charles Van der Meer. They heard him hacking inside the basement tunnel. He did not worry them either. They knew how to take care of Charles.

CHAPTER TWENTY-TWO

Charles Van der Meer lay in a rectangle of light on the basement floor at the base of the steps to the exterior. He was on his side, sweating profusely, his breath heaving. He coughed intermittently. Eventually, the hacking subsided. Gerrard with the light hair approached but stayed in the shadows, away from the direct sunlight, shielding his eyes with a burned hand that looked like the shell of a boiled lobster.

"Charles, you fool," the vampire hissed, bending closer to Charles, coming within inches of the sunlight's oblong splash on the floor. Even the hiss sounded hollow, but now the voice was weak, Charles noted, almost as weak as Charles himself. "Get our cattle back. They can't go far naked above ground. These humans!" He shouted an oath in his foreign dialect, infused with venom, so loud it caused dirt to crumble from the walls.

"I can't," Charles managed to gasp. "Too weak. I'm sorry. I need to rest. You promised to make me strong—one of you. I couldn't climb the stairs right now."

"Damn you!" Eva shouted, rushing to Gerrard's side. The male threw out his arm to hold her back. "We must feed! The light sapped what little strength we had left. Charles, collect your strength. Tonight, take out our friends. Even they are famished and burned, weak from their exertions."

"They'll be impossible to control in the park," Charles panted, looking up at the two gaunt, bloodless figures. Their fine, dusty threadbare clothes hung on them like scarecrow costumes. Their wounds healed slowly before Charles's eyes. The vampiress' eye mostly had been reconstructed. "I had to use the light on them today or they would have torn that woman who died to pieces. Then you would still have no blood."

"Don't be impudent, Charles. We don't need another family member that bad," Eva scolded. She turned to the male vampire and talked to him in their strange, hollow dialect.

"I'm sorry," Charles whimpered, bowing his head. "*They* are difficult to control. They sense my weakness. They don't fear me no more."

After a prolonged silence, as his strength returned, Charles felt emboldened. What did he have to lose? "You promised me. Who else would have gone to the extremes I went through these last few years? The murders I committed. I have kept you safe all this time."

"Then assert yourself," the female said. "Get up and close that door before someone sees the opening and stumbles in. What we don't need now is a junker we can't consume for weeks."

Charles struggled to his feet, using the steps to pull himself up. He gasped for breath. Slowly, he mounted the steps, using his arms and legs like the Whistlers, and crawled out of the basement. The captives were gone. He looked around dismayed. He had no idea where they could have gone they disappeared so fast. It was like they were scattered by the constant hot wind. Using all his strength, Charles lifted the metal door off the ground, stood it upright while he climbed partially inside, and slowly lowered the door on his back while he descended the steps until the door finally shut.

"Good, Charles. Lock the door. We don't want the cattle coming back during the day while we are practically helpless."

Charles locked the door, slid down the remaining steps, and sat at the bottom, holding his head in his hands.

"Come, Charles," the female said. "*We* have work to do."

Charles raised his eyes to her. Anytime *we* had work it was designated to Charles alone. "You must rest during the day with us and tonight take out our friends," she said. Her hollow voice was soft now. It showed as much pity as he had ever seen from her. She caressed Charles's head like a child's. "Poor Charles. You must gather your strength. You must control them and find another human—a clean one. We can't wait weeks for a body to cleanse itself. We need blood now. The vampire disease can barely heal us. *It* demands blood."

"I understand, Madam. I remain your servant," Charles said, bowing to her from his seat on the steps. He was too tired to stand, too unsteady to bow other than from his seated position.

"You are correct. You have been good to us these years," the male said. "Moving to this city was a hardship but necessary to spread our numbers and avoid detection. This accommodation suits our needs better because *we* are different from most vampires. We have a different palate than others like us, younger ones. After you come into the fold, Charles, you'll understand. Meanwhile, we'll need another *Watcher*." The vampire smiled at Charles, revealing his sharp teeth, blackened by time, and stained by blood. "We leave that to your discretion. We don't want a junkie. We would prefer a man but will accept a woman. She would have to be physically strong and able to move our caskets. Above all, we need someone who is not impaired by alcohol or drugs. Someone who will be capable of protecting us during the day, and leading the hunt at night. Someone who can control our friends."

"I will do my best, Master."

Gerrard said, "I can sense your remaining time is limited. The disease in your chest consumes you. Remember, choose this person carefully, because he or she will protect you, too. You have served us well, Charles." The vampire put his long-fingered hand, now withered from dehydration and burns, covered with boils, on Charles's shoulder. The vampire squeezed, causing Charles extreme pain. Charles winced.

"My pardon," the vampire said. "I forget how delicate you creatures are. Soon, however, you will be as strong as many men. All your faculties will increase. You will see in the dark; hear and smell at great distances. Your thirst for blood will consume you. It will burn in your throat and your mind, like nothing you have experienced as a human. And when you drink warm, pure blood, you will experience ecstasy." The vampire smiled again. "The smell, the warm taste in your mouth. The feel of blood running down your throat while the still beating heart clamors. To suck out the lifeblood. To feel the life wane and expire. To sense your victim's terror. That is truly *living*."

Charles looked up at the vampire.

"That was a joke." The vampire grinned. "We are not all morbid. You will see."

"Of course," Charles said. "A joke."

"When I was alive, I was known for my levity," Gerrard said.

"Indeed, he was," the female said, moving closer, taking the vampire's arm. "What times we had."

"Then you knew each other back *then*?"

Charles always feared looking at the undead, but now, with a promise to make him one of them near, the chance to live for eons, free of disease, he smiled at their withered faces. The female still had part of her face missing. Her right eyeball was exposed partially in its socket. It gave her face a lopsided look. The exposed eye rolled in its socket as if it had a will of its own. The blisters on their faces and hands wept a milky viscous, foul-smelling liquid.

Charles grimaced at the sight.

"We aren't much to look at, are we?" the female said. "We've had a few close calls since you became our Watcher, and you know that once we feed we will heal quickly and be radiant again. Our full strength will return. We will be beautiful. Humans will find us irresistible."

"I remember," Charles said. "You have been good to me, and I have served you to the best of my ability."

"And so you will be rewarded," Eva said. "Everlasting life." Her bare, burnt arms dripped the viscous fluid on the floor. She tried to moisten her cracked, burned lips with her marvelously pointed black tongue, but after several circuits of the puffy lips, she gave up.

The evening clothes they wore to feed were frayed, dusty, stained, and shiny from wear. The gown was unraveling at the seams, especially the hem, which trailed long threads. The vampires seemed not to notice or care. The clothes must have been magnificent centuries ago. Perhaps custom-made. Charles had seen them in modern clothes, but they always came to the feeding room dressed elegantly, if not shabbily. He had wanted to ask about washing the clothes but thought water and soap might destroy the fabric, leaving nothing but rags.

Charles breathed regularly now. He turned his attention to the vampiress. "I don't mean to pry, but can you tell me a little about how it was when you were alive? Human?"

The female threw back her head and laughed. The hollowness of it echoed off the walls. Now that they were famished, the laughter seemed more dead and flat than Charles had heard before. "Now, you are talking history," she said. "So long ago." She looked toward the male and patted his arm. "My brother was a giant in his time. Today, merely taller than average. I, his sister, was tall, too, taller than most men. Today, a little more than average height for a woman."

"We have seen many things, Charles. You will, too, as the future unfolds," Gerrard said.

"It should be wonderful," Charles said, smiling at the grinning corpse.

"I hope so," the woman said. "We *lived* in simpler times. The miracles of modern life hold little interest for us. We don't need medicine, air travel, although it can be practical sometimes, television, computers, cell phones..."

"We do like vampire movies," the male quipped, interjecting. They both exploded with their empty, cavernous laughs, then quickly recovered. "The sad thing is we're mostly killed off at the end of movies. There are few vampire heroes. As alluring as we are to humans, no one really loves a vampire. Occasionally, the man upstairs," she pointed toward the ceiling, "arranges to show a movie for us. After the restaurant is closed."

"That explains why you come down the steps sometimes," Charles said. "It makes sense when no one is there. I always thought you were man and wife?"

"You might think that, but we are brother and sister. Even during life, we slept together," the vampiress said. She raised her arms. "We were infamous. Everyone knew about it, and we did little to hide our relationship. The scandal was part of our allure. *What would they do next? What lovers would they take?*" She sat down near Charles and the male leaned on the step rail. "Sex is still wonderful, as you will see. Much better than as a human."

"If I did get it up, I'd go into a coughing jag before I got started."

The vampires smiled. Charles saw they were visibly exhausted. The female's arm blisters were crusted over now. The outline of bones was noticeable under the sagging flesh. Charles wondered who would expire first, he from lung cancer, or the vampires from lack of nourishment. He was afraid they might suddenly turn on him and drain him dry, but he knew his blood was tainted and doubted they would go so far. They were so picky about the blood supply.

"Remember how Bonaparte hated you?" Gerrard said, looking at his sister.

"Napoleon?" Charles was dumbfounded.

"Among other things, he hated me because I was so much taller. He hated dancing with me. He was like a child next to me.

His little legs couldn't keep up. I could have lifted him off the floor and swung him in a circle. Imagine that. The Emperor." The female tilted her face toward Charles and smiled. "I hope you like to dance, Charles. You are tall and quite handsome. We will dance together. I will hum famous waltzes in your ear, and we will dance."

"I don't know if I can dance to a waltz," Charles said, perplexed. "I never tried."

"I will teach you, Charles. There will be so much time. You will see there is time for everything after you are turned. We will dance through the ages. Then we will have wonderful sex. You will see. Sex after feeding is—how do they say it?—awesome."

Her brother tittered. "The good old days, Charles. Yes, we already were old in human years during the French Revolution."

"A wonderful time," the female said. "How we fed. There were so many wounded. Even the peasants. If we took a few it was called witchcraft. When we took more it was called a plague. There were many vampires then. We had lavish galas. So many of us. When the orchestra stopped playing, we copulated on the dance floor. Our gowns were spread out like large fans. The orchestra set down their instruments and copulated. It was nothing to consume a hundred humans in a night and line them up all naked. Their fear was—how do you say it—palpable. Then we left their corpses to rot. How the living feared us! Afraid even to talk about us. All superstitious fools." She clapped her hands and winced in pain.

The couple laughed as heartily as possible. Still, their voices echoed off the walls.

"We were—how do you say it—the toast of the town," the female said.

"No, dear," Gerrard corrected. "The town was our toast."

They tittered again.

"We were from the nobility. We moved among the humans at court and were thought to be eccentrics. The humans feared us and, yet, found us irresistible like they would any vampire."

"Then the humans started to keep records," Gerrard said with a snarl. "If someone disappeared there was an inquest. Vampires were *discovered*. They were no longer merely legends. They learned how to kill us from the ancient folklore. We were hunted down. Many of us were killed. When they weren't warring, the armies of Europe excavated graveyards, supposedly to bury the new dead, and move the old dead to be among their own kind, but in reality, they sought us. They lay aside their muskets and carried shovels and wooden stakes. We found it necessary to split into smaller colonies, groups that needed fewer cattle, and we spread out, and came to America, even the coldest parts of the planet. All the vampires needed was people. *We*, my sister and I, collected the Travelers to hunt for us." He paused to shake his head, as if concerned for their plight. "They are poor, unfortunate, malformed vampires. Freaks. No one wanted them, so we decided to be their guardians. One benefit, if there are any, is they can consume human organ meat. Drink any bodily fluid to sustain them. That way we get almost all the blood. Of course, we try to keep their numbers low, too. We don't encourage adding new Travelers. We need places to conceal them, as we remain concealed during daylight hours. They are so unruly. And, as you know, make so much noise. And, of course, they need enough space to hunt."

Charles suddenly felt a camaraderie with the fiends. Soon he would be one of them and ultimately pass down his experiences through the ages. "I'll get the beasts out tonight. Whip them into submission, one way or another," Charles said. He nodded his head toward the vampires. "We'll take a clean blood from the park or the street. There will be plenty of people around the stadium. There is a baseball game tonight. You'll see. Tomorrow morning you will enjoy your rest. You'll be full."

"We know we can rely on you, Charles," Gerrard said. His voice was hollow and ominous. "We must rest now." He turned and walked across the passage to the vampire crypt. He twisted a stone on the wall and a hidden door swung open. He disappeared inside. In a moment, a casket lid shut.

"One more question, please?" Charles said as the vampiress turned to follow her brother.

"Of course, Charles." She smiled at him.

Charles lowered his eyes. "Are all vampires so picky about the blood they drink?"

"It is a proclivity—is that the right word? "

Charles shrugged and looked at her. "I wouldn't know."

"It is a taste my brother and I have developed over the centuries. Some vampires will drink any blood, human or animal. We have drunk animal blood during lean times when we were hunted endlessly. We have drunk the blood of dead humans. It's not very palatable. You would be surprised what a vampire will do to prevent starving. A vampire's death from starvation is very painful and very prolonged. There comes a point where the vampire can no longer move. The pain and torment will continue for up to a year before the disease inside us succumbs. The disease demands blood, even though we are too weak to move and cannot get it. The thirst is hideous. My brother and I have developed a palate for *clean* blood not tainted by drugs and alcohol, even severe disease. Almost everyone had clean blood during the Middle Ages, except the nobility, who were mostly drunkards.

"That makes sense," Charles said. He looked at Eva and she smiled back at him as if he were a child.

"Because we were noble, we were served, even as children, before we were turned. The idea of having our friends bring us blood in the form of humans, rather than hunting ourselves, was appealing. We could keep the malformed vampires hidden and together. In modern times, it has become difficult to find clean blood. We developed this system," she waved her arm toward the basement and its cages, "to maintain a sense of our nobility."

"I see. That explains a lot." Charles opened his mouth to speak again, but the vampiress interrupted.

"If it becomes necessary for *us* to hunt again, we can do it. We have hundreds of years of experience. We can even return to drinking tainted blood. It might be like an alcoholic having to drink cheap booze rather than the good stuff he had always enjoyed before his life fell apart. Does that help you understand?"

"Yes, Mistress. Thank you." Charles bowed.

"You must rest, Charles. You will need your strength tonight."

"Yes, Mistress."

The vampiress turned and walked slowly to the crypt, pulled the heavy door closed behind her, and locked it from the inside. He heard the large bolt grind against the stone.

The vampires were weaker than Charles had ever seen them. He thought, it might be necessary to hang the food in the feeding room and drain blood from the femoral artery, where it was easier to control the bleeding, and serve the vampires blood in their caskets if they were too weak to rise by then. It wasn't the first time it happened. When they moved to the city, the caskets were lost in transit and took days to find. The vampires were already weak from hunger when they left their last Mid-West home. A funeral director who was complicit fucked up. The wooden crates holding their ornate caskets were mislabeled but eventually found. One was damaged, revealing the casket inside. The other was then uncrated. An inquiry was demanded. Where would the bodies be interred? Who were the deceased? Who wanted the bodies moved? Who authorized the disinterment? Were there diseases to worry about? The beasts had already been transported, temporarily stashed in a rented box truck, which they dented by hurling themselves at the sides and roof. After Dark was still under renovation. Contractors moved utilities to the first floor to ensure there was never a need for *anyone* to enter the basement.

Charles was stronger then, with no symptoms of the lung cancer that began to brew inside him. First, he broke into the city warehouse where the caskets were stored, moved them, and burned down the place. An insurance claim wasn't recorded, so the caskets and their contents were assumed burned to ashes in the conflagra-tion. End of story. There were enough other problems with the fire to concern police and insurance companies. City equipment and records had been destroyed. Charles moved the vampires to an old cemetery near the baseball stadium under construction and a neglected mausoleum he broke into. The beasts captured two people in the park. Charles bound and gagged them, and put them screaming and wailing in the crypt, where the vampires drained them. A third person taken on a separate night was thrown inside the battered truck for the beasts. The desiccated remains, shrunken to the size of children, and their shredded clothing Charles buried near a cemetery wall at night.

It had been a close call. After the vampires emerged from their caskets renewed, Charles was offered the promise of immortality.

Once After Dark renovations were completed, the utilities moved upstairs, cells and soundproofing installed, and a pen for the beasts built, the crypt with the secret door erected, the vampires moved in. Charles destroyed the rental truck by fire. The park near the stadium provided excellent hunting grounds for victims who were seldom seen and wouldn't be missed. The beasts could travel unnoticed between the park and After Dark in the black, moonless hours of night. Charles kept the beasts under control. It was a perfect arrangement. A steady flow of homeless disappeared into cells, where their blood was cleaned slowly through painful with-drawal symptoms, and eventually were consumed.

After working in the funeral home, Charles became accus-tomed to the blood, the tissue splatter, the gore, the smell of death, the appalling vampire corpses, their foul, antique clothing, and the beasts. His reward would come. Everlasting life would be worth it. He saw his father die of lung cancer. He knew what horror prob-ably awaited him with the disease.

CHAPTER TWENTY-THREE

After Dark was booming. Giddy fans bellied up to the bar three deep in their baseball jerseys and hats. There were cheers and high-fives all around. It appeared the marquis outfielder who cost the baseball club a fortune to bring to the city was out of his season-long slump. The equally pricey aging pitcher, who hadn't lasted more than four innings all season, threw a rare complete game shutout on his last outing. Suddenly, things looked rosy for a third-place team. They weren't out of the division race yet, or so the fan base hoped. Even newspaper baseball beat reporters and online sports services outlined ways to the playoffs.

Bo entered After Dark alone. He had taken the last spot in the parking lot. Benjamin the bouncer acknowledged him with a casual nod and didn't ask for proof of age. Just as Bo passed him, the bouncer said, "Hey, haven't seen you in a while."

"Been busy," Bo said.

"Where's your posse? How's my boy red doing?" The big man smiled. "That kid has some serious red hair."

Bo turned and looked him in the eye, something he never did. The bouncer's sheer size, the big hands, the powerful biceps, thick neck, and large shaved head were better left ignored. Someone to walk by without comment for fear of catching him in a bad mood. Answer only if you were spoken to. Above all, be polite. Tonight the bouncer's face was bruised; a line of butterfly strips closed a gash on his forehead. More strips garnished a long wound on his cheek.

"Haven't seen them in a while," Bo said, looking away quickly. Who could have done that to *him*, he wondered? I wouldn't want to see the other guy. He's probably taken up residence at the city morgue.

"Hold on," Benjamin said. He checked three IDs and waved a middle-aged couple through who were bemused by being carded. "You guys seemed real tight. Never saw one of you without all three. You were almost Siamese."

"Well, I had the ride," Bo said.

"A yellow Charger?"

Bo nodded.

"I was outside when you drove by and pulled in the lot. I used to see your car all the time. Sometimes in the lot or across the street."

"I've been busy," Bo said. "You know." Bo tried to edge away from the big man.

"Saw your car has some damage on the passenger side."

"It got hit when I was parked over by the park entrance."

"Hit and run?"

"You could say that."

"Catch who did it?"

Yeah...No, not really."

"Spend much time in the park?"

"Not anymore."

"Ain't safe. Not with the whistling things."

Bo's eyes grew wide. "You know about the Whistlers?"

"Got one out back. Dead. What do you think messed up my face? Want to see it?"

"No thanks. I know what they look like. Know all about them," Bo said. He looked back at Benjamin. "That's what damaged my car."

Benjamin nodded and smiled. "That's what I figured. Found a little bit of yellow paint in the dead thing's fur. Just a speck. I thought where did I see that color before? Then it hit me. Not a curb or a center line. That yellow Charger."

The bouncer checked more IDs, a group of scantily clad women in their early 20s already intoxicated. After they moved toward the bar, Benjamin said, "I'm gonna regret leaving them in, but they do add to the decor. They carry they own ambiance." He winked at Bo.

"I should find a seat," Bo said.

"Listen, I have a break coming up. We'll go out back." Benjamin paused and looked at Bo through the top of his eyes, his head lowered. "I *want* you to take a look at that fucking *thing*."

"I'd rather not."

"But I *want* you to. It's harmless now. I seen to that. You know what I'm talking about? Follow me."

The Bouncer led Bo across the floor, zigzagged through tables full of diners, and to the bar. He put a hand on an old man's shoulder and squeezed. "Pete. Take a hike, man. You had enough. I got a friend who needs a perch."

Pete craned his neck, saw Benjamin, and slid off the barstool, while the big hand rested on his shoulder. Pete didn't say a word, but downed the rest of his beer, and shuffled off toward his closet room.

"Hop aboard," the bouncer said. "No extra charge for the warm seat. Don't move. I'll be back in ten when it's time for my break." Before he left for his post at the front door, the bouncer called the bartender and told her to take good care of Bo. The woman with long blond hair, large black glasses, and dragon tattoos on her sleeveless arms, winked at Bo.

Bo scanned the bar. There was no sign of Lisa. Just as well. It was apparent she was already taken. However, the tipsy girls who just came through the door stood nearby, waiting for seats to open at the bar. One with short, dark hair caught his eye and smiled. She sidled toward him.

"What have you been up to?" she wanted to know, touching his arm.

"No good," Bo said.

She threw back her head and laughed. "Just the kind of man I like. Up to *no good*." She squeezed next to Bo and up to the bar, leaving a gap between her and her friends. Her name was Sam, short for Samantha. She was a nursing student at the university and a baseball fan. She seemed disappointed Bo hadn't been at the game. Sam wore a loose-fitting jersey with the name FARGO emblazoned across the shoulders on the back and pants so short they didn't show under the shirttails. She had long, slender, tanned legs. Sam took Bo's breath when she smiled.

Sam patted her back. "He's my boy," she said. "Home run and a double tonight. I was there. Actually, he almost went yard a second time, but the centerfielder robbed him. Made a spectacular catch. I got his autograph earlier this year. Right here in After Dark." She pulled off her baseball cap and showed Bo the scribbled signature inside the bill, which read, *For Sam, Henry Fargo.* She kissed the handwriting and put the cap back on her head. "I have an internship now, so a doc I know gives me his season tickets sometimes. Like tonight."

They talked more about the game, their majors, and school. Sam and Bo giggled. They couldn't help smiling at each other. Sam's friends wanted to leave and threatened to go without her. Bo said he would give her a ride. He tried to catch the bartender's attention for another round when Bo felt a huge hand clamp on his shoulder. Bo had forgotten about Big Benjamin and his promised return in ten minutes. It had been at least twenty minutes.

"It's break time," Benjamin said, with no emotion.

Sam looked up and seemed dismayed by the bouncer's sudden

appearance. She studied the butterfly strips on his face. Bo apologized. He said he had to go outside for something and would be back shortly.

"I hope you're not buying drugs," Sam said. "If I get caught with dope, even somebody with dope, I'll get kicked out of nursing school."

"No, No," Bo said. "My car was damaged a few nights ago. We're taking a look at it. Sit here till I get back, then I'll give you a ride back to school." Bo smiled at her and slid off the barstool. Sam climbed on. Her friends had gone as the crowd inside began to thin.

Outside, Benjamin loomed over Bo as they walked to the parking lot where cars filed out onto Fifth Street and a few inebriated patrons weaved toward their rides.

"I brought garbage out last night at closing, trying to help Jose," Big Benjamin said as they walked around the restaurant. "Wanted to get my full hour in, because sometimes Bart will send me home early if it gets slow. Then he manages to fuck up my pay. Doesn't pay me enough or takes too many taxes out. You know. He likes to fuck with me the only way he can—with my pay. You have to be a fucking accountant to work here." Benjamin stopped suddenly. "I was just about here when I heard this whistling."

"I've heard it," Bo said. "Know all about it."

"The lot was almost empty by then. Didn't think of anything at first. Thought it was funny. I whistled back. I came out of the enclosure and heard something moving in the bushes." He pointed to a parking lot corner. Then continued walking toward it. "Thought somebody might be trying to fuck with me. Maybe that crazy Miguel. Nobody fucks with me, so I went charging into the bushes, picked up a big ass stick on the way. It hit me before I knew it, out of nowhere. All arms and legs slashing, rolling, spinning. But it already was hurt. I thought there was blood on the fur when I grabbed the thing, but it was too dark to see. It moved in a kind of slow motion. I grabbed its neck and felt more blood.

"It was dark and furry, the size of a big dog only the legs were longer and all out of proportion. It was clicking and snapping at me, and oh my God, it stank. Like I said, it was already wounded. I twisted it around to get away from those claws, the teeth, that bad breath, grabbed those front legs from behind and pulled them back, made them cross. It howled in pain. You could have heard it at the stadium. The bones seemed light and I felt them cracking, popping under the fur. I stretched that mother fucker until I had those front legs wrapped right around its body. It was off the ground and the hind legs were kicking like mad, like somebody in a cartoon starting to run but going nowhere. It wanted to catch me with those big claws. Between screams, those teeth were snapping. It tried to turn its head and bite, but I kept it at a distance, where those choppers couldn't land.

Bo stared wide-eyed and swallowed hard. "I was close to them but not that close.

"By this time, we was both tired. I put it on the ground, face first, and kneeled hard on the middle of its back, planted my knees, all my weight, in the middle of its ribcage. It screamed. Howled. It was ungodly. Like nothing I ever heard. I felt the bones break under its back, come through the fur. Maybe some ribs went inward. My knees were wet with blood. I pushed up and dropped my knees, again and again, with all the power in my legs. My knees went right through its back and crushed the front ribs. It puked a stream of blood just like a gargoyle in a fountain. It coughed on the blood in its lungs and died.

"Just to make sure, I kneed it a few more times. Broke the back legs. I was exhausted, too, when it was all over. Even wounded, that thing was strong. I wouldn't want to fight one that was healthy."

"I wouldn't want to fight even a wounded one," Bo said. "Not touch a dead one."

"Kept my knees planted in it for a good five minutes, even after it was done twitching. It took that long to catch my breath. My legs were soaked in blood. Then I drug it out on the asphalt under the big light." Benjamin pointed to the overhead light on the building. "Spread it out. Turned it over. Examined every inch. Ugliest thing I've ever seen. It had long fangs. Like a vampire. So, I went into the bush and found that stick I picked up. It had a sharp end where somebody cut it at an angle. I pushed that mother-fucking stick through that creature's heart. More air came out of it, like maybe it wasn't dead yet, but I knew inside it was all broke up."

Bo grimaced. Swallowed hard. Returned his stare to Big Benjamin.

"That's when I noticed them little flecks of yellow paint in the fur. I picked some off to examine but lost them when I threw out my pants. They were new pants, too. Just got the mother fuckers. I'm so big it's hard getting clothes that fit right. I saw those flecks of paint and thought of that Charger I had seen around After Dark. Then you drove by tonight and I saw the damage on the door. You put two and two together. I thought maybe you ran over this mother fucker before it attacked me."

They reached the corner under the bright dusk-to-dawn light. Bo watched a cloud of moths fly near the light in endless crazy circles.

Without saying a word, Benjamin crashed into the bushes to haul out the Whistler.

Startled by the noise and Benjamin's sudden disappearance into the dark, Bo backed away from the corner.

Benjamin moved back and forth, cursing all the way. The bushes shook. Limbs cracked. Occasionally, Bo heard a word or two. *Fucking mosquitos, fucking dog-bat, I'll fix you.* He moved deeper into the undergrowth.

Bo was worried. He stepped farther away from the corner. He imagined a Whistler would stink, especially a dead one oozing blood. He smelled only the restaurant dumpster, with its sunbaked garbage, the city's fetid odors, and the restaurant kitchen odors spewed from the strumming exhaust fans. The noise Benjamin made stopped. He cursed loudly. After another minute, Benjamin burst from the undergrowth, sweating, panting, and holding a pointed stick.

"It's gone," the bouncer said. "Somebody stole it."

"Maybe it wasn't dead," Bo said.

The bouncer gave him a look of disbelief. Furrowed his brow. "You should have been here last night. There was enough blood to fill a bathtub. I was drenched in it. That thing wasn't about to get up and walk away. Count Dracula hisself couldn't raise that thing from the dead."

"The other Whistlers must have found it," Bo said. "Drug it away. They hunt in a pack."

"They take the homeless," Benjamin said. He wiped a huge hand over the top of his sweating bald head and looked at Bo. He held his wooden weapon like a spear, one end planted on the asphalt. After a moment, he tossed it into the bushes. "They took an old girlfriend who became homeless. She got into drugs. We weren't together anymore. Still, I looked after her. Tried to find her on the street and slip her a few dollars here and there. Buy her a meal. Then she was gone. Couldn't find her and nobody saw her. I did find a flip-flop in the park I thought was hers. Remember her picking it out at the Dollar Store a year ago when I took her shopping."

"I think the Whistlers took my friends, although I'm not sure," Bo said. "They're gone, too."

"Red?" the bouncer said.

"Yeah. Both my friends." Bo's eyes filled with tears glistened in the parking lot's overhead lights.

There was whistling in the distance coming from several directions.

Benjamin lowered and shook his head. "That's tough, man. Let's get out of here before they take us. The only thing I found in there was a pile of goo. Must have come from the kitchen grease trap. It had to be old because it stank like a mother fucker. Stepped in it, too." Benjamin raised a foot to show Bo his slime-covered shoe.

Bo and the bouncer walked back to After Dark. Inside, the man stationed at the door said, "Nice break, man."

"You have a problem with that?" Benjamin stopped and faced the man.

"No. We're cool. You take as much time as you need, Benjamin."

"Go find something to do. My boy here and me were talking supernatural outside."

The man slid from his seat, smiled, and hurried off.

Bo scanned the crowd. Samantha was gone.

Outside, a white junkie was hawking souvenirs. "Fargo autographed hat. Genuine. Just came on the market. Fifty bucks. Make me an offer." He waved the hat over his head.

Bo spun the man around and grabbed the hat. "Where'd you get this," Bo demanded.

"Fargo signed it for me last month, man. I'm in a bind. Need the cash."

Bo looked inside the bill and read the inscription: *For Sam, Henry Fargo.* "Where'd you get this hat?" Bo demanded. He cocked his arm, fist clenched.

"I didn't steal it," the man cried. "It was on the sidewalk across the street. I picked it up a few minutes ago. I don't know if the autograph's legit. How about twenty? It costs more than that new in shops. It's an official hat, man."

Bo felt his stomach knot. He gave the junkie the hat. He knew he would never see Sam again. No one would.

CHAPTER TWENTY-FOUR

It was almost dawn, and the Whistlers held their latest victim, a clean blood, among them, kept her motionless, barely able to breathe, unable to scream, across the street from the vampire lair's entrance. Two police cruisers had sat side-by-side across from After Dark most of the night, one parked on the sidewalk, the driver-side doors facing each other, windows down, just an inch between their cars' side view mirrors. The police officers drank coffee, ate Chinese food, and moaned about their fantasy baseball teams. Both officers bet against the local team, recalling their dismal performance in past seasons. Now, they weren't so sure about their decisions.

The Whistlers sandwiched the clean blood among their bodies. Only four had hunted. Two had died previously. The remaining two were wounded and too weak to hunt. The Whistlers locked their arms and legs together, keeping the clean blood immobile. This action kept the beasts' mouths closed, as well, and prevented them from scratching and biting the victim. The Whistlers hid among the tall, ornamental grass at the park's edge. Charles Van der Meer dozed nearby, where his occasional cough wouldn't be heard from the sidewalk. Eventually, the cops drove off in opposite directions. The Whistlers' clicking woke Charles. After he collected his thoughts, Charles moved stiffly to the sidewalk and surveyed the street in both directions. Early morning traffic had increased, but thanks to traffic lights on Fifth Street there were still wide gaps between cars. Charles waited for the light to change red a block away. He whistled a familiar command when the street was clear, and the mass of animals holding the woman moved silently across the avenue into the lot next to After Dark. As fast as possible, Charles ran ahead and forced open the ground-level door.

The Whistlers slid down the steps and waited anxiously near the mortuary table. They clicked and whimpered, flexing their backs to compress the young woman more, and felt the warmth of her body. Even in their wounded state, the two Whistlers inside the pen howled when they sensed food was available. The four Whistlers unlocked their arms and legs. The woman breathed deeply suddenly. The Whistlers licked at her body and tore the remainder of her clothes with their sharp teeth. Smelled her scent. Her fear.

"Get away from her," Charles commanded. "Leave her on the floor. Get back in your cell. Do it now." The Whistlers growled, bared their teeth, stared with beady eyes. Charles stepped toward the mass. It moved away, compressed as one unit, drug the woman with it. He picked up a club leaning against the wall near the feeding room door.

The vampires would be no help. Surely, they waited as long as possible, all night, to feed but returned to their caskets, exhausted and disappointed. They would not know the police patrol prevented the Whistlers from crossing Fifth Street until near dawn. Charles hoped the masters would be happy tonight. Perhaps they would reward him by turning him into one of the undead, allowing him to feed on vampire blood, even though he still did not have a guardian for the group.

Charles swung his club at the Whistlers. They retreated

toward their cell, still refusing to drop the woman. They became more agitated. Charles feared they would turn on the young woman, kill her instantly, suck the life blood from her in a frenzy. The Whistlers showed their teeth. Crouched in front of Charles. The vampires would be infuriated if they lost another meal and Charles failed to control the beasts. Meanwhile, the wounded Whistlers howled from their pen. Charles threatened to club the beasts again. They withdrew toward the pen door. The captive Whistlers moved to their pen door from the inside. They snapped and foamed at their mouths, forced their snouts through the bars.

One of the Whistlers on top of the mass climbed off and walked on two legs in its lopsided, stiff-legged gait toward the gate latch. Charles knew in an instant the beast intended to open the gate to free the wounded. They would spill into the room. There would be too many to handle. Perhaps they would turn on him, too.

Charles screamed at the Whistler on two legs. "Get back, you freak. I'll club you, split you down the middle."

The Whistler had a clawed hand on the latch. He turned and growled at Charles. His teeth gleamed in the low light. The beasts inside threw their battered bodies at the door. Like before, it was difficult to open the gate latch with pressure against the door.

Charles looked toward the knife blade switch. So did the Whistler on two legs. Charles loped across the floor for the switch. If he could make it to the switch and engage the light, he would send the beasts scattering to all corners of the basement, their fur and their flesh burning under the ultraviolet lights. He would hurt them this time. Let their foul-smelling flesh incinerate before his eyes. He didn't care that the masters were fond of the creatures. This Whistler was faster than Charles, however. It shoved Charles, who spun away from the switch. He dropped the club and it rolled away with a rattle. Charles slid several feet across the concrete floor. The massed Whistlers seemed to cheer, erupting with a cacophony of whistles and whimpers, moved en masse, away from the door with the girl.

The standing Whistler growled at Charles, and moved closer to him, almost turning sideways with each cumbersome step. However, the beast kept his eyes on Charles. Charles was winded. He coughed. Charles crawled to the club, picked it up, stood slowly, teetered on unsteady legs, and threatened the Whistler again. The creature snarled. Snapped its jaws. Moved closer and positioned itself between Charles and the switch.

"You never did like me," Charles said, shaking the club at the beast. "We'll see about that. Try this one on for size. I got only one chance for a winner."

Charles lobbed the club at the wall. It twirled slowly end over end. Attracted by the movement, the Whistler watched it fly across the room in a lazy arc too high for it to intercept. The club struck the wall flat above the switch, and clattered down its length, engaging the blades between their holders. The basement filled with ultraviolet light. The creatures shrieked in pain and collected at the door to their pen. When he turned off the lights, the Whistlers turned again on him. He turned the ultraviolets on and off three times like a mad scientist in a hidden laboratory until the Whistlers retreated and lined up at the pen. Charles opened the pen door, cracked the animal who defied him over the head with the club and locked them all away.

In the big room, Charles lifted the woman to the mortuary table. She was exhausted from struggling, screaming, and fighting the Whistlers. The beasts had bitten and scratched her and shredded her Fargo baseball jersey. Normally, she would go into a cell and await the vampires' pleasure. Today, she would be stripped, cleaned, and held on the table all day until Charles hoisted her upside down for the vampires to exsanguinate. Although she appeared healthy, Charles decided to take no chances and have her die prematurely. He forced her to drink bottled water to prevent her from dehydrating and to plump up her veins. After she was cleaned, Charles strapped her to the mortuary table and wheeled it into the feeding room. He wanted to ensure the Whistlers had no opportunity to get at her.

Charles was dead tired. He sat on the floor with his back against the door to the feeding room. He held the club in his lap. Inside their pen, the Whistlers, too, were exhausted and lay quietly. Before he dozed off, Charles made sure he could engage the knife blades with the club without standing if there were an emergency.

Hours passed. Charles woke to the noise of the key turning in the locked door at the top of the stairs. Immediately, the Whistlers howled weakly from their den. Charles knew it must be night. The vampires were upstairs and coming down. Charles scrambled to his feet and opened the door to the feeding room. The woman lay naked and still on the mortuary table. Charles first made sure she was still alive by finding a weak pulse in her neck. Then he loosened the straps, rolled her on her side, and cuffed her hands behind her back. He rolled her on her back again and secured her ankles to the chains overhead. He released the rest of the straps and roused her into semiconsciousness by moving her head back and forth. She moaned. Charles forced more water down Sam's throat. That was for the Whistlers. She choked but didn't spit any out. Charles pulled on the chains, raising the body slowly above the table. When her head swung freely, he moved the table outside the feeding room and parked it near the door.

Charles still hadn't regained his strength and leaned against the feeding room wall, waiting for the vampires to appear. However, it was Bart who descended slowly down the stairs, hesitatingly, returning his gaze often up the steps, waiting for his masters. He stopped and waited. He appeared nervous. Meanwhile, the Whistlers howled in their weakened condition from inside their pen. Charles knew the beasts' individual barks and knew only four howls remained.

Slowly, ungainly, the vampires crept from their vault across the basement. They held hands. Their clothes, which they normally filled completely, even when their hunger was fierce, hung on their emaciated bodies. The female's face had not healed where Mad Maggie had dug in her fingers and torn away the flesh. The exposed eyeball still wagged back and forth, as if it were independent from the other.

"Charles! Are you there?" the male called in his hollow voice, which was barely audible as a dry whisper.

"Yes, Masters. All is prepared," Charles called to them. "I have clean blood for your pleasure. A female. She awaits in the feeding room."

Bart reached the basement floor and moved out of the vampires' way. He sweated profusely and covered his mouth and nose with a violet-colored handkerchief pulled from his blazer's breast pocket. As soon as the vampires navigated the last step, Bart flashed a glance at Charles. The woman moaned now, forced a scream, and thrashed in her bindings, swinging back and forth like a clock pendulum.

"Why are you doing this to me?" she called, weakly. "Let me go."

The vampires walked stiffly toward the feeding room. They sniffed the air. Their dark tongues twirled around their dry lips but failed to moisten their mouths. They gnashed their black teeth and looked at each other. Smiled. Bart held the handkerchief to his nose and ran up the steps as fast as his short legs could carry him, slammed shut the heavy door upstairs, and locked it. Charles bowed as the vampires approached the feeding room door. The woman's terror intoxicated the vampires. They sniffed the air more and moaned with pleasure as they entered the feeding room. The woman screamed and thrashed with the last of her energy. The vampires grabbed the hanging body, held her close, and still, felt her warmth, dug their claws into her torso. She screamed. The fiends clung to her and licked her flesh with their pointed, dark tongues. The male pushed his face into the pelvic mound. The female held her buttocks and licked the crack in her ass. In their weakened conditions, the vampires clung to the body, letting it support them. When they could take the pleasure no more, they palpated the victim's flesh with their tongues in search of large veins. Once they felt her pounding heart and coursing blood, the couple sank their teeth into her. Their lips locked on her flesh like lamprey mouths. They gulped her hot blood and occasionally stopped to burp up a mouthful on the floor.

The vampires' strength returned soon. Their healing continued, too. Their tongues twirled around their mouths, swept up blood that spilled on their faces. They relished every slurp, every lick. The male wheeled the mortuary table into the feeding room. He lowered the body to the table and undid the handcuffs and ankle restraints. While life still flickered, the vampires fed again. Finally, they moved away from the body and belched foul-smelling gas into the air. Charles was repulsed and drew away.

"It's time for our friends before this one dies," the female said. "It will be a treat. Release them, Charles."

Charles staggered to the pen door and released the latch. He pulled open the gate and four Whistlers spilled out and limped toward the feeding room. They climbed on the mortuary table and drained the rest of the fluid from the now inert body. They sucked, tore open the abdomen, gobbled flesh and organs. Eventually, the beasts rolled off the table and fell to the floor. They lapped all the fluids on the floor with their tongues until they passed out.

Charles stooped over to look inside the pen. There he discovered the desiccated remains of two Whistlers on the floor. The other four Whistlers had turned on their wounded and weakened pack members and drained them dry.

"Charles!" the male vampire called. His hollow voice already sounded stronger.

Charles came to his side and bowed deeply. "Yes, Masters."

"You have done well, Charles," the female said. Her exposed

eyeball was already covered with new flesh. She looked at Charles approvingly as she licked her fingers and their long claws.

"That was wonderful clean blood," the male said. "The best we have had in a while."

"Indeed," the female said. "I believe you are ready to be turned, as soon as you find a replacement for yourself."

CHAPTER TWENTY-FIVE

Lisa woke in her bed. It felt wonderful to stretch and she couldn't help smiling. It was a day off. She was naked and the sheet under her back felt damp. She rolled over and nuzzled against Jimmy. He, too, was naked and sound asleep. Jimmy breathed deeply, slowly. Lisa smiled and wondered what he was dreaming. Could he be dreaming about their night together? Lisa had laundry and shopping to do, but just now in the early morning, she could just as easily stay in bed all day. They would make love and sleep in tuns until night and then start all over again.

Jimmy rolled on his back and snored softly. She placed a palm over his chest and felt his heartbeat. Then she watched him sleep for a while. Eventually, she rolled out of bed slowly, and quietly, slipped on her short, silk robe, the one she appeared in last night after telling Jimmy she had to go to the bathroom. The romancing, which had already started on Lisa's sofa, moved from the living room to the bedroom.

Jimmy was a gentle lover, unlike the drunk she had known, who took her suddenly and roughly, sometimes tearing her clothes. Then he took her money and left her at home for a night out with his friends. It wasn't uncommon for him not to return for days. That life no longer existed, Lisa told herself, as she scooped coffee into the coffeemaker. A new life awaited.

Soon, Jimmy, wearing only his boxers, came unseen into the kitchen and pressed himself against Lisa's back. He sniffed her hair, untied the robe, and rubbed the front of her body gently with his hands. They returned to bed, leaving the coffee not yet percolated, waiting for the push of a button to start the process. Later, they ate breakfast together at Lisa's small kitchen table, feeding each other french toast with maple syrup.

By noon, they had showered and dressed. The day was already hot and humid. Jimmy had taken off. They left Lisa's apartment with the intent to visit the Lutheran church, gather supplies, and hand them out to the homeless. Jimmy's boss approved of the work he did for the homeless, so taking a day off on the spur of the moment wasn't a big deal. Lisa's laundry and shopping would wait. In addition, they would look for Charles Van der Meer. Lisa wondered whether he would look her up at After Dark. She hoped to find him on the street and secretly follow him. Try to determine what kind of sketchy business he was involved in.

With a back seat full of water, tampons, power bars, socks and underwear, Jimmy parked his car near the stadium. Lisa and Jimmy both took an armful of items to give away and started their trek among the homeless. They moved the car often, in the event someone wanted something they had in the car but did not carry on them. When they went to the car usually a crowd of homeless followed. Another group surrounded his parked car, waiting for his return. Jimmy was well known in that part of the city.

"That's something you don't see every day," Jimmy said, pointing across the street to Old Harriet's sweet box. "A junkie in a toga and green running shoes talking to Old Harriet."

"Maybe we should check that out," Lisa said. She raised a hand to her mouth to suppress a laugh.

"Definitely."

They crossed the street and stepped over an unconscious junkie on the sidewalk. Jimmy shook him until he roused. At least he was still alive. Old Harriet saw them coming and stepped forward.

"Watch the scat," Old Harriet said, pointing at the sidewalk. "Somebody took a dump last night and I didn't have the time to clean it up."

"It's good to see you, Harriet," Jimmy said.

"This one is crazier than Mad Maggie was, may she rest in peace." Old Harriet said, crossing herself, then pointing a thumb at the toga-clad young woman behind her. "Needs a fix. Said she was underground for a week, maybe more. Had terrible withdrawal sickness. She thinks she escaped from vampires. Said, believe this if you will, she came from underground near a circus. Ran all day naked through the streets, hiding here and there. At night, she stole a sheet and these shoes off a wash line. Thinks she's Cleopatra herself, waiting for her chariot to arrive. All hoity-toity. Said she had no help getting away. Nobody gets away from the underground by themselves unless it's Bad Nelson. There's a man who did it."

The young woman blushed.

"What's your name? Where do you live?" Lisa asked.

"Call me New Girl. That seems to work," the young junkie said. She had a small, cute nose and a smile that had not yet been destroyed by drugs.

"We can get you better clothes," Jimmy said, smiling. "I don't have any with me. I usually don't run into people wearing togas."

"It's not really a toga, it's a bed sheet I...borrowed, you know." She ran her hand over the fabric. "I want to take it back."

"You never know what you'll find on the street among the homeless, clothes, no clothes like Bad Nelson, or even togas," Old Harriet said with a knowing head wag. The situation seemed to delight her. She scratched at her beehive hairdo that stood at a rakish angle.

"There is a clothing bank at the Lutheran Church. Do you

know where that is?" Jimmy said. "In the parish house next to the parsonage."

New Girl nodded her head yes. "I been to the church a few times."

"They have some nice things. That's where I got this shirt. I can give you a ride," Jimmy said.

New Girl shook her head no.

"You can't walk around like this," Jimmy said. "The police might pick you up. Think you're..."

Old Harriet interrupted. "That's what I've been telling her," she said, exasperated. "Between the Whistlers, the vampires, the aliens, you don't have a chance dressed like that. You stick out like a sore thumb. It looks like you're asking to be taken. The best thing that can happen is that the cops take you away to the looney bin. But that's not a good scenario, either."

"We can get you help, New Girl," Jimmy said." No one will ask questions. We don't pry. We offer help when you want it."

New Girl shook her head no.

"There might be room in one of the shelters," Jimmy said. "It will help you get settled. Until you're ready to be on your own. At least you'll be safe."

Jimmy stepped away and made a call on his cell phone. Old Harriet moved closer and felt New Girl's toga.

"This ain't a cheap sheet," Old Harriet said. "I bet somebody will be looking for this. And those green shoes. They cost a pretty penny. High end. They didn't come from a flea market. You can see them a block away."

"They're too big," New Girl said, "but they'll do until I find another pair. Can't walk barefoot on these crummy streets. Step on a needle or broken glass, a girl could get an infection that kills her. There's so many germs there wouldn't be a medicine in all the world to cure you."

"We could find you a pair of shoes at the church," Jimmy said, returning from his phone call. "Any kind you like. New shoes, too, that will be a perfect fit. Until then, here's a pack of new socks. They should fit you."

"I'm not crazy about the color," New Girl said. "They don't match the green."

"Even if you don't like the color, it's better than getting blisters," Lisa said. "A broken blister will become a pathway for germs."

New Girl stared at Lisa a moment as if she contemplated microbes entering her body through a popped blister. She took the socks and examined the pack. "I don't have any place to put the extra ones."

"Now wait," Old Harriet said. She returned to her shopping cart and rooted through plastic bags. A minute later she returned, smiling triumphantly with a small purse with a long strap. "The high-class ladies in Pompeii were partial to purses like this, so I've heard. Did a nice job protecting valuables. That is before the volcano blew everything to hell." Old Harriet shrugged her shoulders. "After the volcano, them ladies were all dead, burned to a crisp, the ones not taken beforehand by aliens." Old Harriet slipped the purse over New Girl's shoulder. "This is genuine leather. Looks good on you, too."

New Girl examined the purse and smiled. "It does look nice."

Jimmy stepped away and took a call on his cell phone.

"In the meantime, here are some nutrition bars and water to fill that purse," Lisa said, flipping open the purse and pushing in power bars and a bottle of water. "You don't want the wind to blow it away. A girl can't walk around with an empty purse. What would people think? It wouldn't be..."

"Fashionable," New Girl said. She examined the power bars and smiled again.

"Lady like, too," Old Harriet chimed.

New Girl smiled and felt the purse's weight crammed with food. She found a place inside for the extra socks. Then she sat on Old Harriet's chair on wheels and pulled on a pair of socks over her dirty feet. She replaced the green running shoes and tied them.

"Don't look all that bad and feel better," the diminutive woman said. "Thank you."

A city police cruiser rolled down the street. It stopped after it passed New Girl. She saw the cops and hissed, "Christ. Not again." New Girl hiked up her toga and sprinted away. The police car sat in the street a moment then pulled away slowly in the opposite direction. Lisa and Old Harriet watched New Girl recede in the distance.

"Look at her go," Old Harriet said, laughing, pointing, hopping up and down. "That girl could go to the Olympics. Wait till I tell Hunter John. The cops will never catch her. She'll never go to no looney bin. They won't take her alive."

"She's fast all right," Lisa said. "She's probably faster than I ever was, even when I was in training with the track team."

Jimmy returned to Lisa and watched New Girl turn a corner in the distance and disappear. "Well, I had her a place in the shelter. Guess I'll call back and cancel it."

"I'd go myself," Old Harriet cackled, "to the shelter, to catch up on the latest alien news, but I wouldn't want to lose the sweet box I inherited. Got no paperwork to prove the box is mine. Possession is nine-tenths of the law on the street. You know, it's the way of the world. Plus, things on the street are getting interesting. I don't want to miss anything."

CHAPTER TWENTY-SIX

Charles Van der Meer walked toward After Dark. He crossed and recrossed the street to ensure he wasn't followed, pausing often to scan the people behind him. Satisfied no one trailed him, he returned toward After Dark and cut through the empty lot where the homeless had set up a tent city. The number of structures was ever-expanding and threatened to encroach on the secret door to the underground labyrinth. The tent and tarp colors were vivid. In addition, colorful bags were tied or stuck on the chain-link fence that stood behind the tents. The Whistlers would have to push back the homeless and, in the process, collect more food for the tiny vampire colony of which he hoped he would soon become a member. He'd prefer to keep the basement cages filled and ensure a steady food supply was available. You never knew when a junkie would die on you. Charles had overseen the Whistlers' movements, made sure they were never detected.

When hunting as a pack, a lead animal set the direction. Others followed closely, rubbing shoulders, and trading glances. As they moved, animals in the back climbed forward over the top. Periodically, a new Whistler took the lead, possibly changing direction, depending on what it heard or smelled. Although such movement might seem clumsy at best, the Whistler hunted with the same rhythm in their shuffling gaits. Their thick fur allowed them to slide over one another with ease. From a distance, the group appeared to be one undulating mass, as if rhythmic waves propelled it. Only when prey was targeted did the group disperse to surround the human. Still moving, the Whistler reassembled into one unit to trap a human among their hairy bodies, squeeze the air out of captured prey's lungs to prevent screams and allow a minimum of respiration. Usually, victims were rendered unconscious through terror or partial asphyxiation. When prey was scarce, the unit separated and the animals hunted alone. Whistles brought the group back together when quarry was spotted. The Whistlers moved quickly and almost noiselessly while they returned to After Dark and its dungeon basement. After a successful hunt, the Whistlers, still holding their precious capture, remained hidden, silent, across Fifth Street from the secret door. Charles crossed ahead of them, made sure the surroundings were safe, opened the door, and gave the signal for the beasts to move. Once safely inside, victims were placed on the mortuary table, the Whistlers tore off their clothes, and Charles strapped them down. Victim wounds were customary.

Now, pretending to dip, watching movement in the tent city and on the street from between his legs, Charles waited for the right moment, jerked the concealed door open, and ducked into the stairwell, closing and locking it behind him after the beasts glided through.

Although Charles meticulously covered his tracks, he didn't see Overboard George and Mad Maggie, both now clothed, staying ahead of him, avoiding his ever-watchful gaze. Charles eyed the street behind him but did not pay attention to the space in front. Overboard George and Mad Maggie dipped every time Charles's head turned toward them. They were a couple now and tittered every time they dipped to avoid detection. George farted when he dipped until he ran out of gas. That made Maggie laugh more.

When Mad Maggie and Overboard George showed up naked at the Lutheran shelter, claiming they had been robbed of all their possessions and kicked out of the sweet box they shared, the volunteers shielded their eyes, found them clothes, allowed them to pick what they liked, and let them take showers, although they were remarkably clean, free of scabs, and apparently well fed for homeless people.

New Girl didn't wait to go to the shelter. As soon as they climbed out of the labyrinth, she ran screaming, hands waving over her naked body, hair flowing, her small breasts bouncing, through tent city and down Fifth Street. Overboard George and Mad Maggie held hands in the warm morning light and watched her run until she disappeared in the distance.

"Look at her go," Maggie had said, marching a few steps in place.

"Where the fuck do you think she'll end up?" George asked.

"The nut farm," Mad Maggie cackled. "I'd love to hear the story she tells. They'll have her in two straight jackets. She'll be in for the long count." Mad Maggie nodded her head knowingly. "They'll dope her up and keep her talking. But nobody'll believe a word. They won't even listen."

"That's the problem," Overboard George said, matter-of-factly, giving Mad Maggie's hand a light squeeze. "First of all, they ain't gonna believe anything that spouts out of a junkie's mouth, no matter how true it is, even if they were standing next to her and saw it, too. And second, there is no second. New Girl is naked and crazy, screaming like a loon, running like a jackrabbit. They'll be lucky to catch her. She might end up on the West Coast."

"She'll stop when she needs a fix," Mad Maggie said. "That's when they'll catch up to her. Either the police or the Whistlers. I have to admit I'd like to know how far she gets. That is one fast junkie. Maybe they won't catch her. But she'll have to stop to get clothes."

Within moments, a siren wailed in the distance. George and Maggie sat in the high grass to conceal their own nakedness. A large white ambulance from the county, siren blaring, lights flashing, passed on Fifth Street.

"Think New Girl can outrun an ambulance?" Overboard George said.

"I wouldn't bet against her," Mad Maggie said. "She might be able to outrun a Whistler."

They stood and moved away from the empty lot in search of new clothes.

Mad Maggie and Overboard George sat on the grass, the same spot they shared while they were naked, newly escaped from the dungeon under After Dark. Charles Van der Meer had slipped inside the dungeon and closed the door. Now they were clothed. They knew the door's location. Overboard George was clean. He hadn't had a fix since the night the Whistlers took him. However, he'd do anything for his spoon, a lighter, a syringe, and a bag of dope. Mad Maggie was still mad, but her mind seemed clearer.

They had stayed away from their old haunts, not wanting to be recognized or tempted by the drugs present, and spent several days in the public library, pouring over vampire lore, movies, and articles. Included in their research was a copy of *Famous Monsters of Filmland* from September 1964, which was squirreled away in the archives of rare books they sneaked into. They agreed the magazine was especially helpful. It was the only copy in the archives, probably in the entire library, and must have been left there years ago by a horror-loving kid. Mad Maggie wanted to steal the magazine, or at least rip out the important pages.

However, Overboard George refused. "What if some other lost

soul needs help against vampires? This might have been an omen, a sign. Don't forget, we might not survive this fight. We were lucky once. Maybe it's for another generation to take these fiends down. Maybe in another generation or two somebody might need this information."

Instead of taking the issue, they copied on borrowed paper, verbatim, 28 *Fascinating Facts About the Vampire Count*, including nine ways to recognize him, thirteen powers he possesses, and a half-dozen weaknesses. Neither were accustomed to reading or writing anymore. The exercise took up the better part of a day, cramped their writing hands, and exhausted them.

After they left the library, Overboard George said, "We need food, Maggie."

"Well, we don't have any money. The Lutherans gave us clothes, shelter, a meal, and let us wash up, but no money. That's what we need now—money."

"I got some good grub at After Dark, out of the dumpster," George recalled, looking skyward. "There's a white girl there named Lisa who puts whole sandwiches out there, even little packets of ketchup."

"You crazy! I'm not going back there, not even if you give me a first-in-line ticket at the seafood buffet."

"Do they have one?" George asked.

"I don't know."

"It'll be light for hours. We'll swing by, check out what's there, and get back to the tent we stole. We'll have time to spare. *Or*, we can go hungry."

"I say we boost some food from the first market we pass," Mad Maggie said. "There's a couple of stores where I'm not welcome, because they know I steal stuff, but we'll find a place."

They argued for several minutes, finally decided to visit After Dark, grab anything available, and get back among other homeless, where they believed they would be safe. After Dark's parking lot, filled with cars, baked in full afternoon sun. The dumpster was full and ripe when Overboard George swung open the lid.

"Two fucking salads?" Overboard George said, when he examined the prepared bags inside. "No meat, either."

"They're still cold," Mad Maggie said, smiling. "I know that Lisa. She's a nice girl."

George frowned.

"*Or*, you can go hungry," Maggie countered, suppressing a giggle.

George took the salads, passed one to Maggie, and picked up bottled water from the ground. Suddenly, the dumpster enclosure gate swung open. Lisa stood there with two plastic garbage bags. She dropped the bags and rushed to Mad Maggie, hugged her.

"I can't believe you're here. Both of you," Lisa cried. "I thought you were gone. Missing. Dead."

"Not likely," George said. "We know our way around."

"We were held captive in the bowels of this monstrous building, food for vampires, but Overboard George got us out," Mad Maggie said, triumphantly. "Burned the shit out of those turkeys with their own sunlamps."

"What turkeys?" Lisa said. Now she believed they both were mad. Both high.

"Vampires!" Overboard George said. "I repeat. Vampires. They had us but we got away. Been on the lam since, a few days now."

"I don't understand," Lisa said. "No one goes in the After Dark basement. It's sealed off. The steps are supposed to be rickety."

"That's where the vampires enter," Mad Maggie said. "Real formal in their evening wear. They come in a regular procession. Very regal. We watched them feed on people. Once the victims have clean blood, they're strung upside down, naked, and the vampires drink their blood. Then the Whistlers go in and drain everything else. Suck out every body fluid. Maybe even the marrow out of their bones. Until their bodies are dried out husks."

"That's what they were going to do to us," Overboard George

said. "They kept us in cages until our blood was clean. Probably two weeks or more. Maggie's blood was already clean because she ain't a user. She just crazy. But they didn't know that."

"That's right," Mad Maggie interrupted. "I can act the part of a junkie. I seen enough on the street.."

Taking turns, Overboard George and Mad Maggie explained the Whistlers' role in securing victims—mostly junkies, occasionally normal people—to feed the vampires and themselves. A man assisted the vampires. Cleaned the victims, and prepared them for exsanguination.

"The man is weak," Overboard George said. "We can handle him. We want to go back to the dungeon during the day when the vampires are powerless. That's when we're going to kill them. Stake them through they fucking hearts." Mad Maggie took out the notes they wrote in the library and shook pages of childish-looking cursive.

"This is all incredible," Lisa said. Her eyes were wide. She raised her hands.

"I agree," Mad Maggie said, "until it happens to you. After they're staked, I'm going to carve them up with a sharp knife. Frame their sexual organs, like they used to press flowers in a book. But I expect they'll burst into flames, and there won't be anything left."

"Every word is the truth," Overboard George said. "What reason would we have to lie?"

"You might think it's true," Lisa said, "but you might be imagining it. You might be hallucinating."

"Then you tell me how people are missing," Mad Maggie said. "It's the only explanation. Look at the light poles along the street. They're filled with posters for missing people. They're not all junkies who overdose or move away."

Lisa stared at the two.

CHAPTER TWENTY-SEVEN

Lisa checked her order list for the bar. It seemed every week it grew longer. More people wanted things. A few items she doubted and marked to double-check before she called suppliers. After Dark did not need car polish, but Jose had just bought a car. If he could afford a car, he could spend his own money on polish. Lisa sucked on a root beer barrel hard candy. She loved root beer, and thanks to her the bar now served it on draft. It wasn't Coke, but it had a steady following on tap.

Although the restaurant hadn't opened, Lisa heard the front door close and saw her father tentatively look around, as if he might be an unwelcome patron. He saw Lisa and immediately started for the end of the bar she used as a workstation. Charles Van der Meer looked impressive. Tall, lanky, clean-shaven, black-rimmed glasses perched on his nose. His clothes looked new. No wrinkles.

Lisa was ecstatic. She couldn't help smiling. Her father had kicked alcohol. Charles, meanwhile, showed no emotion, which was not unusual, Lisa remembered. He was soft-spoken and a man of few words when he wasn't drunk.

"Daddy, you came to see me," Lisa said, walking from behind

the bar to greet him. He backed up as she approached. "Sit down in the restaurant. I'll put in an order for you. We can have lunch." She reached to hug him, but Charles caught her wrists and held them.

"I can't. Lisa. I came to warn you. Get out of this place. It's not safe. You should get out of this city. Start a life elsewhere." Sorrow showed in his eyes.

"I came here to find you, Daddy. There's nothing wrong with this place. The dishwasher sells a little weed, mostly to college kids. I'm not condoning it, but it's—"

"As they say, it's the way of the world. Please. The streets aren't safe around here, Lisa. Believe me. I've seen enough. I know enough."

"I don't understand."

"You don't have to. Believe me when I say this is not a place for you."

Lisa searched his eyes but couldn't detect even a hint of what he meant. "Are you involved in something you don't want me to know? You can tell me." Lisa tried to laugh. "I can't imagine you would do anything illegal."

Charles looked at her sternly. "I understand you're a grown woman. I can't control you. But this city isn't safe, and it's going to get worse. Especially this area. I won't be able to protect you."

"I don't need protecting, Daddy."

"You have no idea."

"I have a friend. He has a good job. He volunteers helping the homeless. That's how I met him. If you only knew how many hours I spent roaming these streets, always suspecting the worst."

"You shouldn't have looked for me."

"Would you do it for me?"

"No. I couldn't. I would not be able to help you."

"Daddy, if you're in a shelter, you can move in with me until you get your own place. I need to know where you are. How you are. I want the old times back. Mom's dead. I want a life with you."

"That's impossible," Charles said. He dropped Lisa's wrists.

Lisa turned her head. She heard Bart's quick, small steps growing louder. Charles pursed his lips. Looked scared. Bart turned the corner, rounding a potted tree, and froze. His mouth dropped open. His eyes fixed on Charles. Bart stared for a moment and walked away.

Charles looked at the floor.

"Daddy, do you know him? Do you know Bart?"

"That man? No." Charles shook his head and appeared uncomfortable.

"It looked like he knew you," Lisa said, putting her hands on her hips.

Charles smiled. "No, Lisa, I don't know him. I'm told I look like a lot of people, especially with these glasses."

"Bart looked like he saw a ghost."

"Maybe I am. Almost, anyway. Lisa, I wasn't going to tell you, but I have lung cancer. Same thing as my father, your Pop-Pop.

"We'll get help, Daddy."

"No." Charles was resolute. "I was checked out and it's too far gone. I decided not to take treatment. Live out what time I have as best as I can."

"I heard you coughing," Lisa said. "The other night. You looked exhausted."

"It comes and goes. I know my limitations. Today is a good day–so far. The doctor was honest. She said I have a little time. Surgery was out of the question. Treatments would be harsh and add little time in the end. You know," he paused a moment, "I thought my liver would kill me, the way I drank all those years, but it's my lungs. Of course, it runs in the family. You should get your lungs checked. Just in case."

Charles let Lisa hug him and kiss his cheek. Tears trickled down both their faces. Then Charles asked whether Lisa had heard strange tales about life on the street, among the homeless. She took his hand and moved him to a barstool near her workstation. He sat next to her.

"It's been a while since I sat on one of these," Charles said. Then he smiled. "I fell off my share, too. Almost like a rodeo rider on a bucking bronc."

"There's all kinds of crazy things talked about, especially among the old guys who panhandle for drink money," Lisa said. She looked around and lowered her voice, leaning toward him. "They say there are college kids who beat the homeless with sticks. I've seen the bruises, the cuts. Also that there are beasts that hunt in the park at night, grab the homeless, and take them away. The people are never heard from again. They are drained of blood. Vampires, they call them."

Charles closed his eyes for a moment. When he opened them his eyes were lusterless. "I know part of that is true," he said.

"College kids beating junkies?"

"No. The other."

"Vampires?" Lisa was incredulous. She wanted to laugh.

Charles nodded his head. "That's why I insist you leave the city. Go to a smaller town. There are vampires in all big cities, where people disappear every day and don't get noticed. Where it doesn't get recorded."

"Daddy, you didn't tell me that kind of shit when I was a kid. Now..."

"I never lied to you, Lisa. Do whatever you have to but get out of the city. Take your man with you. Even a man isn't safe in this city."

Her father's eyes looked sad. At that moment Lisa realized there would never be a relationship with her father. The memory of good times the family enjoyed before her Pop-Pop and mother's deaths were all she would have to remember. At least she had found her father and knew what had become of him. Still, he was clouded in mystery. What did he do now that was so secretive? How could he believe in vampires? Are his lungs *and* mind going?

Lisa ran her fingers through her father's hair. "You're getting so gray, Daddy."

He smiled at her. "It comes with age."

They stared for a moment at each other. Charles took Lisa's hand and kissed her fingers. Then he laid the hand down gently on her lap. He pulled off his ring and handed it to Lisa.

"No, Daddy. Not your ring. I don't want this to be goodbye." Tears ran down Lisa's face.

"There will be a time when I won't be able to see you anymore," Charles said. "A time when it won't be safe for you to see me."

"I could take care of you. Cancer isn't contagious. I'm not afraid. I want to help you. You have no idea how hard I looked for you. I was about to give up when—"

"You should be afraid, Honey. Be safe and don't go out at night. Above all, get out of this city."

"It's not so easy. I have a friend now. He has a good job," Lisa said. "He helps with the Lutheran church. Helps the homeless, the junkies. I don't know that he could leave the city or would want to. He has some roots now. The homeless know him. They depend on the supplies he brings."

"There's no way to fight vampires, Lisa. You don't understand. Tell your friend about the vampires. He'll have to leave with you."

"And what about you?"

"It doesn't matter about me, Lisa. This life is over. You must think about yourself. Your future. If you stay here, you won't have a future. Your friend can find another good job in a new city. I'm sure he's a smart fellow. It's the only thing to do. If you have a boy some-day, give him my ring. Say it's from his grandfather. Tell him I love him."

CHAPTER TWENTY-EIGHT

After his escape from After Dark, Bad Nelson remained sober. He moved back with his parents in their home on the city's south side. He hadn't told his parents about his experience with the vampires. He didn't expect them to believe him. Anything he said would be tied to his addiction. Instead, he said nothing.

Asked about his sobriety, Bad Nelson said only, "It was time to grow up. I lost too many friends on the street; so many I can't even give you a number. They all died because of drugs, alcohol, or disease. The friends who never got mixed up in drugs dropped me like a hammer. In their eyes, I'm no longer alive. So, that's the story."

His parents accepted Bad Nelson back. He could stay as long as he remained clean and didn't steal from them, even though he was twenty-six years old.

His parents decided not to push the sobriety subject, especially after he declined to join them in draining a large box of cabernet every day. As functioning alcoholics, Bad Nelson's parents, John and Loretta Manner, both had weathered good jobs long enough to secure pensions, social security, and sizeable 401Ks. The stock market had been kind to the Manners, despite their haphazard investment styles. The Manners didn't vacation, didn't eat out much, drove the same car until it died, replaced it with a slightly better used model, and kept the same furniture they had when Bad Nelson was a boy. They preferred to remain at home, guzzling cheap wine from stemless glasses. Bad Nelson saw his parents' decline but remained silent. However, he did accompany Mom and Dad to the liquor store to buy more wine, "To go along for the ride," Bad Nelson said. He always waited in the car. Sometimes, if they were already drunk, Bad Nelson drove and made the purchases for them, because *happy hour* wasn't regulated by the hands on a clock.

Bad Nelson stayed away from his old stomping grounds near the stadium, away from the users he called friends, and away from the dealers who sold drugs to anyone who had cash. If a steady customer died from an overdose, the dealers showed no remorse. They never attended a funeral or offered a eulogy. There was always a new customer to take his or her place. New junkies showed up in the old neighborhood weekly. The Manners also pretended not to notice the night terrors Bad Nelson experienced regularly. He dreamed not so much of the withdrawal symptoms he experienced or being locked underground in a damp cell, but of being taken by the Whistlers, their foul-smelling breath, their raspy fur, their claws and teeth tearing his clothes and flesh, their bodies compressing him to the point of breathlessness, and the never-ending clicking and whistles he couldn't get out of his mind. His body carried the scars of their bites and scratches.

Now Bad Nelson spent most of his days in the garage at the end of the yard. The garage was too small to hold a modern car and was filled with junk that the Manners accumulated over the years. Most of that junk Bad Nelson collected during his high school years. He was somewhat of a science nerd, wanted to study mechanical engineering, and had even been accepted at State, until booze consumed his life, and his parents kicked him out on the street in July after high school graduation. His senior year was marked by alcohol, addiction to opioids, a break-up with his high school sweetheart, dropping out of science club, abandoning his determination to build a compact potato gun, with prototypes that shot holes in their privacy fence and garage door, and broke windows as far away as two blocks.

John Manner replaced pickets in fences and holes in garage doors and even sprang for a few new windows when Bad Nelson was ratted out. After all, Nelson might work for Winchester or the US government someday, with his degree in mechanical engineering. After drugs got a hold of him, all he got was the moniker *Bad Nelson*.

During the hours Bad Nelson hid in the garage, he was back to perfecting the potato gun. These new prototypes had shorter, narrower PVC barrels, larger combustion chambers, and sparking triggers that ignited propane gas, the kind of gas that came in a canister and a plumber might use to solder copper pipes. The guns didn't launch potatoes anymore but eighteen-inch-long wooden darts with sharpened points hardened by charring. Bad Nelson was determined to wipe out the Whistlers in the hopes his vivid dreams about them would cease. Testing his new guns was a daunting project. He had to drive outside the city to woods and carry his equipment where there were no hikers or campers. Even an errant dart could be lethal at a distance. That was the point, after all. In addition to several guns in development, Bad Nelson needed a supply of darts, propane canisters, and various tools to make adjustments in the field. He had to wait until his parents bought their wine to make his runs to the woods. After the Manners were at home with a fresh wine box between them, it was difficult to move them away from the television watching game shows and endless cycles on cable news. They didn't care that Bad Nelson took the car. He'd stop at Lowe's or Home Depot on the way to the forest for supplies.

On one such run to Lowe's, Bad Nelson saw his high school

sweetheart, Megan Fortune, in the plumbing section. Megan looked young for having two kids in tow, both seated in a wire shopping cart. Her hair was still long and blond with dark highlights. Her eyes were light blue. She had remained as thin as she was in high school.

"Bad Nelson," she said suddenly, almost passing him in the aisle. "Do they still call you that?" The truth was he hadn't seen anyone he knew all summer since he escaped from the vampires and street life around the stadium.

"Some do. The ones who remember me from before." Bad Nelson juggled several lengths of inch-and-a-half PVC pipe between his arms."

"You should have a cart," Megan said. 'All I need is a water filter for the refrigerator. Come on boys, let this man put his pipes in the cart. You can walk."

Megan lifted the boys out and Bad Nelson put the PVC pipes inside the cart. The kids complained about the loss of their ride, but Bad Nelson showed them a quarter that disappeared from his hand and reappeared behind their ears. The boys were enchanted. Stood grinning nearby.

"I didn't expect to buy so much, but I figure I'll need it eventually," Bad Nelson said.

"What have you been up to, Bad Nelson." Megan smiled.

"Not too much. "I've been sober most of the summer."

"That's great," she said. She looked at the floor and then at Bad Nelson. "I've been divorced most of the summer."

They laughed.

"I'm sorry," Bad Nelson said. "It will be tough for you—the boys and you—without a father and husband. Your boys resemble you."

"That's what everyone says. Are you working for a plumber? I see all the...pipe."

"Not exactly."

"You're not still making those potato guns?"

"No," Bad Nelson laughed. "Something different. Something better."

"Oh boy." Megan rolled her eyes and looked away for a moment. "I'll keep my eye on the police blotter in the newspaper."

Bad Nelson smiled. "I'm living with my parents. They're retired now. Until I get back on my feet. Decide what I'm going to do."

"That's good. I'm with my folks, too."

"While I have your cart, I need a few more things. I'll be back in a minute. My parents get worried if I have their car out too long."

Bad Nelson shot down an aisle and picked up PVC cleaner, glue, and more propane tanks. He went to woodworking and secured heavy dowels for the darts, ensuring each was straight. When he returned to the water filter display, Megan and the boys were gone.

"The last thing she needs in her life is a drunk who has decided to devote his life, at least temporarily, to fighting vampires," Bad Nelson said out loud, shaking his head. "I shouldn't have taken off. Should have talked more with her. Told her she looked good. I don't even know how to interact anymore."

CHAPTER TWENTY-NINE

Bad Nelson was at work in the family garage at the end of the yard. Access to the Manner garage was through their short, narrow yard from the house, or a dirt alley, mostly overgrown with trees and high grass. Bad Nelson's family had one of a few such garages that lined the alley and were still usable. Most were in various states of decay, with sagging roofs, collapsing sides, and overhead doors askew that no longer opened. It had been years since a vehicle drove down the alley, let alone parked in one of the garages. Most of the structures were filled to their ceilings with accumulated junk, console televisions, torn furniture, old bicycles, and broken appliances. Bad Nelson's garage, however, was in better condition and had electricity, via a single 12-2 line from the basement that snaked up the home's siding and ran across the yard barely ten feet high in a long, sagging span to the garage.

The electric supply was enough to power overhead lights and a few outlets on the wall above a workbench Bad Nelson and his father had made from two-by-fours and wood scraps when Bad Nelson was a boy before the entire family succumbed to their various addictions. The bench was cluttered with old paint cans, empty boxes, and tools. Still, there was enough room to lay out a PVC pipe and construct a potato gun that now launched wooden stakes.

Bad Nelson had just strapped and glued the ignition chamber, which acted like a rifle stock, to the back of a PVC pipe. He had already drilled a hole in the ignition chamber through which he now snaked the end of a wire that would deliver a spark from the trigger and ignite propane previously pumped into the gun. The spark ignited an explosion that launched the deadly stake. The last step was to seal all the drilled holes with more glue.

Bad Nelson liked working in the garage. It had been his refuge through his childhood and teen years, whether he was assembling model automobiles or continuing his quest for a more potent potato gun.

The Manners had returned from the liquor store run with two boxes of wine; they hated to shop on weekends and found the crowds overbearing. After they were into their first few glasses, the Manners wouldn't care Bad Nelson took the car for a few hours. Sometimes, they didn't know he had gone out after he suddenly appeared in the living room, smelling of PVC cement and the gasoline he used to clean his hands of glue. At one point the Manners accused Bad Nelson of huffing fumes in the garage, as he had in high school on the path to drug abuse, but after Bad Nelson told his parents he was making an advanced potato gun, they seemed satisfied, and the roof over his head was again secure.

Perched on a rusted stool at the workbench, its padding duct taped to keep in the rupturing foam cushion, Bad Nelson waited for his stake gun glue to dry, He sat in silence, afraid to turn on the AM radio he had made in high school for fear it would alert vampires friendlies. Bad Nelson believed the fiends searched the city for him and had legions of loyalists to do their bidding. It might be paranoia, partly due to his craving to get high, but he didn't want to be exposed. If he were caught again, no escape would be possible, he believed. Feigning death wouldn't work a second time.

After Bad Nelson showed up naked at a shelter, sporting a new beard, he secured clothing and began a rambling, incredible story of what happened to him underground. His first days, as withdrawal began, had been a blur. He wasn't sure where he was or what happened. However, he did remember being crushed among the clattering furry animals with sharp teeth and claws. Inside the vampire lair, his clothes were torn off. He was scratched and bitten and thrown in a cell. He remained naked for his entire captivity, fed by a tall man with a hacking cough who hosed him down regularly, brought food, and changed his slop bucket.

More terrifying were the Whistlers that charged his cell, yapped, and clawed at the bars, sniffing him. They were the ones that took him while he dipped alone in the park. He remembered the vampires, too, with their lurid, bloodless faces, sagging flesh, and deteriorating clothing, staring at him, talking among themselves in a dialect he didn't understand. Occasionally, they interjected a few words of English, as if there were no words in their language to express their thoughts. Always, their voices were hollow and seemed to come from inside a drum. The noise rang through the cavernous underground off the stone walls. They prodded him with long, sharp-nailed fingers that often drew blood. They licked those dirty fingers, relishing the collected drops of blood. They sniggered at his nakedness, especially the female. All the time they sniffed the air, delighted in his terror, while he pressed himself against the back of the cell, and rolled their dark, pointed tongues around obscene lips. Then, as if some internal clock warned them, they would leave, walking in a stiff, slow gait, regally, until they were no longer visible at the end of the basement.

After he escaped and was clothed, shelter personnel recorded Bad Nelson's tale, scribbling as fast as they could on legal pads on their laps, glancing between their pages and Bad Nelson, encouraging him with nodding heads, as if in agreement, raising thoughtful eyebrows, watching their pages fill with line after line, and sometimes adding a *Mumph* of surprise. He hugged himself at times, recalling the damp, fetid air, the cold floor on his bare feet, the heaviness he experienced in the dungeon-like basement. After he concluded, Bad Nelson sat breathless, staring at the shelter volunteers. He accepted bottled water fortified with vitamins. The three volunteers grimaced in unison as if horrified by his experience. As Bad Nelson looked from face to face, he noticed his new clothes had the faint odor of mildew.

When one volunteer remarked how well he appeared, Bad Nelson said he was washed with cold water and fed daily. He had a bucket to eliminate waste. The three volunteers nodded in unison as if they were familiar with similar cases. Bad Nelson wondered if he was not the first to escape the vampires and come to the shelter naked. The volunteer who seemed to take charge, Dale, a tall, forty-ish-something man in jeans with a pot belly under his pink polo shirt, asked whether Bad Nelson needed a cigarette. He patted his shirt pocket and the bulge inside. Bad Nelson declined. Dale requested Bad Nelson repeat his story for another worker.

Bad Nelson was exhausted and wanted to know who the person was.

"A friend of the center," the tall man responded. "Someone who would have more knowledge of your type of...experience," Dale added the final word after a lengthy pause.

"I could call her now and, possibly, she could be here in a few minutes," the man said, with a smile and a wave of his pen. "I'm almost certain she would come immediately. Your case is so unusual. She'll want to hear your story."

The other men smiled.

Bad Nelson knew no one believed him. He needed time to formulate an escape plan. "All right. I don't mind telling my story again," Bad Nelson said, cheerily, as if he had nothing to hide, no place to go. "You know, while I was underground, I didn't do any talking. I had nobody to talk to. I was mostly alone in the basement. It was dark a lot. My voice seems a little rusty."

The other two volunteers nodded again as if in sympathy,

stood, smiled, and exited the room, leaving their tablets and pens on the table.

Dale excused himself, too, and said he would make the call to Dr. Carol. He dropped some coins in a plastic cup next to the coffee maker. He told Bad Nelson to help himself to coffee, which Bad Nelson did immediately. He couldn't recall when he last had caffeine. While he stirred in powdered creamer, Bad Nelson smiled and asked for another bottle of water.

"I'll get one from the kitchen on the way back," Dale said. The tall man smiled broadly. "It will be good and cold. Just the thing on a hot day."

"Thank you. I'm a little parched," Bad Nelson said. "All this talking has dried out my throat."

"Of course," Dale said. "I'll be back in a few minutes. In the meantime, relax. There are cookies in that cupboard. Our secretary brought them in. They're homemade. Chocolate chip. Help yourself."

Bad Nelson was thankful he didn't give Dale his real name. As soon as Dale was gone and his steps receded down the hall outside the room, Bad Nelson flipped open the legal pads and saw that one worker doodled while he listened to Bad Nelson's story and the other wrote line after line of incoherent scribbling. Only Dale had recorded Bad Nelson's story and his writing was filled with exclamation points, question marks, and smiley faces.

Bad Nelson clawed the money from the coffee fund jar, a handful of singles and change, pocketed it, grabbed as many cookies as he could hold, and climbed through a first-floor window, dropping to a thick mulch bed below. Bad Nelson looked around to see no one saw him leave through the window and walked casually down the sidewalk. He wolfed down the cookies. He turned left at the corner and bolted. Several blocks later, breathless and sweating, he found a bus stop and used the purloined coffee money for a ride home. At that point, he hoped his parents would accept him.

Bad Nelson tested the newly applied glue and found it was dry.

He picked up the stake gun, and felt its weight. The gun was defi-nitely the lightest and shortest weapon he had made. He used the sight to target an imaginary foe on the garage's opposite wall. Bad Nelson was now ready to take a ride to the woods and fire the new gun.

There was a noise at the overhead garage door. Bad Nelson froze. Was it a knock or was it a scratch? He couldn't tell. Bad Nelson slid from his seat and sidled to the overhead garage door, pressing his ear near the wooden frame. A knock came. Bad Nelson jumped. There was more silence. Sweat beaded on Bad Nelson's forehead. Ran down his back. He listened again. There was silence. If it were his parents, they wouldn't walk around the garage to use the overhead. They'd come through the garage's back door from the yard. Besides, they rarely ventured from their living room recliners after happy hour began, except for piss breaks. He looked toward that door. It wasn't locked. He felt the need to run across the garage and throw the bolt over. More paranoia. Bad Nelson imagined goth vampire compatriots huddled outside for the chance to jump him. Then the knock came again. This time it was louder and longer. It followed by his name whispered.

"Nels? Are you in there? The lights are on. I can see them through the cracks. It's Megan." Another staccato knock followed.

Bad Nelson recognized the voice. Only Megan had called him Nels. "Are you alone?" he whispered back through the door. He imagined the goth horde again, ropes in hand, had taken her captive, held a knife at her throat, and waited to pounce on him.

"Of course I'm alone," Megan whispered back. She sounded annoyed. "Open the door already."

Bad Nelson stooped, grabbed the overhead door handle, and slowly lifted, inching the door up a little at a time. The door had an electric opener, with a control button on the wall, but the motor burned out years ago. He saw only one set of legs outside. The door flew out of Bad Nelson's hand and up to the top of the frame with a bang. Bad Nelson stepped back.

Megan Fortune stood in the open doorway, hands on her hips. "What's all the cloak and dagger? You never closed this door. Preferred to work in natural light. I hope you're not in here huffing. I smell glue."

"I don't huff. I don't want to be seen or have anyone know I'm back," Bad Nelson said. He took Megan's hand, pulled her into the garage, and closed the door.

Megan giggled until she saw Bad Nelson's serious expression. "What's wrong, Nels?"

"You wouldn't believe me. Couldn't believe me. I wouldn't want to get you involved. You have kids to raise."

"Nels, you can trust me. Is it drugs? Booze? Are you in trouble?"

"It's not drugs. Something worse."

Megan lunged for Bad Nelson and hugged him. "You can tell me."

"You'd never understand."

"I will understand," Megan said. She took his hands. "I loved you once. Remember? After I saw you at Lowe's I realized I still love you. Trust me."

Bad Nelson guided Megan to the stool and sat her down. It was the same stool where she sat many times while Bad Nelson fooled with his potato guns and sang along to songs on the radio Bad Nelson had made from a kit. Slowly, thoughtfully, Bad Nelson unraveled the story of his addiction, his capture by the Whistlers, the incarceration underground, and finally his escape. Megan sat upright, her lips parted slightly, while Bad Nelson told the story. When Bad Nelson finished, he took Megan's hands and said, "Do you believe me?"

"Vampires? I don't know what to think."

"If we had been in touch, you would know I disappeared for more than two weeks, dried out, and showed up at the shelter on Milton Street naked. They gave me clothes, but they didn't believe me, either. They were all friendly but wanted me to talk to another person, I think she was a psych doctor. They did everything but measure me for a straitjacket. I escaped that place, too, while they made the call. I didn't give them my real name, so *they* can't trace me."

"And the vampires?" Megan said, with an arched eyebrow.

"They don't know my name, but I know they're looking for me. The last thing they want is for their story to get out. The shelter might be looking for me, too, because they probably think I'm crazy."

"I think *you* believe what you say, Nels. Honestly, I have a harder time."

"Then you don't believe me." Bad Nelson drew away from Megan.

"I want to believe you, Nels, but it is just so...fantastic."

"The only person who believed me was Old Harriet, a homeless junkie. I told her my story, too, when I first escaped."

"How did you get away?" Megan wanted to know. "Do you remember?"

"Of course. Over the two weeks the vampires held me, I went through withdrawal. It was incredibly painful. I was sick all the time. It's the reason I didn't want to get sober. The dope filtered out of my blood. *They* were ready to drain me. String me up naked, upside down in a special room. I had seen others drained while I was down there. They were all junkies or homeless nobody would miss. While I recovered, they brought in another woman. She told me she had been in recovery. Was clean but was out trying to buy a fix. On the night they planned to kill me, I pretended to be dead. I didn't respond to them and was limp in my cell. The man who took care of us poked me with a broom handle and kicked me hard. The vampires prodded me with their long fingers. I didn't react. I was so afraid I couldn't react. From what I learned in the dungeon the vampires don't like tainted blood. No drugs in it. They also insist on live blood. Once I appeared dead, my blood was no longer useful. At least that's how it seemed.

"They had another victim ready—the woman—so, they decided to dump me on the street and drain her. They were in a hurry to feed. Nobody ever checked me for a pulse."

"Nels!" Megan said. "She died in your place?"

Bad Nelson paced back and forth in front of Megan. Threw up his hands. "She was next in line to die anyway. Nothing I did or didn't do had any effect on her outcome. The tall man with the cough drug me outside—it was excruciating being pulled up those steps—and dumped me near the sidewalk. It was almost sunrise. I took off after he was gone. Went right to the shelter all scraped up. And that's the whole story. Believe it or not. But I have no reason to lie to you, Megan. I'm not looking for sympathy."

Megan looked around the garage. "Well, how do you plan to get back on your feet? By making potato guns?" Megan shook her head in disbelief. Her long hair fell around her shoulders. "We played around with them in high school. I think it might be time to move past potato guns."

"They're not potato guns anymore. They shoot wooden stakes," Bad Nelson said, becoming excited, picking up the recently completed gun, and holding it in front of her. "You can see this one is different from the ones we made. Almost every night I have dreams—nightmares—about my time underground. Really, it's almost every time I close my eyes. I think there's only one way to cure it. I'm going after the vampires and their Whistlers. Instead of them hunting me, I'm going to hunt them. Kill them from a distance. I'll be free when they're all dead."

"Nels, you can get into some serious trouble if you shoot someone," Megan said. She slid off the stool and embraced him.

"Don't worry. The Whistlers are animals. The vampires are already dead."

CHAPTER THIRTY

Bad Nelson convinced Megan to come with him outside the city to test the new stake gun prototype. He knew the design would work. However, he wanted to make sure the sights were accurate. A little trimming on the hindsight with his Xacto knife might be necessary. Bad Nelson knew the vampires and the Whistlers were cunning and moved faster than humans. Accuracy was essential. He could not waste shots. They would leave early the next morning. Megan would drive her car. The Manners were determined to beat the crowds for their weekly food shopping trip and needed the family car. Megan had work in the afternoon. Therefore, morning was the only time she was available.

Megan picked up Bad Nelson at 8:00 a.m. Her compact car barely fit down the alley to the Johnson garage. Bad Nelson waited with the garage door open. They loaded three prototype guns into the back seat, along with a supply of stakes, extra propane tanks, and wadding. They drove west of the city to state game lands, where hunting was allowed, although no season was in now. The parking lot was empty. Megan positioned her car where it wouldn't be visible from the highway.

They gathered the guns and equipment and marched into the forest. Bad Nelson had named the guns one, two, and three. Each weapon had a number on the back of the ignition chamber, the gun's widest part behind the barrel, drawn with a Sharpie pen.

The day was already warm, but the forest smelled fresh. It seemed like old times, when Nels and Megan dated in high school. Although Bad Nelson craved a fix, even a bottle of booze, he was determined to stay clean, possibly win back Megan. His future was uncertain but at least he had a plan. Bad Nelson laid out a vinyl tarp and placed the guns and equipment on top.

He took the number one gun, tamped a stake and wadding down the barrel. There was a foam deer target among the trees a hunter had set up for archery practice. Bad Nelson stepped off about twenty yards, with Megan at his side, carrying additional stakes. He inspected all the drill holes to ensure they were sealed. He didn't want a sudden flash outside the gun to burn him. That happened several times in high school when he had been in a hurry to shoot. Then he checked the sights carefully and aimed at the dear target. By pulling the trigger halfway four times, Bad Nelson filled the ignition chamber with propane from the gas tank strapped below the barrel. It was the perfect place to grip the gun with his left hand. The goal for the potato gun had always been to shoot far, if not always accurately. That's the reason his family fence and garage door suffered so many holes. This new prototype was designed to be accurate over shorter distances. Bad Nelson aimed the stake gun at the deer's imaginary heart, just behind the front leg. He pulled the trigger. There was a flash and a *wump*. The stake flew like a missile and severed the deer target in two, just behind the front leg, exactly where he had aimed. Bad Nelson and Megan shouted with glee. They hugged each other as they had in high school when a launched potato surpassed the old record.

At one point during the old high school days they bought so many potatoes old Mr. Crosley at the market asked them one Saturday morning if they were making moonshine. Wanted to know where their still was and how much they would charge him for a quart.

In short order, gun two and three proved to be equally accurate. Bad Nelson whittled the rear sight on gun three to increase its accuracy. After Megan fired the gun, the deer target was reduced to a pile of indistinguishable foam pieces. The stakes inflicted considerable damage. However, the stakes pierced the target and often flew into tree trunks where they shattered into splinters. Some whizzed through the forest and stuck in the soil. The latter were difficult to find but at least could be reused. A half dozen stakes were destroyed in the target practice. Bad Nelson said they would have to be replaced.

Satisfied with the three stake guns, Bad Nelson and Megan gathered them up, along with their supplies, and returned to the car. They sat in the shade for a while, talking about the old days, and drank the remainder of their iced coffees.

"We should get back," Megan said.

"Is your mother watching the boys?"

"Yes. She's been a godsend. Never complains, although she wasn't happy I was seeing you today."

"That doesn't surprise me," Bad Nelson said. "I don't think she ever liked me."

"That's not true, Nels," Megan said, taking Bad Nelson's hand. "She didn't like the drugs, the alcohol, and you dropping off the grid. She and my dad believed we had a real future together."

"Maybe we still do," Bad Nelson said. He rubbed his thumb over the top of her hand.

Megan smiled.

Bad Nelson wondered whether Megan thought he should have talked to the psych doctor. Find out what was wrong with his mind.

"What about your ex? Do you think you'll get back together?"

"No chance of that," Megan said. "He was an asshole. Little better than…"

"Me?" Bad Nelson said.

"You were never an asshole, Nels. You had an addiction problem. He beat me. Threatened the children. Had one affair after another. He gave up his rights to the kids in the divorce. He pays no support. Even though I could use the money, I like it that way because he also has no say in the boys' lives."

"You were all I ever wanted, Meg," Bad Nelson said.

"Me, too, but I made a bad mistake with Mike. He was cruel. You were always kind, even though you had a thing for potato guns."

Both laughed. They kissed. Megan pulled out from the parking lot and drove back to the city.

"I'd like to see you again," Bad Nelson told Megan. "I promise we won't shoot stake guns. I'll have to find a job, too. I'm not sure what I want to do, but I'm certain it's working with my hands. My dad said he would consider financing trade school for a year or two, but not a four-year school. Not now, especially since he's retired."

"It feels nice to dream again," Megan said. "We can make it work. I know we can. As soon as you have a job we can try moving in together.

"I'd like that," Bad Nelson said. "I would like that a lot. And because your boys are yours, I'd treat them like they were mine."

Megan smiled. "I know you'd make a good father. The best."

"Where do you work, Meg," Bad Nelson asked.

"I have a new job waitressing. It's not what I want to do for the rest of my life. I thought of cosmetology or maybe nursing, but I don't know if I'm smart enough. My manager's name is Lisa. She's been nice to me. Helped me get situated."

"You didn't tell me where the job is," Bad Nelson said.

"Oh. It's near the stadium and called After Dark. You must have you heard of it?"

CHAPTER THIRTY-ONE

After work, Lisa left After Dark and combed the streets for Jimmy. She knew he would be passing out supplies to the homeless. It was especially hot. Lisa looked for Jimmy and the wagon in which he pulled cases of bottled water on hot days. The water, stacked high, was warm, but it kept the homeless hydrated. Faced with buying water or dope, most junkies chose dope. She weaved through panhandlers and dippers, stepping over unconscious bodies, searching for Jimmy with one eye on the pavement for used needles. Lisa had her own water bottle she filled at home. Sweat ran down her face. Her arms glistened. Her T-shirt was wet at the neck and under the arms. A thin line of moisture ran down the shirt's back.

Finally, she saw Jimmy, his red wagon trailing behind him. Even from a distance, Lisa saw he was drenched in sweat. His face was beet red. He wore a bucket hat to keep off the sun. He had stopped to pass out water. A grateful crowd surrounded him and helped themselves from the wagon. Jimmy smiled and shook hands, passed out cards with the church service hours. Despite the heat and strong sun, no one seemed ready to move on. A laugh moved through the crowd like a wave at a sporting event. For that single moment, everyone seemed normal, Lisa thought, as she approached. She stopped about ten feet behind the crowd and listened. Jimmy encouraged the homeless to visit the church. Come to a service on Sunday.

"I don't know what today is," one man said, and the laughter rippled through the water-guzzling, malodorous crowd again. Even Jimmy laughed. Jimmy said there was fresh coffee and pastries after the service. Canned goods were available for the taking, too. Bags with new toothbrushes, toothpaste, and floss were handed out. The junkies showed interest as they sipped from the disposable bottles, but Lisa knew few would attend. Some would forget the day, others would be dipping, panhandling, or trying to secure a fix to ward off dope sickness.

If only one or two came and spread the word, Lisa thought, it was a start. There were safe places to go and people who cared. Now it seemed the homeless feared for their very lives. They dreaded the Beaters and the bat-like creatures that slinked along the ground at night, and vampires who let them go through the torture of withdrawal before draining their blood. It was mass hysteria. However, at this moment they were like children in the schoolyard, all getting along, seemingly carefree.

Lisa scanned the group. Old Harriet was on the fringe. Her beehive hair looked like a large pencil eraser on her head and stood above the other heads. Mad Maggie and Overboard George held hands and finally returned to their old stomping grounds near the stadium. Overboard George nodded in Lisa's direction. Mad Maggie waved with the hand that held her half-consumed water bottle. Both looked clean in their new clothes. Someone had given Overboard George a haircut. Mad Maggie's hair had been trimmed, too, and lay clean and flat. The wild tangles she had were gone. She didn't look *mad* anymore. They might be mistaken for regular people, strolling up Fifth Street, perhaps on their way for a night game at the stadium. Lisa didn't recognize the rest of the crowd. Her father was not among them. He was so furtive, she doubted he would stop to see what was going on. He would avoid people, slink along on the street's opposite sidewalk, and disappear before anyone could recognize him.

Just as Lisa was ready to join the group, a couple walked in front of her and took water bottles from the wagon. The woman was Megan, the new After Dark waitress. The young man carried a length of PVC pipe. Lisa thought it odd. What would someone do with PVC pipe downtown? There were no proper drains in the homeless tent city. The couple did not look homeless. The pipe would hardly make a good weapon.

Old Harriet's eyes grew wide with astonishment when she saw the pipe-carrying man. She slipped around the crowd's edge, took him by the arm, and pulled him back to the sidewalk, with Megan in tow. Old Harriet called Overboard George and motioned for him to follow her. He and Mad Maggie soon joined her, along with the PVC pipe man and Megan. They gathered around Old Harriet's chair on wheels, against the chain link fence, away from Jimmy's crowd. Lisa made her move. She approached Jimmy. He was surprised by her sudden appearance. Lisa pointed to Old Harriet.

"There's something I have to tell you," Lisa said, pointing at Old Harriet and her group. "They're all in on it. At least I think all of them are."

Jimmy told the homeless to help themselves to the water. In short order, the water and wagon were gone.

"What is it?" Jimmy said.

"You'll see," Lisa said.

They zigzagged through the homeless and their shelters to Old Harriet's chair on wheels. Harriet was perched on the seat, as much to prevent someone from taking it as to rest.

Overboard George pointed to the man with the PVC pipe. "Are you who I think you are?" George said.

"Most people know me as Bad Nelson. This is my friend Megan."

Lisa looked at Jimmy, and then at the group. "I thought all day about getting everyone together. And here we are. I can't believe it. We should go somewhere we can all talk. It's important we do it privately."

"We could find a place out of the sun, say in the park," Jimmy said.

"No!" most of the group said in unison, horror etched on their faces.

"How about some A/C?" Lisa said. "Ice-cold soft drinks are on me."

Members of the group smiled.

Lisa added, "We can go to After Dark."

"No!" the group chimed louder, this time shaking their heads and raising their palms to indicate a stop.

Jimmy looked at Lisa, mystified.

"I vote we stay right here on the sidewalk, where there's lots of people around," Old Harriet said. "Not people to hear us, people for protection. I don't give a damn about the heat. After all, it's summer. It's supposed to be hot."

"You think you need protection in the daylight?" Lisa asked.

"As much as if it was nighttime," Old Harriet said with a knowing nod of her head and frizzled hair. She scratched at her scalp with dirty nails.

Lisa and Megan shared smiles. Megan nodded her head as if to say, "Believe what you are about to hear."

"I don't understand any of this. Has the heat gotten to you?" Jimmy said.

Lisa moved closer to him and took his hand.

One by one, each told his or her story of captivity and escape. Three lurid accounts of the foul-smelling corpses that lived after death by drinking the blood of the living. After feeding, the corpses were radiant and youthful. When they were hungry they looked like the rotting cadavers they were. Meanwhile, Old Harriet sat on her chair on wheels nodding in agreement, smiling, as if she had witnessed each episode. As the stories unfolded, Lisa twice had to close Jimmy's mouth with her palm when it dropped open in surprise.

Bad Nelson, the first to be taken, was the last to tell his story. After he concluded, Old Harriet said, "Every word you heard here today is the truth. I'll vouch for each and every one, whether they're junkies or crazy. And just to set the record straight, I'm a junkie, too."

Hearing all three stories together, Lisa looked at Jimmy. They still held hands. The idea of vampires, along with her father's warnings, seemed more incredulous than ever. A former drunk, two junkies, and a psychotic.

"What do we do?" Lisa said. "Where do we go? Who do we tell.? No one will believe you."

"That's why we need your help," Overboard George said, pointing to Jimmy. And you," he added, pointing at Lisa.

Mad Maggie and Bad Nelson nodded in agreement.

"I'm just a bartender," Lisa said. "I have no clout. The cops would think I had one too many if I told them your stories."

"I wouldn't know where to go," Jimmy said. "How do you approach people, no matter how well they know you, with a tale about vampires, and expect them to believe you? I wouldn't know how to start."

"You have the connections we need," Mad Maggie told Jimmy. She looked at Overboard George. "We can't go nowhere with our stories. I have a murder rap from when I was a kid. He probably is still considered AWOL. We'd be locked up before we got a word out. Once you're locked up, you just listen. *They* do the talking. Maybe worse. We'd be separated and both be in the psych unit."

"This is what I thought would happen," Bad Nelson said. To

Megan, he added, "Isn't this what I said? We wouldn't get any help."

Megan nodded her head in agreement and rubbed Bad Nelson's back.

"I have my own plan," Bad Nelson said. "It's not a real plan yet, but it's the start of a plan. I'm going after those vampires and I'm going to kill them. I know where their lair is, and I have the means to kill them." Bad Nelson raised his PVC pipe. "See this? I make guns that shoot wooden stakes. They're accurate, too. Aren't they Megs?"

"You better believe it. We destroyed a deer."

"You killed a deer?" Jimmy said. He looked incredulous.

"Not a real deer," Bad Nelson said. "A foam deer made for practice shooting. One stake blew it in half."

"Two more shots destroyed it," Megan said. She threw her arms over her head. "Completely. I shot it, too."

"That's how you kill vampires," Overboard George said matter-of-factly. "Stake them through the heart." He made a fist and drove it into his other palm.

"We know all about it," Mad Maggie said. "We've been holed up in the library during the day doing vampire research. We know their strengths *and* their weaknesses. And don't forget, we've seen them in action. Fought them tooth and nail."

"I don't understand. What kind of research?" Jimmy said.

"In the library," Overhead George said. "We snuck into the off-limits reference section. Where they keep the oldest books. Found a copy of *Famous Monsters of Filmland* ..."

"From 1964," Mad Maggie interrupted.

"A magazine?" Jimmy said, screwing up his face. He looked among the expectant faces, grinning like amazed children. "You can't be serious!" Jimmy threw up his arms in disbelief.

"Sure I am," Overboard George said, as if proud of their exploits.

"It's about movie monsters?" Lisa said.

"I told you we should have taken the magazine," Mad Maggie said, wagging a finger at Overboard George. "We'd have proof there are vampires and second, it would show how to kill them. Photos and all."

"If you don't want to help, that's fine," Bad Nelson said. "Just stay out of our way until the beasts are dead. Then you can go to the police or whoever you want to call."

Overboard George cocked his head. "Just remember, there won't be no evidence, because the vampires will vaporize once they dead." He smirked at Jimmy. "What is it you said, Mags?"

"No *corpus delicti*. They'll be gone in a flash, a poof of fire," Mad Maggie said, spreading and wiggling her fingers in front of her."

Jimmy turned to Bad Nelson. "Do you really have a gun that shoots wooden stakes?"

"I designed it myself from old potato guns I made."

"You could kill someone," Jimmy said, his voice rising.

"That's the point," Bad Nelson said, stepping toward Jimmy.

"That is murder, my friend," Jimmy said.

"It's not a somebody. It's a vampire. It's already dead," Bad Nelson screamed.

Lisa turned to Megan. "Do you believe this?"

"Of course. If Nels says they're vampires, they're vampires." She folded her arms and stared at Lisa.

"I know there are vampires in this city," Old Harriet said. "Bad Nelson told me his story right after he escaped. He was still naked from being underground. He was all cut up. He's got a nice package, too." Her thin shoulders shook with laughter. Her crazy hairdo shimmied.

Jimmy looked back to Lisa. She shrugged. "I'm surrounded by insanity," he said.

"Ain't nothing wrong with that," Mad Maggie said. "I'm with them all the way."

Bad Nelson said, "I have four stake guns. This pipe will make a fifth. Meg and I are expert shooters. We've been practicing. The guns are single-shot and accurate. It takes only a few seconds to load and prime the gas that shoots the stake. I'll train anyone who wants to come along. Megs and I have been making stakes. We have plenty of ammo now. So, who's in?"

Overboard George and Mad Maggie raised their hands, smiling broadly. So did Megan.

"I'm too old," Old Harriet said, "but I'm with you in spirit. Might come along for the ride, though. Be backup."

"What about you two?" Bad Nelson said, pointing the end of his PVC pipe at Jimmy and Lisa.

Jimmy was silent for a moment. Then he said, "I'll go, if it's only to prevent a tragedy. But I don't want a gun."

"I'm in, too," Lisa said. "No gun for me, either."

"Good. You two can carry the extra ammo, some gas tanks," Bad Nelson said. "It looks like we have a plan and it's shaping up."

"We know how to get underground at After Dark," Mad Maggie said. "There's a secret door in the ground in the lot next to the bar. That's how we escaped with New Girl."

"That's how I was drug out to the street," Bad Nelson said. "I know where it is."

"I can draw you a map of the underground lair," Overboard George said. "I had some skill at drawing and maybe two weeks to look the place over from that tiny cell where they kept me. Mad Maggie and I know where the trip is for the lights that burn the vampires and Whistlers. Ultraviolet. Just as good as the sun's rays. We know it works. We used it on them already. That's how we got away."

"That's great, George," Bad Nelson said. "The rest of us, the ones who want to carry stake guns, will have to get in some practice over the next couple of days. Then we'll hit them hard during the day while they're weak."

"Get them in their pajamas, if they wear any," Old Harriet howled.

"While they're in their graves," Mad Maggie said. "That's where you want to get them. In their coffins. Asleep. And I'll need a new knife. A big sharp one. I plan to operate before they sizzle to nothing."

CHAPTER THIRTY-TWO

Bo Bentwood sat on a bench in the park near the obelisk from which he had spied on the Whispers and watched them take a young woman, Benjamin the bouncer's junkie ex-girlfriend. He had no particular reason for sitting at that spot. His sore muscles and ribs had healed after the night the Whistlers chased him. This part of the park had few benches and for the time was clear of junkies, although there was a dipper on the path going downhill. The dipper was so far away Bo couldn't tell if the person was a man or woman, facing away from him, bent at the waist, knuckles dragging the ground. Since TJ and Ridge disappeared, his days were spent alone with no purpose. He had not chased junkies in the park with the kayak paddle since the night TJ and Ridge were lost. The paddle rested in the Charger trunk. The more he saw the homeless, especially during the day, the more compassion he felt for them. After all, they were just people. His friends' parents texted Bo regularly, asking for news about their sons, assuming Bo communicated with the police and continued to look for them on his own. They were eager for any new information. However, Bo knew his friends' fates, and searching for them was useless. The stack of flyers they had given him to pass out, along with a new staple gun and a full box of staples, remained untouched in his room at the frat house.

Bo spent most of his time on the bench with head lowered, avoiding contact with anyone who walked by. He planned to move when the sun hit the bench. The heat would become intolerable. He heard a familiar hack. Charles Van der Meer walked up the path, coughing occasionally. Bo watched Charles pass. Charles paid no attention to Bo as he continued along the asphalt path in a slow gait. Bo watched the man's progress and noted his neatly trimmed hair and clean-looking clothes.

Suddenly, Bo stood and followed Charles. Bo didn't understand why he trailed the man or what he was going to do. He felt compelled to make contact. When he drew within a few feet, Charles seemed not to notice Bo's approach. "Sir. Excuse me, sir," Bo called.

Charles ignored Bo as if there were other people nearby he might be hailing.

Bo called again and Charles still ignored him. In fact, the man quickened his pace. So did Bo. Finally, Bo touched Charles's shoulder. Charles spun around. "What do you want?" Charles said. Then he coughed violently for a while, so hard it sounded like a bark.

"Sorry," Bo said.

"I don't know you," Charles said after he got the coughing under control and spit close enough to Bo's shoe that he jumped back a step.

"I know you don't, but I know you...in a way."

"What makes you think that?" Charles said nervously. "I don't got any money." He turned to walk away. "Leave me alone."

"I know you're involved with the Whistlers. At the very least, you clean up after them."

"You're crazy, kid." Charles took a step and sneered. "What's a Whistler?"

"You took my camera. I watched you. Followed you."

Charles stopped and turned around. "What do you think you recorded in the park? Where were you hidden? In the bushes?" Charles jerked his thumb over his shoulder in the obelisk's direction.

"I recorded plenty. The Whistlers exist. The junkies don't lie. They're not crazy."

"Maybe you're the crazy one," Charles said, raising his eyebrow at the young man.

"I saw the Whistlers take a young girl, a dipper, on the path. I watched the creatures as they moved in one solid mass. I recorded her disappear inside among their bodies. They held her so tight she couldn't escape or even scream. I don't think a strong man could escape from them. *You* took my memory card and the evidence I had. You came by the next day, retraced their path with your poop bag. You found my camera."

"Go to the police. Tell your story to them. You look like a credible young man." Charles grinned.

"The police wouldn't believe me. The last thing I want to do is get mixed up with the police," Bo said. "If you know what I mean."

"I understand," Charles answered, nodding his head. "I avoid the police, too." Charles stuck out his chin at Bo.

"I'd like to know more about the Whistlers," Bo said. "Can you tell me? I imagine any story would be so fantastic no one would believe me." Bo smiled.

Charles looked around, furtively. Coughed his dry, rasping hack. He spit again. "Your story is fantastic. I've never picked up a camera or carried a *poop bag* through the park. I don't own a dog. I'm vigilant for panhandlers and thieves when I walk, careful about my surroundings, and I don't remember seeing you. And I certainly never saw a *Whistler*. I don't go to the park at night. It's not safe. Some of the junkies are bad. Criminals."

"I was walking behind you as you passed the obelisk," Bo said. His voice rose. "I watched you pick up my camera."

"What do you want from me?" Charles snapped. "I don't have money. I don't have your camera."

"I don't want money. I want information about the Whistlers. What they are. How they work. I think you know all about them."

Charles stared and breathed heavily. "Again, I don't know what you're talking about. Leave me alone." He turned again to leave.

Bo caught his arm. "The Whistlers chased me through the park. One got impaled on the gates at the entrance. That one died. Another banged into my car and was injured. My car was damaged. The bouncer at After Dark said he killed one in the restaurant parking lot that was already wounded. Even without camera proof, I know what I saw."

Charles stopped and turned around. He looked defeated like he wanted to retreat but saw no direction to go. "Let's sit on the bench. I need to rest."

Bo and Charles returned to the bench and sat. Charles hacked and spit. Eventually, he was silent. Finally, Charles talked, ever furtive, about their surroundings, and who might be close enough to hear. Charles unfolded a story that started with his wife's death, his road to alcoholism, an unnamed daughter, and many regrets. At times, tears filled his eyes.

Charles said, "I was a fighter, especially when I was drunk. Had trouble with the police and moved around a lot. Always knew when to get out of town. Sometimes in a hurry, whether it was by bus, train, or even my good old thumb. One night, I was in a seedy little bar and picked a fight with a vampire who was hunting. He moved closer and closer to me. Eventually, it was too close. Of course, I didn't know he was a vampire. He kept smiling at me. That made me madder. I won't tolerate a man on a man." Charles laughed a moment and spit. "The fight moved outside and the vampire pummeled me. Gave me the worst beating of my life.

"It was in a heap like Beetle Bailey from the comics. It was cold, so the crowd went back inside and left me on the sidewalk. I even pissed myself. The vampire took me back to his lair. I woke up in a cell, bruised and sore, with a terrible headache. At some point, the vampire returned and thanked me for the best fight he had in years from a human. That's when he told me he was a vampire and was going to drain my blood as soon as it was free of alcohol."

Charles smiled as if recalling the incident years ago. He cleared his throat and continued. "The vampire expected a reaction. Wanted one. From my experience now, most people scream and fight when they know a vampire is going to drain them. But I told him I was ready. My life was wasted and had no more meaning. I think that surprised him, because when I recovered they didn't drink my blood, but introduced me to what you call the Whistlers. We call them the *Travelers*. They're deformed vampires. Ones that didn't turn correctly. They stayed permanently between man and vampire, I suppose because the process got interrupted."

"Retarded vampires?"

"You could say that. The vampire colony was large. Between the Whistlers and the vampires themselves, they kept the cells full. There was lots of blood. The vampire I fought took a liking to me. I can't explain why. Was it because I got a few licks in our fight? Broke his nose for about a minute until it healed by itself? Did I remind him of someone? Who knows? Maybe because I didn't show any fear. He kept the other fiends away from me. He had status in the vampire colony. He wanted me to care for his crypt. The smell was nauseating, but eventually, I got used to it. Next, I took care of the Whistlers and hunted with them. There were more of them then, and I was in better shape. I could keep them in line."

"I don't know how you did it," Bo said.

Charles smiled. "I did. I was able. Eventually, the vampires figured their colony was too big. Too many people disappeared off the street. Regular people. Not just the homeless. The police were investigating. And there was a secret group hunting us, called the Brethren, well-armed, well organized, and well-funded. They killed some of the vampires. The vampires got really cautious. The masters decided to move some of the vampires to other cities, other colonies. I was placed in charge of the move here because the vampires were virtually powerless during the day. A brother and sister vampire team said they would go on their own, take the Whistlers. That's how we all got involved."

"That's too amazing."

"It is amazing," Charles said. He was silent for a moment and continued. "Originally, we had four vampires and eight Whistlers. Two vampires were caught outside at dawn and died. It was a terrible mistake. Their mistake. Not mine. They were new vampires. No experience living as the undead. The Whistlers have dwindled to four. They will kill and eat their own when one is injured and can no longer hunt while they recover. As you said, one Whistler was impaled on the park gate. The bouncer killed another who was injured. Probably the one that ran into your car. Over the years, others have been hit by cars, etc., and consumed by more dominant ones. There is no remorse, no sentiment, among them, among any of the undead."

Charles, who had directed his words down, looked up and directly at Bo. "Now I am to become one of the vampires. I have lung cancer and not much time left. Once turned, I would regain my strength, be stronger than ever, and live through the ages. Never cough again. Imagine that. Never cough again. The masters said they would turn me for my service, but I had to find a replacement for myself."

"Do you have one?" Bo interrupted.

"No. I believe my time is short. I am weaker all the time. Cough more. I must find a replacement soon." Charles raised his hands and dropped them in his lap. "But who?"

"Why not me?" Bo looked into the man's eyes.

"You!"

"I know you all exist. I already knew about the Whistlers. You've filled in the rest." Bo now had a way to wreak vengeance on the vampires for killing his friends. He would have to be careful. Wait for his chance.

"It's not an easy life," Charles said.

"What life is easy? Mine never was."

"You are at the beck-and-call of the vampires. Their needs go before all others. You must ensure they have humans to drain. These two vampires were part of the nobility. Never lifted a finger. Like to be served. When they and our friends are finished with a victim, you must get rid of what's left of the corpse. You must clean the basement. Feed the captives. Carry away their waste. Show no remorse for them. They will cry and plead to be set free. Scream until it hurts your ears. Call for their mothers, fathers, children, loved ones, even God. You will be an accessory to many murders."

"I worked in a hospital when I was in high school," Bo lied. "As an orderly. Did all kinds of things. Empty bedpans. Strip shitty linen off beds. I've even delivered bodies to the hospital morgue. Some were quite ripe. Smelled right through the body bags. As far as a life, I have none. I hate people. All people, especially druggies. I want to disappear from the face of the earth. I want to imagine myself dead to the world."

Charles stared at Bo.

"Have you heard of the Beaters?" Bo asked.

"I have. The homeless talk about them. Coming at night, beating them, sometimes into unconsciousness. Just for the fun of it."

"I organized it. Always had two of my friends along," Bo said. "I used a kayak paddle, which did more damage. The paddle's in my car trunk. I can show you blood on it. My friends used switches. I have no love for the homeless. We found a dead junkie in the park here one night. I beat her anyway. Split her face open. It was just as much fun."

Charles wiped his palm across his face. And looked back at Bo. "You can't tell anyone what we talked about. If you do, the vampires will kill us both. Not just drain us dry, but horribly. They torture victims when they're angry. Medieval torture. Hot brands. They pull them apart. I've seen them do it. The pain is incredible.

That's how they keep the normal, like me, in place. They can be kind, as long as you do what you're told. At some point, they would grab someone to torture just to show you what it's like. So, you're warned."

"I'm willing," Bo said. "I could devote myself to them. Be their slave. It would be better than my life now. Who knows? Maybe someday they will turn me. Maybe you can turn me."

Charles cocked his head. Bo could see the man was thinking. "You would be young. Computer savvy. See things I don't. You might be better able to protect them."

"And you."

"And me." Charles smiled. "I'll have to think about it. Can we meet again?"

"Of course." Bo smiled. "How about this bench. You name the time."

CHAPTER THIRTY-THREE

It was dark. Charles Van der Meer watched the latest victim in his cage under After Dark. The man had been in rehab but was already using again when he was taken two days ago. He was ready to be consumed. After cleaning the man, the new victim shivered on the floor, curled in a ball. The concrete floor had been hosed down. Puke and excrement were washed down the drains, and the basement retained a damp smell. Charles coiled the hose for storage. The consuming room had been cleaned and was ready for use. The vampires were hungry. Charles knew their ways. Even though they slept in graves and wore threadbare clothing, they liked the basement clean. Since the woman died hanging upside down in the consuming room, just before the vampires were ready to feed, Charles was more cautious about his captives' conditions. He did not want to raise the creatures' ire when he was so close to being turned.

Then he heard the secret door to the vampire crypt open. Charles was still nervous when his masters approached, even after all these years of caring for them. He fought a shiver when he felt their approach. Charles smelled the couple and the stench of their graves before they appeared from the basement's unfinished end. The vampires made their slow, stately walk from their crypt to inspect their latest meal. Charles heard their dark tongues spinning against their lips.

"He's a big man," Gerrard said in English as he approached the cages with the female. He and Eva looked at each other and smiled, showing their black teeth. "He has lots of blood. We need a good feed after our recent famine. There will be plenty, even for our friends, who are still not recovered. I would imagine they struggled with this one. That he almost escaped, now that only four remain."

"He is strong and slipped his head from their embrace," Charles said. "He filled his lungs to call for help, but I hit him in the face and pushed his head back among their bodies. The beasts reattached themselves to him. You can see the punctures their claws made. I made sure he didn't lose much blood. He's been quiet since that one outbreak. I just finished cleaning him."

"You have done well, Charles, in selecting this man," Eva said, her hollow voice filling the chamber. She smiled at Charles.

"Will he be missed?" Eva asked.

"No, Madam. He won't be missed. I've already inquired. He must be new to the area. He might have come looking for drugs."

The female nodded with satisfaction.

"Your reward is near. Have you selected your successor?" Gerrard said.

"Yes, sir. His name is Bo Bentwood. I had him through the basement while you slept. He will join me the next time we hunt. I presented him with the same contract I received when I was entrusted with your care. He understands and accepts everything. He is young and should serve us for many years."

"Excellent," the dead couple chimed.

"Thank you, Masters," Charles said, bowing.

The male vampire looked at Charles. "When you say Bo understands and accepts everything that accompanies the job, does he understand humans are cattle to us? That the ones he brings in are doomed?"

"He understands. He has no love for the homeless and he especially hates drug users. He has no problem watching them suffer while their blood cleans."

"What about clean bloods?" Eva asked. "You know how we enjoy them."

"Bo is a student at the university. He is from another state. He told me he has no friends in the city and intends to drop out of school. He intends to drop out of sight. Become invisible."

"Then he has found the right job," Eva said. She patted Charles's cheek.

"Before we turn you, I would like to see these cages filled," Gerrard said. "Even though we have only four friends left, you will need sustenance from the start. We can't expect Bo Bentwood to be as skillful a hunter at the start as you are."

"Masters, I don't know what I think about drinking blood," Charles blurted, lowering his head to the two vampires. "If I had to drink blood *now*, I don't know if I could do it. It seems..."

"How do they say it," the vampiress said slowly, "Repulsive?"

"I don't know what to call it," Charles said, regaining his composure. "It seems so different. So difficult to imagine at *this* moment."

Eva threw back her head and laughed. She stepped close to Charles and cupped his cheek with her palm. Charles felt the cold, the clamminess of her touch. Her flesh so close to his nose smelled of the grave. She ran her long-nailed fingers across the top of his head, through his thick hair.

"Oh, Charles, we must warn you," Eva said. "When you are turned there will be pain, not ecstasy as in the movies. I will turn you in our crypt. We will give you a casket. I will drink your blood, and you will drink my blood. The process will kill you. My blood will poison you. It will be a painful death. Soon, however, you will rise. While you are dead my blood will change your very cells, your brain, your mind. The disease in my blood that holds vampires, that gives them longevity, will consume you. There is no cure. The disease will preserve you forever, or until a human destroys what remains of your dead heart. You will spend several days in a cocoon while the change occurs, while the disease infuses your body and mind."

Charles swallowed and suppressed a cough. He grimaced.

Eva continued without noticing. "You will wake with an unquenchable thirst for blood. That blood keeps the disease alive. It will be amazing. The excitement is thrilling. The thirst you experience will be a hundredfold the craving you had for alcohol. With all your heightened sensations, the smell and taste of blood will be more than you can imagine. You will never be able to get enough. Blood will intoxicate you. Your squeamishness now will seem foolish." She stopped a moment to look at the ceiling. She smiled. "You will laugh as you drain life after life through the endless years, always in the chase to quench that unslakable thirst for hot, fresh blood. Nothing will affect you. You will be immune to hot and cold, sickness. The vampire disease that consumes your being will keep you young and allow you to serve it. It doesn't think as we think. Make plans. It is not—what is the word—sentient. It will do anything to preserve itself."

Charles smiled. "I look forward to that date."

"The sooner Bo is trained, the sooner we can turn you," Gerrard said.

"Masters, do you want to meet him before the training starts?" Charles said.

"We will meet him after he hunts with our friends," Gerrard said. "You must be sure he is capable of this job. Although it is easy for the dead to kill the living, it is not always easy for the living to kill the living."

"I have talked with him at length several times," Charles said. "I believe that although he does not have an addiction problem, he is at a place in life where I was when you took me in. He needs something. A way of life—or death—we can provide."

With tenderness, Eva said, "Yes, Charles, I understand. You were a lost soul when you came to us. It sounds like Bo Bentwood is a lost soul, too."

CHAPTER THIRTY-FOUR

Even the homeless had cell phones, mostly monthly plans they bought minutes for when they had money. Minutes carried over month to month and could be saved. Cell phones were essential to keep in touch with family, which happened rarely. They were more important for reaching out to their drug dealers to coordinate buys. With this network of phones, the vampire hunters arranged to take the cars of Bad Nelson's parents, Lisa, and Jimmy for an excursion to the game lands outside the city to practice shooting the new stake guns. Bad Nelson had made another stake gun and added more wooden stakes to the arsenal. He hoped his mother wouldn't notice the charges he made on her card. Bad Nelson bought a new deer target and chopped off its legs, to make it resemble a whistler in size.

The vampire-hunting team included Overboard George and Mad Maggie, Bad Nelson and Megan. Lisa and Jimmy did not want to carry stake guns but went in the hope they could prevent anyone from being shot accidentally. Old Harriet went for the ride. Mad Maggie opted out of carrying a gun but procured at a pawn shop a machete and a long jungle knife with a serrated blade. Overboard George sharpened both blades. Etches in the machete handle represented kills, Mad Maggie claimed, so the pawn shop owner had told her with glee and a knowing wink.

In addition, New Girl resurfaced. She had traded in her toga and ill-fitting garish running shoes for clothes and sneakers from a shelter. Petite and now sporting purple hair, she blended into any crowd, almost. Although she and Old Harriet were still using, they vowed to be clean for the attack on the vampire den, no matter how strong the urges were to shoot up. In addition to their assortment of weapons, Old Harriet insisted they take her chair on wheels, which was strapped to the roof of Jimmy's car. She didn't want it stolen while she was gone and needed a place to perch. She still looked for larger wheels to make the chair navigate better. Overboard George had drawn plans to replace the small wheels.

After they reached the game lands parking lot, the vampire hunters carried the guns, stakes, and other equipment to the edge of the woods, where they could shoot but remain hidden from the road. They weren't worried by the noise the guns would make because each shot was accompanied by a not-so-loud *wump* as the gas in the ignition chamber exploded. When pressed about what weapons they would carry, Jimmy said he would get a wooden harpoon. Lisa said she would do the same. Within minutes Mad Maggie cut down two remarkably straight saplings with her machete. She and Overboard George stripped off the leaves and cut sharp points on both ends. In the end, all agreed it was a shame to kill two beautiful trees, but they might be needed to decimate the vampires. They had to be prepared for anything.

"Your harpoons have a nice weight and balance to them," Overboard George said. "Good for thrusting or throwing." He demonstrated thrusting, stabbing the air while keeping the back ends low, before slinging them some twenty yards, where the points stuck in the ground. "The thing is if you throw one you lose your weapon. Better throw it only as a last resort. It's better if you thrust." Overboard demonstrated again. "Keep the back end low. Stab uphill.

Aim for the heart." Then George coached Jimmy and Lisa on the harpoon's use. Lisa's staff was shorter than Jimmy's. Both soon became proficient at pivoting, striking with one end and with the other, stabbing imaginary foes as Overboard George had instructed, but neither could throw the weapons far or accurately.

"To be honest, we hope we don't need these harpoons," Overboard George said. "If we need them the fight will be more up close and personal than I'd like it to be. I thought you two would be more like reinforcements, ready to bring us more darts or gas. Just remember, if you use them harpoons picture their dead hearts on their chests and aim for that."

"I like that plan," Jimmy said. "We'll be where we can see everything."

Overboard George smiled.

After seeing the harpoons in action, Old Harriet insisted on having her own to defend her sweet box, and she soon had one. She danced around the clearing, whooping, and stabbing at the air. "Want my sweet box?" she howled with delight. "Take this and this and this!"

Old Harriet soon became winded and settled down. She never noticed her harpoon had blunt ends. She climbed on her chair, but its small wheels sank into the thick pine-needle floor and toppled, spilling her to the ground. Once the deer target was assembled, however, she wanted to stab "the creature," but Overboard George wouldn't let her, threatening to take back his sweet box if she didn't behave.

Meanwhile, Bad Nelson laid out his tarp in the shade of pine trees and arranged the stake guns and their projectiles. The vampire hunters crowded around the tarp to inspect the weapons and their sharp missiles. Just then a loud car, unseen but heard by the group, flew into the parking lot and slid to a stop on the gravel. Bo Bentwood exited his Charger and followed the trail of many feet through the high grass. Soon he stood before the group. Old Harriet ran to his side.

"This is..." Old Harriet thought a moment but seemed to lose her words.

"Bo Bentwood," Bo said. "I think we all know there are vampires in the city. I know I do."

The vampire hunters, except for Lisa and Jimmy, nodded their heads in agreement and seemed to relax. They gathered around Bo and shook hands. Bo and Lisa recognized each other from After Dark and traded awkward stares for a moment.

"I see you got my text," Old Harriet told Bo. She smiled.

Bo nodded and told the group, "Old Harriet invited me. She said I might be interested in a way to kill the Whistlers and the vampires."

"We have all we need," Bad Nelson said. "They're lined up there," he added, pointing to the stake guns.

Bo walked to the tarp where the weapons were organized. "They look like smaller versions of potato guns," Bo said. "My friends and I made one years ago. Ours was pretty crude, but we had to stop before we got into trouble. Destroyed too many things."

"I know what you mean," Bad Nelson said, smiling.

"Our plan is to ambush the bastards in their underground lair, in the daylight, where we can corner them," Overboard George said. "They'll be powerless anyway."

"You can't believe everything you read in *Famous Monsters of Filmland*," Jimmy said. "If there are vampires, we don't know what we're up against."

"We know all about vampires," Mad Maggie said, defensively. "Everything we need to know."

Everyone looked at Jimmy in disbelief. Lisa turned to him and took his hand. "I think we should get to the bottom of this before we organize any attack," Lisa said to the vampire hunters. "These stake guns seem like they're lethal. What if we hurt a real person?"

"I've seen the Whistlers take a girl in the park," Bo said. "I know they're real. They almost got me, too."

"Ever shoot a gun?" Bad Nelson said.

"A few times," Bo answered quickly.

"That's good. It's more than most of them here."

"I'd rather get a .357 Magnum," Bo said, "instead of one of these homemade guns."

"A .357 Magnum is like shooting a rubber band at a vampire, despite its power. You need a wooden stake to kill one," Overboard George said.

Bad Nelson picked up a stake gun and started the training. He began with some basic safety. "You don't want to shoot one of us," Bad Nelson said. "Never, never, never point one of these in another person's direction, unless you intend to shoot him. Wait until your target stops."

"Don't try to shoot a moving vampire," Overboard George interrupted. "They move so fast all you see is a blur. That's when you'll kill one of us, swinging a stake gun all around."

Bad Nelson demonstrated by waving the gun back and forth. "Make your shots count. These guns aren't automatic. They're single shots and it takes a few seconds to load a new stake and prime the propane gas in the combustion chamber. Don't pull the trigger before you get the stake fully seated inside the rubber gasket and add the wadding, or you'll shoot a stake through your hand. Maybe take off a couple of fingers."

Mad Maggie inspected her hand. She touched her thumb to the other digits.

Bad Nelson sweated but seemed to enjoy his job as an instructor. He explained each part of the stake guns. How to load them and fill the combustion chambers with gas. How to ignite the gas with the triggers. How to change gas tanks. Most importantly, he explained how to aim the weapons. Each of the group took a turn shooting at the deer target. All the shots were taken at close range. There would be no long shots in After Dark's basement and no need to elevate the rifles. Point and shoot. The deer target was reduced to a mound of foam pieces after everyone had one shot. New Girl and Overboard George were especially adroit at loading and firing the stake guns. After a couple of tries, the fleet-footed New Girl's small hands could load, change a propane tank, and prime a gun as fast as Bad Nelson. Even Lisa and Jimmy reluctantly took turns loading and shooting the guns. Just in case. They seemed to cautiously enjoy it. Old Harriet howled after she took a shot, heard the slight thump of the blast, and felt the small recoil. Mad Maggie shot, too, but still maintained she would carry only the machete and jungle knife.

Eventually, the group moved their armory to a corner of the tarp and sat to eat lunch. It was shady and sweet smelling among the trees, quite different from the city. The breeze moved the branches overhead and made a comforting noise. Occasionally, pine needles fell to the ground. Not everyone could fit on the tarp. Some settled on the thick carpet of pine needles. Bo dropped beside Lisa. Jimmy passed out water bottles and sandwiches. Lisa had crept into After Dark early before Bart arrived and Pete stirred from his closet. She avoided the CCTV cameras and made food for the group. If he noticed, Jose the cook wouldn't say anything about missing food.

"You worked at After Dark," Bo said to Lisa. "I haven't seen you for a while. You still there?"

"My hours were changed to the early shift," Lisa said after swallowing a bite of hersandwich. "Megan works there now, too." Lisa pointed to Megan where she sat close to Bad Nelson, sharing a story, heads together.

"Good food," Bo said. He chewed slowly, methodically, as if trying to think of something else to say.

"Excellent roast beef," Mad Maggie said, between lip smacks. "It'd be better with a little au jus."

Lisa frowned. "Sorry. I didn't have the time."

"I remember seeing *you* when I worked nights," Lisa said. "You were usually with two other guys. One guy was cute and had red hair."

"You think *he* was cute?"

278

"I do."

Bo twisted his lips and looked toward

Jimmy stood patiently while Mad Maggie showed him the notches in her machete handle.

Old Harriet had righted her chair on firmer ground and perched on it. She held her sandwich with two hands.

"The Whistlers took my friends, including TJ the redhead. I didn't see them taken, but I know the Whistlers got them. My friends disappeared. Never showed up again. I know they're dead."

"I'm sorry," Lisa said.

"Yeah. Me, too. They were good guys. I miss them."

"I'd say we're just about ready, vampire hunters," Bad Nelson announced from his seat in the pine needles. "Everyone did very well. Better than I expected. I think we should have another practice session, then we'll move as soon as we figure out how to get those doors open in the field. I've tried them several times. Once they were open. Twice they were locked. It's the only way in or out, as far as I know. The other entrance is from inside the restaurant. That won't work. We can't parade through the dining room with our guns to make the attack."

"We can't attack unless we know the door is open," Overboard George said. "Mad Maggie and I know where the door is, too, but we always found it locked. We can't carry these guns around the city day after day until we find the door open. We're bound to be seen and turned over to the cops. And there are no safe places to hide them. Hell, Bad Nelson and me made a map of the interior. Very detailed. Made copies, but the map ain't any good unless we have a way in."

Mad Maggie said, "If you want my opinion, we should stop sharpening stakes and start making torches." Maggie stood from her corner of the tarp and addressed the group. "Screw the police. Just like in the movie *Frankenstein*, we should organize the homeless, give everybody a torch, and march on After Dark. Burn it to the ground like the villagers did the windmill. After the blaze is roaring, we'll fling the torches and disappear in the crowd. Nothing gathers a crowd like a good fire. The vampires will burn to a crisp. We won't need Bad Nelson's stake guns. Let the blood they stole from the living boil in their veins, vaporize into the sky." She raised her hands over her head and wiggled her fingers.

Everyone was quiet a moment as if thinking about Mad Maggie's proposal.

"You have a point, Mad Maggie," Overboard George said. "None of us will have to worry about not surviving the ordeal. I hope you all understand there's a chance some of us won't survive."

"I see only one problem," Jimmy said. After a pause to get everyone's attention, he added, "After Dark is brick. We'll never catch it on fire with torches."

"We'll soak the place in gasoline," New Girl said, raising a fist in the air. "You know how to make any bombs, Bad Nelson?"

Bad Nelson shook his head. He seemed dejected as if their attack plan was heading nowhere.

"How about the natural gas for the water heaters, the ovens, the grill?" Megan shouted. "We can blow the place up from the inside, bricks and all. Bury the bastards so deep they'll never claw their way out."

Smiles appeared on some faces. Jimmy shook his head. "What about the people inside? People eating. Waitresses. Office workers upstairs. An explosion could burn down a city block. What if a fire spread across the street to the stadium?"

"We'd be fucked," Mad Maggie pronounced slowly. Then she smiled. "But only if we get caught."

Bo stood. "I thought you had solved getting inside After Dark. I took it for granted. It would have been the first thing *I* would do. I know, or I *will know* how to get inside from the field."

"Go on," Overboard George said. "Let's hear your idea."

Bad Nelson and Megan perked up.

"What Old Harriet doesn't know, which developed since I first talked to her, is that the vampires have plans to turn the man who takes care of them. He has lung cancer and needs to change soon—into a vampire—or he will die."

Lisa dropped her harpoon.

"*He* controls the Whistlers, hunts them in the park to collect victims for the vampires," Bo said. "It's a perfect setup. The homeless disappear. No one knows where they go. They might enter rehab or a shelter, or even move away. Go with a family member. Or die from disease or an overdose. In a little while they're forgotten because the people they knew overdose or move away. Then they're gone, too. It's like the ones taken never really existed."

"You're very caring, Bo," Old Harriet said. "I'm glad you came today."

"Actually, I wasn't that caring until recently, until I lost my friends and saw what grief it caused their families," Bo said. Then he added, grinding his teeth, "Now I just want to get even."

"Bo, do you know the man who takes care of the vampires?" Lisa asked.

"I do. He plans to train me to take his place."

"How?"

"It's too long a story to tell now," Bo said.

"Do you know his name?"

"I only know his first name. It's Charles."

Lisa collapsed.

Bo reached for Lisa, but Jimmy was already at her side. Bo looked incredulous.

"Lisa's father is named Charles and he has lung cancer," Jimmy said.

Lisa buried her head in Jimmy's shoulder and sobbed. "No wonder he wanted me to leave the city. He warned me about vampires. I thought he was crazy. How can this get any worse?"

The vampire fighters crowded around Lisa to comfort her. They stroked her hair. Rubbed her back. Bo Bentwood cried.

"Once the undead claim him, he won't be your father," Mad

Maggie said. "He would drain you the same way a kid downs a milkshake. A quote, I believe, from *Famous Monsters of Filmland*."

Overboard George nodded.

After everyone recovered, Bad Nelson said, "So what's your plan, Bo?"

"They want me to hunt tonight. With the Whistlers and... Charles. I'll try to make sure we don't get anyone and ruin the hunt. Then I'm supposed to get another tour of the basement. Learn how to lock and unlock the secret door outside. My plan all along was to get inside and fight the vampires alone. Kill them one by one, in their coffins. Your plan with more fighters improves the good guys' odds."

Jimmy cradled Lisa in his arms. "I don't know whether there are any good guys here."

CHAPTER THIRTY-FIVE

It was 6:30 p.m. Bo Bentwood sat on the bench near the obelisk, waiting for Charles Van der Meer. He drank from a water bottle Jimmy gave him earlier that afternoon when they shot Bad Nelson's stake guns in the game lands. It was hotter downtown in the park than in the forest. Now the humidity was intolerable. He sweated sitting on the bench. Ridge had been a sweater too—even in the winter. Ridge rarely wore anything long-sleeved. Never wore a hat or heavy coat, not even on the coldest days. He had laughed at Bo's gloves, scarf, and fur hat with ear flaps.

What he wouldn't give for a nice cold day, one when his breath was visible and his nose ran. He thought about that fur cap, a gift from his parents at Christmas when he was a freshman. He lost the hat at the first college party he attended after Christmas break. Someone stole it, he believed, and although he looked around campus for weeks, checking around him the bobbing heads of students on their way to classes, he never saw the hat again and bought a stocking cap he could stuff in a coat pocket. Bo thought he might like to skin a whistler with Mad Maggie's jungle knife to make a new fur hat complete with ear flaps. The fur would be warm but perhaps too stiff to be comfortable. And what about the smell? Would it be possible to rid the fur of that fetid odor he smelled when the Whistlers were on the hunt? He might have to take the fur to a taxidermist, one who could sew him a new hat. He'd have both a trophy, a warm cap, and one hell of a story.

Bo was distracted by his thoughts. He didn't notice a dipper twenty feet away on the asphalt path who had pulled down his jeans and defecated into his pants. Nor did he notice a couple filming a documentary about the homeless. Down the path a trio of men huddled on the ground, their needles ready, to syphon dope from a spoon heated over a cigarette lighter flame. All three smiled and were expectant, waiting for the crystals to transform from solid to liquid. Simple, potentially deadly chemistry.

Suddenly, Charles was in front of Bo, looking down, watching him intently. "You ready, Bo?"

"All set." Bo tried to smile but he imagined his lips held a grimace.

Charles checked his surroundings, ever vigilant. "You must be careful. Always. Never let your guard down. You can't tell who might be watching, following. Like I said, there's a very organized group of vampire hunters. I haven't noted any here, now, but I imagine they are spread out across the country. If they got the chance, they'd kill you or me just as soon as a vampire."

"I think you're paranoid," Bo said. He stared at the man he now knew was Lisa's father. He saw the resemblance. Of course. Lisa looked like her dad. The same nose. The same eyes. He had been handsome. She was beautiful.

"Listen, this summer four people escaped from After Dark. It was my fault. I was weak. After they were gone, I expected the police to arrive with warrants, but nothing ever happened. Probably no one believed their stories. They might all be dead from overdoses. Maybe they were scared straight and moved to another city. I'm always watching for them. I imagine they follow me. What I wouldn't do to get those four back in the basement after I change, after I'm strong. Invincible. I'd throw the big black man in a cell. Keep him for the masters. There's lots of blood in him. The others I'd tear apart. Drink their blood until I couldn't hold any more. I'm realistic, though. Seeing those four back in the basement will never happen. Never. It's just a dream I have."

Bo stood and faced Charles. Even stooped, Charles was slightly taller. "I thought I'd give you another tour of the facilities, first," Charles said. We must wait until the sun goes down to take out our friends. To hunt. They will be excited. They're recovered and strong again."

"Why didn't we meet at the park entrance? Then we wouldn't have such a long walk in this heat," Bo complained.

Charles smiled. "Don't like the heat?"

"I don't like this humidity."

"The walk will let me explain things you will see when we get downstairs," Charles said. "The lock on the exit door in the lot, the lock for the masters' crypt. It will help you remember them. Hear first, see later. That's how I learned." Charles stopped and turned to Bo. "You make a serious mistake with the vampires and they will kill you in a second. Drain you dry. They don't tolerate much."

"I understand," Bo said.

They continued down the path. The single dipper had revived and was gone, including his pants full of shit. Of the junkie trio, two dipped. The third might have managed to walk away and could be dipping or on the ground behind a bush.

Charles and Bo continued down the asphalt path. "The walk lets you see if anyone is trying to follow," Charles said. "The shortest path isn't always the best. Keep your eyes open."

They walked silently for a while. Charles coughed and cleared his throat. "I like to get a view of the park before a hunt," Charles said, finally. "See how many people are around. Look for some likely candidates, although the numbers can change in a minute, especially if there's a game. You might like a certain target, an easy mark, you think, only to find it's gone when you return later with our friends. When that happens, I let it go. Think that's one that got away for another night. You'd never find him or her. Never know in what direction they went. The other thing is, now that there are only four of our friends, it's better to target smaller, weaker people. But, once the beasts get going, they pretty much pick their own prey. You can't decide for them."

All the talking winded Charles. He coughed and cleared his throat. Charles stopped again and faced Bo. "The other thing you must do, regardless of whether you're a baseball fan, is to learn the schedule. Know when the team is on the road or at home. Know what time the games start. Check what the weather forecast is. That way you can predict crowds, even possible rain delays. Know what time to release our friends. You don't want them hunting when there are mobs of people around. You can't let them be seen, although they're pretty good about hiding, blending in. It seems natural to them."

They continued along the path, and Charles detailed the many requirements that would be part of Bo's new job. "If you ever have a question, don't hesitate to ask *me*. Even after I am changed. *Never* ask the masters if you are unsure of something. It makes you and *me* look bad as if I didn't train you well. Or you were too stupid to learn. Understand?"

Bo nodded.

"The masters were intelligent people in their old lives. Nobility. They look down on the common man. They don't tolerate stupidity." Charles continued his instruction. Eventually, they neared the park entrance.

Bo saw the stone columns from which the iron gates hung topped with their pointed shafts. Bo said, "Doesn't it bother you? Taking people from the park to be killed. These people are somebody's kids. Somebody's mother or father. Some of the homeless are old enough to be grandparents."

Charles motioned for Bo to follow him to an empty bench, where they sat. "There was a time in that other place before we came to this city, it bothered me watching the people we took to die. Then I saw the lives the junkies led. The way they lied and stole. Eventually, I didn't see them as people. It became shopping for groceries, although the clean bloods give me a twinge from time to time. Even now. After all, you would think they have some kind of meaningful life. A kid might be waiting for them to come home. Not be able to understand why they don't come back."

All the time he talked Charles surveyed the surroundings, craned his neck to look this way and that. He continued. "The vampires pay me well. They will pay you well. I could have a Mercedes Benz, if I wanted one, a big one, too, if I had a driver's license. The man I replaced retired when he got too old to care for the colony. After he trained me, he took the wealth he accumulated and moved to Florida. Took up golf. As far as I know, never contacted the vampires again. Why would he? It was like retiring from a job. One day you are there, and the next day you are gone. I intended to retire someday, too. Get away from this city and all its stink. Far away. Never look back. Go somewhere near the water. The ocean, where there's a boardwalk to walk and sit and smell the salt air. I like the salt air. In the back of my mind, there was a hope that, if I could find her, Lisa and I could..." He stopped.

"But you got sick," Bo said.

"I got sick." Charles lowered his eyes. "Retirement was no longer an option. I had been loyal to the colony. Made the long move here. Everyone survived. Even all our friends made the trip."

"So now..."

"The vampires are rewarding me. Turning me into one of them. I can stay with them, move to another colony I like that might have an opening, or go off on my own. Some vampires like that—being on their own. Responsible for only themselves. One thing is paramount. Defend your colony at all costs. It is part of the vampire code."

"You could still...*live* near the salt water."

"Yes. It might take years to get set up near the ocean, but time will have no meaning."

This time Bo managed what he thought was a genuine-looking smile, but he suspected Charles would not live to be turned. Not survive the ensuing war. He didn't feel sorry for Charles, but he was sorry for Lisa. Despite Jimmy's presence, Bo still had feelings for her. Bo knew what it was like to lose someone close.

Charles stood stiffly. "It looks like the coast is clear. We'll walk down the sidewalk until we reach a point across the street from the field. We'll cross there. When no one is looking we'll go through the door to the basement. There's a lever that will unlock it from the outside. It's not a perfect arrangement, but we usually keep the door locked, especially now that people know about it. The vampire crypt is near the bottom of the steps. There's a hidden lock on that, too. You will see. I will show you."

Charles and Bo crossed the street and entered the grassy lot. "The other thing you have to watch for here is the homeless," Charles said. He coughed several times and spit. "When they're awake they sit in those tents and watch everything. Always looking for some advantage. If they ever found the entrance and the lock it would be like..."

"A zombie apocalypse," Bo said, smiling. *Better than torches and natural gas*, he thought.

Charles forced a smile back "Better believe it."

<hr>

THEY LEFT the sidewalk behind and crossed the lot next to After Dark. Suddenly, Charles whispered, "Now! Go fast!" Charles trotted ahead. He kneeled and felt around in the long grass. "Here it is, Bo. A lever. Pull it."

A small lever, metallic and thin, rose from the grass. Charles flipped it forward. It clicked. He scrambled back a few feet and searched through the grass again until his hand caught a handle. He looked around quickly and pulled the handle. A door covered with grass swung open. "Get in!" Charles commanded and without hesitation, Bo charged down the dark stairway. Charles followed in an instant, dropping the door behind him. It was the fastest Bo had seen Charles move. He pulled another lever and locked the door.

Once inside, Charles sat near the bottom of the steps and coughed and spit. He looked up at Bo. His eyes were watery from the coughing spell. "Never let anyone see you enter or leave. Understand?"

"I understand," Bo said. "Never."

Charles showed Bo the vampire's crypt door, undistinguishable from the surrounding rock wall. It lay about ten feet beyond the base of the steps.

"This is the latch," Charles said. He put his hand on a rock that appeared cleaner than the rest jutting from the wall. "Give it a twist, like this," he continued, simulating the action. "This door weighs tons, but you can open and close it with one finger. It will lock automatically after it closes. Sometimes, *they* leave it open a little, probably to let out the stink, but they don't seem to mind the smell. At least not that I can tell. I've never seen them breathe unless they're sniffing something."

Charles smiled again, as if Bo were a new playmate and he was eager to show him his toys. He motioned for Bo to follow. Beyond the steps was a door in the wall with a lever handle. The Whisperers attacked the door immediately, throwing themselves into the iron bars. Bo recoiled.

"They won't hurt you. I won't let them," Charles said.

"What the hell are they?"

"Vampires," Charles said knowingly, jutting out his chin. "When they were turned, it wasn't successful. For some reason I don't understand, they get stuck between man and beast. It doesn't happen often, so I understand, but when they get stuck it's permanent. The vampires treat them like children. Call them *our friends*. They have all the vampire senses, hearing, smell, that sort of thing.

They are strong, but their brain power is diminished. They understand what you say but can't talk. They communicate among themselves with clicks and whistles. To me, it's a limited language. Basic skills. The vampires don't even know."

Charles roared an indistinguishable command, and the Whistlers fell silent and retreated away from the door.

"Sometimes they listen," Charles said. "Sometimes they don't." He walked over the damp concrete floor, passed the cages, to the feeding room. He picked up the club leaning against the wall near the door. "They fear this club," Charles added, hefting it like one might feel the weight of a baseball bat. "Give one a rap over the head and the rest will fall in line. If they really get out of line, do this."

Charles engaged the knife switch. There was a small spark on the switch and the room filled with bright ultraviolet light. "This will burn the shit out of them. They'll be back in the pen in a second. It's the same as daylight."

"And the vampires?"

"Same thing. But you never want to throw this switch when the vampires are here. Enough exposure will kill the vampire and our friends. That's how three of the humans escaped. One managed to throw the switch. It was daylight when they did it, so nobody could follow, not the vampires. They kicked the shit out of me, so I was too weak by the time the ruckus was over."

Three people in cages moaned at the bright light. Two women and a man. All were naked. Bo stared in disbelief and then looked away.

Charles pulled Bo away from the cages, where the people would not hear. He hissed, "You have to show strength with these people. Some are con artists. One guy pretended he was dead. I slapped and prodded the shit out of him. He wouldn't twitch. We thought he was dead and his blood was useless. The vampires can drink blood from the dead, but these two don't like it. We dumped the body outside and he took off.

"If he was a junkie, he's probably dead now. OD'd," Bo said, without emotion.

"It's unpleasant to look at them, but you have to keep a close watch on their conditions. Some will hurt themselves by banging their heads against the bars. Some have scabs they pick. They can get infections. One dude I had was the picture of health. Came down with pneumonia and died. The masters don't like to miss a skillet, especially when they look forward to draining a particular person. They come in often to see what's on the...menu, especially after they sense we have taken someone new."

The man and one woman pleaded for help. Asked for drugs to combat their withdrawal symptoms. Charles returned to the wall and disengaged the knife switch, returning the basement to its former dimness. "Three in the cages is good," Charles said. "Once I am turned you'll have to have at least two, preferably three, in various states of detox all the time. Occasionally, you can take a clean blood, if necessary, but clean bloods can raise an alarm when they go missing. Their families get involved. Want investigations. Usually, nobody misses the homeless. The masters like clean blood better than detoxed blood. Apparently, to them, there's a difference. We took some clean bloods over the summer. Maybe too many."

"That's interesting. Good to know."

"Another thing, these vampires are old, hundreds of years old. They could drink junkie blood full of dope, but they prefer the clean blood they remember from centuries ago, when all blood was basically fresh, clean. The colony we came from drank tainted blood. These two did only as a last resort. Then they started to take the junkies and let them detox. Had our friends do the hunting."

"Connoisseurs?"

"Something like that," Charles said. He smiled and put a hand on Bo's shoulder,

"The other thing I do is take a turn in the park when our friends don't hunt. Sit near the homeless to hear what they're talking about. I might even pretend to have passed out. Slump down a bit on a bench. Right now, I can tell you everybody is on edge. There's talk of Beaters, who attack the homeless, and Whistlers, which means our friends have been seen and heard. I don't like it. Do you think you understand everything?"

"I think so," Bo said.

"After I'm turned, I will go through a period of hibernation. It lasts a few days, maybe as long as a week. It depends on how much vampire blood I drink and what is my body's condition when I'm turned. A cocoon will form around me. During that change, I mustn't be disturbed. That's how most of our friends are made. Their bodies are disturbed, and they come out half-formed."

"The process is like a moth?"

"A butterfly," Charles corrected Bo. "I will emerge a vampire."

CHAPTER THIRTY-SIX

"ONE THING ABOUT OUR FRIENDS," CHARLES TOLD BO, WHILE his hand rested on the Whistlers' door release lever. "They can consume any liquid in the human body. Flesh, too. And they'll eat just about anything: rats, cats, dogs. The masters take most of the human blood. They" – Charles motioned to the clicking and whistling animals – "will consume the rest. What blood is left, bile, urine, even stomach contents. When they're done, the body is a mere shell, completely dehydrated."

Bo felt woozy. The room began to spin.

"Need a moment?" Charles said, smiling again. Bo thought the old man enjoyed making him sick.

"Go ahead."

Charles pulled the lever and opened the cell door. The Whistlers, now recovered, charged from their cell. They crowded around Bo, sniffing him, clicking, rubbing their bodies against him, rushing around and through his legs. Charles let the Whistlers see his club, which he smacked against a palm.

Charles screamed. "Do you want to hunt tonight!"

The beasts swirled around one another and moved to the

bottom of the basement steps. They paused, crouched, and watched like dogs waiting for a command.

"This is your new master," Charles said, pointing to Bo.

"Do they understand?"

"They understand. Sometimes too well," Charles said. Then he screamed at the beasts. "He is younger and stronger than I am! He will put you in your place. Now grovel before him, before he beats you and turns on the light that hurts."

The Whistlers whimpered and lay flat against the floor, all with their faces turned toward Bo. One by one, they crawled to Bo and whimpered more. Licked his shoes in submission.

"They acknowledge your leadership. Touch their heads," Charles said. "That means you accept them."

Bo cupped a palm and stroked each of the Whistlers' heads as if they were dogs. Their fur was stiff, bristly. One by one, they retreated to the bottom of the steps. Again, they sat and looked toward the secret door to the outside, expectant, waiting for the command to hunt.

"You must never show any weakness," Charles said. "Treat them roughly. Beat them with the club when necessary. Beat them when it is not necessary. You must keep them in line. They are not pets. Use the light, if necessary, but never when the masters are present. The vampires have a soft heart, if there is such a thing, for these creatures."

"I understand," Bo said, nodding, sweating, flushing.

Charles looked at his watch. "It's not quite dark enough. We'll wait a half hour." He handed Bo the club. "You should sit on the bottom step with them. Let our friends get accustomed to you. Show them the club. Let them see who's boss. They'll understand."

"I hope they don't have fleas or even ticks," Bo said, examining his fingers where he caressed the beasts.

"They keep one another clean. Despite their disgusting eating habits, and even though they stink, they are remarkably clean, unlike the masters." He nodded his head toward the closed crypt door.

Bo walked to the steps, through the Whistlers, and sat down. The beasts crowded around him. They licked at his hands and arms. One showed his fangs. Bo recoiled.

"You have to remember, they're always looking for some weakness," Charles said. "Keep a close eye on them. I wish the grinning one had been among those killed. Life would be easier. He will always test you. The others will follow his lead."

The Whistler that had bared its teeth turned to Charles and growled. Bo rapped it over the head with the club. "Back in line, or I'll bash in your brains," Bo shouted.

"No matter how hard you hit them, it hurts only for an instant," Charles said. "Still, they don't like being hit. Just like a vampire, they heal on their own. You can't do any harm unless you pierce their hearts."

The beasts dropped to the floor. Charles smiled and winked at Bo. Charles moved away to the feeding room and climbed on the mortuary table. He leaned against the wall and rested. He sighed and then coughed a few times. In a moment he appeared to sleep.

Bo looked around the basement. Foul-smelling creatures lay at his feet. Charles snoozed on the table where vampire victims were stripped of their clothes and trussed up. Then there was the feeding room, the site for exsanguinations, with its block and tackle secured to a wooden beam. Chains, leather straps, a black apron, and long gloves were affixed to the wall. High boots sat on the floor under the gear. Beyond Charles, the cages lay in shadows with whimpering junkies wracked with withdrawal pains, their pleas for help unheard. Charles slept through it. Across from where Bo sat, the vampire crypt was quiet behind its secret door.

How will I ever survive this ordeal, Bo thought. He was overcome by the basement's rank odors. His head pounded and he sweat profusely. How his friends TJ and Ridge must have suffered in their last hours of life in this fetid room. Despite his terror at being in the squalid basement, Bo decided to fight on, no matter what the cost, to get even with the vampires and their beasts. The other members of their vampire-fighting group would make similar sacrifices when they stormed After Dark. His job now was to learn as much as possible about the place to ensure their attack would find no surprises.

After a while, Charles stirred, looked at his watch again, and slowly, painfully slid to the floor. He approached Bo. The Whistlers dozed but jumped to attention when he approached. Bo, too, felt groggy after sitting so long. The basement's oppressive air seemed to crush him.

"Ready, Bo?"

Ready," Bo said. He thought *anything to get out of this place.*

Charles kept checking his watch as if there was an optimal time for exploring the exterior world. While they remained inside, Charles showed Bo a series of hand motions to control the Whistlers. Calling outside in the park would give up their positions. The silent signals were essential. Charles repeated the motions, making the Whistlers move, stop, crouch, and attack. Bo used them himself and the Whistlers responded. The beasts seemed to understand obeying him would result in a successful hunt and food.

Charles had Bo run through the signs again, the last being a charge on the cages. The junkies screamed in terror as the beasts hurled themselves against the bars. Bo pointed toward the ceiling. Charles shrugged. "No one can hear what goes on down here," Charles said. "I suppose if you were to lay on the floor or near the floor you might hear a scream, if conditions were right, but normally...nothing. Do you hear the DJ upstairs? There's supposed to be one tonight. Loud enough to split your head open."

"I didn't hear any sound from upstairs," Bo said.

Charles smiled. "You see? This is a perfect location."

"As long as it remains a secret."

"Yes. As long as it remains a secret," Charles said. He stared at

Bo for a moment. "Make sure you never compromise our position, or the masters will drain you very painfully." Charles checked his watch again. "It's time. Let's go."

Bo used the hand signals to return the Whistlers to the steps. They lined up expectantly, clicking their teeth, licking their lips, and whimpering.

"There can be only one hunt master," Charles said. He nodded his head. "That will be you. The friends will follow your orders only because you will open the doors. This should be easier because there are only four. Unlock the door and open it slowly. Look around. Make sure no one is close enough to see us. If someone is there, drop the door and lock it. If the way is clear give the sign for them to emerge. They will fall into line outside. They will lie flat on the ground. When there is a gap in the traffic, we'll cross the street into the park. Use your hand commands. They will watch you. Understand? When all is safe, you give the command, and they will follow us into the park."

Bo nodded. He climbed the steps and pulled open the latch. The Whistlers became agitated. Whined louder and clicked. Bo gave them the sign for quiet and they became silent. Only an occasional low click could be heard. Slowly, Bo pushed on the heavy door. He poked out his head. Instantly, he smelled fresh air. For once the city smelled good. He looked around. Saw no one. Inched the door higher. Still, no one was in sight. He opened it far enough to climb out. Bo looked down the steps into the dim light. The Whistlers sat expectantly, waiting for his hand signal. Charles stood farther away. Bo gave the signal, and the Whistlers sprang up the steps silently and dropped to the ground in the high grass. Their eyes returned to Bo. The beasts were silent. Their grinning mouths exposed fangs. Finally, Charles climbed the steps, inspected the surroundings himself, climbed out, nodded his approval, and closed the door.

It was after midnight. The home team had a day off after two series on the west coast. Traffic was light. After Dark looked ready to close. Bo moved across the empty grass lot, trotting, bent over at the waist. The Whistlers inched forward on their bellies behind him, always watching for their next cue. He motioned for the four beasts to stop. They did and remained silent. Bo approached the edge of the sidewalk and dipped, facing the street, watching traffic in both directions. It seemed odd seeing traffic upside down, but it was something he would have to do until his gang was ready for the big fight. Finally, the traffic lights turned red in both directions, temporarily stopping traffic on Fifth Street for two blocks. Bo crossed Fifth Street and gave the Whistlers their hand signal to follow. The beasts outpaced him, their claws scraping on the asphalt, until they galloped into the park's high ornamental grass. Charles waited on the opposite side of Fifth Street and eventually crossed, bringing up the rear.

A Whistler clicked and Bo immediately gave the sign for silence. Bo moved along the asphalt path. No one was in sight. Bo walked thirty yards before giving the signal for the Whistler to follow. They crawled noiselessly on their bellies. Bo continued up the path. The Whistlers kept pace behind him in the grass. Charles followed at a distance, occasionally dipping if he felt something was awry. Ahead, where the path branched to the left, the usual junkies had started their small fire. They talked and laughed in deep, low tones. Suddenly, the Whistlers darted to the side, running two-by-two. As they ran, the beasts changed positions, the back ones moved in front. They moved quickly and noiselessly. Bo panicked. They were gone from sight. He had no means to give them a hand signal. Then he saw them moving ahead of the campfire. They returned toward the path. Bo realized they had skirted the junkies and were ready again to hunt. The beasts crouched and watched him. Bo saw their eyes shine. Bo looked back at Charles, who nodded his head and motioned for him to continue up the path.

Bo caught up to the Whistlers and passed them. They lay still in the grass until he signaled them to follow. Soon they were back to their old routine. Bo roamed the path. The Whistlers inched ahead behind and to the side. They reached a rise where a young female dipped silently. A garbage bag lay between her legs. An overhead light provided wan illumination on the spot where she stood. A man, probably drunk, weaved down the path toward Bo. He stopped to look at the dipper, then continued. Did he want them to take her? Was there too much light? Could he control them? Deny them an easy mark? Find another one?

As the drunk approached, his erratic walk changed, and he confronted Bo. "Can you give me a few dollars for a meal?" the man asked. He was hunched over and clasped his hands as if in prayer.

"Not tonight," Bo said.

"I'm so hungry. I'll take anything you can spare."

He drew closer to Bo, blocking his path.

"Get lost," Bo said.

The man pulled a knife from his pocket. Suddenly the drunk act was gone. "Then I'll take your wallet, asshole." The knife had a long, thin blade, and flashed in the light from overhead.

When Bo backed up the man advanced. "No place to go," he said. "Give me the wallet. Make it easy on yourself."

Without realizing it, Bo gave the hand signal to attack. The Whistlers covered the man in an instant. One creature bit the hand holding the knife. The weapon hit the asphalt with a clatter. The pack, with the man sandwiched between the two layers, disappeared into the darkness. The only noise was the knife hitting the ground.

Charles caught up with Bo. "Good work," Charles said. "This one might be a clean blood. But who knows? Looks like the type that won't be missed. Scum bag. We'll head back to the basement. Stay on the path. Our friends will follow with the prey, through the darkness. You won't hear them, but they will be there, always watching for your commands. When we get out of the park, cross the street and open the door. Return to the sidewalk to signal our friends the coast is clear. Stay away from the door entrance until after they're inside. They are very fast. You don't want to get knocked over and fall down the stairwell. Their claws can easily disembowel a person. Even you. By mistake. They're all business when they have a captive."

Bo and Charles exchanged glances. Charles said, "I'd say your first hunt was an easy one and successful."

Bo followed Charles's instructions. The man was conveyed inside After Dark's basement within minutes. The street was quiet. No one was aware the knife-wielding vagrant was gone. After the basement door was locked, Bo put the stiletto knife he picked up inside the feeding room on a shelf alongside other relics taken from victims.

The man screamed and thrashed as the Whistlers tore off his clothes, scratching him severely. This noise caused the trio of junkies in cages to shriek. The vampires left their crypt within moments. How they relished the terror among the group. Their pallid faces appeared smooth and waxen because they had fed the night before. They both had broad smiles.

Bo was aghast. He recoiled but the female caught him from behind so fast he didn't see her move. "Charles, he's so young." The female smiled and pressed her dead, cold body against Bo. "Don't be afraid, little one." She squeezed Bo against her, restricting his breathing. She smelled his body and licked his neck and face with her long, black tongue. Bo gagged at her fetid breath. "What I wouldn't give for a drop of your blood."

"Masters, please. The man is scared," Charles pleaded and moved forward. "He did well on his first hunt."

"I see," Gerrard said. He inspected the new male, now in his cell, and returned to sniff Bo casually and approvingly.

Bo tried to recoil, but the female still had him in her grasp, not so crushing now. She grabbed his head and stared into his eyes. "Come with me," she demanded.

She released her grip on Bo. Bo relaxed and followed her toward the crypt, as if in a trance.

"Masters!" Charles implored, stretching out his arms.

The female stopped and turned around. Then smiled. "Don't worry. Charles. I'm not going to eat him." The female laughed. "You must be turned, and he must procure us more cattle. He's a virgin. I can smell it. I will taste him and make his first time special, although he will not remember the sex. That is how it is with vampires. He will remain a virgin, too, because we are dead." She laughed again. After looking into her eyes, Bo followed obediently.

CHAPTER THIRTY-SEVEN

The female vampire took Bo by the hand and led him toward the crypt. Several times she leaned in to kiss and lick his neck, letting her cold lips linger on his skin.

"Do you know how to open the door?"

"Yes, Master," Bo answered, as if in a trance. He wanted to run. The steps to the exterior were close, but he found himself powerless to the vampire's will.

"Excellent. Charles has been a good teacher in such a short time." She ran her fingers through Bo's hair. "Open the door and let us in."

Bo opened the hidden latch and let the heavy door swing open. Once inside the crypt, Bo closed the door. It locked automatically. The crypt was larger than Bo had imagined, but it had a low, stony ceiling, just high enough for him to stand. Eight caskets lay in a row, all with the lids open. All were empty. The air smelled of death, like the vampires' noxious odors.

Bo wanted to run. He tried to run for the door, release the latch, and sprint up the steps to the outside world. However, he could not move. His legs were heavy. Impossible to lift. He wanted to shout for help but couldn't. All he managed were a few whimpers as tears rolled down his cheeks.

"Don't be frightened, young one. You will survive this," the vampire said. She pinched his flushed cheek and smiled. She looked in his eyes again and demanded, "I want you to undress. Everything."

Bo obeyed. The vampire stripped off her gown and clutched Bo, held him close. "The human heart. So wonderful and yet so short lived. How it moves the living blood to every cell. It's all so amazing." She pulled Bo closer. Her breasts were erect. She cupped Bo's buttocks and pressed his groin against her.

"No," Bo managed to say. He felt the corpse's cold, hard flesh against him. Her long, pointed tongue licked him, imparting its sticky, malodorous coating on his skin.

"You will obey everything I say, Bo. You are now my slave. You will hear my call and you will come to me immediately. I will enjoy your body with its little thumping rabbit heart and coursing blood whenever I like. You will not resist me. You will lie in my grave. We will pleasure each other. I will taste every inch of your flesh and sample your sweet virgin blood."

* * *

Bo woke in darkness. He was naked and lay on his stomach. He was groggy, but his nostrils stung with the smell of the vampiress. He moaned and coughed. He tried to crawl to his hands and knees, but his head bumped a hard surface. The thump sounded like wood. The bump jarred open whatever was over him, admitting a sliver of dim light. He moved his right hand to better balance himself and pressed on the cadaver's abdomen. A soft moan and more stench belched from the mouth. Bo gagged. The knife of dim light slashed across the vampire's face. Bo saw her staring, lifeless eyes, parted lips, exposed fangs, and a thin trickle of blood that ran from the corner of her mouth.

Bo stood, screaming, throwing open the casket lid violently. He was lightheaded, but in that instant, in the wan crypt light, he saw the naked female stiff inside the casket where he stood. The male vampire rested in the next casket. The door to the basement hung open. Bo turned to escape. His buttocks and shoulder ached. A wound on his stomach seeped blood.

Bo threw himself from the casket. The female caught his ankle in a vice-like grip. Bo fell forward and hit his head on the floor. Slowly, laughing, the female vampire pulled Bo back and gently lifted him inside as if he were a doll. She held him still and licked the cut on his forehead. "I am not finished with you, young one. We have much to do. I have much to show you." Bo struggled until she looked into his eyes again. Bo relaxed. His mouth grew slack, and she closed the casket lid.

Charles entered the crypt and picked up Bo's clothes. He returned to the basement. He folded the clothes and put them in the feeding room. "I never had such bad luck," Charles mused. He pursed his lips. "Must have been the cancer."

⁂

Bo emerged from the casket. He was still groggy. The room spun when he stood, causing him to sit again. There were bite marks on his shoulder and torso. There was blood on his sore buttocks where Bo imagined there were more puncture wounds. He was covered with the foul-smelling slime from the vampire's tongue. He whimpered again, moved to the door, and unlatched it. He entered the basement, saw Charles, limped toward him, and swooned. Charles caught Bo and helped him to the mortuary table. The captives shrieked in terror. Charles took the club, ran to the cages, and beat on the bars. After the captives fell silent again, Charles returned to Bo.

"She turned me into a vampire," Bo cried. "That fucking bitch made me a monster."

"Did you drink her blood?" Charles said. He sounded nervous, Bo imagined, because he was the one who would be turned. "Did she feed you?"

"I don't know. I can't remember much. I get paralyzed when she looks in my eyes."

Charles took a step back. "She can mesmerize you with her mind. That's what they call it. Are you hungry?"

"Starved. How long was I in there?"

"Almost three days," Charles said matter-of-factly. "You're very pale. She drained you good. You won't become a vampire unless you drank her blood. She must share it with you. What are you hungry for?"

"Cheeseburger. A double. No, triple meat."

"That's a good sign." Charles disappeared into the feeding room and returned with a large bottle of orange juice and a paper bag. "Start with this. This is what the Red Cross gives when you donate blood."

"That wasn't a donation," Bo said. "I was raped."

"Cock sore?"

"Feels like it was torn off and sewn back on."

Charles smiled. "Yeah. So it is with vampires. They have incredible strength. I was afraid she might kill you by accident. I've seen it happen."

Bo took the orange juice and gulped half it down. Charles pulled a box from the bag and produced a large burger. "It's a triple. From After Dark. Lucky choice. I figured you'd need it if you ever came out alive."

Bo took the burger and took a huge mouthful. In short order, he consumed the burger and drank the remainder of the orange juice. Then he leaned back against the wall.

"If you were a vampire, you couldn't eat regular food like you just did. That's a good thing," Charles said. "She said she wanted you living to herd the cattle. It had to be difficult for her to stop. Not to drain you completely. Certain things really turn on vampires. A virgin's blood, male or female, especially an adult, which is more rare. The other thing more precious is newborn blood. Even though it wouldn't be much, compared to an adult, a newborn's blood would be the creme de la crème. It's supposed to give a vampire tremendous strength."

"I have to get this stuff off me. God knows what it is. It smells awful."

"It's a secretion of some kind," Charles said. "Don't think it's harmful, although one guy they drained got a rash from being licked. Anyway, he didn't last long enough to discover if it was anyway lethal."

Bo slumped over. He looked at Charles. "God knows what kind of venereal disease I got from her. Christ. It could be the black plague."

"Well, I don't think there's too much to worry about there either," Charles said with a smile. He touched Bo's shoulder, the one without puncture wounds. "They're dead. Just corpses. I don't think any bacteria or viruses would live on them or in them, other than the vampire disease."

"You know for sure?"

"No. Not for sure. I'm not a doctor. But it makes sense. Don't you think?"

"I hope so."

Charles showed Bo a shower he rigged for himself in the basement and how to mix the hot and cold water. Bo felt better after eating and taking a shower. However, he was still weak and lightheaded. He dressed and rested on the mortuary table. Assured the Whistlers would not hunt tonight, Bo slipped out of the basement before dark and with difficulty, walked to his car, and returned to the frat house. After three days in the vampiress' casket, Bo knew tomorrow there was a meeting at 1:00 p.m. in Bad Nelson's garage to lay out the final plans for the assault on After Dark.

CHAPTER THIRTY-EIGHT

Bo eased down the side street, Balm Avenue, and stopped suddenly at Forger Way, little more than a dirt, trash-strewn path overgrown with trees. The street sign marking the corner was rusted and leaned at a forty-five-degree angle, apparently held up by vines that climbed from a nearby wooden utility pole. Bo gunned the engine a couple of times, as was his habit, enjoying for the moment the Hemi's roar, and turned off the engine. He locked the car and walked slowly down the alley, passing dilapidated garages on both sides. There was not a part of him that didn't ache, either bruised or punctured or rubbed almost raw by the vampiress. He feared some of the bites might be infected. He hoped the Neosporin he applied worked. Still, he pressed on down the deserted alley. He couldn't wait to stake her with one of Bad Nelson's guns. Bo would claim the female vampire as his target, his personal kill.

Bo walked almost half a block before he saw Bad Nelson, PVC stake rifle over his shoulder, waiting outside the open door of his family's garage. Bo tried to manage a smile as he approached, waving to Bad Nelson. Bad Nelson waved back and looked at his wrist at an imaginary watch.

"Thought you were a no-show," Bad Nelson said, when Bo approached. "Everybody's here."

"Traffic, man."

Bad Nelson closed the overhead garage door as soon as Bo was inside. The rest of the group stood or sat around the garage. There was Old Harriet perched on Bad Nelson's workbench stool, Overboard George and Mad Maggie, New Girl, hardly more than a sprite, Megan who sidled over to Bad Nelson, and Lisa and Jimmy. They all showed looks of concern.

"What the hell happened to you?" Overboard George asked Bo. "You look like death warmed over. Did the Beaters get you?"

"It wasn't Beaters, it was the vampire. She raped me and sucked my blood for three days in her crypt. In her stinking coffin that reeks of the dead. I can't get that smell out of my mind. I imagine it's still on my body, even though I've practically lived in the shower and threw all those clothes away."

Old Harriet slipped from the stool and sniffed at Bo. "Nice. Old Spice, I think. You don't stink. Even your breath smells good. I wouldn't mind having a go at you myself."

New Girl tittered.

Bo scowled at Old Harriet and peeled off his T-shirt to show his wounds. He turned around and exposed an ass cheek and its puncture wounds. "I *feel* like the Beaters did get me...or at least what I imagine it feels like."

The group gasped. Before Bo could pull up his shorts, Mad Maggie slid off her seat and stepped to his side. She touched the inflamed buttock and felt the wound. Bo winced. "That's what they look like all right," Mad Maggie said, searching the group's faces. The others moved closer to Bo to do their own exams. "I've been in the basement, remember, and I've seen the wounds on ones they drained. Those marks are bites."

Overboard George said, "That's a vampire puncture. Mad

Maggie and I seen them drained right before our eyes. First, the vampires and then the Whistlers get the rest. In the end, the body is shrunken and dry as a mummy. The whole body looks like one of them shrunken heads. Only the whole body is shrunk."

Bo unfolded the long story of his captivity to the group. They listened in silence, except for a few gasps from time to time.

"If that's true," Lisa said after Bo finished his story and showed his wounds, "it means he is or will become a vampire." She looked from person to person.

"That's not how it works, is it, George?"

"No. Tell them, Maggie," Overboard George said.

"I still have a problem with this whole vampire thing. It defies logic," Lisa said.

"Me, too," Jimmy said. "I think it's outrageous."

"There are vampires, aren't there New Girl?"

New Girl nodded like a bobblehead figurine.

"To become a vampire, a *real* vampire has to let or *make* you drink its blood," Mad Maggie said. "That vampire could have drained Bo for weeks, months, years, as long as she let him live. He would remain a human, too weak, too depleted to escape. If he died without drinking the vampire's blood, Bo would be as dead as anybody else who keels over."

Jimmy stepped to the center of the crowd. He shook his hands over his head. His voice got louder as he spoke. "How do you know all this...*stuff*...This vampire lore, these so-called facts about vampires?" He looked at each of the members.

"Humph!" Mad Maggie said, throwing her own hands into the air. "Where else? *Famous Monsters of Filmland*."

"No. No. No!" Jimmy screamed. "We can't plan an assault on *vampires*—I can't believe I'm saying this—based on a horror movie fan magazine. It's ludicrous."

"I don't see a problem," Overboard George said.

"Me neither," Bad Nelson said.

"I'm with Nels," Megan added. "If Bad Nelson says so, I

believe there are vampires in that basement, right underneath where Lisa and I work."

"I know what I saw," New Girl said. "I was there, too. I heard the people scream. Seen them hung upside down. Heard the vampires and the Whistlers gulping and sucking everything out of them. I seen emaciated corpses. It wasn't no drugs. It was real."

Jimmy looked at the floor a moment, composing himself. Everyone waited. "Is there any chance you could have hallucinated all this? The drugs you were on. I mean...the withdrawal sickness? I'm no expert, but the idea of vampires is a lot to swallow. For me, at least."

"Exactly. That's my point," Lisa said. "We want to be perfectly sure about what we're saying. What we're doing."

"I wasn't on drugs when I was in that basement," Bo said. "I don't do drugs. That vampire had me in a trance. I don't know how she did it. I don't remember most of those three days. But I know I was inside her casket, in the dark, with her. With *her*! All that time. When I tried to escape, she pulled me back inside. She moved around inside like a snake. She could bend herself over and move up and down its entire length over me. Her body was hideous. The flesh was cold. Dead. She bit and scratched me all over."

"I believe something *happened* to you," Jimmy said. "It's obvious you were bitten. I'm not saying that's not true. I can't justify in my own head that we force our way in and shoot anything that moves. Vampires or not."

"You're going to have to shoot before it moves," Bad Nelson said. "They can be extremely fast. Move in a blur."

"To be honest, I don't like our chances after seeing them in action," Bo said. "I thought I could get in that basement, subdue Charles, and stake the vampires in their caskets, one at a time, then turn on the Whistlers. I already knew they could be killed. After she had me, I thought I was going to escape, but in an instant, she had me by the ankle digging in her claws and I was back in the casket with her. She has tremendous strength. When she stared into my eyes, I was helpless, couldn't say no to anything she told me to do. I stripped off my clothes in front of her and climbed into her casket. Then she climbed in on top of me and closed the lid."

"You backing out?" Megan said.

"Never," Bo said. "I want to stake that bitch and watch her die."

"She's already dead," Mad Maggie corrected, waving a finger in the air. "She'll most likely be consumed by fire and leave a small pile of ashes, so don't get too close. You can't explain vampire exposure in the burn unit."

"Famous Monsters?" Jimmy asked.

"*John Carpenter's Vampires*," Mad Maggie said.

Jimmy sighed. They were silent for a while. The fluorescent light above the workbench flickered and hummed. A large fly buzzed around the garage, making endless laps. Everyone seemed to watch its path but none seemed to have the energy to swat it. With the overhead door closed, the garage became stuffy in the day's heat. Bad Nelson moved to the door and opened it. The heat from the outside poured in. Everyone seemed exhausted, but at least the air smelled fresher.

"Another thing I wanted to mention," Overboard George said. "Mad Maggie and I are taking torches when we attack. Two each. We already got them made. Saw a YouTube video in the library. There's more if anyone wants one. They'll burn for about fifteen minutes. We tried one already. Timed it ourselves. I know this wasn't a popular idea, but it's part of *our* plan."

"Not that nonsense again," Jimmy said. "You can't rush in there with torches. It'll attract a mob. Christ! You can't tell who'll you shoot. The purpose of having a plan is for *everyone* to follow it." He chopped one hand against an open palm. "We all have to know what the other people are doing and when they're doing it. That is essential. We can't act like a bunch of freelancers."

"If we have any advantages, it's numbers and surprise, especially by going in during the day," Overboard George said, "when they're mostly helpless."

"They can move around during the day," Bad Nelson said. "But they can't enter direct sunlight. That's lethal."

"I've seen *her* move in the day," Bo said. "Not necessarily fast. And she's still strong. She handled me like a rag doll."

"I'll carry a torch," Old Harriet said. She dropped from the stool and joined Overboard George. "I'll set those old clothes you claim they wear on fire. They'll go up like a Roman candle. I'll burn them to skeletons."

"What about you, Bo?" Jimmy asked. "What if *she* wants *you* to fight us, defend the vampires, their lair?" He paused a moment and ran his fingers through his hair. "I don't believe I just asked those questions."

"I don't know. She told me she can summon me at any time. Even from far away." Bo said. He felt drained. He looked toward the ceiling. "When I was there, I did what she told me, without thinking. It never occurred to me that taking off my clothes and climbing into a casket, with its stains and smells, was wrong. I did it without question. I couldn't stop."

"I think they knew better than to try mind control on me when I was there," Mad Maggie said. She pursed her lips and then added, "Yeah. It wouldn't work. I'll push my torch up that bitch's snatch. Catch her bush on fire. You can't mind control a maniac."

"Mind control won't work on somebody already crazy," Overboard George added, smiling, taking Mad Maggie's hand. They smiled at each other. "Everyone knows that."

"I want all of you to understand. I want to kill that female vampire. I want to stake her with one of Bad Nelson's guns," Bo said. "If for one second it appears I am defending the vampires, don't hesitate. Stake me. Promise me."

"You can count on it!" Old Harriet said, pumping her fist in the air. "Not that I want to see you harmed. I just decided I want to carry a gun, if you have an extra, along with my torch."

Lisa and Jimmy traded worried looks.

"I have enough parts. There will be a gun ready for you when we move, Old Harriet."

Old Harriet smiled at the group and returned to her stool. She looked thoroughly satisfied.

"One more thing," Overboard George said. "If we're going to do this, everybody has to be sober. No booze. No drugs. Not even one hit on a blunt. Understand?"

The group nodded heads in unison.

"That's what I want to see," Overboard George continued. "Maggie don't use, but I've been clean since our ordeal. It's not that I didn't want to, or couldn't have, but I resisted the urge with Mad Maggie's help. And I helped her think clearly. I know New Girl slipped a little, but she's back on the right track." Overboard George looked at New Girl and leaned closer to her. "Isn't that right, New Girl?"

"That's right. I'm clean and going to stay that way."

The group applauded and New Girl smiled and curtseyed somewhat awkwardly, eliciting a few laughs. Mad Maggie said, "Overboard George and I decided that if we have one vice together it's only going to be menthol cigarettes."

"That's right, New Girl. I could use a Kool right now. I understand not everybody here has a problem," Overboard George said looking around and pointing, "Lisa and Jimmy, Megan, and Bo. And of course, my Mad Maggie. So, what I said doesn't apply to you all."

Bad Nelson stood and retrieved the map he and Overboard George had drawn of the underground lair. He apologized for it not being drawn to scale, "But I didn't have a tape measure up my ass or the time to use one."

The group laughed. Old Harriet doubled over and slipped to the floor. Bo helped her back on her perch.

Bad Nelson bent over the map. The vampire hunters crowded around him. He pointed to each feature. The steps they would descend. The hidden crypt. The feeding room. The cells. The steps to the restaurant. The blade switch for the ultraviolet lights. He described the Whistlers' cage and its lock operation.

"Again, the map's not to scale," Bad Nelson said. "Especially the spaces between things. Just keep it in mind when we're inside if you have to shoot or escape."

"It looks pretty darn accurate to me," Mad Maggie said. She winked at Bad Nelson.

Bad Nelson grew serious. "I've given this attack a lot of thought. And this is what I've come up with. If anyone has any objections or has a different idea, now is the time to express it. Don't wait until we're going down those steps to change directions. Understand?"

The group nodded.

"Everyone will have an assignment. And everyone *must* execute that job," Bad Nelson said.

Then Bad Nelson outlined his plan. While his parents were passed out, Bad Nelson would deliver the stake guns at night by car to Overboard George's tent. The torches would be stored there already. The next day, the vampire fighter teams would pick up their weapons, at five-minute intervals, starting at 10:00 a.m. Bad Nelson reasoned most people who worked would be at their jobs. It would be early for most homeless to prowl the streets, and After Dark would not open for another hour. The vampire fighters would go to their designated starting points. He hoped the attack wouldn't take more than an hour.

"If we're in that basement more than an hour, I don't know that we're coming out," Bad Nelson said.

Bad Nelson said the vampire hunters would approach the vacant lot and its trapdoor from different directions. The teams would be Overboard George and Mad Maggie from the north, Lisa and Jimmy from the south. Bad Nelson and Megan from the east. New Girl and Old Harriet, also from the south, somewhat behind Lisa and Jimmy. Bo would arrive first, find the door, and unlock it. As everyone assembled, Bo would throw open the door. With the secret door opened, Bad Nelson would light the torches. Overboard George, Mad Maggie, Bad Nelson and Bo would enter first, because they were familiar with the basement. Next, New Girl would lead Megan and Old Harriet inside. Because they refused to carry weapons, Lisa and Jimmy were assigned to stand guard outside and control the door. Bad Nelson would open the whistler pen. He and the others would fire from the entrance, staking the beasts. While the group reloaded, Bo would open the hidden crypt lock and swing open the massive door. The group with its reloaded charges would storm the crypt and stake the vampires in their caskets at point-blank range. After an all-clear call from Lisa and Jimmy outside, the vampire fighters would disperse and meet at Bad Nelson's garage to turn in their weapons.

Bad Nelson said a practice run wasn't possible for fear the group and its complicated plan would be discovered. Each vampire hunter would have to remember his role and execute it without failure. Each person repeated the plan until each knew his or her part. Lisa and Jimmy continued to trade worried looks.

"Easy-peasy," Old Harriet said, finally, after she was the last to recite the plan's details.

"We understand what has to be done," Bad Nelson said. "All that's left is to decide when to make our move."

Friday was chosen, two days away. Lisa and Megan were off. Jimmy could take a vacation day. The rest were unemployed.

CHAPTER THIRTY-NINE

The next day Bo felt queasy. He chalked it up to nerves about the impending attack on After Dark and his ordeal with the female vampire. Thinking of her made him nauseous. More of his memory had returned. He recalled her cold, hard body against his. The odor of decaying flesh inside the casket. The crusty casket lining. Her tongue inside his mouth. He gagged at the thought of that tongue's hideous slime and its foul taste. The pop of her fangs breaking his flesh, finding a vein, and sucking his blood. The sound of her pleasure as she drank. Her cruel eyes locked on his when she demanded sex again and again. However, he had no memory of the act itself. No recollection of pleasure.

He was still sore from the tryst with her in the casket. In the privacy of his room at the frat house, he doused the infected puncture wounds with alcohol, which stung mightily, and smeared them with ointment, which stuck to his clothes after he dressed. He wondered if his body could ever clear the vampire's impurities. Bo sat on his bed and sobbed.

Suddenly, Bo felt a compulsion to go to After Dark. His mind had no reason. There was no need, but still he knew he had to go. Drive downtown, park on Fifth Street, walk to the empty lot, unlock the latch hidden in the tall grass, throw open the door, and descend the steps into the basement. It was not necessary to hunt. There were sufficient captives inside the cages even though one or two might be exsanguinated by now. The vampires and the Whistlers should be resting in the afternoon. Bo decided he would instead visit Bad Nelson in his garage. Heft the stake guns. Practice swinging the weapons, finding targets, and sighting them in. He knew no matter how fast he could swing the gun, aim, and fire, the vampires would be faster.

Bo liked Bad Nelson and considered him and Megan friends. Perhaps Megan would be there, too, if she was not waitressing at After Dark. Lisa was working more than likely, too, as was Jimmy. Bo thought of his friends TJ and Ridge. Their parents wanted to do another flier hand-out. They were busy making copies and talking to police officers on the case. By the time a meeting was arranged the After Dark raid would be completed and the vampires extinguished. Bo hoped some evidence would remain to prove the vampires existed and what happened to his friends, to provide closure for their families. Perhaps shreds of their clothing could be found in the pile that accumulated in one of the basement corners.

Bo reached his car, turned on the engine, and let it warm for a minute. He stopped for gasoline on his way to the city and squeegeed off the windshield while the tank filled. He tried to stretch his sore muscles in the process. Once more on the road, he roared down the interstate. Instead of taking the exit for the city's south side, where Bad Nelson lived, he veered off suddenly to the left, using the stadium exit, cutting off another driver, who hit the brakes and his horn. Immediately Bo realized his mistake and tried to turn around and head back to the south side, but he couldn't. He drove around the block—three times—but still headed toward the stadium. His hands seemed stuck in place and the steering wheel was uncontrollable.

Sweat streaked Bo's face and soaked his clothes. His hands shook on the steering wheel. As much as he wanted to change course, he couldn't. His mind told him he must go to the vampire lair. Her bidding must be obeyed. The more he resisted, and struggled to turn around the car, he felt it increasingly difficult to breathe. He screamed. Tried to hit the brakes, but his foot only pressed the gas pedal more. The car bolted ahead. It was all Bo could do to keep the Charger under control. He passed car after car. Finally, as he reached downtown, the car slowed, and Bo got some control back. The tightness in his chest eased when he pulled into the municipal parking lot near After Dark. He found a spot, turned off the engine, and slumped over the wheel.

Despite his fatigue and the grogginess he experienced, Bo climbed out of the car and locked it. He was soaked with sweat. He moved unsteadily at first, but eventually regained his footing, and crossed Fifth Street. He entered the empty lot, carefully, scanning for anyone who might watch him. After he was sure no one was near, he dropped to his knees, felt through the long grass, and found the door latch. The lock was open. Bo took one more look around before tugging open the door and dropping inside.

The captives wailed immediately, imploring him for help, pleading to be let go. It was obvious they recovered from withdrawal and had seen more than they wanted. Their cries increased, including those from the man Bo had taken with the Whistlers.

"Shut the fuck up!" Bo hissed. "I can't help you."

"What will they do with us," the knife-wielding man screamed. "You were the one who brought me here. I gotta get out of here. I can't stand it."

Bo retrieved the club from where it leaned against the wall near the feeding room door and beat on the cages, screaming for the captives to be quiet. He raked the club across the bars. The captives shut up suddenly and looked at the exterior steps. The large door to the crypt swung open. Bo streaked across the basement and hid behind the feeding room's open door.

The female vampire entered. The captives whimpered, crouched in their cells. She sniffed the air, paused, and giggled. "Bo, you answered my call, after some small resistance. I said you would come to me whenever I called. You are mine. The same way these cattle are mine." She waved her arm toward the cages and walked closer to Bo's hiding place. She smiled, exposing her dark teeth and fangs. "However, you are special, Bo, lovely. And now you hide from me. I hear your little rabbit's heart thundering away so fast it's difficult to count the time between beats. I hear your shallow, nervous breathing. I feel your anticipation for a return to my grave. *Time.* What meaning does it have for us? For you, it is your beating rabbit heart. The flow of your delicious blood. Always circulating. Always fresh. Always sweet in your young veins, waiting for me. And for me, time is *nothing*. It has been nothing for centuries. Still, in a small, amusing way I envy those who keep time, who track the days and years, celebrate a new year, a birthday." She stopped for a moment and scanned the basement. "If it were not for the mortals who keep track of time, I would not know how old I am. Isn't that strange, Bo, that I would be dependent on mortals? They already serve as food and as caretakers, but also, as guardians of time, which to me has no meaning."

She threw back her head and laughed. Her hollow voice rang off the walls. The captives screamed in horror from their cells. The vampire howled louder. Behind the door, Bo quaked. She rushed across the room in an instant and shut the heavy feeding room's metal door, exposing Bo's hiding place.

"There's my little rabbit," she said cupping a palm under Bo's chin, then taking his head in her hands. She licked his sweating cheek, imparting her tongue's slime on his face. Bo immediately wiped it off with his shirt sleeve. He looked at her and trembled.

"I have so much to teach you, my little rabbit, but unfortunately not today. We have work to do. Come."

The vampiress turned and walked toward the crypt. The

captives howled. For a moment Bo thought of running for the knife switch, engaging the bright lights, burning the bitch to a crisp. However, he doubted he had the strength or the speed to make such a move. The switch was too far away. It grew farther away with every step. She could catch him in an instant and rip him to pieces. Bo followed closely, obediently, unable to flee, with no escape route available. She walked slowly, in her stately manner, her gown, soiled at the bottom, trailing on the floor threads and bits of fabric at the hem. There were loose stitches at the seams and fabric worn thin in places, almost to the point of producing holes.

As they approached the crypt door, the vampiress, now serious, said, "We've encountered a problem, Bo. Charles became ill suddenly. His cancer has spread quickly, unknown to us or him, other than that infernal coughing. To Charles, *time* was paramount. Rather than lose him, we turned him. Gerrard supplied the blood. Because of Charles's *disease*, it took a considerable amount."

They stepped inside the crypt side by side.

She pointed to the male vampire in his casket. "Gerrard drank from one of the captives, just enough to restore his strength. The captive will be allowed to recuperate before we *finish* him." She licked her lips and twirled her obscene tongue around her lips. She stroked Bo's head and ran her long nails down his back. Bo shivered. The male vampire was extremely pale, waxen, like a life-sized candle. All he lacked was a wick.

"Charles is over here," she said, pointing to a closed casket. She turned to Bo and smiled. "He is recovering, too. Turning is not easy. Gerrard and I laugh at the vampire movies we love to watch, where an innocent dies and pops up a full-fledged vampire after a few seconds. The actual turning is an ordeal. It's complicated."

She opened the casket. Charles was encased in a cocoon that looked like the vampiress' tongue slime. The cocoon undulated in a regular rhythm. The open casket smelled putrid, and Bo recoiled.

She clutched Bo and pulled him to her, cradling him with an

arm around his back, pressing him against her side. Her strength was incredible. Bo winced in pain. She seemed not to notice his discomfort. "Charles found the vampire odors repulsive at first, but he soon became accustomed to them. You will, too, in time."

She released the pressure on his body and stroked his head again, running her long nails through his hair.

"When will Charles be...done?" Bo said, completing the question after a pause.

"You can never tell with these things," the vampiress said, thoughtfully. "Tomorrow, I think. Why do you ask, little rabbit?"

"Just curious."

"Well then, you should know this is the critical period. Inside the cocoon. This is how vampires, or your so-called Whistlers, are made. Any disturbance and the process might go awry. A Whistler results. For example, should we have to move the casket to another location, Charles would surely become deformed. If I slam the lid, it could have an effect. In a way, at this moment Charles is like a souffle. She smiled at Bo. "Even under perfect conditions, there can be a malformation. Just like in a human birth. But this *turn* seems to be going quite well. How do you say it? It's a casebook."

"Yes. That's it," Bo said. He swallowed with difficulty.

Slowly, gently, the female vampire closed Charles's casket lid. She patted and smoothed her palm over the top.

"This is why I brought you here," she said. "To let you know about Charles. He will no longer hunt with our friends. It is up to you to bring us cattle. Not tonight, though. Too many cattle require too much food. They cannot get suspicious upstairs. At least not until we bring more likeminded humans into the fold. Then it might be possible to increase our number here in the city. There are so many who can go missing without a trace. You will be paid well and at some time in the future, you might want to retire. Live out your natural years in comfort. How I will miss you as a young man with your sweet-tasting blood. Incidentally, the key to the cells is hanging on a hook on the feeding room door's left side. At some point, you will need it."

"Charles showed me."

Bo realized he might be able to escape from this fiend unharmed. He said, "Won't having too many people upstairs be dangerous? To you?

"Your concern is flattering." The vampiress placed a palm on Bo's chest. "Little rabbit, you must learn not to fear me, for it is you who will take care of me. If I moved my hand at this moment, I believe your little pounding heart would crash through your chest. That would be such a pity because I have grown fond of you."

Bo backed away. "I should be going."

"So soon?"

"I have things to do."

The vampiress raised her eyebrows and pursed her lips. "What kind of things? The things young male rabbits do?"

"Sort of."

She smiled at Bo. "You should only care about serving me. This colony should be your main concern."

She took Bo by the shoulders and turned him to her. "Before I let you go to do your *things*, little rabbit, you will pleasure me, and I will pleasure you. Then I will take a small sample of your delicious blood, because you have not yet recovered from our last encounter. Look here."

"No," Bo shouted. He backed way.

"Bo. Come to me." Her empty voice rang off the crypt walls and its low ceiling.

Bo swayed, as if suddenly dizzy. He complied.

"Undress," she demanded.

She was already naked by the time Bo untied the shoelaces of his running shoes. She tore off his clothes in a frenzy. Slime from her mouth ran down her chin. Bo whimpered. She sank her fangs into his shoulder, clamped her parted lips over the wound, and sucked blood. She gulped greedily, but after a few seconds pulled her mouth away, resulting in a large pop from the suction. She used her tongue to lap up blood on her face and Bo's body. She picked him up like a doll and threw him into the casket. Bo moaned and cried softly. She was on top of him in a second.

CHAPTER FORTY

Lisa and Jimmy lay in her bed. He stretched, rolled over, and held her. She sighed. "I could stay like this forever," she said. "No worries. No problems. Just us."

"My thoughts exactly," Jimmy said. They kissed and embraced.

Finally, Lisa said, "I have to get moving. Coffee?"

"You read my mind."

Lisa slipped into her skimpy robe, with its flowered pattern, and went to the kitchen. Jimmy lay in bed for a few minutes before getting up. He ran a hand over the bed's sheet, still warm and slightly damp from their exertions. He smiled and put on sweatpants, part of an ever-growing assemblage of his clothes accumulating at Lisa's apartment. Jimmy joined Lisa at her small kitchen table for coffee.

"Then it's settled?" Lisa said, after pouring coffee in two mugs with puppies on the sides.

"Yes. This whole idea of storming After Dark is crazy, especially with torches," Jimmy said. "For as nice as they all are, for as much as I like them, we have a bunch of half hopped up crazies who think vampires are inside, kidnapping the homeless, draining their blood. It's insane. If one starts shooting those potato guns with wooden stakes, they all could be whipped into a frenzy. Turn the guns on one another. You saw the damage those guns can do."

"It is farfetched," Lisa added. "But what about Bo and his wounds. The bruises?"

"To me, it looks like he was in a fight," Jimmy said. "He reminds me of the type of guy who's always trying to get laid. Maybe he tried to pick up the wrong girl. One who was already attached."

"The puncture wounds he showed us?"

"They could be self-inflicted." Jimmy raised an eyebrow and made his eyes grow large, as if saying, 'get my point?' "We don't know Bo any better than we do the rest. He could be a psycho, or just looking for attention. The punctures didn't seem that deep, but they certainly add credence to his claim. And I don't like the way they look...infected. The perfect thing to inflame the crazies who do research with a horror movie fan magazine and believe every-thing they read. Plus, they talk like the "Horror of Dracula" is a documentary, a credible one at that, instead of a low-budget horror movie. From the Fifties, no less."

Lisa smiled. "I like them. I like them all. If there's one bright spot it's the fact that while they're consumed by fighting vampires they remain sober. It gives them purpose. I hope they can eventu-ally find another purpose, a better one, to occupy their time."

Lisa reflected a moment, then added, "It is strange that there would be a hidden trap door in the ground next to After Dark. They all seem to know about it."

Jimmy smiled, reached across the table, and took Lisa's hand. "That might be another imaginary thing. I can picture us all converging on that lot, stake guns loaded, torches lit, only to find there is no door, spending hours on our hands and knees. Maybe the vampires moved it. At worst, we end up shooting one of our own or starting a brush fire. The only reason I'll be there is to make sure *that* doesn't happen."

"And if there is a trapdoor?"

"Who knows? The door might have been designed to accept deliveries, away from the building and its...commerce, back when horse-drawn wagons were used. You know, horses shit a lot and don't care where they do it."

Lisa laughed. They showered together and dressed. The day was already hot. They left Lisa's apartment and drove in Jimmy's car toward the stadium. The trunk was loaded with bottled water, protein bars, tampons—and today, two cases of canned sardines in mustard sauce and bags of plastic utensils. You never knew what might get donated for the homeless, Jimmy said. They pulled into a parking place on Fifth Street near After Dark where trees in the park temporarily shaded the morning sun.

"What would criminals think if they broke into your car?" Lisa said, looking through the rear window after she got out.

"Criminals wouldn't be interested in my car. Not even for parts," Jimmy said.

They crossed the street and entered After Dark's main entrance. Bart swooped from table to table, checking the place settings before the 11:00 a.m. opening, and didn't see them at first. Jimmy stood near the door. Lisa tracked him down.

"Bart, I need to talk with you."

"What a dedicated employee. Coming to work on her day off," Bart chimed. "I think I can find some gratis work for you to do. Just a little."

"Lisa smiled. "It's serious, Bart."

"Oh no. I hope you're not leaving us." Bart stopped. He looked worried. Placed a hand over his heart. "I can't do anything for more money, not now, anyway, not that you don't deserve it, but I'd have to give everyone a raise. And not everyone deserves a raise. I always say, let them work harder for tips."

"This is serious."

Bart looked from Lisa to Jimmy waiting by the door. Jimmy walked toward them. Bart motioned for the two to follow him to his office. Jose and Miguel watched from the kitchen. After they were inside the office, Bart closed the door and waved his arm in the direction of two chairs.

Once they were all seated, Bart adjusted the knot in his tie and laid his small hands flat on the desktop. "What is so serious with you," Lisa?" Bart smiled.

Lisa introduced Jimmy. She told Bart about their work with the homeless. She began a long preamble about passing out water and tampons, which caused Bart to blush. Lisa knew she lost Bart's attention when his eyes glazed over. That's when she hit the important part and raised her voice.

"There's a group of homeless, mostly from the greater neighborhood, mostly drug users, some alcoholics, and a few with mental conditions, who believe vampires live in the basement."

"Who?" Bart interrupted, half-rising from his seat.

"Vampires."

"Ah, yes. Of course," Bart said. He sat and smiled at the couple. He looked nervous.

"The vampires have beasts who kidnap the homeless at night, and hold them in cells in the basement *here*. Apparently, the vampires don't like tainted junkie blood and drain their blood after the withdrawal symptoms end and their blood is clean. Several of these people claim to have been prisoners here and escaped."

Bart's mouth opened but he said nothing. Then he scratched his chin as if buying time for an answer.

"I might add that *we* are skeptics," Jimmy interjected. "This group has planned an attack on After Dark tomorrow morning with stakes and torches. I think they're all crazy. We're afraid they'll hurt someone or even themselves."

"That's preposterous!" Bart said, slamming a palm on his desk. "It's insane. Torches? They'll burn down the neighborhood. Possibly the stadium. This very building. It's historic."

"That's why we're here," Lisa said.

Beads of sweat rose on Bart's forehead. Wet rings appeared on his purple shirt under the arms.

"We didn't want to go to the police without you knowing," Jimmy said. "However, *you* might want to call them."

"No. No. No," Bart said, wagging his tiny index finger, and pushing his wheeled chair backward. "No. No. No. No police. That will be scandalous for the business. You were right to come to me." Bart lowered his head and thought for a moment, pulled his chair back to the desk. "Who would like a Diet Coke? It's my only weakness."

Bart ran for the door and disappeared before Lisa and Jimmy responded. "Do you think he'll be back?" Jimmy said.

"He's a big Diet Coke fan," Lisa said. "That's all I see him drink. He'll be back."

"I know this isn't the Alamo, but this building will be attacked tomorrow," Jimmy said.

They waited in silence for several minutes. Bart returned, struggling with the doorknob before finally entering with three large glasses of fountain soda. He closed the office door with a kick. He set down the glasses, for Jimmy, Lisa, and himself, then pulled paper straws from his shirt pocket and coasters from a back pocket.

"Do you always carry them around?" Jimmy joked.

"Hardly," Bart responded with an imperious tone.

Bart sat behind his desk, opened the straw, shoved it in his glass, and took a large suck of the diet soda. "That's better," he said after he finally finished. He waved his hand for Lisa and Jimmy to join him. They peeled off the paper from their straws and sipped at the Coke. Bart retrieved their paper straw sleeves with his tiny hand and dropped them in a waste can under the desk.

Bart seemed more relaxed than he had been since Lisa's story started. "I reiterate, there is no need for police intervention. What would it take to convince this group to call off their attack? To understand there is nothing sinister in this basement, except cobwebs and perhaps a leaky pipe." Bart shrugged his shoulders as if seeking help from the couple.

"I don't know," Lisa said. "They seem determined to carry out this attack."

"How many know about this? How many attackers will there be?" Bart said.

Lisa counted off the names in her head. Overboard George and Mad Maggie, Bad Nelson and Megan, Bo, Old Harriet, New Girl, and them. "There are nine attackers if everyone shows up and you include us, but we were not going to attack, just show up to ensure nobody goes crazy and nobody gets hurt. As far as I know, we nine are the only ones who know about all this."

"Interesting," Bart mused. "And gossip on the street. How do you account for that?"

"We, actually *they*, were trying to keep this attack a secret," Jimmy said. "You know, loose lips sink ships."

"I see." Bart looked at the ceiling for a moment and returned his gaze toward Lisa. "Excellent. Nine attackers. How many people would it take to overcome vampires?" He cocked his small head toward Lisa. "How many vampires are here...supposedly?"

"They think two, maybe three, plus the Whistlers, maybe four or five of them."

"What's a Whistler?" Bart's voice showed skepticism."

"The Whistlers are things that hunt the homeless. Bring them to the basement. Apparently. And they claim several have been lost over the summer," Lisa said. "Killed."

"Their knowledge is very detailed. Supposing for a minute there are vampires, what do you think are the odds of such an attack working?" Bart said. He folded his little hands and leaned over the desk at the couple.

"First of all, we don't suppose there are vampires," Jimmy said. "If we could get a look at the basement, maybe we could convince the others there is nothing down there."

Bart pointed a finger at Jimmy. "That's an excellent idea, Jimmy. Excellent!" Bart said, smiling.

"I was under the impression the steps to the basement weren't safe," Lisa said. "That's what everyone has always claimed."

"We had them replaced, probably when you were off," Bart said, matter-of-factly. "Mexicans. They work like demons. Had the steps demolished and carted off and new ones replaced, all in one long day."

"It's strange no one talked about it," Lisa said.

Bart chuckled, then laughed more. "I wouldn't expect anyone to talk about it, my dear. It wasn't gossip." He smirked and wagged his head from side to side. "Gossip is the only thing talked about in this joint. You know that, Lisa. After all, if the staff doesn't use the steps, then they have nothing to complain about. Now, finish your drinks and we'll all go to the basement. I'm very busy."

Bart drained his soda, sucking air noisily, then waited, smiling, for Lisa and Jimmy to finish off their glasses. Lisa licked her lips and shivered.

"That Coke tasted funny, don't you think?" Lisa said.

Jimmy smacked his lips a few times. Shrugged.

"Mine tasted fine," Bart said. "You know me and my Diet Coke. I'm a connoisseur. Pete just tapped a new one."

Bart rose, burped, and excused himself. He pulled a large key from his pant pocket and showed it to the couple. "Our passage is this way."

Bart led the couple from his office, toward the kitchen, and the large door to the basement. He looked around to see who might be watching, before inserting the key in the lock and, with difficulty, turning it.

Bart pulled open the door and let Lisa and Jimmy descend the stairs first. Bart closed the door and locked it. Lisa turned around and stopped halfway down the steps. "Is that necessary?"

"Of course," Bart said, sounding wounded by her question. "Suppose a patron looking for the bathroom fell down these. That would cause another attack, one by their lawyers. And we *all* would be looking for new jobs."

Bart descended, almost pressing them forward. Lisa continued. Jimmy was already at the bottom. "Is there a light down here? The place is dark," Jimmy said. "I can't see a thing."

"Stay where you are," Bart answered. "I'll have to find the switch. This isn't my residence, you know. I come down here once in a blue moon."

Lisa reached the bottom of the steps. She found Jimmy's hand and held it. Bart slowed his progress.

"It smells down here, like something dead," she said. "I suddenly feel a little woozy. It must be the smell."

"It does stink," Jimmy said. "I feel funny, too." He put his arm around Lisa.

"All closed basements have odors. Probably a dry drain lets in sewer gas," Bart said. "It should pass in a minute. Actually, I don't mind the smell. Hardly notice it."

Jimmy guided Lisa forward a few steps in the dark. "How about those lights!"

"Of course." Bart's voice receded. Then there was silence.

"Bart. Are you okay?" Lisa whispered. Silence followed.

Lisa walked toward the shadows where Bart had disappeared. She called again. Jimmy pulled her back. He called Bart. Suddenly, the space was filled with light. The captives howled immediately.

"There are people down here," Lisa said. "They're naked." Then she passed out. Jimmy caught her and lowered her to the floor. He kneeled over her. He looked up at Bart, who stood nearby.

Jimmy tried to stand. Sank to his knees again. "You drugged us," Jimmy said. He collapsed, too.

"Indeed. You two will make a nice temporary addition to our menagerie. The masters will be pleased." Bart smiled. "Two down and seven to go. We'll meet the rest of your group tomorrow. A hundred of your deadbeat friends couldn't handle our hive. These ancient vampires could wipe out this entire city."

The captives continued to howl, imploring Bart to let them go. He got the hose and sprayed them with cold water until they shut up. Now there were only a few whimpers. Bart dragged Jimmy, who had collapsed over Lisa, toward an empty cell. He did this with great difficulty, managing to budge Jimmy only a few inches at a time.

"Where are these handlers when you need one?" he called into the empty darkness.

As Bart struggled, the crypt door opened, and the vampires glided out and approached the cells. Both were dressed in their threadbare eveningwear.

"Masters. I have two clean bloods for your enjoyment," Bart said. He bowed and continued to tug Jimmy's wrists.

The male vampire grabbed Jimmy's shirt and picked him up with one hand until his feet dangled in midair. He walked Jimmy to the closest empty cell and dropped him inside. Then he picked up Lisa and threw her on his back. He started for the next cell and stopped suddenly. He sniffed the air and then Lisa.

"Bart!" the male vampire shouted. Bart shrank away toward the upstairs steps. "You have done exceedingly well. Your reward will be great." Bart stopped his retreat and stood frozen. The vampire grinned. "This one is pregnant!"

"What!" the vampiress screamed. She rushed to Lisa and smelled her body, burying her nose in the clothing. "Strip her, Bart. I want to make sure. There must be no mistake."

Bart said, "But..."

"Do it!" she demanded.

The male vampire put Lisa in a separate cell, laid her on the floor, and stepped back. Bart rushed to Lisa, kneeled, and unbuttoned her blouse with trembling hands. He sweated profusely. His purple shirt was soaked. He looked nervously at the vampires and Lisa as he continued the strip. After she was naked, Bart crawled away. The vampiress picked up Lisa by the arm and held her like a ragdoll off the floor. She smelled Lisa's body slowly, deeply. She licked her breasts. Then she sat her carefully in the empty cell.

"Lock the cell doors, Bart," she demanded of the little man.

Bart ran to the wall, retrieved the key, and locked Jimmy and Lisa's cells. He shrank away again.

"Well?" Gerrard said.

The vampiress turned to the male and smiled. "She's pregnant. So recent she probably doesn't know yet. The baby is barely detectible, but her body is already changing."

The male clasped his hands. "When was the last time we fed on an infant?"

"In Prague," she said. "So many years ago. Such a magical period. What a magnificent ceremony. There were so many of us then." The vampiress closed her eyes and shuddered. "So many we were allowed only a thimble full of pure blood. Its taste still burns in my mind. Bart! Come to me," she called.

"Please don't hurt me, Mistress." He minced toward her on his diminutive legs.

"Don't fear. I don't want your cocaine-laced blood. I can smell the drug on you." She took Bart in her arms and squeezed. He screamed in pain. She released him immediately and let him drop to the floor. Bart scrambled away and stood, brushing off his clothes.

"Bart, she must have special care. She will need bigger quarters down here. Good food. She will carry the baby to term and deliver. Then while the infant is still slippery, we will consume the child, the blood of which will give us incredible strength. More than even now. I am very proud of you, Bart."

Bart smiled and retreated a few steps.

The vampire walked to Jimmy's cage, where Gerrard lifted Jimmy, with his arm through the bars. He sniffed Jimmy. "This is the father," Gerrard said. He offered Jimmy's body to the vampiress. She approached, sniffed him through the bars, and stepped away. Gerrard dropped Jimmy on the floor. His head hit the empty slop bucket.

"I smell his sperm in her now, probably from a morning

coupling," the vampiress said. She looked at Gerrard and tittered. "This will be truly wonderful."

"What about the man?" Bart asked, pointing toward Jimmy.

"His work is done," Gerrard said. "We'll consume him tomorrow."

"Will Bo know what to do?" Bart asked.

"Bo will know," the vampiress cut him off. "I have trained Bo personally."

She and Gerrard laughed. She smiled at Bart, revealing her black teeth.

Bart recoiled.

"Come here!" she demanded.

Bart obeyed.

The vampiress patted Bart's cheek and pulled him closer. "It might be necessary to give *you* some instruction personally."

Bart sobbed. "Whatever is your pleasure, Mistress."

She let Bart go and he shrank away, ready to return up the steps. "I do have bad news, Masters."

"You know we don't like bad news," Gerrard said. Still, he smiled at Bart.

"There is a group of homeless who know about our colony," Bart said. "Among them, I believe, are the four who escaped over the summer. They plan to storm the basement with stakes and torches tomorrow morning" Bart waved his arm toward the cages. "These two told me of the plan just now. Of course, I came immediately to tell you and brought them with me."

"How would they get in?" Gerrard said. He looked skeptical.

"Bo might be involved with them," Bart said. "Bo's the only other who knows how to get in. How to enter the crypt. Be warned, Masters."

"How many infidels are there?" Eva the vampiress asked.

"Nine with these two," Bart said.

Gerrard and the vampiress looked at each other. They clapped their hands, threw back their heads, and laughed. Their hollow voices filled the chamber. The captives cried again.

"You're a fool, Bart," Eva said. "In one campaign Gerrard slaughtered a hundred armed men in an hour with his bare hands. How they shrieked in terror. Then we drank the blood of the wounded until we could hold no more."

"Of course, Mistress," Bart said. He sweated more and stuttered, "I understand they don't have a chance against you."

"Charles, if he is fully turned, could handle seven of these homeless...junkers, with their stakes and torches. Let them come. Leave the door open. We welcome them. This will solve all our problems. The escapees will be returned, and their friends and those they have confided in will be eliminated. Double them up if we run out of cages. We will have—what do they call it—a homecoming." Gerrard spoke to Eva in their native dialogue. She listened and answered. They talked for several minutes. Although he couldn't understand the language, Bart knew an important plan was formulated.

Finally, the vampiress looked at Bart, who recoiled a few more steps. She said, "We are in agreement that there might be more than the nine who know about our colony. Prepare us to travel with our friends to another city. Make sure the means to convey us has space for the pregnant one." The vampiress was quiet for a moment. She turned suddenly to Bart, adding with a hiss, "We will not leave her behind!" she hissed. "Never!"

"And Bo?" Bart's voice quivered.

She looked toward Gerrard and back to Bart. Her eyes were hard. She pronounced each word separately, distinctly, in her hollow voice. "As for Bo, I do not believe my little rabbit would betray us. He may become a casualty of war. I have not decided. Still, I have grown so fond of him. As of this moment, I expect to take him with me. He is in my casket now."

CHAPTER FORTY-ONE

Bo crawled from the casket and fell to the floor in pain. The vampiress lay naked, eyes staring, the hint of a smile on her face. Or was it a smirk? Bo couldn't decide. Had she been alive, Bo would have lusted over her body. Well-fed recently, her skin was flawless, like alabaster. Her face was young and beautiful. Her hair was glossy. However, Bo knew the flesh was hard and cold, the teeth stained almost black from centuries of drinking human blood, the canine teeth long and sharp. Her eyes were dark and hard, hypnotic in their stare. He was repulsed by the corpse but still could not take his eyes off her as he made a slow, painful retreat.

Her ragged gown was draped over the casket's open lid. It smelled and was crusty in spots. Bo's only thought was escaping. His clothes lay in shreds on the crypt floor. New scratches and puncture marks stung. Old wounds still ached and barely had begun to heal. Most were infected. Charles Van der Meer lay in *his* casket still encased in a chrysalis. The metamorphosis from human to vampire was not yet complete. However, the chrysalis was no longer soft and undulated. It was hard and nearly transparent. The exterior was cracked. Charles moved inside, stretching his legs, opening and closing his hands, turning his head slightly, this way and that. Charles looked more like a corpse than ever.

Bo grabbed his shoes, opened the crypt door, limped through the opening, and closed it. The captives whined when they saw him run through the basement naked. They begged for mercy, a chance to escape with him.

Lisa and Jimmy were among them. Lisa pointed at the key on the wall.

"Get us out of here. There's the key," Lisa implored.

"Come on, Bo. They'll kill us," Jimmy screamed. "They know about the attack. Bart told the vampires. I heard him. I believe the group. We have no chance against them. It'll be a massacre. They're too strong. Please!"

Whether he didn't see Lisa and Jimmy or couldn't understand them among the cacophony of cries from the captives, Bo ignored the prisoners and turned his back on them to rummage through the clothing pile. Most of the clothes were shredded. Some didn't fit, and there were women's clothes, too. Heaps of shoes, sandals, flip-flops, underwear, winter coats, scarves, hats, all mixed. Eventually, he found a dirty shirt and blood-stained jeans he could squeeze into. Near the top of the pile he recognized Ridge's blood-soaked T-shirt, torn from collar to hem by the Whistlers, poked with holes, and one of TJ's sneakers, He could not bring himself to touch them, bring them along to show their parents. He backed away from the pile, clutching the clothes he had found for himself.

After he was dressed, Bo took one fleeting look at the cells, and saw Lisa naked, her crotch shaved—for Jimmy, no doubt, he thought—holding out an arm to him through the bars. Jimmy shook his cell door furiously and screamed. Bo bolted for the exterior steps, threw open the trapdoor at the top, and let it slam shut after he was outside. The howling from inside died immediately, no longer audible above ground.

The sun was up, well above the horizon. A light breeze stirred trash nearby but couldn't hide the impending day's heat. The attack would start soon. Bo expected to see the vampire hunters converge on the lot from their various directions, murder in their eyes, weapons in their hands. He knew PVC pipes, bottled gas, wooden stakes, and torches, would be ineffective against the dead, even during daylight when the creatures were at their weakest. He wondered whether he had the strength to fight. If any of them would survive. Loss of blood and infection had weakened Bo. He felt feverish. He dropped to the ground, sat cross-legged, and cried. How could this have happened to him? He had left Lisa and Jimmy to die in the basement. Saved his own skin.

Bo lost track of time. The next thing he knew Bad Nelson shook his shoulder. "What the fuck happened to you?" Bad Nelson said, incredulously.

"The vampire."

"Again?"

Bo nodded his head.

"You're in no shape to fight the undead. You'll have to wait outside with Lisa and Jimmy."

"I think they're going to be no-shows."

"What do you mean?" Bad Nelson said.

There was a pause. Finally, Bo said, "It's just a feeling. They didn't seem to like the plan."

"They promised to be here," Bad Nelson said, almost whining. "Safety in numbers. Remember?"

Bo shrugged his shoulders. "I just got a feeling about them."

Bad Nelson pulled his stake gun and a backpack to Bo's side. "There's extra stakes and gas canisters in my bag." He opened the top zipper and showed Bo. "You can drop it inside the hole if we need anything."

"Got it," Bo said.

"Don't let the bag hit anybody."

"Of course."

Bad Nelson looked through the nearby grass. "Where's the door?"

"I'm sitting on it. Here's the handle." Bo pulled up an oblong metal handle by his side. "The lock's already open. I think they're waiting for us."

"How would they know? Who would tell them? This whole operation has been secret."

"It's just a feeling I have."

Bo pulled a stake from the backpack and inserted it through the door handle to keep it exposed.

"Were you down there?"

"Just for a second."

"How's everything look?"

"Quiet." Bo shook his head back and forth as if disagreeing with his own words. "They have a bunch of people in cages screaming to get out. I had to leave."

"You didn't free them?"

"No time," Bo said. "Plus, they're all naked. Can you imagine that? A half dozen bare-assed people jumping out of a hole in the ground? The key to the cells is hanging on the wall. It's big. You can't miss it."

"We'll have to put someone in charge of getting the key, letting them all out," Bad Nelson said. "I know what it's like. We can't leave them there."

"Some good news," Bo said. "The new vampire is still in some kind of a cocoon. He'll be easy to dart. You can see him inside it. Just shoot where you think the heart is. The female was catatonic when I left. I don't know whether she'll wake. Whether she can sense what's going on. Her coffin is open. The male was in a coffin with the lid closed."

Bad Nelson smiled. "Like's his privacy, huh? This is going to be a walk in the park."

"I doubt it, but I hope so," Bo said. "Be careful. These are good people."

Bad Nelson said, "I made my rounds. Everybody's in place,

except for Lisa and Jimmy. The rest of them are waiting for my signal."

"Signal?"

Bad Nelson pulled a bottle rocket from his backpack, lit the fuse, and held it over his head. A flare shot into the air and burst with a bang into red and blue colors, followed by smaller cracks.

"What happened to ten o'clock? So much for secrecy," Bo said. He looked up at Bad Nelson in disbelief.

Bad Nelson looked at Bo with contempt. "Do you have a better way to get everybody moving at once when they're so far apart? Smoke signals? The sound won't be noticed. How many gunshots are there on any given day."

Bo smiled back.

Overboard George was the first to appear crossing Fifth Street. Mad Maggie was at his side. Both carried PVC stake guns and torches. When Lisa and Jimmy didn't show, Megan picked up Old Harriet and New Girl, who waited aimlessly in their initial positions. The five converged on the trap door flawlessly, all jogging the last couple of yards to reach Bad Nelson and Bo. All were armed with PVC guns and extra stakes. Old Harriet wore a bandana and had her face covered with camouflage paint. "I got this," she said pointing to the face paint, "from Hunter John." Her beehive hairdo stood erect, recently redone.

"Everyone ready?" Bad Nelson asked, looking from face to face.

Each gave a single nod of his or her head.

"Are we waiting for Lisa and Jimmy?" New Girl asked as if the attack wouldn't be possible without them.

"They were skeptical from the beginning," Overboard George said. "They're not going to show. If they do, they can help with the mop-up. They can hose the ashes or the goo, whatever's going to be left, into the drains."

"I knew they couldn't be trusted," Old Harriet groused.

"They're probably spilling their guts at the police precinct right now."

"Let them," Mad Maggie said. "Who's going to believe a story about vampires? Let them tell the whole story. Let the story go back to Transylvania. They'll be in straight jackets before they're finished, confined in a rubber room. It's safe to say we're on our own, and that's just the way I like it."

Overboard George looked around the group. "My friends, welcome to the madcap world of fighting the undead. Let's get it on."

Before they opened the basement door, Bad Nelson told the group Bo would take the place of Lisa and Jimmy outside, and pass down more stakes and gas, if needed. After seeing the disheveled Bo, no one complained or commented.

"Looks like you had a rough night," Overboard George said. "Hope you can remember the party you came from."

Bo shook his head and rolled off the trap door.

"One more thing," Bad Nelson said. "There's hardly a cloud in the sky. That will give us a large square of sunlight on the floor at the bottom of the steps. Bo, make sure this door stays open. The sunlight will protect us *if* the vampires make their own attack."

Bad Nelson nodded toward Bo. With difficulty, Bo raised the door and gently let it fall back against the ground. Only the hinge creaked. One by one the vampire hunters stepped inside and descended the steps. At the bottom, Bad Nelson showed the others the protective oblong of sunlight on the floor and used his arms to make a square in the air. The vampire fighters nodded that they understood. Bad Nelson pressed a finger to his lips, indicating silence. He looked to his vampire hunters. Each sweated profusely.

"That smell again," New Girl said. "I don't know if I can take it."

"You'll do fine," Overboard George whispered. "You got me by your side. Remember, today you have a way out."

New Girl smiled and nodded.

Outside, Bo perched on the open door, ensuring it would not close. He held Bad Nelson's backpack on his lap, opened and closed the zipper to ensure it worked freely, ran his fingers over the stakes, examined the points on a few, and hefted the extra gas canisters. Bo looked over the stairwell. The shadow of his head appeared on the floor in the sunlight safety zone. Finally, he breathed a sigh of relief and pulled back.

From below, the captives began wailing.

"I'll shut them up," Overboard George said, running to the cages, shouting at the captives.

"No! Come back," Bad Nelson shrieked. "We need you here."

Mad Maggie tried to join Overboard George, but Bad Nelson pulled her back into the light. "We have to take care of the Whistlers first. We need everybody. Pay attention! I'm going to open the pen."

Bad Nelson ran to the pen and grabbed the lever. The Whistlers threw themselves at the door, baring their teeth, snapping their jaws, as if they knew they were under attack.

"Charge your weapons," Bad Nelson called. "Get ready to shoot!"

There was bedlam in the basement. The Whistlers snarled. The naked prisoners wailed. Overboard George screamed at the captives and banged one of his torch handles against the bars. It had no effect. Bad Nelson couldn't open the Whistler door with one arm. He dropped his weapon to use two hands. He gave a mighty tug. The Whistler pen latch opened a few inches.

In a frenzy, the Whistlers nosed through the door a few inches and began squeezing through. Bad Nelson retrieved his gun, aimed, and shot the first Whistler through the gate in the shoulder. The beast yelped. Stopped. Howled in pain. Bad Nelson seated a new stake through the tight-fitting rubber gasket and recharged his gun's compression chamber. The beasts behind bit the wounded Whistler, and pushed it through the opening. Old Harriet and Mad Maggie unleashed their stakes, both striking the wounded beast.

One dart pierced the heart and the animal rolled over dead. Bad Nelson shot the next creature that came through the gate. It whimpered, quivered for a moment, and dropped dead. The dead beasts melted into a viscous, foul-smelling liquid, in which some of the bristly hair still floated. The last two Whistlers slipped on the goo and threw themselves through the gate.

New Girl and Megan fired their guns. One dart missed, striking the wall and splintered into many sharp, fast-moving pieces. The second stake hit one of the beasts in the mouth. It chased the women into the sunlight, choking on the wood, and burst into flames as it hit the rays. The heat scorched New Girl's purple hair. The fourth Whistler turned on Bad Nelson. Crouched. Growled. It was hit by four stakes in quick succession before it could pounce. It dropped dead without a sound and bubbled into a putrid pool on the floor.

"Reload! Reload!" Bad Nelson called. For the first time since the fight began, no one could fire a gun. "Back to the steps!" he instructed them. They dropped back into the sunlight and seated new stakes, charged their guns' combustion chambers. The vampire hunters breathed heavily, sweated, smiled at one another, and even giggled.

"Too bad Hunter John's missing this," Old Harriet chirped.

Hearing the commotion, Bo crawled to the edge of the doorway. The vampire fighters were crowded into the sunlight. They kept their backs to the steps. Bo saw the steaming puddles on the floor. Heard only the captives' screams. Figured the Whistlers were done. Overboard George was missing, but Bo heard him screaming at the prisoners. The captives just got louder. Bo called down the steps, "How's everything going? There's a hell of a lot of noise."

They all looked up at Bo. "The Whistlers are gone," Old Harriet said with glee. "All reduced to slime and hair. Even the bones decayed in front of us. What a fucking sight!"

"That's great. Thank God, you got them." Bo looked quickly at the sky. "You better hurry. It's clouding up in the...west, I think. Getting windy, too. You're going to lose your sunlight."

"We got the sun lights down here," Mad Maggie said with a grin. "I already used them once."

"Still, you better hurry," Bo said.

"The crypt's the next stop," Overboard George yelled, after rejoining the group in the sunlight. The captives still screamed, so much so that no voice was coherent.

"What about the prisoners?" Mad Maggie said. "Why didn't you leave them out?"

"They're safer in the cells for right now," Overboard George said. "They caught Lisa and Jimmy, too."

Old Harriet looked up the stairs. "Throw me some water."

"Don't got none," Bo called back.

The crypt door burst open, banging off the wall behind it. The fighters gave a start. The vampiress, wearing a long glove, reached into the square of sunlight, grabbed New Girl, and threw her to Gerrard.

"I'm getting the pregnant one," she hissed, "before one of these imbeciles shoots her. Kill the rest!"

Gerrard caught New Girl. "My little lost lamb has returned." He smiled, sniffed her, exposed the neck, and sank his teeth in. New Girl whimpered and coughed once. The vampire hunters stood stunned. Gerrard took several mighty sucks and tossed the limp body away. Blood trailed from New Girl's neck while her body arched through the air. Blood streamed down Gerrard's chin, and he burped a mouthful on the ground, along with a piece of bloody flesh ripped from New Girl's throat.

"Shoot the mother fucker!" Mad Maggie screamed.

The group unleashed their stakes at once. Gerrard, in a blur of movement, batted the stakes away, splintering them against the walls and floor.

Bo looked on from above hidden by the doorframe. He turned

repeatedly from the action in the basement to the sky, watching the clouds progress above him. They crept closer to the sun.

"Reload," Bad Nelson called as if he were an infantry commander in an old movie.

As the group recharged their combustion chambers, the direct sunlight disappeared behind a cloud.

"Your protection is gone," Gerrard laughed, in his chilling hollow voice. "Let's see how brave you mortals are now.

In an instant, Gerrard grabbed Mad Maggie, the closest, and flung her across the basement toward the crypt. She landed hard on her gun, which snapped in half. With the wind knocked out of her, she crawled into the crypt, expecting the vampire to follow. She raised her gun only to find the stake had fallen out of the broken barrel. She grabbed the stake. She raised to her knees, still trying to suck air back into her lungs.

Meanwhile, Gerrard turned to Bad Nelson, who had loaded his dart and shot. The missile hit Gerrard. The vampire backed away in disbelief, looking at his impaled hand. Gerrard grimaced. He hissed, exposing his black teeth. As he reached for Bad Nelson with his good hand, the sun came out and burned his flesh. The vampire howled and retreated from the light.

"Gerrard!" Eva called her brother from the basement's opposite end.

Gerrard turned in surprise, a blur, but it was too late. Mad Maggie, with a stake in hand, launched herself at the male vampire. Mad Maggie was in full flight, off the ground, the stake ready in her cocked arm, by the time the vampires saw her. The stake hit his spine, slid to the side, penetrated his ribs, and struck the heart as the female vampire arrived at his side to watch him burst into flames. Mad Maggie hit the floor, rolled, blackened by the corpse's ashes. Eva recoiled from the flames.

Overboard George pulled Mad Maggie into the light-filled oblong. The vampiress howled in disbelief. She glared at the group.

The sunlight faded, as the edge of a cloud passed before the sun. Then it reappeared, only to fade again. The vampiress waited with anticipation for the direct sunlight to disappear completely. She rocked back and forth toward the steps, ready to launch herself as soon as the sun disappeared. Instead, the string of clouds moved on and the sunlight returned with full force.

"Stake the cunt," Overboard George cried. Mad Maggie pulled her machete. They shot. The stakes clattered off the wall and floor. Hit nothing. There was no blood on the floor. Eva outraced the darts to the feeding room, where she threw the door closed behind her and locked it from inside.

The group members looked at one another in disbelief. "Reload," Bad Nelson choked. "I never saw anything that fast. She was faster than a blur."

"There was no blur that I seen," Overboard George said.

"Maybe she just disappeared," Old Harriet said. "They say a Sasquatch can do that, disappear when it wants to. I saw it on the television." She raised a finger in the air. "Watch for orbs. She might be in an orb."

"There's another vampire in the crypt," Mad Maggie said. "In a cocoon. In a coffin. I seen him."

The group reloaded, charged their weapons, and moved toward the crypt door in unison. They leveled their guns. Overboard George joined Bad Nelson, and Megan to fill the doorway. Old Harriet with her stake gun and Mad Maggie with her machete stood behind the front row. The group coughed on the fetid odor that still escaped from the crypt. The chrysalis exploded in hundreds of glass-like shards, covering the vampire hunters. Charles Van der Meer stood naked in the casket. His thin body was waxen, wet from the amniotic-like fluid that coated him. He stepped out to face them. He looked at their faces and hissed. He clenched and unclenched his hands. Long nails grew from the fingertips. Long canine teeth extended from his gums. He stopped. The vampire hunters stood frozen for a moment. Charles coughed and expelled black tumors from his lungs, spit them on the floor.

"Well, ain't this special," Overboard George said, "a fucking new release." He fired a stake that passed through Charles's stomach and came out his back. A vile, black syrupy substance seeped from the wound. The other vampire hunters unloaded their guns, striking Charles in the torso. One dart pierced his heart. Charles's expression changed from a sneer to one of surprise, before his body was consumed in flames and fell back into the soupy fluid in the casket.

Old Harriet looked around proudly, smiling. "I must say, this is the *best* vampire killing I ever attended." She added as an aside, "And the fucking last one, I hope."

They withdrew from the crypt and its noxious odors, and returned to the sunlight on the floor, which was now longer and narrower.

"We gotta get those people freed," Overboard George said. "I'll get the key and let them out. The rest of you keep your stakes trained on that door. Stay in the sunlight. Start firing if that door moves an inch, makes one rattle."

Overboard George crept across the basement and plucked the key from the wall. He went to work opening the doors and releasing the prisoners. The incarcerated clamored again, unwilling to wait their turn, everyone calling to be let out immediately. The prisoners ransacked the clothing pile for something to wear. Jimmy was the only one who had remained clothed. He found Lisa's shirt and pants in the arms of another woman. He pulled them away from her and returned them to Lisa, who dressed immediately.

While the captives climbed the steps to the exterior and freedom, blinking, shielding their eyes from the bright afternoon sun, Lisa and Jimmy remained inside with the vampire hunters, within the ever-closing rectangle of light. The couple couldn't remember how they got in the basement, or how Lisa was undressed.

"I can't be sure, but I think Bart was in on it," Lisa said. "I just don't know."

"My mind is a blank," Jimmy said. He shook his head.

"Let's stake the little fucker, that Bart," Old Harriet said. "Bring him down here and shoot him a little bit at a time. That's how you get to the truth. He chased me away from that dumpster out back. Wouldn't let me have a thing. 'Save your money and buy something,' he says to me, all hoity-toity."

Mad Maggie shouted, "Let me give him a kick in the pills before you stake him."

"I'm sure he's long gone," Overboard George said. "He's the type that never gets caught. We'll deal with Bo when we get outside."

After more talk and banter, Bad Nelson said finally, "What do we do now? Wait her out? She'll have to come out at some point. Eventually, she'll have to eat again."

"She might be too fast for us, even with the stake guns," Old Harriet said. "I'm all for ending her miserable existence, but she outran our stakes."

"She won't outrun a bullet," Mad Maggie said. "I'll put one between her ears. That'll slow the bitch down. Then we'll stake her"

"Bullets don't work on vampires," Megan said. After a pause, she added, "Supposedly."

Mad Maggie raised her index finger in the air. "If we notch a cross in the bullet tips, it will take the bitch down. Lead is soft. I seen it in a movie." She paused to scratch her head and think. "Might have been *Blade*, but I don't remember. It'll come to me, though. It always does." She looked at Jimmy.

"If you say notches on bullets work, I don't doubt it, Mad Maggie," Jimmy said. "I'll never question anything you say. As far as I'm concerned, *Famous Monsters of Filmland* is the Bible when it comes to vampires."

Mad Maggie and Overboard George smiled. George said he knew where to get a revolver and bullets. They prepared to go get them.

"I'll stay as a guard," Old Harriet said.

"If she decides to come busting out of that feeding room, all of us together won't stop her," Overboard George said. "Let's all go for the gun and bullets. We'll take our chances she'll still be here when we get back. Before it gets dark. She can't go outside now, anyway."

"You guys have any objections?" Bad Nelson asked Lisa and Jimmy.

"None," Jimmy said. "The way you guys handle stake guns, you're all sharpshooters in my book."

They started to file up the steps to the exterior. "Damn!" Overboard George said. "We forgot to light our torches. Too much excitement going on."

The group laughed.

Bo was missing when they got outside and closed the door. Bad Nelson's backpack remained on the grass. There was no trace of Bo. The basement captives also evaporated into the crowd on Fifth Street. It appeared none wanted to stay near After Dark.

CHAPTER FORTY-TWO

THE NEW WHITE VAN SAT AT THE LOADING DOCK, ENGINE running, gas tank full. Two burly attendants stood nearby, stern and solemn. Both had long, thick mustaches and curly black hair. They wore jeans and carried pistols in holsters on their sides, hidden under dark hoodies. An oversized casket, new and shiny, nearly filled the back of the vehicle. Bart stood across from the attendants in a spiffy suit, with a white shirt and purple tie. Near him were two five-gallon buckets that had contained dirt from the original grave of the vampiress.

She lingered in the shadows. Although it was evening, there was still enough light to bake her in a few seconds in the rays of the direct sun. "Bart, I was thinking," Eva said. It was the first she had spoken since arriving at the loading dock. "I want this Lisa and her baby. *She* has cost me my brother Gerrard. I will postpone this trip. If you move her schedule back to working in the evening, I can capture her myself. Take her with me."

"I don't know if that is wise, Mistress," Bart said. "Too many things could go wrong."

"We agree," one attendant said. The other talked to her in the ancient dialogue she had used with Gerrard.

She answered curtly in the strange language. Her tongue rolled around her lips. Her eyes were dark and hard. The men fell silent and bowed their heads.

"Perhaps," Bart started.

"Not perhaps." The vampire cut him off. "I want Lisa to suffer for what she and her friends did to our haven. I want her to watch her baby sucked dry the minute it is born."

"There will be other pregnant women," Bart said. "You can have your pick."

"Silence!" the vampiress screamed.

Bart retreated. The attendants remained silent with their heads bowed.

"I want Lisa. I want to murder her friends, that little band of junkers that killed Gerrard. You, Bart, can track them down, and I will kill them."

"I don't like them any more than you do, Mistress," Bart added, "but once they get back on the street they probably will kill themselves with overdoes and disease. That kind of death will be more painful and prolonged, like torture. They will see it coming, and realize it, but not be able to do anything about it. Their addictions are that powerful. Almost as powerful as you are."

Eva thought for a moment. "You might be right about the friends," she said. "Though not all of them use drugs."

"If you like, Mistress, I and my brother Kazmer will return here after you are safe, when things get colder, as they say, hunt them down and end their lives," the attendant said in English, so Bart would understand. "We can capture Lisa and bring her to you in the new colony."

"Of course," the vampiress said to Lazlo. She smiled, not a hint of her anger remained. She spoke to the men in her language. They answered humbly and bowed as if they suddenly felt honored. She called each to her, put her hands on their shoulders, and kissed the tops of their heads when they bowed. The men backed away solemnly, stole glances, and smiled at each other.

"So, Bart. We will take your suggestion. Go soon. Even now," the female vampire said. "When our plan is complete Lazlo will contact you. Everything will be put in place, and you will help."

"Yes, Mistress. It will be my pleasure to make you happy," Bart said, bending slightly at the knees as he talked.

The vampiress took a step from the deeper shadows. "He is here." She smiled again.

Bo climbed on the loading dock. He was flushed and sweating.

"What took you so long, Bo? We are waiting."

"Traffic," Bo answered, mechanically. He looked at the casket already in the van and at the two attendants. "It looks like you're all set. You don't really need me."

"Oh?" the vampiress said.

"I thought you needed help loading the van. That's what I heard in my mind," Bo said, tapping the side of his head.

"I see we need to train your mind, Bo. Come to me."

"You don't need me anymore. I can't. I don't want to."

"Come here, little rabbit."

Bo obeyed, hesitatingly. He half-staggered toward Eva. "You told me, through your mind, that you are leaving the city," Bo said. Still, he walked toward her. She pulled Bo's head closer and whispered in his ear.

"No. Please, no."

She tore open Bo's shirt, scattering buttons across the dock. "Look at me!" she commanded. Bo obeyed, looked into her eyes, and his mouth became slack. She mussed his hair. "Now, do it."

While Bo undressed, leaving his clothes in a pile on the dock, Eva returned a few steps to the casket and pulled out a leather strap.

The attendants looked at Bo's nakedness, the bruises, the infected puncture marks. Kazmer said, "Is he what they call a junkie, Mistress?"

She smiled. "No Kazmer. He is what they call...*my pet.*" She affixed a leather collar to Bo's neck. "Maybe someday you will understand how sweet a virgin's blood is. This will identify Bo as mine in the new colony. No one will dare touch him. *No one!*"

Bo stood naked, unable to move. He wept.

The brothers smiled.

Bart sniggered.

The vampiress pressed a palm against Bo's chest. The other cupped a buttock. "My little rabbit. How your heart beats so furiously. I heard it thumping just now as you approached. I heard your heart this afternoon. Why didn't you protect me? Was it your plan to fight against me? To kill me and be free?"

"Of course not. They were already in the basement when I got there. They had those guns. I was afraid."

She looked at him and smiled. "I believe you, Bo. Just as well you weren't hurt, little rabbit." She mussed his hair again. Pulled him closer. Smelled his fast, shallow breath with apparent interest. "I've already lost Gerrard and Lisa. I wouldn't want to see your sweet blood spilled."

"Lisa?" Bo asked. He coughed at the stench rising from her.

"Temporarily. I will get her back. Soon, I think." She smiled. "Then the three, or should I say four, of us will be together. At least for a while. You will be a busy little rabbit serving me." She touched his nose playfully with an index finger. "But you will remain my virgin and supply only me with sex and your sweet blood. No other human or vampire will ever have you."

She whispered again in his ear.

"Please don't ask me."

"Go now, Bo. My grave calls you. Wait there for me."

Bo obeyed. He stepped into the van, crawled into the new casket, and lay on his back. He cried silently, occasionally emitting a sob. Tears filled his eyes and ran down his face.

The vampiress turned to the brothers. "How was your plane ride?"

"Very nice," Lazlo said.

"We watched a movie on the flight," Kazmer said.

"We came immediately, of course, and bought the van and the casket. We have everything we need for the trip."

"Imagine that?"

"What, Mistress?

"Humans flying. It's such an odd thought. They think we fly, you know." She threw back her head and laughed. Bart and the brothers laughed, too.

She was serious again. "You know the route?"

"Of course," Lazlo said. "We are taking all back roads, where no one will recognize us. Hardly anyone will even see us. There will be no traffic cameras. We have license plates for the states we will pass through. We even have magnetic signs for the van that will...advertise businesses. There are plumbers, electricians, auto parts, and so on. All made up, ready to use, but none of these businesses really exist."

"Excellent. You have done well on such short notice. How long will it take to arrive?"

"We will travel slow, Mistress. No speeding. No traffic tickets. A week or more."

"I have Bo, and Bo will need food," she said, thoughtfully. "I want to keep his blood sweet and fatty. You must supply fast food for him. Cheeseburgers, I think they are named." She twirled her tongue around her lips as if licking Bo's blood from her face.

Lazlo bowed. "So it will be, Mistress. We eat cheeseburgers ourselves."

"Lovely. Did you hear, Bo? A week to travel. We will be alone, like newlyweds. Of our time we will make—how do they say it?— the most of it."

About the Author

Dean Alan Conrad is a former newspaper reporter and columnist. He is a graduate of the Pennsylvania State University with a degree in English. He lives in Pennsylvania and always has been interested in everything spooky.